D1025631

Rhiana

MICHELE HAUF

LUNA™
www.LUNA-Books.com

LUNA™

First edition May 2006

RHIANA

ISBN 0-373-80234-X

www.LUNA-Books.com

Printed in U.S.A.

Holly LaMon, Alice Countryman and Nita Krevans,
incredible women, each in their own manner.

CHAPTER ONE

Western shore of France—1437

The face of the limestone wall was not sheer. Juts of jagged rock poked out like gooseflesh on a cold man's arm, which made for good handholds. Feet bare, for better hold, Rhiana balanced on a helmet-sized shelf of rock. Her back and shoulders pinned to the wall, with outstretched arms, she clasped the uneven surface.

Her heartbeat thudded. A whisper of early-morning breeze curled into the strands of red hair come unbound from the leather strips she used to wrestle her waist-length curls from her eyes. Her skull vibrated with the constant pulse of excitement. This was the sort of endurance test she craved.

One misbalanced step would see her plunging to the rocky seashore below. Rhiana did not remark even a flutter of fear in her breast. No mincing, faint-hearted female be she. Tears and fright were her sister Odette's mien.

'Twas the wee hours of the morning, just past lauds. A few white-bellied seabirds coasted over the somnambulant waves below. A silver sky, this day. The moon had fallen behind the distant line of centuries-old oak and elm that topped the cliff with a thick emerald cap. Only the tides below that hugged the shore with intermittent *shushes* marked the time.

This was the hour it slept, the moments between the moon's descent and dawn's rise. Rhiana's trainer had taught her to observe and understand the beast, though she had only once before had the opportunity, and that had been brief.

Opportunity had again come, but not without risk.

The creature inhabited the caves wending beneath the mountain that shielded the village of St. Rénan on the north side from the brisk sea storms that frequently arose in the winter months. Caves labryinthed for leagues throughout the mountain, poking out dozens of exit holes along the craggy limestone wall facing the sea.

The wall of stone to which Rhiana clung.

Swinging her right shoulder, she shuffled her feet on the small jut, rotated her hips, and swung her body around. A deft move, which placed her nose to the wall of rock. The stone smelled like the sea, salted by centuries of wind and wave. Dashing out her tongue, it tasted dry and salty, much like last evening's fish stew cooked by Odette. Her sister should keep to the medical arts she so liked to dabble in, and leave the cooking for…well, certainly not Rhiana. 'Twas their mother, Lydia, who created marvels from flour and sugar.

She moved onward. And down.

A wide ledge served as opening to one of the caves, and it stretched out below her like a minstrel's stage. Yet it was a dangerous leap. The castle's finest acrobats might form a tower of four men to broach the distance. A precarious descent.

"I can do this," she muttered to the stone wall. Wasn't as if she'd never before made this climb. "Slowly but surely."

With fingers curved to strong hooks to cling for hold, Rhiana managed another cautious move. She slid her right leg out and tapped a small jut with her toes, testing its stability. Bits of rock crumbled away. Quickly, she retracted and bent her left leg. The toes of her right foot found a more secure spot. The rhythm of her heartbeat remained steady—focused. She worked herself lower.

'Twould be better to fashion a rope ladder and secure it high. Would that she had so clever an idea before making this perilous descent. But she would certainly remember it for future visits. Sure as the snow always fell in winter, there would be future visits.

Pray she survived this day to see that future.

The scrape of her scaled armor against the stone cautioned Rhiana to go slowly. Mustn't make overmuch noise. The creature's hearing was excellent. As was hers. The only thing known to muffle its senses—and hers—was fire and smoke.

It wasn't so much that she heard the sound of the beast's heartbeats in her ears and processed it as noise, rather, the pulse beats of life echoed in her blood as if an ancient stirring of instinct. All her life, Rhiana had noticed, before all others, when a dragon had nested in the caves of St. Rénan. Even as a child of five she had alerted her stepfather to a dragon flying the distant skies.

Only now was she capable of doing something about that eerie cognizance.

Now she determined the distance for a jump was right. Fingers dry and dusted with limestone powder, she secured a good fingerhold on two craggy dents of rock, and dangled her legs over the cave opening. The muscles in her arms stretched to a luxurious ache. Biceps strained, but did not threaten mutiny. This task was to her mettle. Such inner power, it felt good. Strength—it was her boon.

"*Admit it!*" Memories gushed back from childhood. She'd

held her best friend, Rudolph against the wall, her wooden practice sword to his gut. *"Say it!"*

"I surrender!"

"Not that, Rudolph."

"Oh. Must I?"

"Yes!"

On the verge of tears, Rudolph's lips trembled, but he managed to say, "Girls are better than boys."

Letting go, Rhiana landed her feet and immediately rolled to her side and shoulders, making a complete tumbling circle across the smooth, stone landing. To roll lessened the impact and spread it throughout her body, minimizing the hazard of broken bones. Her trainer had taught her the acrobatic move. She was indebted to Amandine Fleche for the summer he'd spent helping her to master the skills required to perform such tasks. For she constantly sought danger and answered its call.

As well, the call to seek fire ever tempted.

Scrambling to the edge of the cave opening, Rhiana pressed her back to the magnesium-flecked wall that arced and curved about the half moon of blackness. The entrance to hell, the villagers named any and all of the cave openings dotting the seashore.

The scriff of her armor against stone was muted thanks to the leather tunic upon which the scales had been lashed. Paul Tassot had designed the armored tunic, fashioned from the iridescent indigo and violet scales removed from Rhiana's first—and only—kill. The scales were impervious to blade, bolt and flame, though she rarely worried for flame.

Many leagues of tunnels and snaking passages wended through the darkness, eventually forming the narrow tunnels that led to the penetralia deep beneath the heart of St. Rénan. Never before had more than a single beast nested within the caves at a time.

Here, standing at the mouth to the cave, the vibrations pulsing in Rhiana's blood amplified. Mayhap she had gauged the heartbeat incorrectly? Could there be…more than one?

"Pray to St. Agatha's veil there be but the one," she murmured.

This day she would not enter the darkness. She had but come to mark out her suspicions and verify what the entire fortressed village of St. Rénan feared. A dragon had once again come to nest in the caves that opened onto the sea.

And while past years had proven little interest to the dragons—none had attacked the village for over a decade—this time it was different.

Yesterday evening, Jean Claude Coopier, the village ferrier, had been snatched from his very boots by a vicious dragon. Indeed, Rhiana had noted the empty boots, still standing upright as if a man wore them, as she passed through the field of vivid pinks to the north of St. Rénan on her trek to the caves. Jean Claude had been the third villager taken in five days.

Taken wasn't exactly the word for…murder. A second man had been found—well, parts of him had been discovered at the edge of the forest. A third had been plucked up and dropped into the sea, never to be rescued.

A carnivorous hell had settled into the caves.

Dragons had ever troubled St. Rénan—the hoard drew them. Or it once had. For two years the caves had stood empty. Not since the summer of Rhiana's training had she seen a dragon. The people had become complacent. The festive hoard-raids had flourished. Even youngsters banned from the raids had begun to trek to the massive caves to sneak about, and the very few returned with a glittering gold coin as proof of their daring. Of course, the youngsters were aware only of the hoard that lured the dragons.

Two days ago, St. Rénan had battened down. Rhiana felt the

changed attitude as a tangible shiver in her bones. The people feared. A fear which grew stronger every day, for this time, it was different. Never had the dragon so boldly hunted people. Once, a man need fear danger only should he stumble into the caves and upon a sleeping dragon. History told the creature had to be aggravated to attack. It must sense danger to itself or its offspring. And very little posed danger to a dragon.

One dragon was easily endured, for the beast rarely remained long. Being social animals, the voracious rampants required the company of their kind while they were young and wily. Only the elder, maxima dragons chose to inhabit a hoard and nest for decades, never leaving, content to exist alone in torpor.

Never, in Rhiana's two decades, could she recall a dragon purposefully swooping down from the sky to snatch up a helpless and flailing body.

No man in St. Rénan dared step forth to challenge the beast. Such boldness was the slayer's vocation.

Yet there did happen to be a slayer in residence.

For many years Rhiana had felt a stirring in her blood. Mayhap, since the very day she entered this world near the warm licking flames of the massive hearth fire in the castle kitchens. The hearth was so huge a grown man could step inside it without bending his head and shoulders. The warmth of the constant blazing flame ever entranced her. Visits to her mother, Lydia, who worked in the castle kitchen, were long and frequently silent, for Rhiana would sit before the flames and become transfixed.

When she was three and her mother would leave her to her stepfather's care in the armory, Rhiana would sit before the glowing brazier. Once, she had grabbed for the entrancing flames. Paul, who had just turned to speak to her, let out a shriek and lunged to jerk her hand from the flame. The hem of her sleeve had frayed and burned, yet her flesh had not. Paul had never told Lydia, for he had been remiss in watching Rhiana.

One would think Rhiana had learned a lesson then. But no, it happened on a few more occasions; each time Paul would remand her and shake his head. He'd lost his fright over her strange compulsion to flame, but never his astonishment.

Fire chaser, her stepfather had taken to calling her, when no one else was around, for most would use it as an oath against an arrogant slayer. Ever enchanted by fire, and not afraid of harm.

As for a fire-breathing dragon? This day, Rhiana would stand tall before danger and show it her teeth.

Stepping out to the center of the landing, she marked her steps. Ten paces. Which made the landing about twenty paces squared. It likely served as a main entrance. There were dozens of openings in the rock wall that hugged the sea and stretched for leagues beyond Rhiana's sight, though this was the only one she'd ever explored.

The cry of a seabird soaring overhead distracted her momentarily. And in that moment the shadows within the cave grew darker. The entrance to hell had never before felt so ominous.

Gifted with Lucifer's flame... Or so legend told.

Sage scented the air. Sweet and heady, a familiar scent, but never before in so voluminous a concentration. Ancient scholars said that sage could expand one's lifetime to the point of immortality.

Rhiana didn't believe it. No one lived forever.

The fine hairs at her wrists sprang upright. Sensing the ominous presence before seeing it, she lowered her gaze to search the black void. Crouching, she centered her balance. All power manifested in her belly, her female center. From there she drew up her strength.

Tilting her head, she listened. The basso heartbeats pulsed out a tormenting tattoo.

The distinct scent of the beast curled through Rhiana's nostrils. It tasted bitter and warning at the back of her throat, and spoke on slithering hisses. *I am here. You cannot stop me.* Attack scent, that. Once before she had scented it, sharp like the sea, innate and feral. And once before she had vanquished the threat.

Spreading her legs and squaring her hips beneath her shoulders for a firm stance, Rhiana reached behind her back and unlatched the crossbow from the leather baldric slung from shoulder to hip. Specially designed by Paul, and forged completely of steel, the crossbow bore not a sliver of wood that might easily be burned to ash. The string? Fashioned from finely braided dragon's gut, as well, impervious to flame. A cumbersome windlass was not required to draw taunt the string on this precious bit of weapon. Flexible at rest, the dragon-gut was easily pulled to notch, yet shrank tightly for a forceful release.

She notched an iron bolt into place. But she would not fire unless the beast proved a threat. It could be wandering in a sleepy daze, have mistakenly scampered out to the cave opening. Despite their deadly nature, Rhiana revered the dragons. Elegant, wondrous creatures of flight and flame, she felt an affinity toward the scaled beasts.

"Not of hell," she murmured in awe.

'Tis a wicked enchantment, surely, that birthed them. An enchantment that, much against her intuitive calling, lured her to arms.

The click of curved ebony talons, stealthy, marking its pace upon the stone cave floor, told Rhiana this one did not approach in a somnambulant daze.

She slid her free hand over the dagger secured at her hip. The handle was fashioned from an ebony dragon talon.

Emerging into the pale grayness of the pre-dawn, one scaled paw studded with deadly talons rattled out a warning staccato. Indigo scales glinted even in the feeble light. All about, a heavy silence thickened the air. Not so much as a lap of seawater against the stones on the shore below could be heard.

And then, from out of the dark void, the beast's head swept forward. The size of two field oxen and rimmed in hard indigo scales and juts of deadly spines was the skull. The horns stabbing out from the temples were small, no longer than Rhiana's forearm, but weapons she respected. Tusks at the corner of the mouth were but short picks spiking to the sides. 'Twas a rampant, young and wild, many decades of growth still required to reach the elder maxima's size and docility.

But no less dangerous to a man's mortality.

Thrusting back her shoulders and lifting her chin, Rhiana declared, "I am come! Let us begin this dance of will and strength."

The beast tilted its head, for a moment seeming to wonder at her words.

Rhiana did know they could speak the mortal tongue no more than she could read their beastly thoughts. Yet, Amandine had told her the maxima had such ability.

Focusing on the pattern of ridged scales between the eyes, shaped like an inverted cross, she readied her aim.

A hiss of sage-tainted smoke billowed from the nostrils in a creepy fog. So sweet, their breath. Intoxicating, should one lose focus and succumb. Smoke dulled her senses, but she knew it had the same effect on her opponent.

The beast drew up tall, its head rising as it stretched up its long neck.

Rhiana anticipated its next move.

Defiant in her stance, she merely smiled as the creature's head lunged and the jaws opened wide. Deadly maws targeted her feeble size. A filigree of amber flame danced upon the air. One moment it formed a wisp of steam at the corners of the dragon's tusk-pointed jaw, the next, it formed a rippling cacophony of heat and fire and evil that encompassed Rhiana's body.

Heat, smothering, yet intoxicatingly dreamy, wavered images of the world before her. Amber wall of stone on fire. Distorted crystal sky. A frenzied blotch of scale and fang behind the wall of flame.

Standing amidst the fire Rhiana could not breathe. Her lungs expanded, then sealed up. Her chest felt bloated, stopped up. Her senses began to shut down. But she did not fear.

Fire. 'Twas her vitae.

As the last tendril of flame extinguished, Rhiana confidently raised her crossbow and sighted in her mark. The dragon, its head still lowered as if to attack, held its wide gold eyes at a level to her shoulders. Inverted cross in sight above the top of her bolt—perfect.

She released the trigger. The heavy steel bolt hissed through the sky and landed the target. There, in the center of the beast's skull, right between the eyes—the kill spot, a direct entrance to the brain through a fine seam in the skull. Cursed by Heaven for its fall from grace.

Impact forced the creature up onto its powerful hind legs. The belly of soft, semipermeable violet scales glittered as the first beams of sunlight broke the horizon. Great pellicle wings scooped the air, the force of wind pushing Rhiana back a few steps. She marked her position. Fire did no harm, but a slap from a wildly flailing wing could push her over the edge.

And then, it tumbled. Over the side of the cliff it soared with little grace. Once an elegant beast of flight, now it crashed upon the stones and boulders below with a bone- and scale-crunch-ing sound that sifted up dust and caused the seabirds to cry out the death of its winged compatriot.

A quick death, that.

Rhiana, still standing her ground, waited for the calamity to settle. Breaths huffing, a smile formed.

Swiping a palm across her face she nodded, and then propped the crossbow against her shoulder. "'Tis not a good day to be a dragon."

CHAPTER TWO

The beast had landed the shore; its upper half, including the neck and skull, had plunged into the sea. No bones or scales to claim this day; the tide would carry away the carcass before nightfall.

From within the blackness of the cave opening another heartbeat yet pulsed, but she did not sense the second had been wakened by the attack.

A second? Truly, there was another.

Was it the mate? The fallen dragon was female, evident in its bright coloring. It was the male that protected the eggs, and which was in need of dull gray scales. Never had Rhiana seen a dragon egg. Or a male, for that matter.

Topside, after a perilous climb up the cliff face, Rhiana rushed across the open meadow to the forest and retrieved the thick wool cloak she'd secreted behind the twisted trunk of a burned-out oak stump. Swinging the cloak around her shoulders, she then followed the purlieu of the forest a league back to the battlement walls.

The sun dashed a gold line across the horizon and even from

a distance Rhiana heard a rooster crow the morn. Beads of dew danced at grass-tip blades like faery finery. The morning smelled fresh and salted with the slightest tang of sage.

As she walked, she pulled the leather tie from her bound hair and shook it over her shoulder. True, dragon's flame did little harm to her flesh and hair. But she hadn't yet discovered a fabric that could withstand the heat, be it dragon flame or a simple hearth fire. The thin cambric tunic she wore beneath the scaled leather armor had burned away during her flaming, proving the wool cloak a necessity.

This armor was remarkable. Fashioned by her stepfather Paul, the leather cuirass was more a tunic that covered chest, back and the tops of her shoulders and arms. Secured at the backs of her arms and down her torso with leather straps, the thin strips were stitched through with fine mail wire to allow malleable strength that couldn't be burned away. As for the mail chausses, Rhiana had made them herself, utilizing double rings instead of the usual single ring method. Rarely did she wear but hose beneath them—heavier chamois braies were unnecessary—for the thick mail protected verily, even one's modesty.

Rhiana felt she might wear merely the armor, baring more flesh than any maiden should, for it would save on damaged clothing. But she must be cautious. Should she be spied in such attire, surely there would be a price to pay.

All in St. Rénan knew of her industry. They had seen her tromping about in the armor and wielding her dagger. "She's an odd one," they'd mutter to themselves. "Always has been." Why, some had mistaken her for a boy when younger, for her antics and attraction to all things muddy or slimy, and her frequent play with makeshift weapons.

Yet, all in St. Rénan believed the real slayer who had been visiting the village two years earlier had taken down the dragon. A dragon Rhiana had slain. At the time, she hadn't felt the need to correct perceptions, for she'd been so excited, the elation of the kill had far outweighed any glory the villagers might have bestowed. Instead, she'd gladly stood back while Amandine had collected his dragon's purse from the hoard council as payment for his kill.

Praise and acknowledgment mattered very little to Rhiana, only that her loved ones were kept safe. For without family, what had one left?

The village walls were sixty feet high and fashioned from massive bricks shaped from the same ocher limestone that frilled the seashore. Four towers set at each direction of the compass punctuated the battlement walls, with wide parapet walks stretching between them all. The walls completely closed in the village, for it was small, yet growing, though none had chosen to build outside the walls for the dangers were real.

Avoiding the drawbridge that crossed to St. Rénan's barbican and main entrance gates, Rhiana skipped along the curtain wall to the north entrance, close to where the artillery stored dusty trebuchets and long-forgotten cannonballs. It was rarely used, for siege and battle were nonexistent.

A narrow plank, no wider than two fists, stretched across the dry, yet deep, moat, attracting only the most deft and balanced.

Steadying herself with but one outstretched arm, Rhiana danced across the wobbly plank. The scaled armor clicked softly and her mail chausses *chinged.* The sound of mail in motion made her smile. It signified all things chivalrous and adventurous to her. Halfway across she lunged into a bounce. The plank wobbled, digging up plumes of dry earth at either end. Lifting one foot out before her, Rhiana performed another bounce, landed her foot and skipped quickly to ground and the thick iron door.

She glanced back at the expanse of moat she'd crossed. A satisfied nod followed. Every opportunity to danger must be met.

Rudolph manned the barbican in the early morn, but his watch didn't start until prime, so Rhiana had coerced him to guard this door. Rudolph was a lifelong friend and fellow cohort in today's mission, for 'twas his brother Jean Claude who had been snatched from his very boots.

A double rap to the thick iron door with the heel of her crossbow, was followed by Rudolph's husky, "Who goes there?"

The lanky young man always tried to lower his voice and speak slowly, as Rhiana had suggested would make him sound more imposing.

"Fire chaser," Rhiana replied, the previously decided password. It was a nickname only Rudolph and Paul used, yet Rudolph was not privy to her most exotic secrets, as was her stepfather.

A blinking eyeball peered through the squint hole. The door opened and an arm lashed out to grip her by the wrist and tug her inside the battlement walls. Slammed against the closing door, Rhiana smirked at Rudolph's theatrics.

With a scatter of blonde hair poking out from beneath his tight leather skullcap, he glared his best glare at her, then, with a sniff and a nod, stepped back, assuming modest nonchalance. "My lady."

"Rudolph." She chuckled and tugged unconsciously at the wool cloak. He did not know what she wore—or did not wear—beneath. "Do you not recognize my voice, that you must every time treat me as a possible intruder?"

"It is my task, my lady, to protect the village from impostors and brigands."

When they were children he'd once accused her of pressing him to always play the knight when he much preferred to be a minstrel or village fool. Mayhap their play battles had some influence in his chosen profession of guard, or so Rhiana liked to believe.

"You serve Lord Guiscard well with your astute attention to detail."

"Think you?"

"Indeed."

Pleased with the compliment, Rudolph bowed in affirmation. Then with a nervous tug of his cap, which never did cover his overlarge ears, he grew more serious. "Any dragons?" he wondered.

"One less, thanks be to my trusty crossbow."

"My lady, you are a gem!" Eyes stretching up the battlement wall to her side, Rudolph said with less enthusiasm, "If only you had been near when Jean Claude was taken."

"Rudolph." She clamped a palm upon his shoulder. Wheat dust smoked out from his brown tunic; he spent his nights romancing the miller's daughter in the shadows of the flour mill. "Your brother was a benevolent man, ever eager to set aside what he was doing to aid, be it building or chopping or even singing during the village's frequents fêtes. There is no doubt, in my heart, Jean Claude sings with the angels this day."

"You are ever kind. I just…keep wondering how awful it must feel to be snatched up in a dragon's maw."

A thought Rhiana had had many a time. It was what had kept her alert and deft in the face of danger.

Rudolph stomped a boot upon the packed dirt ground. "Forgive me, I am well and fine. No tears, no tears."

Sniffing, he resumed a defensive stance, arms crossed over his chest, and a guardlike frown upon his face. A familiar pose, for Rhiana had often pushed him to tears with her teasing. Because, most certainly, girls *were* better than boys.

"Thank you, Rudolph. I continue to rely upon your discretion."

"But wait!" He blocked her leave with a dancing step to the right. "You said *one* less. What does that mean? One less? Less than more?" His voice warbled. "Be there more…dragons?"

"Shh, Rudolph, you'll wake curious ears." They both looked down the aisle of houses that snaked along the battlement walls. But a strip of sunlight glowed upon the slate rooftops. "I am not positive, but I think there is another."

"Another," he panted out. Straining to keep his voice to a whisper, he muttered, "Go back! Kill it, fire chaser! Do not let this day pass without banishing hell's evil. It will continue to stalk our village!"

"Rudolph." Rhiana sighed.

Should she have remained? Walked deep into the darkness of the cave and explored, seeking the other dragon?

No, the other had slept surely. Else, would it not have flown out to avenge its mate's death? She had sensed no immediate danger. And what if it had been male, protecting a newling? She did not kill indiscriminately.

"I am on it, you can trust me."

"Girls are better than boys," he tried with a teasing lilt to the statement.

She winked and gave him a quick hug, then strode past him and into the narrow back alleys twisting about behind St. Rénan's strip of artillery and armory shops. The buildings were constructed of timber posts and beams, but overlaid by slate or fieldstone. A decades-old edict declared all buildings must be of stone and all roofs of slate or tile. Best defense for a village oft ravaged by flame.

A cock again crowed the morning and dogs yipped in response. The delicious smell of baking bread unearthed a ridiculous hunger in Rhiana's belly. Dragon slaying was hard work and required a hearty meal. She must to home to catch the last bits of Odette's breakfast.

A twig rolled off an overhead rooftop and tapped her on the shoulder. Must be from a bird. But yet—she paused and searched the sky. One must never become complacent. So many noises in this village forged of stone and earth and as little wood as possible. She spied a dash of gray skirts.

"Mother?"

Rhiana skipped around and hid behind a tightly woven wattle arbor. Her mother made her way to the castle kitchen. Lydia walked a swift pace, and kept looking over her shoulder. As if she thought she was being followed. Strange.

Rhiana scanned the area. No one else out so early. Hmm…

Her mother had been different the past fortnight. Avoiding Rhiana more than usual. She was most brisk with their conversations. 'Twas almost as if Rhiana had done something to affront Lydia. But she did not know how to ask if there was a problem.

Lydia's dour gray skirts swept out of view and behind a wall of hornbeam.

Rhiana sighed. "Something is amiss with her."

As she walked onward, the clangs of the armourer's hammer sang out like a childhood lullaby. Truly, such racket was lullaby matter to her. Since she was very young, Rhiana had spent her days toddling about Paul Tassot's legs, asking him questions about every step in the process of creating armor, playing with the old yellow mongrel that slept beneath the stone cooling tank, thriving in the atmosphere of the shop.

The song of the hammer beat out a rhythm in her blood. Hard metals being coaxed into smooth, elegant curves, and blades that could kill with but a slice? How exciting! The red-hot flames and the glow of heated iron? Mesmerizing. Wherever there was fire, Rhiana felt soothing comfort. And the exquisite reassurance of gold, on the rare occasions Paul worked the supple metal to a fine sheet to leaf armor, ever beckoned.

Rhiana slipped into the shop and padded across the swept stone floor. The armory was circular, the south half sporting the brazier and works in progress. The north half was set up with a massive oak table for detail and leatherwork.

Bent over the flame, Paul concentrated on a curve of metal heated to vibrant amber. Paul Tassot was Rhiana's mother's husband. He was not her father, but had married Lydia when Rhiana was three.

Rhiana did not know her real father. For all purposes, a man had been in her life from the time of her birth until she was two. One Jean Cesar Ulrich Villon III; he was not her father either, though he had been married to her mother. Villon had abandoned her and her mother without reason or word. Lydia had cried for a se'ennight following. Even so small, Rhiana had wondered would her mother's tears flood their home and sweep them both out to the sea, never again to be found, and so far away from flame and the family she loved.

As she grew older, many questions busied Rhiana's thoughts. But when asked, Lydia Tassot would not speak of Rhiana's origins. Rhiana suspected her mother must have been violated, or, in her more lusty imagination, she wondered had her mother an affair with a powerful lord or a fancy traveling courtier.

Either way, Rhiana had taken to Paul Tassot, who had been a mainstay in her life for twenty years. Just riding the end of his fifth decade, he possessed kind blue eyes that never looked upon Rhiana with the exasperated frustration Lydia's eyes often held. And he was supportive of her quest. When Lydia scoffed at Rhiana taking off with a slayer to hone her skills, upon her return, Paul would question her every lesson with great fascination. What is he teaching you? Do you feel confident? How can I help? And under his breath—touch any flame this day?

Paul looked up from his task. "Ah!"

After an incident with sickness last summer all of Paul's hair had fallen out. Now, recovered and healthy thanks to Odette's infamous comfrey poultice, he continued to shave off the new growth. Rhiana liked his shiny bald pate. It was soft and round, like his giving heart. The man embodied integrity in his simple manner and devotion to his family.

He flashed her a brilliant smile, and with a shrug, worked his shoulders against the rounding hours leaning over the anvil forged into his muscles. A nod of his head summoned Rhiana to his side.

The glowing curve of iron he held with tongs could not be left unattended, so he divided his attention between it and her. A forceful pound of the hammer clanged the molten metal and sparks danced out like fire sprites.

"Come from the caves?"

Rhiana nodded as she reached behind her waist to itch at the leather points securing her tunic to the mail chausses.

"Was it as you suspected?" he asked.

"Yes, and no. There may be more than one of them," Rhiana explained. "I didn't have a chance to focus and count, but certainly there could be another."

"Another?"

"Yes, I sensed another heartbeat after— Oh, Paul! I took out a female rampant."

"You did?" He winked and smiled broadly. So much pride in that look. Another pound. Sparks glittered in the air between them. "So the armor is good?"

Rhiana dropped the wool cloak to a puddle around her feet. The entire armored tunic glittered with the mystique of the beasts. Fashioned from dragon scales, the iridescent disks changed from indigo to violet beneath the sun. Paul had smoothed the sharp edges and pierced holes in each scale with such care. After much trial and error, he'd discovered the only tool capable of piercing the scale was an actual dragon's talon or tooth. He'd designed a small inner tooth, which the beast used for ripping its prey apart, as a punch.

"It's remarkable."

Rhiana felt no embarrassment standing before Paul in the flesh-baring costume. But the backs of her arms and a narrow slit down each side of her torso showed. Paul had worked with her to fit the scales to her body to provide maximum movement along with minimal weight and excess attire. It was he who had suggested she wear a thin tunic beneath, for her modesty, but they both knew Rhiana would be sewing many a tunic should her slaying skills ever be called upon.

"Change in the closet," he said, turning the curve of molten iron, held with a pincers, to begin working the opposite side. The dry metallic scent of heated iron was most pleasant to Rhiana's senses. "The gown you keep stashed in there waits. Did no one see you reenter the village?"

"Rudolph is most discreet," Rhiana called as she slipped into the tool closet and closed the creaky wood door.

"Only because you have cowed him over the years," Paul said. With a laugh, he again hammered at the supple metal.

They both felt it important to keep Rhiana's slaying discreet. Certainly the threat to the village must be dispatched. But so many had difficulty accepting a female as a powerful and strong force.

It dumbfounded Rhiana. Why should she not be allowed to perform the same tasks as men?

Inside the closet, her eyes strayed across the items on the many supply shelves. Splaying her fingers across a tray of wire rings she'd fashioned a few days earlier made her smile. Crafting mail, she enjoyed. Almost as much as slaying.

She unfastened the leather straps placed from armpit to hip neatly concealed with overlapping dragon scales. The leather tunic slipped from her body, baring her breasts. Tugging out the slips of burnt tunic from around her neck and at her waist, she tossed them into the waste barrel.

Exhaling deeply, Rhiana thrust back her shoulders and lifted her arms over her head in a languorous stretch. So alive, she felt. Vigorous and strong. A flex of her arm bulged the muscle above her elbow. Like a man's muscles, she mused. Constant training with the sword and working with Paul kept her muscles hard. And that hard work had paid off.

The moment she had stood before the dragon, defiant, had truly been a pinnacle. For her only other kill had been assisted. This one was all her own.

"I'm a real slayer," she murmured. "Finally."

A folded blue-gray gown waited on the shelf. For emergencies, which is why she hadn't left one of her two pairs of braies—she used those daily. Bits of dried lavender fell from between the folds as she shook it out.

Slipping the ells of soft damask over her head, Rhiana shimmied into the plain gown. Once silver vair had rimmed the hems of her sleeves, but the fur tickled overmuch, so she'd stripped it and gave it to Odette to sew onto a pair of house slippers. Rich as the village was, traders rarely visited, so fur of any sort was highly valued.

She stroked the gold coin suspended around her neck on a thin leather strip. Barter was the only form of purchase; coin had little value.

Shucking the mail chausses in a chinking pool about her bare feet, she then peeled down the wool hose, which were still connected to the points of her tattered tunic, fried to a crisp as they were. The softness of the damask fluttering about her legs felt ridiculous. So light, not at all protective. The gown was…not her. Many were accustomed to seeing her wear braies and tunic, but on occasion she did wear a gown. Only a gown caressed her waist and bosom and revealed to a man that, indeed, she was a woman. *Look at me,* she felt the gown called when she wore one.

And what be wrong with seeking a man's attentions?

Still, many whispered as she strode by, defying propriety in her comfortable male costume. And to even consider her ambition? A female who dons armor and wields a crossbow? Insanity.

Carefully, she placed the armor upon the wooden stand and covered it with a tarp of boiled leather. While every man in the village was aware of her passion, they had not seen this latest armor made by Paul. Even those who looked to her with hope for their safety would be horrified. Women simply did not tromp about in mail and armor, acting powerful and flexing their muscles as a man.

Tossing her hair over her shoulder, Rhiana stepped back from the armor. Thick, loose curls tumbled across her back and swept about her waist. Ever teased as a child for her red hair and freckles—surely a witch, be she—Rhiana had come to accept her differences, but only after being assured by the village hag that she was not a witch.

Something so much more…

The hag, known to all as the Nose, after reading Rhiana's future in the flames of a hearth fire, had flashed her a frightened grimace and shuffled her out from her cottage.

So much more?

Indeed.

CHAPTER THREE

As opposed to setting up a small bake shop in her own home, Rhiana's mother worked in the castle kitchen. Lydia rose before the sun and wandered home late in the evening. It was a labor of love, for Lydia was the castle's pastry chef, and delighted many with her designs fashioned from sugar, nuts and honey. Holidays such as Lent and Midsummer, were made all the more festive with Lydia's creations gracing the high table.

Odette, Rhiana's half-sister, would be either at home fretting over some bits of lace to attach to her sleeves or in the castle kitchen sampling Lydia's wares. Odette strove for little in life, save a plump waistline to attract a fine and fruitful husband. Though she did favor the medical arts—stitching up wounded knights landed high on her list of activities.

None in St. Rénan strove for much more than a simple life filled with all the luxury that could be managed. Thanks to the hoard, the village thrived. Where most cities and villages paid the taille to their lord, St. Rénan had developed its own form of reverse-taille, paying to each citizen a yearly stipend. One would think the entire city lazy and roustabouts, but that was not so. Every able body worked hard, and in return celebrated the fruits of their labors with fine furnishings, elegant clothing and always food on the table. Starvation was not something the people of St. Rénan understood, for should the crops be poor one summer, a trek to a neighboring village, or even a sojourn to the debauched city of Paris, to purchase food was undertaken. Anything could be had for a price.

The Hoard Council, formed by Pascal Guiscard three decades earlier, monitored the disbursements and insured none in the village became slackards. If you did not pull your weight, you did not receive the stipend. Very few were thrown into the dungeons for shirking their duties. The village was small, working as a companionable hive. All guarded the secret with a blood oath taken before Lord Guiscard upon their sixteenth birthday.

Bi-yearly hoard-raids were celebrated with a fête and great bonfire (which, Rhiana mused, was lit in defiance of the dragons). Though, not many had been venturing beyond the curtain walls the past few days.

So Rhiana's trip through the city this morn was met with little but the stray pig from Dame Gemma's stables snorting in the onions and cress planted outside the woman's three-story manor. Children were kept safe behind closed door, or close in sight splashing in a nearby puddle or playing stones with a neighboring child.

Rhiana gave no regard to the half-dozen knights who marched purposefully toward her—in full armor, as usual. Though Lord Guiscard's knights were called to little warfare, and even less martial exercise, Rhiana had decided they wore the full armor to look opposing. And to attract the opposite sex. There were many marriageable young women in St. Rénan; wenching was one of the knights' favorite exercises.

Champrey, Guiscard's seneschal, strode in the lead. He was hounded by a rank of hulking shoulders and rugged, dirty glares.

The men in the village were so desperately primal. Baths were rare, for the claim of little physical exertion kept them clean. Yet, much as Odette was always complaining of the knights' awkwardly amorous attempts to seduce her, Rhiana had never fielded an unwarranted touch from any. She knew what the men thought of her. Not right, mayhap a witch. Certainly not feminine. She did try, when she thought of it. But emulating Lady Anne's walk always saw Rhiana tripping over her own feet.

But did the men in the village, at the very least, see her as a woman?

Obviously not. It was only when Rhiana had developed breasts that Rudolph's father had admonished him not to play with her. She was a girl, not the boy his father had thought her. Fortunately, Rudolph had never cared one way or the other. Their friendship remained strong; like siblings, they continued to taunt, torment, and love one another.

Rhiana craved a kind look from a man—any man who was not Rudolph or Paul. And, perhaps, not so kind a look as a promising one. Something that said to her, I favor you. Your strength does not frighten me. I can accept without fear or jealousy.

For those were the reasons no man approached her. They feared her independence. They were jealous of her strength.

Sighing, and striding onward, Rhiana realized the band of knights had stopped before her. Armor clattered and gauntlets clinked about sword hilts. Not a one would make a move to allow her passage.

"Demoiselle," Champrey sneered. He did have a way of sneering his speech. It ever gave Rhiana a tickle. He wasn't half so villainous as his lord and master, but he certainly tried to compete. "My lord wishes an audience with you."

"Oh? Well, but I've—" A hungry belly to fill. And a certain lusty baron to avoid.

"Immediately."

What could Lord Guiscard want with her? Had someone witnessed her entry into the village, sans proper clothing and wearing but the dragon scale armor? She was ever vigilant of the men who sat in the towers placed upon the battlement walls.

"I was on to the kitchen to speak to my mother. Does Lord Guiscard wish me to speak to Lady Anne?"

Rhiana often visited Lady Anne. Upon her arrival three years ago, the lady of St. Rénan had taken a liking to Rhiana and frequently requested she tend her in her solar. Anne allowed Rhiana to comb her hair and plait it, one of the rare feminine skills Rhiana possessed.

"Hold your tongue and follow me, wench."

So that was the way of it, eh? She hated being labeled wench.

Shrugging, Rhiana followed Champrey's sulking steps, and as she did, felt the ranks close about her. Lifting her skirts to keep the mud from lacing the hem, she cursed her lack of shoes.

An escort to Lord Guiscard? No good could come of this.

They entered the castle through the iron doors that stretched two stories high. Grinning stone gargoyles sporting lion heads and eagle bodies overlooked the human cavalcade. A three-legged mutt bounced past Rhiana as she moved swiftly through the great hall. Rushes were scattered upon the stone floor, but she did not notice the fennel and mint mixture Lady Anne insisted be sprinkled over all.

Normally Rhiana's keen senses picked up every smell, almost to the point of annoyance. 'Twas nerves, she knew. Anxiety dulled her senses. She did not like being called to Lord Guiscard, unless it concerned Anne. In truth, a summons to speak *only* to Guiscard had never before happened. Foreboding tightened the muscles in her jaw.

The keep was a grand room, four stories high, and capped

with a vault ceiling that captured triangles of colored glass between each of its sectioned ribs. The painted sky, Rhiana had named the stained-glass ceiling.

The yellow Guiscard crest—a red salamander *passant guardant,* and in the lower quarter of the bend sinister a green cricket; a combination of both houses' coat of arms—fluttered from banners hung upon the walls low enough to brush a mounted knight's polished bascinet helmet.

Along the west wall hung a series of tapestries depicting the dragons' fall to temptation with the dark angels, and the resulting hand of God touching one on the forehead, cursing them with the kill spot ever after.

Always the great hearth at the north end of the room blazed; now, some four-legged beast turned upon the spit. While the village consumed an inordinate amount of fish, the occasional land-roving boar or deer was blessedly welcome.

The high table was set with gold candelabras and gold place settings. The lower table was not set up, and would not be until later this evening. For as much as the village was ensured wealth, there remained a fine line of social hierarchy. The baron did not boast a full court with lords, ladies, minstrels and such, but he did have his inner set of trusted alliances. And while most of the villagers were always welcome at the lower table, many found the settings and food at their own homes of equal taste and wealth.

Rhiana spied Lord Guiscard's elegant dagged emerald velvet surcoat and made a beeline through the crowd of assorted craftsmen and gossiping ladies to him. She knew it would not be truly proper to approach him in such a manner—without being announced—but whenever she sensed trouble it was better to face it straight on, than linger and fret about it.

"My lord Guiscard!" Champrey, yet struggling through the crowd behind her, hastily announced Rhiana's approach.

Narcisse Guiscard, baron de St. Rénan, turned. To his right, an iron torchiere shaped like a dragon's head flickered, though the sunlight beaming through the colored glass overhead brightened the room sufficiently. Narrow brown eyebrows lifted in lascivious manner upon spying Rhiana, but his wondering expression quickly crimped to a frown.

Even ugly moods could not dampen his elegance. Rhiana always caught her breath at sight of him. So young and attractive. She fancied him her age, but he must be years older, for his father had been sixty-two when he died five years earlier.

Tall, lean, and wrapped with muscle, Guiscard stood, feet spread and thumbs hooked at a hip belt of interlocked gold medallions. Thigh high boots, revealed by a sweep of his surcoat, emphasized long legs wrapped in parti-colors of emerald and black. He wore not the fashionable pudding-basin cut that had the men shaving the backs of their heads up to ear-high level. Long dark hair was braided at the baron's ears to keep it back from his face. Possessed of bright blue eyes and cheekbones sharp as any blade, he easily slayed all females who fell to his allure.

Sapphires glinted at his fingers and along the gold chain that strung from shoulder to shoulder. Rhiana lingered on the gold. She liked gold, its brilliant and warm veneer. To hold it in her hand made her feel safe—comforted—strange as that sounded.

It was with great willpower she resisted reaching out and touching the finery that glittered everywhere on Lord Guiscard.

The baron had taken command of the castle upon his father's death five years earlier. Pascal Guiscard had succumbed to fever after eating rotten fish, and following months of suffering, had died after three decades of benevolent rule over St. Rénan. He had been known for his gentle yet precise ways. It was Pascal who had discovered the hoard, and he who had chosen to share it with all.

Narcisse Guiscard shared his father's attention to detail and possessed a forced kindness, but there were things about him that put up the hairs on Rhiana's arms.

"Ah, the Tassot wench. Our very own rumored dragon slayer." He spat the words through teeth clenched tighter than the fists at his hips.

She would not deny the truth. But until now, Rhiana had not known the castle was aware of her slaying activities. How could they know of this morning's kill? Had Rudolph—?

Mayhap now she could explain the situation to Lord Guiscard, perhaps even suggest he loan her a few strong knights. If there was another dragon, as she suspected, she would require assistance. For where there were two, could there be even more?

"My lord," she said, and bowed.

Her unbound hair spilled to the floor as she did so. The tresses were not clumped with mud, which relieved her, but certainly they were in need of a comb. The only time she was aware of her lacking femininity was in the presence of a powerful man.

The men standing around the baron, smirking and handling all manner of shiny weapon from ax to bow to leather-hilted sabre, focused their attention on the woman who so boldly approached.

Oh, but the bravado heavy in the air put her to guard. Absently, Rhiana slid her palm over her left hip. No dragon talon dagger to hand.

Guiscard glided out from his entourage and met her in the center of the keep. The clean lavender scent of his soap attacked her senses as if a fox dashing for the rabbit. Now she smelled everything, from the fennel and mint rising about her skirt hem to the barrage of musk that claimed the keep as a man's domain. Women belonged in the kitchen and the laundry, she had heard Guiscard say before, or as ornaments decorating their man's arm.

Curious blue eyes preened across Rhiana's face, and then tilted a smile at her. Not a generous smile, most always devious.

"Tell me," he said, "what it is about slaying dragons that intrigues you so? Be it the danger? The fight? The desire to touch such fierce evil?"

"Is not the desire to see my family safe enough of an attraction?"

"But you are a woman. Women do not gallivant after dragons. Why…" He glanced over his shoulder to a fellow knight and murmured, "Women are to be made sacrifices, no?"

A few snickers from the men enforced Guiscard's cocky stance. A shrug of his broad shoulder tugged tight the gold chain across his chest and with a distracting *clink*.

Drawing in a breath, Rhiana grabbed back the courage and focus she had initially held. "My apologies for being so abrupt, my lord, but is it possible we may discuss the business of these dragons come to nest in the caves?"

"Dragons in our caves, my lady?"

"Three men have been devoured in five days."

"You said dragons, as in, more than one?"

"Mayhap." A surreptitious glance about saw many more eyes had become interested. She did wish to alarm no one, especially the women, so she lowered her voice. "Do you not wish it put to an end?"

The baron now regarded her with a lifted brow. Utter arrogance seeped from him as if the lavender scent. "And you propose to be the one to end it? My lady, I had not thought to entertain such a humorous farce this morn, but I thank you heartily for the amusement."

He touched her chin with a finger that glittered with enough gold to serve a peasant family for an entire year, and lifted her head to look directly into her eyes. The look was familiar, and dreadsome. On occasion Guiscard caught Rhiana as she was entering Lady Anne's room. A silent capture, which held her against the embrasure outside the solar, his blue eyes eating her apart with unspoken lust.

"You've been to the caves," he said. "This morning? My men report seeing you leave just after lauds. Your return was not remarked."

She would lie to no man, for integrity of word was important to her. "I did, my lord."

"Such boldness to tromp about a dragon's lair."

"I killed one rampant this morn. But there may be another. I…sensed its presence."

"Just so?" He spread his gaze across her face. A curious look. Fascinated or horrified? "You *sensed* another? Without sighting it? Sounds…magical, to me."

"I have no magic, my lord." She wanted to follow with, "I am not a witch," but best to leave that word unspoken. For once heard…

"Who gave you permission to do such a thing?"

Permission? Rhiana gaped. To protect— To— Why, to see her family safe? She did not know what to say to that.

"You say there are others?"

"Mayhap," she answered. Still at a loss—he expected her to *ask* before slaying a danger that threatened the very people of his village?

"So you are not sure. And yet, you boldly approach me with these ideas of another. You frighten us all, my lady."

"I do not mean to. I only wish to protect—"

"Against imagined evils?"

"They are not imagined!"

"Did you see this other dragon?"

"N-no, but I—" Blessed be, why must the man be so difficult?

"You are not like other women."

How many times had she heard that statement, and always as an accusation? It deserved the usual response. "I try, my lord, but sewing and cooking does little to satisfy me."

"Ah?" He delivered a smirk over his shoulder. A few knights snickered. "Well, if it is satisfaction you desire…."

Oh, but she'd put her foot in it with that one.

"Is there a reason you had me escorted to you this day, my lord?"

"Indeed there is." Mirth fell at Guiscard's feet. The air of his forced humor instantly hardened. "I was boldly woken by my seneschal this morning with news of your foolhardy deed. Besides the rude awakening, I feel your cut against all in the village. How dare you take matters into your incapable hands."

"But, my lord—"

"You are forbidden to prance about playacting at this nonsense of slaying dragons."

"No one is playacting. You can find the carcass on the shore to the north."

"I believe you, and I am horrified." He said the last word with such drama, any who had not been discreetly listening now stared boldly at Rhiana. "How many others?"

"One."

"You are sure?"

She nodded. Not sure, but willing to trust her instincts.

"I will not abide you to go near the caves. And should I hear you have gone against my wishes, I will have you chained and put in my, er—the dungeon."

"But, my lord, the innocent people! Who will protect them?"

"That is what slayers are for."

"A slayer?" But she was… Well, she wanted to be—no, she had slain two thus far. She was a slayer! "It will take well over a fortnight to call a proper slayer to St. Rénan. In that time half a dozen more will be plucked out from their boots. I can do this! I am—"

A woman who chases dragons.

The words caught at the back of Rhiana's throat. Why could she not boldly declare her mien?

"And who will protect you?"

Her? Protection? The man did no more care for her welfare than he concerned himself with the crumbling infirmary that desperately needed repair.

"You, my lady, will heed my warning, and thus get yourself into the kitchen, where you can be taught proper skills such as kneading and sweeping and whatever else it is you females do. Isn't that where your mother works?" A glance to Champrey verified. "Indeed. It is high time the woman trained her child to be the female she appears to be."

The very nerve of him!

With nothing but snickers, male eyes bared, and weapons circling her as if a pack of hungry dogs, Rhiana thought the wiser at protest.

Nevertheless, her passions always ruled over her better sense. *Girls are better than boys.*

"I refuse to stand back and allow the dragons to take another life when I can stop it!"

The baron whipped a dagger glare from his arsenal. "You raise your voice to me, wench?" he hissed out of the side of his mouth.

Rhiana focused. She had become irate, her heart pounded, her shoulders tight. Lowering her head, she breathed through her nose, coming to accord with this ridiculous demand. Guiscard was a fool. Yet notions of a woman's place were not unusual—to a man.

"It appears you have great concern for the womenfolk in your village. I can accept that." No, she would not, but small lies were sometimes necessary. "Have you called for a slayer, then?"

Guiscard shrugged.

"You cannot dismiss the danger!"

"Champrey."

At a nod from Champrey, three knights surrounded Rhiana, not touching, but it was evident they would wrangle her to their bidding if she spoke so much as one more word out of order.

A simple kick to their knees and a fist to a few jaws would serve her anger well.

"Now." Guiscard sighed, and ran his fingers through his hair in an utterly vain display. "Will you be a good girl and listen to your betters?"

Betters? Rhiana required proof for that statement, but knew not to ask for such.

"Very good." Guiscard took in the masses of hair spilling over her shoulders to her elbows.

The look made Rhiana clutch her arms across her breasts. 'Twas not a condemning look, more luxurious. Either one, it made her skin crawl.

Not sure if he considered, or if he merely played the moment out for effect, she waited nervously as the man stepped back from her and studied the floor, hands to hips. Finally he lifted his head, and again slipped close, so close Rhiana smelled his intentions, and they were not sincere. "Be you a witch?"

"N-no, my lord."

"Come now, time to tell the truth. You've bewitched my wife." He lowered his voice to a whisper, "You have bewitched me." Spinning and stretching out his arms in declaration, he stated, "Obviously, you've the power to bewitch dragons to lie down before you and seek death."

All eyes in the keep fixed to her. Chitters and smirks rose amongst the rough scent of power and dirt and rosemary-tainted curiosity.

"I have but skill and dexterity, my lord. I have been trained to know the dragon, its habits, its hunting rituals—"

"And yet you could not foresee the deaths of the three who have been taken from our bosom?" Allowing that fact to settle in, Guiscard grandly stalked the floor. "You know nothing, wench. Now, will you walk from the keep to tend the feminine skills, or must I have you arrested and thrown into the dungeon?"

"I will walk from the keep, my lord." But she would vow fealty to no man. Especially one who risked the lives of innocents through his ignorance. "Good day to you."

And she turned and walked away, feeling many eyes on her back, and likening it to a nest of hungry dragons. But these dragons did not kill for sustenance, no; these dragons toyed with women for their humor. They had put her in her place, upon a shelf to be regarded only when chores needed be done or fancy be met.

Not allowed to slay the dragons?

She'd see about that.

CHAPTER FOUR

What manner of soul did she possess?

That she had physical differences from others could not be dismissed. So she had red hair and freckles. Ignorance caused others to tease her. The color of one's hair did not make them evil or unclean. There were many in the village with red hair. Of course, it was not so bold as Rhiana's, as if sun-drenched garnets. And she could not disregard her unusual eyes. Only those who really looked at her noticed. She did not call attention to the fact one eye was gold, the other green. Lydia's eyes were green. But when Rhiana asked, Lydia would not verify if her father's eyes had been gold.

At the end of a stretch of houses, in the row facing the gardens, stood the chapel. Entering the always open doors, Rhiana genuflected toward the front of the church, then straightened and dipped her fingers into the fount of consecrated water. There was no permanent priest, but the one who traveled along the coast was currently in residence at the castle for a fortnight.

Tracing a cross over her forehead, she whispered a Hail

Mary. Confession must be made soon; it would erase her venial sins, but not the mortal ones. So she did not sin mortally.

Or so she hoped.

Could slaying dragons be considered a mortal sin? She did not know if, by taking the life of a dragon purposefully, she robbed their souls of divine grace. God had cursed them. What grace could they have? Did they even possess a soul?

There were a few benches near the door. Most ladies brought along their own simple velvet-cushioned *prie dieu* to place in the nave. Rhiana liked the open space. No clutter, no sign of the riches upon which the village thrived. Just simple peace.

Striding to the front of the small church, she knelt upon the stone floor and pressed her hands together.

A wooden cross hung over the altar, supported by ropes on either arm of the cross. Carved from limewood and not oiled, the wood bore a few holes from burrowing insects, but that only gave it more charm, Rhiana mused. It was far from the grandiose cross embellished with rubies and gold that she had seen in the castle chapel. She did not care to worship a gaudy master.

Lord Guiscard's penchant for finery oftentimes made her wonder if Lady Anne were not just another bauble in his collection. For truly, it was as if he had plucked her out from a treasure box. With no family to name, and no origins to claim, the woman had arrived in St. Rénan three years earlier, already wed to the baron. (Yet, for all purposes, she had claimed the grasshopper as her family sigil.) Barely seventeen at the time, Anne had spoken little, yet her round dark eyes had seen all.

She had reached out to Rhiana one eve during a hoard-raid fête, drawing her close into a hug.

"So pretty," Anne had said of Rhiana's hair. "Like fire. I like fire."

That was all Rhiana had needed to hear to comply should Anne ever request her presence.

Though she was hardly an orphan, Rhiana felt an affinity to Anne. They were two alike, in a manner she could not quite decide. While Anne's mind was not always her own, and she often flighted from reality, Rhiana could sense the young woman's distinct need for belonging. To understand.

For Rhiana longed to understand.

"What am I?" she whispered now to the cross. "Why do I…?"

Not burn.

The preternatural trait must always be hidden from others. Rhiana would not speak of it, except to Paul, and only then when they were assured no others were close to hear.

Upon her sixteenth birthday Rhiana had forced herself to visit the Nose. The old woman had earned her name because she was always nosing about, had her nose into everything, and knew more than most even knew about themselves. The Nose moved in the shadows, held stealth in her breast, and yet, was no more threatening than the elder widow she was. She was not a witch, though mayhap a sage of sorts. Empyromancy is what she practiced, reading the future in the flames of a hearth fire or the wild ravages of a bonfire. The Nose lived at the south edge of the village, apart from all the rest, not caring to participate in the hoard-raid festivities, but quietly accepting her portion of the yearly stipend and pocketing it in the rags she chose to wear. Her participation in St. Rénan's way of life was the fertilizer she created to cover the castle gardens that produced some stunningly large vegetables and abundant medicinal herbs.

After staring at Rhiana from across a table covered in moth-eaten cor-du-roi, squinting and sniffing as if determining her species, the Nose shot upright and declared her not a witch, but something so much more. Pressing a palm before Rhiana's face, her withered fingers had moved like spider limbs testing the air, and then retracted as if stung by a bee in her web. With a shrill cry, she'd hastened Rhiana from her home and admonished her never to return.

Not a witch.

Something so much more?

But what then?

Touching the moist line of the cross she had traced onto her forehead, Rhiana now mused that it matched the kill spot on a dragon's skull. Put there to remind the beast of what it could never have—divine grace.

Legend told of fireless dragons that long ago roamed the earth. Then the dark angels fell. And the dragons, enticed by the wicked creatures that had defied their God, had mated with them. In punishment, He had reached down from the heavens and touched the dragons' foreheads. Their first offspring had been born breathing fire, a gift from the angels of hell—Lucifer's breath—and an inverted cross upon its brow, the kill spot, a punishment from heaven.

Had she been put into this world specifically to slay dragons? It felt right. When she stood before a fiery beast and defied it with her crossbow and sheer mettle Rhiana felt in her element.

Why Guiscard insisted she not continue, she could only guess was because she was female. Surely, if a male dragon slayer offered to defeat the nest of beasts, the baron would agree to the offer?

"Would he?"

She'd not gotten that feeling from him. For some reason, Rhiana sensed Lord Guiscard would do nothing to stop the imminent threat to St. Rénan. And that feeling unsettled her.

Shuffling to sit on her haunches and spreading her legs out before her, Rhiana rested her elbows on her knees. Hardly a ladylike position, especially with the gown rucked to her calves, but she was alone.

There was some part of Narcisse Guiscard that Rhiana understood on a deep inner level. Gentle and patient, he cared for Lady Anne like no other. That he had even accepted a woman not always of her mind into his life spoke untold compassion.

And yet, each time Lord Guiscard looked at Rhiana she felt his desire crawl across her flesh as if a seeking insect. A duplicitous man. And while that very look was exactly the kind of regard Rhiana craved, she would not answer its plea.

"Never," she whispered. Not from a married man. Not from any of the knights in the village who had pledged to Guiscard. They were all so brutish. The sort of man Rhiana desired must understand a woman, above and beyond her eccentricities. He must not be a brute. Yet, he must practice chivalry. An equal? It was too much to hope for.

Bowing her head she summarized a silent prayer. Thanks be for her strength and skills. Please to keep her family safe and all others in the village she loved and cared for. Paul and Odette. Her mother. Rudolph. Anne. Yes, even Guiscard, for he did love Anne.

And send understanding. Knowledge. Or mayhap, merely acceptance for the unknown.

Crossing herself from forehead to stomach and shoulder to shoulder, Rhiana then stood and glanced out the narrow stained-glass window to her left. The village actually echoed with voices. A good thing to hear after days of silent terror.

On the other hand, if the villagers became complacent only ill could come of their fall from vigilance.

Sweeping up her skirts, Rhiana strode toward the back of the chapel, but noted a glint of steel lying on the floor below the final bench. A leather-sheathed broadsword. The hilt was wrapped in scuffed black leather. Must belong to one of Guiscard's knights, ever hopeful for a skirmish.

Rhiana drew it halfway from the sheath. The blade held more than a few dings and scuffs. A well-used weapon. Hmm, then it could not belong to any in the garrison. There had been a time when the garrison fought to protect the city from marauders and sea pirates. But the port had closed decades ago, and now the city rarely saw travelers of any sort.

Though it did not bear his mark on the pommel, Paul would know to whom this sword belonged. A small flared rooster crest be his mark, taken from his great-grandfather's coat of arms. 'Twas Paul Tassot's proof mark, a sign the armor he'd made had been tested by arrows and was impenetrable at a distance of twenty paces.

Sword in hand, Rhiana set out for the armory. The noon sky brightened her mood. A flash of brilliant white glanced off the bronze roof topping the bath house. Not a single cloud this day. The only thing that could make the day better would be a bit of rain to drench the crops on the south side of the curtain walls.

"I've killed it!"

That declaration sounded too ominous to be a good thing. Rhiana dashed for the bailey where a small crowd had gathered. They surrounded something that moved and struggled about on the dirt courtyard. Was it a fallen horse? She could but see a flailing dark limb.

"Stomp its head!"

"Have you another arrow?" someone cried. "Get me a dagger!"

Rhiana pushed between two teenage boys and spied what had caused the commotion. A shout burst from her mouth before she could even summon sense. "Back! All of you! What have you…"

Plunging to her knees, she splayed out her palms before the struggling beast. Gawky and thin, it resembled a gargoyle nesting the castle tower come to life. It had taken an arrow in the pellicle fabric of one of its supple black wings.

"Rhiana?" Paul's voice, as he pushed through the crowd. "What is it? Oh…"

"It is a newling," Rhiana said to all, hoping an explanation would cool their lust for its life. "A baby dragon." The crowd gasped in utter horror. "It will harm no one. Why, it is no larger than a dog. Who shot it?"

Protests against self-protection and thinking it was a big bird shuffled out in nervous mutters.

"It is a dragon!" Christophe de Ver snapped. He'd sought to join the garrison, but his awful eyesight kept him from earning his spurs, and resulted in more than a few tumbles and visits to Odette for stitching. "You killed one this very morn, my lady. Why are you so keen to keep this one alive?"

So word of her kill this morning had already breached the masses? Couldn't have been Guiscard's doing.

"It is but a babe," she said. "Can you not see it is helpless? Was it you who shot it?"

Christophe nodded proudly. Rhiana must, for once, be thankful that the man's myopia had altered his aim.

The newling mewled. It struggled to sit its hind legs. Its wounded wing shivered and stretched. It was completely black, the scales shimmery, yet supple. Easily pierced with an arrow.

"Bring it to the armory," she heard Paul say. "We mustn't keep it overlong."

"We must kill it!"

"No!" Rhiana stood and bent over the newling. "We will remove the arrow and tend its wound. Then we must release it, or its mother will come looking for it."

"Its mother?" Someone spat. "There are more dragons?"

"She will come anon!"

"And whose fault is that?" She could not argue with the idiocy of these people. And their cruelty. To bring down one so small? "Paul, can you lift it?"

Her stepfather knelt before the newling, and sweeping his arms around the thing, managed to cradle it into his embrace. Vision blocked by the spread of a good wing, Paul hoofed it quickly to his shop. Mewls scratched the sky, and the circle of villagers followed their steps to the armory. Rhiana closed the door on the curious faces and followed Paul into the warmth of the shop.

He set the newling on the wood floor before the brazier where solid ingots of iron waited his coaxing. "It may like the heat," he suggested, and stepped back to stand beside Rhiana. The twosome shook their heads as the creature stood, and then stretched out its good wing. It squeaked loudly as its attempts to stretch the wounded wing resulted in it wobbling and stumbling to land on its tail. Then, with wide black eyes that seemed to beg for tenderness, it scanned its surroundings.

"This is not good."

The newling rubbed its hind legs together. The horny projections on the backs of its legs created a piercing stridulation.

"Immensely not good," Rhiana agreed. "Let's get the arrow from its wing and send it on its way. That sound it makes… I think it is calling for its mother."

Rhiana tried to hold it carefully without embracing overmuch, or making it feel captured, while Paul cut the wooden arrow with a clipper and carefully drew it from the wing.

The newling continued to stridulate. And Rhiana kept a keen eye to the open window. She looked beyond the horrified stares of the villagers and to the sky. Clear. For now.

"There." Paul stood back, holding the two pieces of arrow. "Set it free."

"Should we not cauterize the wound? It could become infected."

"Rhiana, I want that thing out of here."

"Very well, but what if it cannot fly?"

The newling stretched out its wing and shrieked.

"Then it can walk home. Take it to the parapet and release it. Or shall I do it?"

"No," she said. "I can."

The newling dropped to the ground like a rock.

Leaning out over the crenel between two merlons, Rhiana cried out. She should not have expected the small dragon to be able to fly with a hole in its wing. Yet, it wobbled off, away from the battlements, stridulating occasionally.

"Be quiet," she said, but knew the hope was fruitless. "I should have carried you home. Oh, what—"

A cloud soared overhead, streaking the parapet Rhiana stood upon in a fast-moving shadow. Much too quick for rain—

Tensing at the shiver shimmying up the back of her neck, Rhiana did give no more time to wonder at the weather. 'Twas no cloud. Nothing could move so swiftly. Save, a dragon. And not a small, wounded newling, but mayhap…its mother.

CHAPTER FIVE

Steps picking up to a run, and skirt clutched to allow for longer strides, Rhiana headed down the spiraling stairs to the bailey. As she ran, yet another dark shadow crept across her path. A violet-winged creature dove toward the ground. *Inside* the castle walls.

Shrieks filled the air, both of the dragon kind and from humans.

Rhiana cursed her lack of crossbow and the cumbersome skirts. A glance to the shadows of the tower where they'd found the fallen newling spied the sword she'd found in the chapel. Lunging, Rhiana grabbed it. Drawing the sword from its sheath, she abandoned the leather slip in her wake.

The rampant's wings flapped, swirling a gush of wind throughout the bailey. Dry, dusty earth coiled up in small tornadoes. Its cry was as a thousand eagles. Looking for her newling? Had it not seen the small creature wobbling along the battlements?

Likely, it had, and now it sought revenge for the injury done to her offspring. Stupid Christophe, to have shot at the newling!

Landing briefly, the rampant filled the bailey with a wing-span that stretched from the outer steps of the castle to the cooper's shop that sat across the way. The violet beast lifted up from the ground and flew away as quickly as it had landed. The struggling limbs of a man dangled from its maw.

"Inside!" Rhiana yelled to all those foolish enough to yet be out in the streets. "Close your doors and hide under your beds. Grab the children. Run!"

She passed Myridia Vatel who cradled her newborn son to her bosom. Her house stood around the corner; she would make it.

Thudding to a halt before the castle steps, Rhiana searched the grounds. Deep gouges from the rampant's talons carved out the pounded dirt amidst meager hoof marks left previously by horses. No sign of a struggle. The beast had simply lighted down and plucked up its meal. Make that *her* meal. The rampant had been another of the boldly colored females.

A distinct chill scurried up Rhiana's spine. She had seen *two* shadows move overhead.

Sweeping her gaze across the sky, she searched for the second shadow.

"My lady, seek shelter!" Antoine, the cooper, cried as he closed up his shop window, dropping the hinged canopy with a deft release of the screw and bolting the slats securely.

"Anon!" Rhiana called, having no intention of going anywhere.

"Where are you?" she muttered, her eyes fixed to the sky. No clouds. Blinding sun. Pale blue, this day. Gripping the sword firmly, she yet held it down along her leg. "Show yourself, pretty lady. We had no intention to harm your youngling. Scoop it up into your wings, and fly from here. If you do not…"

Rhiana would be forced to make an orphan of the newling.

She could sense the presence in her blood before sighting a dragon. The pulse beat 'twas like a war drum heard long before it marched into sight. Though she had not remarked the danger when she'd set the newling to flight. Awe had lessened her focus.

Now her blood tingled beneath her flesh. Yes, two of them; one, flying away, a man clutched in its talons, but the other was yet close.

The sun's brilliant touch suddenly ceased. Impulsively ducking, Rhiana knew but one thing could block out the sun so swiftly. A creature swooped overhead. Indigo scales glinted as if jewels. Another female.

Instinctively falling forward, Rhiana landed in a crouch and rolled to her back. Close, the beast swooped over her. She looked up and viewed the belly scales. It skimmed above her, a serpent snaking through the air, incomparable in size to any land beast.

The dagged tail swished near her face. The sharpened spikes that decorated the tip, as if a mace head, sliced open the air.

So close. Had she not gone to ground, vicious talons would have plucked her up. A horrible death, that.

The indigo rampant's landing shook the ground. Rhiana rolled to her side. Beneath her palms the earth moved as if startled. She and it were the only things moving in the wide circle bailey before the portcullis gates.

Still she wielded the knight's sword. But it would serve no boon until she could broach the distance to the small target between the beast's eyes.

The dragon bowed its head, prepared to breathe flame.

Reaching out, Rhiana's hand slapped onto a fist-sized stone near her foot. Fingers curling and determination fierce, she claimed the weapon. In a fluid movement, she rose to stand, and thrust the rock overhead as if a catapult.

Direct hit between the eyes! The beast's head wobbled and dropped to the ground.

"Yes!"

She'd knocked it out. But for a moment.

Tugging the bothersome skirts from around her ankles with her left hand, and right hand lifting the sword, Rhiana charged. Bare feet pressed the dirt ground, swiftly gaining the felled beast. The huff of sweet sage encompassed her as she advanced the horned snout. Gasping, she swallowed the dragon's essence, sweet and heavy upon her palate. *Just breathe, and be lost…*

"No!"

Leaping onto the beast's nose, she raised the sword in both hands over her head. The beast's snout was studded in thick armor-like scales of indigo. The scales did not make for a secure hold, and her feet slipped to either side of the snout. Assessing that loss of balance, Rhiana knew in but a moment she would sit astride the skull. And so she plunged the sword into the kill spot, fitting it horizontally within the inverted cross and feeling no resistance as she tilted the blade upward to angle back through the brain.

The creature gave a mewl much like the newling's helpless cry. Wisps of flame snorted across the bailey grounds. The head wobbled to a death pose. The movement tilted Rhiana from the skull and she landed the ground in a graceless tumble.

The tiny death mew replayed in her thoughts. That she'd had to kill this wondrous beast!

With a shove of her hands, she righted herself and looked upon the havoc. Blowing out a breath, she shook her head sadly.

Could this kill have been prevented had the newling not been harmed? She did not like to murder an innocent beast, but its companion had taken one of the villagers, and surely this one would have done the same.

"She killed it!" a gleeful cry from a child Rhiana could not see startled her from the dreadsome thought.

"Hurrah, for the dragon slayer!"

Standing and brushing off her gown, she then retrieved the sword with a tug. Two kills in little over eight hours.

You are a slayer. Revere them, but do not mourn their passing.

Those words, spoken by Amandine Fleche, had been the most difficult to hear, but Rhiana knew they were meant to keep her from succumbing to such overwhelming guilt she might never master her profession.

And so she nodded, acknowledging the beast for its glory and beauty, and then dismissed it as the predator it was. Pride rose as she stood over the felled dragon. Steam gently misted in sage whispers from the nostrils. Glitter of enchantment twinkled in the blood spilling down the sword blade and soaking the hem of her dirt-smattered gown.

Nodding, satisfied and pleased that this one would not have the pleasure of taking a human victim, Rhiana wondered would the other return for another kill.

So soon? Pray not. Surely the female would be appeased and must tend the injured newling. For now, St. Rénan was safe.

Rhiana turned and walked right into her stepfather.

A small band of villagers had pressed into the courtyard. Wondrous eyes and pointing fingers speared her with a curiosity Rhiana understood as less than condemning and more thankful. Though their expressions remained wary. It was the children who danced and poked a stick at the fallen dragon's tail.

"Leave it be!" she called. "Respect it in death."

"You are safe," Paul said and he took her into his arms.

Dropping her sword arm, Rhiana spread her free hand around Paul's shoulder. "I was not able to get the first one. Who...who did it take?"

He shrugged and lowered his head to whisper, "We'll not know until his widow cries out his absence. They came so quickly."

"It was because we had the newling. They invaded the sanctity of the village. My home. Our home."

"Shh, Rhiana, you could not have prevented what happened, even had you sensed their arrival. Nothing could have stood in the way of this attack." He always knew what to say. Paul looked for the right in any situation.

Murmurs rose around her. Some condemning, others relieved. Would they blame her or help her?

Mothers pulled their children from the beast, while the cooper and the goldsmith paced around the head.

Rhiana turned to address those who had began to circle the dead dragon. They were frightened but curious. Calmly, she coached, "There is an urgency required. We must destroy the beasts that would pluck us from our own homes, so daring they be. A slayer is needed. I will serve you well, if you would allow it."

"Your skills are impressive," Christophe de Ver said, "but rumor tells there is an entire nest of the dragons."

"An entire nest? Who says so?"

"The Nose!"

Rhiana jammed the sword tip into the ground, frustration dulling her regard for the valued weapon. The Nose had been most industrious!

"Rumors be just that," she said. "I have not counted more than the three we have all witnessed. This morning I killed the one who stole Jean Claude away, and now this one."

"There is one left! I saw it fly off with a man!"

"They will not stop. And there is the newling," another villager called. "They are breeding! Soon they will nest below our very feet!"

"Nonsense," Rhiana quickly admonished to bestill the stir of nervous whispers that moved about like fire catching on tinder. "We mustn't fear them getting so close as beneath our village. They cannot drill up through solid rock and earth. And the hoard at the edge of the north caves is enough—"

"That hoard is pitiful!"

"It needs to be destroyed," the goldsmith muttered.

Rhiana stared down the flinching gazes and turning heads. They were worried and frightened, because they didn't have all the information, and could only make guesses to what all thought a horrible fate. Best to involve them, so they could know the enemy and learn how to vanquish it. "Who volunteers to aid me?"

Many gazes dropped, and the remainder looked off to the sky. Nervous hands claimed a child clinging to a leg or patted a spouse's shoulder.

Of course, it was a ridiculous request. These men were not warriors or knights, they were simple craftsmen and fathers and sons. They had families to look after. The best protection they could offer was to stay alive themselves.

"What of Lord Guiscard's knights?" Myridia called. "They spend their days hunting and depleting the food stores and their evenings wenching. Should they not be pressed to aid the village in its most dire need?"

Indeed. And yet, would the baron grant the garrison's resolve to the village? He wasn't keen on slaying dragons for a reason unbeknownst to Rhiana. Mayhap if it were *his* idea, and a woman was not involved…

"Perhaps Lord Guiscard should be approached," Rhiana offered, "by elders he trusts and with whom he will hold confidence. I intend to set out for the caves this day in an attempt to determine if there be more than the one remaining. But if I were accompanied by knights on horses, wielding weapons, more the better."

She returned a look to Paul. That he held such pride in his pale blue eyes toughened her strong stance and made what seemed an impossible job a bit less overwhelming. Why could not Lord Guiscard put as much trust in her as her stepfather did?

"We will speak to Guiscard." The cooper stepped forward, removing his leather apron and handing it back to his wife. "I and Paul, yes?"

Paul nodded and winked at Rhiana. He and Antoine both served on the Hoard Council. Mayhap a few others could join them.

"Excellent." She handed the sword to Paul. "I know not who this belongs to; I found it in the chapel."

Paul took it and wiped the remnants of dragon blood onto his forefinger. He rubbed them together in admiration. "Promise you will wait until we return, Rhiana. I will do my best to bring back an army of men for you to lead."

"Yes!" the crowd agreed eagerly.

And though their enthusiasm was heartening, Rhiana could but nod and walk on. This day would bring her no aid.

A runner had been sent to check the caves. Soon the baron would know what, exactly, occupied the caves and how voracious it was.

Narcisse Guiscard tossed a pheasant bone stripped of tender meat onto the small pile growing on the floor below the high table. The mongrel attending the pile growled and flopped to its back, tail between its legs. Make that *leg*. The poor mutt had but three legs. No interest in the thin twig of bone after it had consumed enough to equal half a dozen complete birds from all the table scraps combined.

Dragging his fingers across his crimson hose to wipe away the grease, Narcisse then leaned in to nuzzle into Lady Anne's hair. A scatter of loose dark tresses tickled his nose. She smelled like no thing he had ever known. Rich, sweet, alluring. And damaged. It was that bit of instability that excited Narcisse. For as fragile as she was, her core was powerful. Yet, he knew she hadn't the awareness to tap the core, so frail was her mind.

She responded to his caress with a kiss to the crown of his head. A lingering sigh fluttered across Narcisse's forehead.

"You are troubled, my love? Why do you pick so at your food this eve?"

"There is much to wonder about," Anne said in the drifty, not-all-there voice she often engaged. Her frequent slips to wonder, increasingly more often, troubled him. Soon she would not be his at all. The notion devastated.

She had never truly been his. But whence she had come, he could only imagine. And sometimes he did imagine—to his own great horror.

"I am never so hungry as you, lover." Another sigh lifted her bosom. The creamy white damask paled in comparison to her daisy-white flesh. And there, where four fine gold chains draped across her throat, did her flesh glitter.

Slurping back a hearty draft of rose-hip wine, Narcisse smacked his lips and gestured to the bottler who stood at post behind him to pour another round.

"Do you imagine," Anne said, turning into Narcisse and snuggling her head against his neck so they two shared each other and none at the lower table could be privy to their conversation, "she will come to me today?"

"She?" As he'd suspected, Anne wondered after the Tassot woman. While he'd thought their friendly relationship necessary to Anne's very mental health, now their contact troubled him. The fire-haired woman threatened his ambitions and

Anne's very peace of mind. "Anne, dearest lover, I fear the Tassot wench may have stumbled into some trouble."

"What sort? Is she ill? Fallen? Have you verified as much?"

"No, but when last I spoke to her she nattered on about chasing dragons. Can you imagine anyone wishing to harm those delightful creatures?"

"They have returned to nest in the hoard?" Anne clapped her hands gleefully. "They are so very pretty. I want one, husband. Please, oh please, I want a pet dragon to chain upon a delicate silver chain, as my own."

She traced a finger along the fine silver links that circled her waist and dangled to her diamond-bejeweled slippers.

Narcisse stroked his fingers through Anne's long tresses. Colors beamed down from the stained-glass windows and onto her hair. The glint of sapphire emerging from the dark strands shimmered like stars in a midnight sky.

"A dragon is far too large for your delicate chains, my love."

"I would be most careful! And I would not send it to fetch me gold or trample my enemies."

"You have not a single enemy. You shouldn't tax your head with dark thoughts, Anne. Promise me you'll spend more time in the solar sitting in the sunlight? It is good for your humors, the Nose says so."

"The Nose says too much. She doesn't know everything. She doesn't know what Rhiana told me. She said…." Lady Anne paused, and in that moment of silence Narcisse could almost hear her mind flutter off tangent. How to understand her hidden thoughts? "Kiss me, lover."

He did. And Anne's lips were sweet with wine and unuttered sighs. And menacing with the secrets her mind tightly held. He would discover later, when she lay naked beside him after lovemaking, what she had learned from the bewitching dragon slayer.

"My lord!"

Grimacing at Champrey's abrupt shout—the man ever approached without warning and did so at such inopportune timing—Narcisse reluctantly pulled from Anne and sat back in his chair. "What is it, Champrey?"

"There's been an—" he eyed Anne cautiously "—er, altercation."

"Let me guess," Narcisse drawled. Hooking a knee over the arm of the chair and lazily sulking back against Anne's shoulder, he tapped a pinkie ring noisily against the gold-plated arm. "Cecil, the falcon master has been found soused and naked, draped over the well, yet again."

"Not quite, my lord." Champrey winced. "A dragon has been slain. Again. Here, in the very courtyard of our village."

CHAPTER SIX

After checking that Odette had not a clue about the attack in the bailey, Rhiana then sought Lydia. Her mother had heard of the attack, but only afterward—when the fires were blazing in the kitchen, little else could be heard outside her small interior world.

Now Lydia shivered in a way that always made Rhiana want to draw her mother into her arms for a hug. But she never did. How to touch an enigma? 'Twas blasphemous, yet at the same time, so tempting. Would she find the answers to her questions wrapped in her mother's arms?

Yes.

But not right now.

Instead, Rhiana explained, should the dragons again come, Lydia and Odette must remain in the castle for their safety. Should they be on the streets, they must enter the first house possible. They mustn't risk trying to run home, for the dragons were swift and seeming hungry for the first human close enough to snatch.

Lydia nodded and agreed, her focus averted by rolling the

fine flour and sugar pastry out on the cool stone table. An excuse she must return to her baking was taken with an accepting nod from Rhiana. Her mother did never face adversity, but instead, looked away. If she could not see it, then it could not harm her.

They two were so different. Where had she gotten her mind to chase dragons? Certainly not from Lydia.

"You are off then?" Lydia wondered.

"Yes." For a few moments Rhiana stood there, sensing the tension, the unspoken words. Of late Lydia had been even more distant, almost as if she wished that by not looking at Rhiana she could make her disappear. "Good day to you, mother."

The fire in the armory was low; Paul never doused it unless he was to be away from the shop for more than a day. The curved walls of stone were lined with half-finished swords, plates of armor for every portion of the body, and spurs twisted in ruin and in need of repair. Paul did all the metalwork for the village's knights. A quality product—once requested by King Charles VII himself—kept him busy. Though he was not so busy as an armourer who furnished an active garrison, which suited Paul just fine.

Paul wasn't in the shop. Rhiana recalled his offer to go to the castle and speak to the baron with a few others on the Hoard Council. She must assume he would return without the news she so wished for. Guiscard would not put forth a single knight to aid her. She knew it as she breathed the air.

Sitting before the worktable, Rhiana propped a foot on the highest rung of the stool. The heat of the fire warmed her ankle.

Most unladylike! she could imagine Odette admonishing. Your skirt rides to your knee!

With a smile, Rhiana straightened and put down her foot.

She assumed a vain pose, hand to her hip and lips pursed. That was how Odette and Lady Anne did it. For some reason, the feminine always felt wrong on Rhiana. But just because it felt wrong did not mean she could not strive for it.

For all purposes, she was well beyond the marrying age. Yet, many in St. Rénan married in their later twenties. Rhiana figured this was because the pickings were so slim. She had no intention living life alone and unhappy. Sure, there was room in her family's home, should she wish to remain with mother and Paul. But she did not wish it. Independence tempted.

You have independence. Would you give it up for a man?

"Never. The man I marry must accept me as a partner, not chattel." It wasn't very likely she would find such in this village.

Sighing, she turned to prop an elbow on the table and splayed out a scatter of mail rings. She traced a fingertip around a close-to-perfect circle of wire. She fashioned the rings herself, hammering and drawing to first form the wire. Wrap that length about a steel dowel and cut the rings. A hole punched in one end of the delicate ring was then riveted to the opposite end, but not until actually weaving the mail. Tedious, but fulfilling work.

Years ago, Paul had decided that if Rhiana were to linger about the armory so often then she may very well learn the trade. Much as she'd wanted to learn the real work, pounding out metal over a hot flame, Paul's generosity had not allowed him comfort in teaching her that dangerous task. A man's labor, he'd say, 'tis sweaty and hard on the muscles. No work for a female, no matter her mettle. So small, less strenuous mail-work it was. But no less satisfying to see the finished product.

Drawing one ring out from a scatter of hundreds of rings, Rhiana tapped it impatiently. There was at least one other dragon out there. It had snatched up a man from the bailey this afternoon. One rampant should prove little trouble to take down, whether or not any of Guiscard's knights came to aid her.

Yet, who was she to endanger the village should she fail?

And why was Guiscard so adamant she not attempt the task?

"Why am I thinking failure?" she asked herself.

Would it not be better to at least try, than to not try at all? To wait for a slayer—a man—could prove too long.

Indeed. She was not the person to toe the line, then step back and wait for another to push out ahead of her. A dragon must be slain!

Lifting her head and clasping her hands about her shoulders, Rhiana closed her eyes. Summoning deep within those tendrils of the unknown that ever challenged her, she found the well of ambition, of honor and valiance that brewed.

Ambition she had been born with. It had kept her skirt hems dirty and her eyes focused to adventure. Honor she had witnessed in the skill and grace of Amandine Fleche, and in Paul Tassot's heart.

Valiance is something she would ever strive for. To stand boldly in the face of danger, no matter the consequences.

Rhiana murmured the phrase Amandine had taught her two summers earlier, "Memento mori."

'Twas Latin, and meant: Remember that you must die.

It wasn't so much a morbid statement as a reminder that all life eventually comes to an end. Live it, before it is stolen from you. Seize it! "Meet all challenges," Amandine had said to her. "For in the end, you will then look back and know you did truly live before death."

Rhiana liked the phrase and thought of it as her motto. In fact, Paul had engraved it into the twisting dragon design that graced the stock of her crossbow. It served a reminder to her—and an epitaph to those dragons that fell courtesy of her crossbow bolt.

Hooking her foot upon the high stool rung and nodding to herself, Rhiana's smile grew.

"No dragon is invulnerable. They all have a kill spot."

And where there was a way, Rhiana was determined to find it.

A spring mist fell upon the bailey, beating down the loose dust stirred up by hooves and feet, and wetting the limestone castle walls to a dark sludge color. Narcisse waited inside the main doorway beneath the grand arches that bore the Guiscard family crest in gold medallions fixed to the stone. Champrey had sent a squire to retrieve his rain duster. One thing he could not abide was rainy weather. It made him sniffle and gave him the shivers.

The duster rushed to his side, the squire bowed and then helped slide it up Narcisse's arms and flipped the heavy velvet hood upon his head. The generous hood completely shielded Narcisse's face. He favored the foreboding menace look. Anne said it granted him power. But he already had power.

"Let's be to it, then."

He strode outside, followed by his entourage. At least six knights at all times to protect him from any who thought to protest their lord and master. Rarely were they called to arms, but the security could not be overlooked.

Narcisse had heard the whispers: the son was nowhere near so valiant as the father. Never make a benevolent lord.

And why should he? Everyone had exactly as they wished. There was no need for him to step beyond and show great mercies or benevolence. They had it all!

Oh, what a miserable life to be so satisfied. One must desire. One must…crave. And Narcisse did crave, which set him apart from all others.

"The beast was dragged from the bailey," Champrey explained. He winced at the increasing rain and hunched his shoulders where water ran in rivulets over his brushed leather gambeson. "Took eight destriers to do the task!"

A massive beast lay at the bottom of the castle steps. Narcisse skipped down them. "*Mon Dieu!* What has been done?"

Ignoring his fallen hood, he bent over the carcass of scale, horn and talon. That someone had felled so magnificent a beast. Narcisse understood the threat to innocent lives, but no one could know what a boon the dragon served him.

"My…life," he murmured. "What have they done?"

Oh, but there! There, between the eyes, yet leaked thick, dark blood from a horizontal cut in the transverse of the cross, a mark put there by God himself.

'Twas the first time he'd been so close to a dragon. And yet, he embraced the idea every evening. To look it over and marvel, yes, marvel, must be done. Indeed, they were deadly; a bane to a man's well-being, why, his very mortality.

Narcisse scrambled over the meaty hind legs—thick as a log hewn for housing. Groping his way around the outstretched wing, he swung down to kneel before the belly. A small dragon, about six horses combined, yet to stretch out the tail would surely add twice the length. The belly scales were pale, like burnished gold, and they glittered even under the assault of the rain.

Pressing his palm to the slick scales, Narcisse slid his hand along them, moving toward the hind quarters of the beast, as the scales overlapped, so as not to cut his flesh on the sharpened edges. Minute warmth yet remained; he could feel it.

About him, his men strode around the massive beast, commenting on its lack of fierceness now it was dead.

"Not so ferocious now, is she?"

"Look here at the tail," Gerard Coupe-Gorge said. "I could make myself an ax with this odd dagged scale. That would bash nicely through enemy skull."

Why the man remained in St. Rénan, when he lusted so mightily for blood, was beyond Narcisse's reckoning. But he would endeavor to keep Gerard in his lists, and not make an enemy of him.

Tracing his spread fingers over the belly, Narcisse turned his back to keep his motions covert. He drew away his hand and studied it beneath a hunched tent of his duster. Upon his palm glittered a thick coating of the finest substance. Dragon dust. A rare treasure in this village that thrived so magnificently. None were aware of its value.

Smearing his palm over cheek and nose, Narcisse inhaled deeply of the God-forsaken dust. He could not determine potency, did not feel anything. It had no taste whatsoever. He tested now. No, just a bit of saltiness he evidenced from his own flesh.

"A great loss." He knelt back on his haunches and scanned the beast's body. If it sat at the bottom of the steps for more than a day it would begin to rot and stink. The flesh could be eaten. The scales could be used in some manner. The tusks and talons could be fashioned into cups and dagger sheaths and be drenched in gold.

"Was it the wench who thinks herself a slayer?" Thinks— hell, she *had* slain. Narcisse knew of no knight in the garrison so bold. Save, Gerard.

"Indeed, my lord," Champrey answered. "The demoiselle Tassot. Two dragons attacked the city this afternoon while you feasted. They swooped from the sky and right into the courtyard. The first dragon snapped one of our court musicians up. This one…well, you see."

"I do see." Narcisse tapped the belly, wincing at the loss this would cause him. His quest had been detoured. He muttered lowly, "And the wench took it down."

"Many witnesses recall, with great theatrics, watching her run up the beast's skull to plunge her sword into its brain as if St. George himself."

Witnesses declaring her triumph? Narcisse smirked. So she had developed a following. "Impressive. The people revere her now?"

"In a manner. They are not sure what to think of a woman so bold. But we have always known she is different."

"Yes, different."

"And powerful."

"Powerful?" Narcisse must suppose she was strong to have accomplished something like this. He had watched her grow from a dirty-faced child ever in trouble and being teased, to an independent young woman who would rather go off on her own then do as normal females did. She was…untamed.

A bit like Anne. Beguiling.

And she had slain two dragons in a single day. The woman must think herself quite the swagger.

"But there are more?" Narcisse stood and thinking to wipe off the dust, could only hold his hand by the wrist. The precious commodity must be preserved.

"The Tassot woman insisted she had slain one earlier by the sea, but my scouts report no evidence. The runner tells there is but the one that got away with the musician, my lord."

Champrey would never speak the runner's name, they both knew he was able, swift, and devoted to Narcisse. If gold could not buy one's allies then promises to portions of land could.

"Just the one then?"

"He claims it. It is quite extraordinary, for that means—" Champrey tallied on his fingers "—there were three."

"Many more than we've seen at one time." If he had known sooner the riches that nested so close, Narcisse would have sent out half the garrison to the caves. As it was, he could still take advantage of the situation.

One remaining? That was all he needed.

"We cannot allow this woman to persist with her delusions," Narcisse stated firmly. He must be careful with a situation such as this. Champrey, while his right-hand man, did not always agree with his politics. "She could…harm herself."

"She is quite skilled, as proof is evident, my lord."

Narcisse coached the tic tugging at the corner of his mouth to remain still. If there was another dragon, it could be his only chance for a continued supply. Small hope. But one, it seemed, he would be forced to cling to.

"Oh!"

All eyes looked up to the castle door. Looking frail in winter-white damask, Anne stood, her dark hair spilling down to her waist. The rain did not reach her beneath the arch of the doorway. Hands pressed to her mouth, wide eyes screamed what her voice could not manage.

"Bring her inside!" Narcisse ordered.

One of his knights responded, rushing up the steps, clinking mail and sword sheath punctuating his urgency.

"It is dead!" Anne shouted. "But you cannot— Oh!"

Her body wilted to a faint. The knight landed the top stair. He lunged to capture her about the waist before her head hit stone. "I have her, my lord!"

"Careful, Gerard. Watch her head. Bring her to the solar."

Regret twanged at Narcisse profoundly.

He knew Anne's affinity for the dragons. She, well…she related to them in a manner he could not fathom. Every evening at matins she said prayers for them, and then received a blessing of holy water. Without her blessing she could not sleep, and would roam beside the bed—for the chain kept her close—until the morning hours found her literally slumped on the cold stone floor. She pined to go to the caves. Always she spoke of the nest below her bed—for the caves wended about beneath St. Rénan. But there were no nests below. Narcisse knew not even a small dragon could permeate the narrow caves, but Anne refused to believe.

She should not have witnessed this spectacle. It was all the Tassot wench's fault.

Bending and pressing both hands to the dragon's tumescent belly, Narcisse gave orders. "Drag it to the kitchen entrance. We shall feast heartily for days. Preserve the skull, the talons and the scales."

"Very good, my lord." Champrey signaled to his men to man the ropes tied about the dragon's legs and head. "As for the slayer? Do you wish to have a word with her?"

Straightening, and for the first time noticing his hair was wet for the fallen hood, Narcisse sneezed. Wretched rain. "Can she be brought to me posthaste?"

"Yes, my lord."

CHAPTER SEVEN

Rhiana ran home and quickly changed to braies and a plain woolen tunic and boots. She strapped her talon dagger at her hip and then returned to the armory to don the scaled armor.

The sky darkened early this eve, for she tasted rain in the air. She left St. Rénan through the door guarded by Rudolph while the knights inside the castle ate the evening meal and, at the same time, groped a voluptuous wench.

It took but half an hour, her strides sure and swift, to broach the top of the mountain that capped the caves. Four megaliths marked the grounds as if a king's crown. Keeping to the purlieu of the forest, she marked a spot beneath a massive twisting beech tree. Sending her companion to flight with a nod, she watched as the pisky flitted toward the cave opening. Sitting, she then propped her crossbow over her wrist, she closed her eyes to listen. For a heartbeat.

For challenge.

There, within the depths, beneath the earth and stone and centuries of vegetation fluttered the heartbeat. *Heartbeats*. Focusing, she picked out more than one, for each one was unique as a name or color.

Seven. That is how many heartbeats she counted. But she could not be sure, for some dragons might have burrowed deep into the labyrinth of caves below her resting place.

Mon Dieu. So many?

Did her senses play tricks with her? Was it just the one final dragon, and she interpreted it as so many additional beasts?

Again Rhiana closed her eyes. Breathing slowly, releasing each exhale on a lingering sigh, she quieted her core, which opened her to receive the sounds of life all around. Birds and squirrels, even a fox close by, were easily ignored for their rapid pulses registered as a high, agitated tone as they all sought shelter from the sprinkling rain.

'Twas a low bass pulse that fixed in her veins and matched her own heartbeat—that was the dragon. One, just below, and two to her left. Many more behind, some sleeping, others moving about. They were there, below her.

The villagers will be horrified to learn this. That their nightmare was far from over? But she must not keep it secret. Knowledge was power, and she would never keep them in the dark when all must know vigilance must be increased.

But why so many? All females? And with the dwindling hoard? Was it a doom, traveling in seek of a permanent home and nesting place? They could not have it here! She would not allow it.

But what could one woman do against so many?

A fine mist pelted the long spring grass spiking up at forest edge. Nestled at the base of the beech tree, Rhiana was protected from most of the rain by the canopy of thick glossy leaves. She didn't mind getting wet. Enjoyed it actually, for the raindrops slipped over the scales on her armor and made it glisten.

It was the sound of raindrops plinking upon the leaves and ground that interfered with her concentration.

Content to wait out the weather, for she knew the dragons would not fly this night, Rhiana settled against the smooth trunk, wrapping her wool cloak about her shoulders and the armored tunic.

The pisky she had sent to reconnaissance the caves shimmered through the raindrops, its wings iridescent even in the nighttime, though the heavy droplets hampered its flight. The creatures were as common as butterflies but usually avoided human contact. Thanks to Anne, Rhiana had learned to communicate with them and win, if not their trust, at least their curiosity. Of course, a bribe was never sneered at.

Landing her shoulders, the violet pisky sat for a moment. Its tiny huffs were audible as beats inside Rhiana's head. Patiently, she waited. And in thanks she pulled the small lambskin of fresh cream from her hip pouch and opened it before the pisky.

Fluttering to the edge of the lambskin the pisky drank heartily. After its repast, it flew up to Rhiana's head and sat upon the crown, belly nestled into her thick tresses and arms dangling over her forehead. It began to tap upon her brow, and Rhiana counted.

"Nine?"

So there were two she had missed. Perhaps they slept more deeply, had chosen to hibernate. Or had they come to build a nest? Mayhap the two were males? Or they were maximas. The elder dragons infrequently took to the sky, choosing to nest upon the hoard and store up their energy. Their heartbeats became very sluggish. Rhiana had never opportunity to mark a maxima.

It was the young rampants, vigorous and voracious that flew the skies, reveling in their energy and seeking the kill in small field animals. They did not require the safety and rejuvenation of the hoard so often as the maximas.

For it was the actual hoard, piles and piles of gold and silver and pillages of fine metals that served the dragon's lifeline. All replenished their vitae at least once a day by sliding slowly over the mounds of gold. The metals reacted with the sensitive belly scales, alchemizing rich vitae that permeated their scales and entered their very veins. Rhiana understood little of the actual workings of the transmutation, but it was how Amandine had explained it to her.

If kept from a hoard for overlong a dragon would eventually die. The oldest and largest of dragons needed a constant source of vitae. Though they were most powerful and could be so large as the castle keep, they needed little in sustenance beyond the hoard.

Nine.

So now she must plan how to take out nine dragons before they destroyed the entire village by slowly plucking up person by person. For, it seemed the beasts were intent on claiming humans, as opposed to livestock.

Singularly, was the only way she might defeat any of them. How to draw them out one by one? She may be able to handle two, but only with a distraction to keep one of them busy. But not a distraction as they'd had this afternoon.

With a flutter of its wings, the pisky buzzed her ear, and then spiraled upward to find a dry nesting spot amidst the glossy leaves.

To her left the heather meadow emitted a heady perfume. The rain-soaked blossoms oozed scent like a censer swinging through a church nave, Rhiana's eyelids grew heavy. There was nothing more she could do this evening. The rain would keep back the dragons. They felt the rain as did the piskies; heavy upon their wings. She would dream upon it. Oftentimes she would fall asleep thinking of a trouble, and by morning, the answer became clear.

Standing and tugging down the scaled tunic, she lifted her crossbow to prop over her shoulder. The trek back to St. Rénan was one long league.

Raising a hand to wave thanks to the pisky, it was then Rhiana noticed the shadow cross before the brilliant midnight moon.

One rampant would not be kept back by the rain.

Crossbow drawn, she tracked the flight of the dragon above the sight. Finger tapping the trigger, she held. Utter calm befell her. She would not fire until it flew closer. The bolt could not travel so far; it would be a wasted shot.

She never panicked. But even so, her heartbeats fluttered like a pisky's wings. Rain splatting off her nose and eyelashes made her blink, yet Rhiana held firm.

"Come thee, I bid you," she murmured as the dragon's shadow grew larger in her sights. "I'll not tease you with a dance. Quick and painless, I promise thee."

A burst of flame escaped the dragon's nostrils. Had she moved?

Planting her feet and stretching out her right arm, elbow crooked and fingers firm upon the trigger, Rhiana drew in a breath.

The dragon swooped low, skimming the field. Mayhap it did not sight her, but only blew flame to warm a chill caused by the rain?

When she could smell the vigor stirring the blood of the beast, Rhiana touched the trigger. The bolt released. The dragon banked upward sharply. Target diverted. The bolt found its place in the wing.

"Blast!" Quickly working to reload, Rhiana kept the dragon's trajectory in peripheral view. It hovered above the treetops, as if a fly suspended in a web, and then, it dropped.

She followed the dragon's landing. Mid-fall, the bolt dislodged from the pellicle fabric stretched between the wing bones. The beast landed hard upon its left rear foot, then staggered and fell to its side in the center of the heather meadow.

Scampering over the twist of beech roots, Rhiana stealthily stalked through the brush and to the meadow.

The dragon growled and hissed out fire, but it did not call out the bellowing cry that would alert others of its kind. Was it so smart it did not want to bring others into danger? Or had she hurt it that much with her misplaced bolt?

Moonlight beamed upon the meadow, alighting the heather and grasses like a wilderness stage. Its wounded wing stretched out and flapping at the air, the other wing tucked tightly to its body, the dragon walked, tripping occasionally and landing its head in the thick violet stalks. It struggled, but made its way to the edge of the meadow, opposite where Rhiana stood.

Using its preoccupation as cover, Rhiana carefully stepped across the meadow in the dragon's wake. Crossbow held ready to fire, she kept behind and to the left. The beast wobbled to the right.

Anger-scent strong, the dragon's energy permeated Rhiana's own flesh. A hard vibration of power pressed her quickly forward, eager to claim her prize.

A vicious snap of its head took out a tenderling maple at the forest edge. The dragon insinuated itself into the trees, crushing sticks and breaking branches in its wake. It made a horrible noise but had yet to cry out.

Rhiana chuckled softly. It would never sense her presence until it was too late. She simply had to follow it, and when it finally exhausted itself, make the killing shot.

"Can you come that?" she whispered.

A massive jut of stone concealed the dragon's retreat. Megaliths dotted the top of this mountain, making childhood play exciting when the dragons were not in residence.

Rhiana trod up to the huge boulder and pressed her shoulders to it. Slipping along the slick stone wall she gained the corner round which the dragon had passed. She did no longer hear its shuffling steps and dragging wing.

Did it wait on the other side of the stone? Through all its struggles and noise, had the beast remarked her?

Whispering a prayer to St. Agatha's veil, she drew up the crossbow. Closing her eyes, she listened. But her senses were drugged with the dragon's anger. She could not fully concentrate on noise. And so, it was now or never.

Swinging around the corner, Rhiana drew the crossbow on target with a pair of human eyes.

CHAPTER EIGHT

A steel bolt—set between two intent eyes—aimed at Rhiana's nose. She followed the weapon from glinting tip, down the crossbow stock, to a finger poised upon the trigger. Rain splattered the wooden shaft of the crossbow. Moonlight sparked in the very human eyes mirroring her own deadly gaze.

It took two breaths to realize she stood, not before a dragon, but a man wielding a crossbow. Where he had come from, she did not know.

"Stand down," Rhiana demanded.

The man's eyes narrowed and one dark, wet brow arched in defiance. "On my honor, my lady, you do not look like a dragon."

"Neither do you resemble a fire-breathing beast. Lower your weapon, if you will."

"You first."

The man's mail coif was pelted to his scalp by the increasingly heavy rain. And those eyes, she wagered they were blue, though she could not determine for the darkness.

Still she held her aim.

Avoiding looking at the tip of the bolt, Rhiana summed him up. Dressed head to toe in black leathers with steel spikes studding the coat of plates and his wrists. Broad-shouldered and tall as she, he must be a knight. But she did not recognize him as any from Lord Guiscard's garrison.

"If you be honorable you would stand down first," she sputtered in the pouring rain. "I must be on to the dragon!"

"It slipped down that tunnel."

A nod of his head indicated the wall of stone to her left. Rhiana noticed the slit of blackness that must lead to the lower caves. She had never before remarked the tunnel. It had to be recent.

The muscles in her arms began to stretch and protest her position of aim, but she had no intention of backing down. Her thumb slipped from the trigger. Shivers, caused by the chill rain, echoed through her body. But her intentions were perfectly aimed.

"Are you not a knight?" she shouted against the heavy rainfall. "Pledged to serve your lord, and to protect women and children?"

That got him. The man slowly lowered his crossbow. The usual weapon, fashioned of hard wood with a steel band and fixings.

Stubble marked his narrow jaw. An angry nose, bent to the left, shouted of previous injuries. Completely soaked, the rain softened what Rhiana suspected would prove a rugged complexion. Not an entirely distasteful face.

Or it may be Rhiana was cold, wet and starting to hallucinate, for the air wavered with the cloying heather and the distinct odor of the dragon's sage essence.

"You surprise me, my lady." The man stepped back a few paces to stand beneath an oak tree. There the rain was half so strong, so Rhiana joined him, yet kept the crossbow waist level and pointed at him—ready. "The last thing I would have expected to find upon this mountain, besides dragons, is a woman wielding a weapon as if a warrior."

Rhiana slicked a palm over her scaled armor. The dragon scales glimmered in the moon's light.

"Who are you, sir? And why are you tramping about the forest with a weapon? Lord Guiscard looks unkindly on those who would hunt his deer and boar."

"I am dragon hunting."

Now he set the crossbow against the tree trunk, and crossed his arms over his chest. His gauntlets skittered over the rows of narrow steel studding his leather coat of plates. Rhiana had once fashioned the plated armor, but preferred chain mail, for she could shape it to fit a body exact.

Peering curiously at her, his gaze worked such a hypnotic fix upon her, she found herself stepping closer. Right up to him.

"I wasn't sure if dragons had reinhabited the caves here at the seaside," he said.

"Reinhabited? You've hunted here before?"

"Not me, no, but I've been told these caves are rich and attract the fire-breathers. I had thought to check for myself—with success! My shot to the beast's belly was most effective in bringing it down."

"Your shot?"

Gape-mouthed and stunned, Rhiana spun a look to the dark crevice where the dragon had disappeared, then back to the man. He had a fine opinion of something that was not his to claim.

"'Twas my bolt which felled the beast. An arrow to the belly penetrates merely fat. Nothing more than a bee sting to the creature. But to fly with a torn wing?"

"I beg to disagree, my lady." He splayed a steel-plated gauntlet before him in explanation. "A deep wound to the belly on the younger rampants penetrates easily to the lower organs. My bolt was enough to disorient the dragon. It has been wounded, mayhap, seriously. Likely now it will be an easy track."

Rhiana chuffed out laughter. "You plan to track the beast into its lair?"

"Of course."

Cocky, self-important— Be this man a slayer? For only one trained and experienced would consider so dangerous a tactic.

Had Lord Guiscard held good on his claim he would call for a slayer? But that was only this morning when Rhiana had spoken to him. This man had not been summoned to St. Rénan.

"Be my guest," she offered. "I shall stand in wait of your triumph."

Only a fool would be so, well, foolish.

A nod, and tilt of his crossbow against his shoulder, and the man began to march toward the tunnel entry framed by the rain-slick megaliths. The lackwit planned to enter the cave, teeming with dragons. Nine of them, by Rhiana's estimate. Of course, he could have no idea there was more than the one he claimed to have felled.

The idea of a stranger come to hunt dragons in her territory put up Rhiana's hackles. And that he did not grant her the fell-shot?

"There are many more inside!" he called. He slapped a palm to the stone near the razor-slash entrance that could very well plummet to the very fires of hell. The gauntlet clanked dully against stone. "I guess a dozen."

"Nine." Rhiana stepped into the rain and tramped across the slick grass to join him. How did he know there were others? Fascination prompted her to learn more. "How long have you been here, sir?"

"Just arrived."

Then how could he possibly have determined… "What be your name?"

He bowed grandly, palm to his chest. As he rose, he performed a sneaky, but chivalrous move by lifting one of Rhiana's hands to his mouth.

She almost pulled away when she realized he planned to kiss it, but curiosity stayed her. It was a knight's manner. Chivalry, and all that bother. He merely bussed her flesh with his closed mouth, wet with rain. Heat tendrils traveled up her arm, disturbing her as equally as they excited her. It was the closest she had ever come to a kiss.

"My lady, I am Macarius Fleche, dragon slayer."

Rhiana tugged back her hand. Fleche? But that was…

"Actually," he continued, "I am the *greatest* slayer in all the land, which includes the English isles, all of Italy and the upper parts of Spain. I remain unmatched by any who claim the same occupation. I've twenty kills to my record, all within a decade."

Twenty kills? Impressive. Two a year. What a prize the doom below their feet would offer. Said prize, being more than mere notches to his crossbow. For slayers who took out a dragon were promised all they could carry from the hoard as payment. It was an unspoken rule of the land.

Macarius Fleche. That name…

"Know you Amandine Fleche?" Rhiana tilted her head to dissuade the raindrops from her lashes. "He is a dragon slayer."

"Was." And the man's face changed, the twinkle in his eyes flitting away. With a hook of the crossbow over his shoulder he paced away from Rhiana, walking the expansive curve of the megalith.

Was? But that would mean—

Rhiana rushed after the slayer. "He is dead?"

"Last summer," the man called.

Mon Dieu, Amandine was dead?

There waited a horse behind the megalith, hobbled beneath a copse of maple, and soaked to the hide. The horse bristled its back as Macarius attached his crossbow to the flanks and secured it with a tug to each of the leather belts. The man then turned to Rhiana.

"You are the female dragon slayer I have been told about." A statement. He did not wait for her response. "I did not believe it. And yet now, mayhap there be some tidbit of truth to it." He stretched his hand up her length. "Very fine armor. Remarkable even. Rather, I can believe in the possibility of a female slayer, but there yet remains the proof of it."

Well. Not at all pleased with his indifference, Rhiana took a step toward him, and then marked her anger. Now was no time for arguments. Besides, she need prove herself to no man. Most certainly not to one who considered himself *the greatest.*

"What be your name, my lady?"

But of course, she was being rude. How easily a foul mood clouded her better senses. Odette would surely admonish her for playing the ruffian when delicacy of manner was required to attract a man's eye.

Not that she'd any intention of enacting her pitiful powers of attraction.

Lifting her chin proudly, she declared, "Rhiana Tassot. I *am* a dragon slayer. And I have no cause to prove it to you. Now, if you'll excuse me. I am off to my home. The weather bechills me, and the wounded rampant will not show again this day, to be sure."

"St. Rénan?"

Reluctant to answer, Rhiana knew it was the closet village for leagues. "Yes."

"I am headed there myself." The man mounted the horse

and reined it toward Rhiana. He bent at the waist and offered a hand. "I can carry another rider behind me."

Staring at the black leather palm of his gauntlet, Rhiana vacillated. 'Twasn't as if the plague crawled across the leather. But the offer made her sort of crawly inside. He had demanded proof of her skills. Had almost cast her aside as an impossibility, and so, of little concern. He was as all other men, bullheaded and prideful. Believing women belonged slaving over the hearth fire, or sweeping out their men's dirty boot-prints, or moaning beneath them between the sheets.

The greatest slayer in all the land? Ha! And how many kills had he marked in the past day? Likely, zero to her two.

Cocking her head to the left, Rhiana shook it in answer. "I favor walking. It keeps me strong." With that, she marched off toward the walls of St. Rénan.

For the longest time, Rhiana was aware the man followed her from a distance. Marking her long strides with a slow pace that surely put his beast to misery for the rain. The trek down the mountain went swiftly. Over the decades a path down the counterscarp that wedged a gouge all around St. Rénan, made for a quick, if plummeting walk. Her pace continued across the field of rape that would be harvested for oil and grain come autumn. She would not turn to look at him. That is what he wanted, no doubt, a pleading look.

Eventually the man passed her by, tipping a nod to her, and then pressing his horse to a canter for the village drawbridge.

It was then Rhiana stopped and fisted her hands over the scales that ended just below her hips.

"The daring…"

Well, he had offered her a ride. She should not be angry for that.

But why did it miff her he'd not offered a second time? As he'd passed her by? She would have turned him down again.

Of course! But he could not have known that. Any man would have continued to press her to accept a ride. A gentle man who believed in chivalry, grace and honor.

"Macarius Fleche, eh?"

The surname was common. There was a Fleche who fashioned arrows in St. Rénan. He could not be related to Amandine Fleche. Not once, while training her, had Amandine mentioned a son or other relation.

Amandine was dead? How? When? This man had announced his demise with little regard. He could not be a relative, for would he not have shown some emotion?

Struck to her very heart, Rhiana's tears mixed with the rain as she trudged onward. Her belly began to ache with an inexplicable hollowness. She had lost without having been aware. The old man had taught her selflessly, giving to her the gift of his skills, and asking in return that she strive to be the best.

"I have become quite good," Rhiana murmured as she stalked, wet and weary, onward.

But the best? She had only begun her adventures in dragon slaying. To take her measure now would not be fair, especially when matched against one who had been slaying for a decade.

I am the greatest slayer in all the land.

"We'll see about that."

CHAPTER NINE

He passed by a set of boots, slumped over, but as if standing in wait of a knight to jump into them and race to action. The main gate to the city was imposing, stretching three stories and mounted with a barbican lined in spikes. The entire stretch of battlements was mounted with spikes.

Macarius wondered did the city see siege. Seaside villages often invited pirates and plunderers merely because access was so easy. And yet, the very air seemed so still. Complacent.

His mount pawed the ground impatiently as he again called out for notice, and finally got an answer.

"Who goes there?"

"Macarius Fleche, the great—"

"You are a stranger," droned back at him from somewhere behind the stone walls. "No admittance."

He looked about. Not a soul to be seen or heard, save the woman tromping through the field behind him. Pretty, be she. But a woman stalking dragons at night and in the rain? "I seek an inn to stay for the night, if you please."

"All strangers must be vouched by a resident and accompanied as well."

"But—" Macarius searched for the squint hole behind which he might find an eye that belonged to the obnoxious voice.

"Display your weapons, stranger!"

Obliging, for he was tired and did seek a bed, with a frustrated sigh Macarius drew out his sword and moved his mount to reveal the crossbow.

"Insufficient proof of affability. And not even peace-tied!"

"What? Why you—"

Rhiana walked up behind Macarius and kicked the portcullis door. "Open up, Rudolph. I will vouch for this man."

Silence followed. The woman did not look at him. Macarius could not decide if he were pleased or put off that she was attempting to aid him.

"Very well, my lady. But I never get to turn anyone—"

"Rudolph!" She gave another brute kick to the door and it started to rise on squeaky ropes and pulleys. With a grin to Macarius, she strode inside.

Macarius Fleche rode into St. Rénan upon his sixteen-hand white destrier displaying all the posture of a great and mighty knight. He was a great knight. He'd earned his spurs from Charles VII himself in the unending battle against the Burgundians to rule Paris. His battle sword, Dragonsbane, worked for the good of many. It erased a scourge mere men could never dream to vanquish. As the last of the legendary dragon hunters he had traveled to this particular walled city after hearing tales from Amandine of the female who slayed dragons.

A female slayer? Nonsense. No woman had such fortitude.

Macarius had been determined to see her with his own eyes, to judge if Amandine were merely making a tale or if he had dreamed a woman in his aging thoughts. Surely the old man had a penchant for a well-rounded woman. But Amandine had generally tupped them, not trained them to slay fire-breathing dragons.

And what to think now he'd looked upon the woman?

Rain pouring upon their heads, she'd stood defiantly at forest's edge, solid steel crossbow aimed at him. At him! For a moment Macarius had little doubt, if prompted, she'd touch the trigger. Fright tended to make females goosey and irrational. And then to boldly refuse a ride? And wearing armor that looked as if it were fashioned from dragon scales. She had no right to wear the scales without the kill!

The air inside the battlement walls bustled with an odd tumescence. His mount taking the dirt road in careful clops, Macarius inspected the buildings and houses. Most were two or three stories, very large and spacious. All of stone, even the rooftops were slate or tile. No thatching or wood structures. Interesting. All of stone? Rather smart, he mused, for a village that must be frequently set upon by fire-breathing dragons.

Meows from a gather of mangy cats sang a wretched tune beneath a dripping slate tiled roof. Shop fronts were closed, wooden boards pulled down and tied for the evening. Macarius neared the castle courtyard and noticed the blazing iron torches shaped like dragons. Banners swayed in the minimal breeze. Distant pipes called to revelry. Indeed, merrymaking stirred behind the castle walls.

There were almost a dozen dragons nesting but a league to the north. Did the village fête in the shadow of such danger?

Were they aware? But surely their female slayer must have alerted them? Else, why ever would she be so quick with him at the gate if she had not rushed to warn them all?

Amandine had not given him details of his stay in St. Rénan, only that it was a happy summer. He did never elaborate; so many secrets he kept to his breast. But Macarius knew the old man had likely a woman, or two, reason enough to stay a while in any city. But he could not imagine Amandine taking the young woman he had met as a lover. He did possess decency. So what had called him to the woman?

Whistling to direct his mount to the left, Macarius spied a thin young man doddling outside a cart stacked with firewood.

Upon question, the squire in ragged green hosen—but a spit-spot clean tunic—informed Macarius the villagers had gathered in the castle keep to celebrate the kill. A dragon had been slain in the courtyard this afternoon. Lord Guiscard invited all to celebrate and drink and eat for days. Dragon meat would be passed around until all had filled their bellies.

Mayhap the woman *had* slain a dragon. And this day? Hmm... Of course, Macarius required proof of the act. Likely the village men had rallied and taken down the beast.

"And," the squire added, "it be much safer than walking about outside. The dragons will swoop down and bite you right out of your boots."

Macarius had noted the boots sitting just outside the battlement walls.

"So, boy," he leaned down from his high mount, "you know there are other dragons?"

"To be sure! They fly the sky waiting for a man to forget his caution."

Macarius nodded in agreement. He straightened in the saddle. That familiar surge of adventure teased his muscles. Such fortune to arrive at a dragon infested city.

Nine dragons, the woman had said. And how had she counted?

"My thanks," he said to the young squire. "Will you lead me to your lord?"

"Indeed, sir."

* * *

Alive with merriment, music and much ale and smoking meat, the keep was crowded from wall to wall with most every resident of St. Rénan. Dragon meat was tender and savory when cooked right, Lydia had once told Rhiana. Still, no amount of cajoling would convince Rhiana to taste the meat. It was difficult enough to account herself for the sin of killing. And it wasn't as if dragons were bred for consumption, like a lamb or even cattle. But she did not discount others for joining in the feast.

Rudolph skipped by her, a hunk of dark meat on a stick clasped in one hand and a giggling female's derriere in the other. Rhiana returned his wink and then found herself sliding her palms over the pale ocher tunic and braies she wore.

All about her couples were dancing and whispering in each other's ears and some even kissing. Dulcimers decorated the air with lively rhythms that enticed women's hips to swivel and the men to circle about them. The women wore their hair in braids and curls and crowned their temples with delicate flower garlands. No wonder they attracted a curious suitor, Rhiana decided, the sway of their skirts and the tinkle in their laughter was an entrancing thing. So utterly female and beguiling.

And here she stood, being passed by, almost as if a ghost, by every male in the room. A hard lump at the back of her throat made a swallow difficult. "I…" *Want,* she thought. *What they have.* To be fancied by a man. To know a man's regard.

Should have changed to a gown—

The sudden gush of fire close behind Rhiana made her spin. There, near the hearth, stood Sebastien de Feu, the fire juggler. Wearing brown leather braies—he never wore a shirt; fire hazard—the dancing fire tricked across his muscled chest, drawing Rhiana's interest. In each hand he held a five-pronged torch that resembled a dragon's claw, glittering with flames at each of the five talons. Swishing the torches before him painted brilliant white dashes and circles and zigs in the air to delight all. Children danced around him, unsuccessfully held back by their mothers.

Sending a charming smile to Rhiana, he then breathed upon one of the torches and sent the flames gushing over heads and toward the center of the keep.

Compelled by the beauty of the flame, Rhiana stepped closer. She forgot her masculine attire. Why, she forgot the festivities. All that mattered was the flame dancing through the air, swishing hot breaths across her face as she moved even closer, until she stood so close a child called out for her to mind her distance.

Sebastien's grin defied the difficulty of his stunt. Though he wore a steel helmet fashioned with bronze laurel leaves around the perimeter to protect his long black hair, Rhiana had noticed previously he also wore many a scar from burns. The most prominent on his left forearm, which stretched to a thin pink sheen, because his muscles were so bold and tight.

"You are entranced, *douce et belle?*"

Shaking her head out of its tizzy, Rhiana realized Sebastien spoke to her. *Douce et belle.* Too pretty a moniker to place to her, but he was ever kind to her, and always willing to talk.

He leaned in toward her. She could hear the fire torches hissing behind his back. The scent of the oil he used to keep the torches burning sizzled in the air. And the scent of him, oil mixed with his intense and dark presence, almost overwhelmed Rhiana.

It could be the smoke and flame; they always disturbed her senses.

She touched a stone in the nearby hearth wall, for balance. Consciously tugging the hem of her tunic, she could not meet the man's dark eyes. Dark like the lava stones in the caves, she knew, for whenever he was not noticing her, she noticed him.

A flutter in her breast troubled, and suddenly she could not find her voice.

"My lady? Have my flames burned your tongue silent?"

She shook her head. A tilt of her chin caught his eyes, and she held his stare for a few moments. Feeling her neck and face flush with warmth, Rhiana convinced herself it was merely the close presence of fire.

So close, the fire, and in the form of muscles and sinew and beguiling dark eyes.

"You never talk to me, *douce et belle*. Do I frighten you? I would like it if you would say but a few words."

Frightened by something so wonderful as flame and… and…him? Rhiana began a grin.

"My lord, the dragon slayer!"

Suddenly alerted by the seneschal's voice, she turned from Sebastien's beguiling eyes and stood on tiptoes to see about the keep. Dancers who reveled and made merry parted as a stranger entered the keep.

Finding an audience with the baron of St. Rénan proved easy enough, even after the squire had abandoned him for the lure of hot dragon meat and a game of sticks. Macarius had merely to sight in the high table amidst the revelry of drunken lackwits. The glint of gold tableware could not be missed.

Macarius strode through the grand hall glittered with golden fixings and freshly strewn rushes. Fresh flower garlands draped the doorways and the backs of chairs. Tapestries on the east wall depicted the dragons' fall from grace with the evil angels. A particularly grand dragon skull, gilded around the circumference of the eye openings, hung high on the wall over Lord Guiscard's chair. The upside-down cross indicating the kill spot glittered with rubies set in gold.

Studying the beast's skull, he determined Amandine

might have been responsible for that one. He knew of but two other slayers in Europe, and rarely did they venture close to the sea, for the added hazards, such as the cliff-side entrances to the dragons' lairs and, well, there was the sea and all its dangers. Amandine had liked to travel the coast, knowing the greatest challenge always offered the most satisfying results. Besides, he'd once told Macarius of the sirens. He had not seen one himself, but what riches he would give to see a flash of scale and to catch a pretty green smile.

Sirens. Macarius nodded. Yes, he would like to see the sort, and would, surely, for his travels took him far and wide. What a catch that would make, eh? He would commission a massive tank and display her for all to see when finally he settled and built his own castle upon the sea.

But enough of that nonsense. He had a more urgent commission to gain. If there were so many dragons, that could only mean one thing—the hoard, which attracted the beasts, must be tremendous.

The seneschal who had seated himself to the right of the lord whispered into his ear and gestured toward Macarius. His reputation obviously preceded him for the baron nodded and grinned. How joyous this village would be to receive him into their arms!

"My lord Guiscard." Macarius bowed grandly before the damask- and silver-lace festooned high table. His gauntlets clicked against the sword sheath at his hip. Flames from the many wall torches glittered across the mesh hauberk skirting in dags below his coat of plates. The very flesh on the left side of his body pinched with the movement of so grand a bow, but Macarius was accustomed to pulling a face over the pain. "I am delighted you have bid me welcome into your home."

Guiscard twisted his fingers, ringed with sapphires, and

studied Macarius with vivid blue eyes. "My seneschal tells me you are a dragon slayer?"

Did Macarius detect a note of *boredom* in that tone? Must be the abundant wine, and a night of festivity surely altered a man's sense of generosity and need for protection.

"I am indeed a slayer, the greatest in all the land. Macarius Fleche. I travel constantly, and mark no city, village, or demesne my home. I have followed my father's profession, and before that, his father. I once worked with a partner, but alas, he has fallen to the bane of our profession. Therefore, I am the last of a most fearless and revered breed."

"I see. Quite the pedigree."

Macarius bristled proudly. "I've patents if you wish to look them over."

"No. Just get to the point, Fleche. What brings you to St. Rénan? Do you not see we celebrate? If you wish to join the revels, be my esteemed guest, but if you've another reason for interrupting…"

Macarius snickered at Guiscard's bantering disregard. A glance about found the entire keep had settled to observe and whisper. So let them! This day their lives would alter for the better, thanks to his skills.

"My lord, and good people of St. Rénan—" Yes, involve them all. It only increased his esteem. "I understand you've a dragon problem."

The woman sitting to Guiscard's left—very nearly in his lap—reached for a sugared sweet and pressed it to her thick red lips. Her dark eyes held him with an intense fascination that bordered on eerie.

Guiscard gave a dismissive sway of hand. "Eh. St. Rénan has always been known to harbor dragons. You've seen one…"

Such complacent disregard!

"But, as I am given to understand," Macarius said, now a bit quieter, but still firmly, "not for some years. Yet the dragons have returned to the caves overlooking the sea."

"You purport to know our village well."

"My father spent the summer here a few years back. He waxed effusively on the gorgeous meadows strewn with fragrant meadowsweet, and of your hospitality, my lord."

Best to lay things thickly, Macarius knew.

"Seems we've a rash of eager slayers, of late," the baron announced.

"My lord?"

Another dismissive shrug.

Macarius felt the eyes of all upon him. Beaded hennins draped in silks of all colors tilted in interest. Men wielding pewter mugs of ale, and a woman's backside in the other hand, paused to listen. Still the musicians played, but quieter, background accompaniment to the show before the high table. At the rear of the keep a man holding elaborate fire torches held a pose of interest, his arms high to light him like a gilded statue. Even the three-legged mutt wending its way through the crowd seemed interested.

Macarius did not mind the attention. Stand back, one and all; he'd show them his skills. Who dared to put a challenge to the greatest slayer in all the land? He'd snatch that challenge up with his teeth and spit out the booty for all to admire.

Lord Guiscard stretched forward in his chair. "We don't need you, Fleche." He flicked his multi-ringed fingers at Macarius. "I bid you leave as quickly as your mount can carry you from the village."

"But—" Macarius wasn't able to get out a protest because two behemoth guards gripped him by the shoulders and literally dragged him—boot heels tunneling through the rosemary rushes—from the keep.

"Lackwits!" Macarius shook his fist at the buzzing crowd. "You are all in danger! They will not leave you alone!"

He spied the woman who claimed herself a slayer, leaning against the hearth, one hand to her hip, and a smirk stretching her lips.

What was her name? Well, he could not call out for she seemed as humored by his embarrassing exit as all others.

Flung bodily outside, Macarius caught himself from a fall against the stone balustrade on the top step. "We don't want you. Begone!"

The doors to the keep closed with a clank of iron and a hiss of dust.

Stumbling across the rain-slick stoop, Macarius stepped to the side and down the steps. Torchlight beamed across his face. He flicked away a nuisance moth.

"I will not be gone. Someone has to slay the dragons."

"It is a brave man who can stand before a beast of fire without flinching."

Macarius swung to observe a man who appeared to be an armourer, for his leather apron and darkened face and hands. He held a heavy hammer and slapped it in his palm. Did he threaten him? Be this his punishment waiting?

Macarius strode past the man, but was joined at his side. He allowed the accompaniment, because he wasn't sure where he was going, and didn't want to ask directions. There must be a tavern where he could get some beer and fall asleep on a bench. It couldn't be considered livable if the town did not have at least a tavern or two.

The armourer matched Macarius's strides. Hooking up his horse's reins, he did not break pace. "Why are you not inside, fêting with the rest of the lackwits—er, people? There is much wine and idiot laughter to be had behind those walls."

"I choose not to laugh at death," the man offered.

Macarius paused. He did not turn to the man, but stared off into the midnight sky. So many stars. Twinkling at him like a woman's eyes leering over the steel shank of a crossbow. Or did they smirk at him? She *had* smirked at his embarrassing exit.

He would not be so easily put out from the village.

"How many have died because of dragons?" he asked the armourer.

"In the past five days…four. One this very morning in the bailey. It is dragon meat the castle roasts this night."

Macarius swung to peer into the man's eyes. Rimmed in black soot, the splay of lines at the corners of his eyes showed white against his brown flesh. "Dragon, eh? A bit gamey for my taste, but if seasoned well and salted for weeks it can serve an exquisite palate. Who took down the dragon?"

"A slayer." The man walked onward, thumping the air near his thigh with short hammer beats. "But she needs help, whether or not she will admit it."

She? Suddenly breathless, Macarius rushed after the man. "I have seen this woman. Red hair and a strange coat of armor that glistens under the moonlight."

"You could mistake her for none other, that be the truth of it."

"She had counted the dragons, and claims there are at least nine more!"

"She has a manner to her. She can sense the beasts. Hear their heartbeats."

Yes, yes, Macarius knew as much. He was so honed to tracking the beasts he could smell them leagues away and guess their sex merely by sniffing the wind. But that another had developed the skills he'd thought to possess exclusively?

"How know you this woman?"

"She is my stepdaughter. And who be you, monsieur? You look ready for a dragon yourself."

"I am Macarius Fleche."

"Fleche? Be you the son of Amandine Fleche?"

"The one and the same. My father…trained your stepdaughter?"

"Two summers ago, just beyond the forest that laces the mountain. Her name is Rhiana. I am very proud of her."

"I see that. And so what is the quandary with Lord Guiscard? He refused my offer to slay the dragons."

The old man shrugged. "He chooses to overlook dangers to his people while he remains safe behind his walls of thick stone. Rhiana is selfless. She will fight for us all. But I fear for her. There are many more dragons than we'd initially thought. Nine, you say?"

"Yes! And how ridiculous for a woman to think she can take them all down herself!"

Now the man leveled a formidable gaze on Macarius. Macarius would not argue any man who wielded a hammer and a stern eye. "She is a warrior, man. And you will do well to stand beside her, not before her."

Duly warned, Macarius nodded and dismissed himself to locate bed and board.

A warrior woman?

No woman was going to stand before him and make him look the fool.

CHAPTER TEN

"You've the instincts for the hunt," Amandine said, as he swung a long fighting staff fashioned from limewood toward Rhiana. "It is almost as if you think like a dragon atimes. It startles me you can determine their intention before it is evident."

Dodging to avoid the staff's trajectory, Rhiana spun and delivered a whack with her rosewood staff to the return swing of her trainer's weapon. "I can feel their flight as if in my own muscles."

"Yes, instincts," he repeated. "A marvel—ouff!"

Knocked to the ground by an expert swing of Rhiana's staff, Amandine Fleche hit the dust with a pouf of smoky dirt rising about him. Rhiana, dirt smeared and sweating after an afternoon spent beneath the hot sun training, offered her hand to help up the old man.

Not so very old that she worried for his health or breaking a bone during their sessions. Amandine was a hearty, strong man who had faced many a dragon in his time and yet stood. Which was saying a lot. The average span of a slayer's life usually stretched no farther than his ability to avoid flame. He had

Michele Hauf

arrived in St. Rénan a month earlier as the pinks had begun to blossom in the meadow. He'd watched her that afternoon as she had run across the gap-toothed merlons dotting the battlements. Rhiana often took them by catapulting forward on her hands, body flipping over her head and landing one merlon with her feet, then swinging onto the next hands first. A feat that still garnered worried shouts from Rudolph. When Amandine had accompanied her to Paul's shop—Lydia didn't like strangers in her home; of course, she never blinked an eye to the many knights whom Odette frequently doctored—telling her tales of his slayings, she had listened, enraptured.

A simple question, "You have always known?" had drawn Rhiana's confession.

Yes, she had always known she was different. That the few dragons she had seen in her lifetime had set her blood to a blaze. That she knew she could get close to them, and would not fear. And yet she knew little about the actual dragon.

Amandine had taught her all she needed to know. That dragons lived centuries, but only the largest and eldest ever grew to full maturity—the maxima. It was the young ones—the rampants—that tormented the villages, snatching up the unwary and flaming the crops. They were beasts, nothing more, chaotic, dangerous, and feral. He'd also explained that it was the males that guard the nest, and the females who hunted for food.

But the old dragons, now they were a spectacle. Amandine had once seen a maxima. As large as the castle keep, he'd guessed the beast had roamed the earth two hundred years. He'd found it spread out across a great hoard deep within a cave at the southern border of France. The maximas became rather sluggish in their longer years, but yet remained a force. It was rumored the elder dragons could communicate with mortals, bechance, they could even shift to mortal form during the night of a blue moon.

For what purpose, that change, Amandine had not known. He suspected it was to walk amongst mortals, mayhap to learn their secrets.

Amandine had not the heart to slay the mighty beast. For he'd thought he'd heard its voice in his head. *I seek not your vengeance, only your understanding.* And so he'd left the creature to its nest of gold and instead, had slain a male rampant on his path back up to ground.

Amandine had taught Rhiana an array of physical skills in the three months he'd stayed at St. Rénan. Swift of foot, that be a slayer's forte, for dodging flame was of highest import. How to breathe softly, yet use one's entire lung capacity. Such breathing clears the head, Amandine had coached, and opens one to the unexpected, also, it allows silence and stealth.

Rhiana had given the breathing a try. Indeed, when she most needed to concentrate and focus, breathing served a powerful accompaniment.

Now, she woke from her dreams with a start. Tears trickled down her cheek. Morning sun beamed a white triangle across the foot of her trundle bed. She'd dreamed of her trainer. And now to be told—with so little compassion—he was dead. Amandine had come to be a figure of authority and kindness, much like a grandfather, in Rhiana's life.

Who was Macarius Fleche?

Dragon slayer, yes. Arrogant and self-serving, obvious. Beguiling? Well, she would not say so out loud, but…

But who was he really? It could not be coincidence that *two* slayers with the surname Fleche had come to St. Rénan. Could it? And why did she care to discover more about the handsome man who had almost shot a bolt right between her eyes?

The day promised full sunshine after yesterday's cleansing rain. Rhiana tugged the blue damask gown over her head, tightened the laces at her shoulders and the right side of her waist and stretched her arms wide to open her chest and breathe deeply of the sweet morning air.

She always slept with her window open. Better to hear approaching danger, and to note the changing times of day merely by scent.

This day a cool sea breeze undulated across the linen panels hung on the north wall of her bed chamber. Odette had embroidered pink cabbage roses along the panel borders. Very little in the house escaped Odette's fetish for the ornamental.

Save me, Rhiana thought with a smile. Though Odette had tried many a time to curl Rhiana's hair or braid flowers into her red tresses, Rhiana had ever slipped out before the decorating could begin. Though, she was intrigued by the henna designs the Nose painted on Odette's hands and feet. Many of the village women went to her for the same. It was a Persian ritual, Lydia had once told her.

Plucking up a small pebble of white gesso, she stood before the stone wall that paralleled her bed. Riddled with her tiny, precise scribbles, the wall drew her concentration first thing every morning. She enjoyed marking out letters. Books were few and rare here in the village. Besides integrity, knowledge was high on Rhiana's list of personal value. There was a small library in the castle, rumored to hold Pascal Guiscard's collection of dragon lore, but the one time Rhiana had broached Anne about being taken there, Anne had sighed dramatically and consigned books to a lazy man's mien.

Pressing the chalky stub to the stone, Rhiana carefully underlined the statement she'd written out yesterday morning: *memento mori*.

Remember that you must die.

"Memento mori," she repeated, and smiled, to think of yesterday's success. The gauntlet had been laid down. It was either the dragons or herself. She would die to see her family safe. Yet, she felt she had so much to live for, so many wonders to experience, and so she said a prayer for longevity.

Giving but a glance to her flat-soled damask shoes by the door, Rhiana tossed the gesso to her bed and padded barefoot down to the second floor where Odette sat against the hearth, snoring. Four years younger than she, her half sister had a habit of waking at dawn with Lydia to chat with her while she dressed and readied to leave for the castle, then immediately falling asleep wherever she had been sitting following Lydia's departure. Tiny amber lines snaked around Odette's wrists. She must have visited the Nose last night before the festivities in the castle. Odette always wanted to look her best for any interested man.

Behind her, the spice cupboard remained unlocked, no worry for thieves come in search of saffron, vinegar or pepper. Every one in St. Rénan had exactly what they needed. Below that the table was set with a cooling loaf of bread and some rose-petal-dotted almond milk pudding.

Rhiana dipped a finger into the creamy concoction. She loved the simple treat. Stealthily, she lifted a spoon and dipped that into the bowl, quietly consuming the entirety while Odette slept. The moment of luxury seemed too rich. Her mother's concoctions almost made her weep. So perfect, and smooth, and crafted with such love.

It was that care and attention to detail that ever troubled Rhiana. That she had never received equal attention bothered. How to win her mother's love?

Why do you think so? She loves you, only, she loves you in a quiet manner.

"Mayhap," Rhiana said, as she set the spoon inside the empty bowl.

Finished, she crept past Odette toward the steep stone stairs that curled to the lowest floor.

"You will protect us?"

Startled at the sleepy question, Rhiana paused in the stairway and looked back to her sister. Blond curls tousled about her head in a ridiculous crown of femininity. Eyes closed, she wiggled her nose and tilted her head against the stone hearth to readjust her position.

"From the dragons?" she prompted.

"Er…" Never before had Odette shown interest in Rhiana's calling. Usually she snickered when she'd see her leave with crossbow in hand. "I shall try."

Now Odette opened her eyes, and shrugged a palm up her opposite arm. A foot stretched and rotated at her ankle. A kitten waking from slumber. "Please try very hard."

It was the closest to a plea Odette would ever manage. And so innocent, yet laced with the real fear Rhiana felt ran through the veins of every person who walked behind the walls of St. Rénan.

"I will fight for my family's safety ever and anon, good sister."

Satisfied with that declaration, Odette smiled sleepily and drifted back to doze.

The morning was quiet this day. Rhiana passed under the horse head sign of the harness maker, and jumped to tap the gilded pill sign outside the apothecary's shop. But the cooper and a pack of mongrels snoozing before the closed tavern were all who disturbed the air. Most must be sleeping late after a night of festivities in the castle.

Skipping and jumping, she hummed a bit of the exotic music the musicians had played last night. Lady Anne had insisted the baron import musicians from a gypsy village that edged the northern sea, for she loved the rhythms and chanting. Sensual and alive, the twisting, tangy beats agreed with Rhiana as well.

Brief thought diverted to Sebastien and his flaming repertoire. Did he dream of dragon fire like Rhiana did? Likely not. Men's dreams were not so fantastical. So then, did he dream of a particular woman who stirred his fancy?

He ever tried to make her speak with him, and was always winking at her. *Douce et belle.* The moniker, even to think it, stirred tingles in her belly. Mayhap he used it with all women? Pray not. It was his exclusive name for her. Yes? A handsome man, Sebastien, but yet, Rhiana wasn't sure if her attraction to him were for his physical appearance, or the flames he mastered with such ease.

For truly, flame bespelled her.

Rhiana scanned the battlements as she walked. It was foolhardy to post men at the postern towers, for they would be a hungry dragon's first stop. But surely, a dragon-proof cage could be developed, something that would house a man safely. And he could wield a horn to alert all.

And what fool should volunteer for such a task?

As she entered the cool shadows of the chapel, Rhiana tilted her head, alert. The quiet solitude of the building felt different this day. The straw covered floor tickled beneath her bare feet. Dipping her fingers into the blessed fount of holy water, she then genuflected and traced her forehead.

Beams of light cast dust hazes across the well-worn benches at the back of the chapel, but there, up near the altar, a man lay on his back, his length stretching one bench complete. There were two benches; they were usually kept to the back of the chapel. Had he dragged them near the altar? One arm dangled, his hand bent to parallel the floor. His black leather coat of plates gleamed, each silver stud riveted to either end of the finger-long plate capturing the light. As Rhiana walked closer, the dancing metallic light glinted at her.

Macarius Fleche. She thought the name to herself. *Macarius*. An interesting name. It remained on the tongue long after one had spoken it. Intriguing? Mayhap. But this man had shown her no such beguiling talents as juggling fire.

Quietly drawing up to the end of the bench, she bent over his head and studied his upside-down features. The nose was long and set plainly upon his face, but not so thin to signal vanity. It had been broken once, she guessed, for the crook at the middle that set it in an eastward direction. Thick black brows dashed to peaks at their centers, granting a devilish wink to his closed eyes. Dark stubble above his slightly parted mouth matched the stubble shadowing his jaw and the back of his head.

Rhiana lingered upon the side of his face, where, as she followed the stubble down his neck and beneath his ear, she saw a thick scar emerge from under the gray wool gambeson he wore beneath the plated coat. 'Twas not a thin wound, possibly from a cutting blade, but rather, stretched a wide path from under his ear. Had he been burned?

By a dragon. The knowledge came to her as if a chalk scribbling on the wall. She knew it as truth.

Pointing a finger to touch the thick silvery flesh, her breaths moved softly over her lips. Using her breathing techniques, she stilled her presence and became very stealth. Carefully, ever so slyly, she pressed the pad of her finger to the rigid, scarred flesh.

Heat flushed through her finger, scurrying over her wrist and up her arm. The sensation moved so swiftly Rhiana hadn't time to know it was a reaction, but merely took it as the sunlight beaming through the window and heating to great intensity.

Macarius startled. Rhiana stumbled backward and landed the bench opposite where he lay, an awkward landing that might have toppled her to the floor did she not place her feet firmly and her hands behind her to grip the wood bench.

Scrambling upright and drawing out his sword from its steel scabbard with a *shing,* Macarius turned on her. His reach, extended by the sword, touched her chin. Lips sneering, his teeth gritted tightly. "Who be you?"

"Stand down, man! You know me."

He blinked and shook his head to chase away the sleep. "The woman who slays dragons. I should have known."

He retracted his sword, but did not resheath it. Instead, he laid it before his knees on the bench he now straddled.

Not willing to completely yield the match, Rhiana mused. Always ready. As should be a man of his profession.

"Did you sleep in the chapel?" she asked.

"I did."

"Were you not welcomed into Lord Guiscard's company?" She knew the answer—had seen his tossing-out—but a mischievousness to his arrogance could not be ignored.

"Seems the lord of your fine village has no interest in exterminating the dragons that intend to wreak havoc upon his people." Macarius eased a hand over his face, and rubbed a thoughtful thumb along his beard stubble. "Why is that?"

Mimicking lack of knowledge with a tilt of her chin, and a shrug, Rhiana casually said, "How should I know the mind of so powerful a man as Lord Guiscard?"

So Guiscard had no intention of hiring a slayer. And should one arrive? Guiscard had refused his services. What was the baron to?

"Does not your lord baron know the dangers? What fool refuses this offer I make? It is for the good of all!"

"Mayhap he is oblivious to the dangers. We've not been visited by dragons for years. The last beast, about two years ago—Lord Guiscard was away during that time—well, I killed."

"Really." Macarius looked her from toe to crown. A blatant summation. An interested look. The kind of look that should make a woman blush. But he wasn't holding fire torches, nor did he wink at her.

And Rhiana did not blush. In fact, the man's stare fascinated her. His intentness changed his rugged face to an appealing boyish charm. A face that did not so much threaten as entice.

"And now you intend to take out your dozen dragons single-handedly?" he prompted. "Can you come that?"

"I did not say I could do as much. And there are only nine."

"Nine. Twelve. It is still very much. Of course, you cannot slay them all. Only a woman would be so foolish to even—"

"I said I could not do it myself. Do not even attempt to chastise me for speaking truth."

"You…need assistance?"

Rhiana shrugged, then turned to face the wooden cross hanging above the altar. A spider web stretched from the cross to the rafters, the delicate gossamer filaments wavering in and out of the sunlight.

An invitation, he sought? She did not know the man. And the little she did know of him put him a brazen, cocky male who served bravado more fully than humanity.

A foolish woman? The man had no idea whom he spoke to.

She bowed her head into her palms, attempting to call some serenity to her troubled thoughts.

"If you do not answer me, my lady, I shall persist—"

"I am praying," she insisted firmly. That called his silence.

Well, *now* she would begin to pray.

Rhiana closed her eyes and muttered a Hail Mary for yesterday's fallen dragons.

She revered the great beasts. Yes, even as she was slaying them. They were creatures of old and ancient enchantment.

Someday she would stand before an elder dragon, and like Amandine, she prayed for the mindful presence to allow it to live. To draw upon its centuries old knowledge, and to become more peaceful for having done so.

Might she witness its transformation from beast to man? Amandine had said it was legend, but had never witnessed it with his eyes. For what reason would a dragon shift to the shape of a man? Would it not be weak and vulnerable in such a state? How fascinating to even consider!

Aware of an overwhelming male presence, Rhiana flicked a glance to the left. Macarius waited for her prayers to end.

What had he asked? Ah, yes. Help.

Never had she thought the offer of help would be so beguiling. Should not a partnership be of mettle and strength? Yet, to imagine working alongside him stirred desirous feelings. He was a fine man to look upon. And that scar. What had happened when she'd touched it? 'Twas almost as if her body had been surrounded by the dragon's flame—she had felt the heat, could taste the flame. And yet, this burn had touched her inside.

In a rustle of creaking leather and shifting steel plates, Macarius stood. He resheathed his sword with another loud disturbance. His boot heels took the stone floor in precise clicks as he walked toward the back of the chapel. Without turning, Rhiana determined he did not leave. Still waiting? 'Twas fine he'd not simply walked out. That meant he was not so easily put off by her attempts to ignore him. A challenge met; he had earned her regard.

Standing and turning, Rhiana faced Macarius, who stood shadowed in the arched wooden doorway. The chapel was the only building in the entire village with visible wattle and daub inner structure. It was the oldest building, and was regularly overlooked when repairs were done, for its structure was sound—but a fire from within could eat away the dry wattle branches with ease.

Macarius broke the sharp silence. "Usual morning tierce," he said, "or request for strength to continue your quest?"

"Both."

Rhiana approached him. A subconscious notion found her smoothing a palm across her stomach and down her hip, as if flattening out a wrinkle. Bother, there were so many wrinkles. Where to begin? It was odd, but she ever felt out of sorts wearing a gown. Not right. Certainly in no means to have a conversation about slaying tactics with a man.

Blowing out a breath, she summoned courage. For standing before Macarius Fleche alone, and in vulnerable dress, she felt at odds. Unlike the sure anxiety she felt when standing before a fire-breathing beast.

Go on, her conscious coaxed. *Ask for help.*

"Of course, it is obvious I cannot take down all the dragons myself. Mayhap even two slayers will perish before we are half through the doom."

"We?"

Rhiana shrugged. "Mayhap we can share ideas on how to protect the people of my village?"

"Besides packing them off to a new location? Or nailing them all secure behind their doors until the dragons learn they've but to set the city aflame to roast their meals?"

"Do not be so morbid. We are very safe in our homes. Have you not noticed the stone structures?"

"False security dies upon a flaming stone, my lady. You cannot keep the flames from igniting a great death pyre after the beasts have crushed you beneath your flame-proof stones." He leaned against the wall of the chapel and tapped the portion of branch that showed because a chunk of dried mud had fallen away. "No false hope here, I see."

He cocked his head wonderingly, and preened her up and down for a moment, and then with a soft, more personal tone, asked, "Why not pretty baubles and fancy gowns trimmed in lace and fur?"

Rhiana understood the question.

Accompanied by a sigh of utter frustration, she answered, "Baubles tend to break and scatter. Gowns, as you can see, are cumbersome and tend to require mending far too often."

"Dusk-blue damask, the color of a rampant's scales beneath a high-noon sun. It becomes you."

She straightened at his comment. The timber of his voice touched Rhiana inside her breast. Twice now he had touched her, without making a move.

And that she succumbed to fancy words suddenly smacked her from her silly girlish reverie. "This gown is overtired and old."

"Nonsense. The color is exquisite. But not so remarkable as your flame-colored hair. You embody flame, my lady."

He was so on the mark it frightened her. So she must divert his aim. "This hair ever troubles me. I should plait it from my face."

"No," he said quickly. His hand moved toward her face, but it jerked back to splay across his plated coat.

Touch her not, or touch and risk propriety. Just one brave move, Rhiana thought with fierce desire. Be this man the bold knight her heart sought?

"I begin to understand you must charm the dragons to your killing bolt. Such a vision of flame must attract the beasts as if to their own fire."

She tilted her head forward, looking up through her lashes.

"If you intend to ply me with silly words then leave now, dragon slayer, for I'll not allow bold flirtations to interfere with my quest."

"You think I flirt with you, my lady?" The boyish charm returned with a quick smile. A smile that grew to his sky-blue eyes. "Mayhap I was. Forgive me." His posture stiffened and his hand fled to the hilt of his sword. Boldness be wary. "Indeed, something so important as dragon slaying should not be muddied with common flirtations. You said something about we. Does that mean you'll accept my assistance?"

"Will you have me believe you'll but assist? Have you not intention to command this quest, hoping I shall toddle up behind you, yet keep out of your way?"

"That's about the mark of it, my lady."

As she had guessed.

"Then you are on your own, dragon slayer. I've a village to make safe before I draw another bolt onto my bow. God grant you good day."

And stepping out into the warm morning sunlight, Rhiana dismissed the slayer to the ranks of nuisance. Mayhap Lord Guiscard had been right. The man could serve St. Rénan no assistance this day.

"My lady Tassot!" Champrey rushed up alongside Rhiana's long strides. Together they took the path toward the armory. Champrey tugged off his gloves and slapped them into his palm. Just behind them a scatter of baby ducklings scurried across the path to a muddy reprise. "Your presence in Lady Anne's solar is requested."

"I shall come as soon as I have…broken my fast." Not a good excuse, and she knew it. But she had so much to do, to think on.

"This order comes from Lord Guiscard. You will do well to accompany me immediately."

Rhiana stopped and looked to Champrey. *Guiscard* wanted her to see Lady Anne? Hmm… Mayhap Anne was in a mood. The baron trusted Rhiana with her, for she had witnessed her flights from reality many a time. But he usually managed his wife very well, was almost possessive in keeping her in his arms and not allowing any other to share her madness.

And after sending her away with a warning to ignore danger, and instead concentrate on the feminine arts, what was the baron to?

Hmm… Well, she would heed the request. It was for Anne.

Following Champrey, Rhiana watched as Macarius strolled out from the chapel and stood beside his horse. The slayer's eyes followed hers until she turned her head away. Still, he watched her, she could feel his regard upon her shoulders.

Plunging a hand through her long curls, Rhiana drew out the bothersome locks and let them fall slowly, freely across her back. A move she had seen Anne perform many a time.

Look you, fine knight, she thought. Drink of me, but not to quench your thirst, only to summon it.

CHAPTER ELEVEN

Accustomed to free rein within the castle, Rhiana gave Champrey the slip and traveled the cool narrow halls until she arrived at the south facing solar in which Lady Anne spent most of her time. The cusped entry door—influenced by the Persian motif Anne adored—was open, and Rhiana, when peeking inside, did not spy Anne's maids or hear commotion that gave clue anyone was within. Exotic incense perfumed the air. Rhiana knew not what spice or oil produced the scent, but she did think she could eat it from the air, so delicious it smelled.

"I wonder where she is?" Mayhap, she yet had not risen? Why then, the summons?

Lady Anne always greeted Rhiana in the solar. Rarely did she summon her to her bedchamber. Just as well, Rhiana had more than once encountered the baron when in Anne's chambers, and he never lost opportunity to put an advance to her. In fact, Rhiana suspected he took wicked thrill in teasing her right beneath Lady Anne's nose.

"Oh!" Rhiana's shoulder hit a giving object. She spun to

look into the frowning face of Lady Anne. A face half concealed by a gorgeous posy of creamy lilies, rosemary and
white ribbons. "Oh, my lady, forgive me." She bent one
knee and lifted her skirts as she bowed for longer than was
necessary. Without looking up, Rhiana offered, "I am so
clumsy."

She had appeared as if from a mist, like a wraith, but so
much more beautiful.

Young and dark of hair and eye, Anne Guiscard embodied fragility. Made of porcelain, Rhiana had once decided.
Perfect in every way, thick curly hair accented her fine bone
structure. So fine, in fact, her face was all lines and bones,
the flesh taunt and thin upon her face. Anne commanded
all eyes when she graced the high table or on the rare occasions she rode down to the village mounted upon the coal-
black destrier that defied Anne's vulnerability with its
powerful build. But for her waifish appearance, she walked
as if a goddess, hips swinging and her entire body moving
like a song.

The personification of the feminine, she—with the flaw of
instability.

"The dress suits you," Lady Anne offered in a deep, husky
voice that always felt like liquid velvet to Rhiana's ear. That
Anne was younger than Rhiana—who was twenty-three—surprised, only because, despite her affliction, she did command
her position with an easy authority.

Rhiana straightened and smoothed a palm over her gown,
rimmed around the hem with a lacing of dirt. "It is simple, but
serves me well. Not so fine as your gowns."

She lowered the posy, and swung it absently. "You could have
a fine gown, if you wish it."

"I know." And she could. "Fine things do not feel right on
me. Like…"

"Like the water upon my feet," Anne said. She gave a small shiver. "So ugly, the feeling. I fancy I would make a horrible mermaid. What think you?"

"I think we should, all of us in St. Rénan, miss you dearly should you dive into the sea and swim away."

Anne considered the notion.

"Lord Guiscard asked me to tend you. Is everything well with you this day, Lady Anne?"

She lowered her dark eyes on Rhiana. Long lashes dusted her pale flesh. Gold dust glittered at the corners of her kohl-rimmed eyes. Anne strode around the tufted chaise where often she lingered in the sun before the trio of stained-glass windows. In her wake a delicate silver chain trailed, attached in a circlet about her waist.

Lady Anne liked to wander; that is what Lord Guiscard told the people of St. Rénan. She walked in her sleep, and not a few times, she had breached the castle walls only to be found wandering the purlieu of the forest. It was no cruelty to chain up a loved one to keep them safe, but usually Anne was only chained at night.

Though she was not attached to anything in particular. Hmm…

Lady Anne noticed Rhiana's dismay. She lifted the silver links, caressing them and counting as a child orders out their precious trinkets.

"Sometimes he forgets to remove it before leaving in the morning." Luscious black curls spilled across her face as she tilted her head. "Stand tall, Rhiana, my bold and brilliant-haired warrior. Let me look at you."

Lady Anne stepped up to her and placed her hands aside Rhiana's cheeks. Her touch was fey, like so many lost dreams twinkled with stardust. The rosemary seeped in exotic waves from the posy. And in Anne's eyes smoldered another unreachable dream. Flames so brilliant Rhiana wanted to dive into them and shed her mortal coil.

Love here. You belong.

"Have you had a good life, Rhiana?"

"Good?"

"Has it been awful?"

"Oh, no, my lady. Well…no." Teasing and forgotten hugs Rhiana could easily suffer. As well, the occasional lusty lord. She lived the life she desired to live. She trusted the future would grant her all that she could desire. "It has been…a life."

"I see." Anne drew a swath of hair over her face. Imperious brown eyes peeked between the black tresses, a she-panther peering out from tall grasses. "It could have been better?"

Rhiana shrugged. Accustomed to Lady Anne's oddness, her swings in demeanor, she strode a few paces toward the stained-glass window. The brilliant yellow pane attracted her, and she reached out, but did not touch. "I have never been beaten, and have not gone a day without bread. I am strong and able to look after myself, so I am fortunate."

"You are very lovely," Lady Anne hissed in a covetous whisper.

Rhiana dipped her head. "Think you? My hair and freckles have never served me well. Certainly not to attract a handsome knight."

She trailed a finger along the stone embrasure. She thought of Anne as a sister, at times. Someone so different, and yet, those differences cried out for acceptance.

"It attracts the dragons."

Rhiana jerked her gaze to Anne. To have heard such a statement twice in so little time… And yet the flames she had seen in Anne's eye were gone, shuttered by lush lashes.

Lady Anne shrugged. She clutched the chain and approached the window embrasure to stand beside Rhiana. "The sky tempts in pale blue," Anne said in singsong. "A match to my lover's eyes and the rings upon his fingers." A tilt of her head revealed an arrow gaze and tight red lips. "Did you kill the dragon yestereve? The pretty indigo one left upon the castle steps like a sacrifice to the gods?"

"I—I did." Aware of Anne's reverence for the beasts, Rhiana cautioned herself. But she would not harm this woman by telling her lies. "I left it where it lay, near the portcullis. Lord Guiscard's men dragged it to the steps—"

"Assassin!"

Rhiana stumbled backward, catching herself against the wall. The urge to draw up her dagger in defense tempted. But Rhiana wore no weapon, and mores the better, for she did never wish to draw it upon Anne.

Anne lunged into Rhiana's space, her breath hissing and tainted with raspberry wine. "You cannot destroy those fine creatures. They are loved by me!" She rapped her chest with a fist. "I *covet* them, can you not understand?"

"It is not wise to covet—"

"I shall do as I wish!"

Blackest eyes buried malevolent daggers into Rhiana. She did not speak to rationality, and so Rhiana must be cautious.

"Lady Anne, truly the beasts are to be revered. And I do—"

"Reverence does not culminate in bloodshed!"

"They threaten the village. The beasts have killed four in so many days. Four people, my lady. Do you comprehend? People. Real, flesh and blood, laughing and loving souls. They had families. Families who now mourn the loss of a loved one."

"They mourn, but they do not suffer," she insisted with an imperious huff. "All in St. Rénan are assured their hoard share."

"You do not understand, Lady Anne. There is more to recovering after a loss than mere coin and distracting labor. It is life and love…emotion. We cannot allow the beasts to snatch up another soul. What if one should pluck up your husband in its deadly maws?"

Anne simply stood there. Rhiana should not have used so horrible an example. Not once had she witnessed the baron be anything but patient and understanding with Anne. His kindnesses to his wife were counterweighted by his cold public persona.

"Lady Anne, I am so sorry. Please, I beg your forgiveness."

"So," Anne said on an ugly sneer. She skipped across the room and settled onto the chair before an unfinished tapestry strung tightly across a standing loom. "You are a dragon slayer?"

Rhiana closed her eyes and tilted her head back against the stone embrasure. "It is all that I know."

"Yes, yes, all that blather about doing what must be done. Did the Nose announce your fate?"

Rhiana smiled at Anne's guess. Had her mood softened? Had she come out of her anger?

"But of course, that old hag thinks to know so much."

Rhiana knew Anne and Narcisse employed great faith in the Nose. Often she was secreted into the castle in the dark of night. Anne had mentioned more than a few times that she mustn't eat the evening meal because the Nose had determined her stars were not correctly aligned that day.

"I am—" Rhiana drew back her shoulders and boldly declared "—a fire chaser."

"Mercy," Anne whispered in a delirious trill. She leaned forward at the waist, eagerness stretching out her neck. "Such delicious excitement. Are you not frightened?"

"Truthfully?" Rhiana was more frightened of Lady Anne's wicked mood swings. "Yes and no. I am confident of my skills, and yet, the beasts are mighty."

"So mighty as to take you out with one hearty crunch."
Anne's giggles fluttered like pisky wings through the air.

Amidst the mad gaiety, Rhiana looked across the room and
spied a distorted reflection of a wild-haired savage in a broken looking glass. Herself. Looking as ravaged as Anne's soul
must be.

"If that is what fate requires for the protection of the innocents, I gladly sacrifice to keep them safe."

"You sound like one of Narcisse's vapid knights. Always the
right phrase to seduce a cow-eyed maiden. But do you think
a single one of them truly believes in his own words?

"Tell me," Lady Anne persisted. Silver links *chinked* between her fluttering fingers. "Have you a *connection* to the
beasts?"

To explain this to one not in her own mind? "Of a sort.
I…know them. Instinctively."

"I see." Anne turned on the padded cushion. Her cheeks glittered, for she wore pulverized gold dust on them to please Narcisse. A panther painted and perfumed for his pleasure. The
panther sighted Rhiana in the mirror and purred from behind
the fragrant posy. "Shall I tell you what I know about them?"

Rhiana stepped up behind Anne to touch the ends of her
glossy black hair. "Why yes, my lady. That would please me."

Lady Anne then whispered, "I can keep secrets. Narcisse
thinks to know his afflicted lover. He believes this stupid chain
claims me for him and him alone. It does not. I will find them.
I can speak to them." Spinning upon the stool, she gripped Rhiana and hugged her desperately about the waist. "Do not slay
my lover. Promise me."

Her lover? Narcisse?

Babbles of nonsense from an ill mind. Rhiana shook her
head, fighting her revulsion to the madness, and wanting to
comfort at the same time. Fearing Lady Anne should burst out

in tears, she thought quickly. "Did you summon me to tend your hair? I shall plait it for you."

"Yes, plaits!" Surrender to another thought, so easily, and welcome. "But not so tight. Pretty and flowing, like fire, your hair."

Lost to strange demons dancing a dalliance in her head, Lady Anne swiveled on the stool to face the mirror. The chain slithered upon the stone floor as her swinging leg moved it rhythmically.

As Rhiana took up four parts of thick black hair and began to loosely weave them, Lady Anne let out a sigh. "Have you taken the sacraments lately, Rhiana?"

"No."

"But I know you go to the chapel daily," Anne sighed. "I have a man who reports to me."

Interesting bit of information. Why was it so important for Anne to have Rhiana watched?

"Do you touch holy water?"

"Every morning before I enter the chapel."

"That is good. One must receive His touch daily. It is all that keeps a soul sane."

Thankful to be away from Anne's flighty oddness, Rhiana stopped by Paul's shop and agreed to watch the fire while he retrieved faggots of wood for this afternoon's work. Much as she needed to be active, planning, she would never refuse Paul assistance.

Settling before the worktable, she eyed the blazing fire. It crackled and plumed out a delicious scent that tempted far stronger than a midsummer's feast.

Fire chaser, is what Paul called her. And just now, in Anne's solar, had been the first time Rhiana had laid claim to the title. Fire chaser.

"It is what I am," she murmured. "No person or force can change that, or alter me. I defy any man to try."

A scatter of mail rings decorated the pocked wood table. Counting out nine rings she placed them in a row before her. Placing a small length of wire she'd trimmed from a ring to the side of the rows symbolized herself. So small and narrow against the wide, round rings.

Propping her chin in palm, she searched her thoughts. What she needed to do was observe their coming and goings from the caves. To mark the younger, weaker ones—if there were any. Did they fly alone? Two had joined forces yesterday afternoon after hearing the newling's cries. Had the newling healed? Would it suffer? What if they all attacked at once?

"Ready to bury some dragons?"

Fingers slipping through the militant rows of rings, Rhiana twisted about to see Macarius Fleche standing in the doorway, a silhouette, for sunlight brightened him like a sort of deity.

"Ready," she muttered, lost in a girlish thrill at seeing a handsome knight.

CHAPTER TWELVE

Macarius tossed a gauntlet onto the worktable next to where Rhiana had laid out the mail rings. She immediately noticed one of the plates had come unhinged over the wrist.

"Is the armourer about?"

"Paul is out. I can fix this. It but needs a new rivet."

Macarius snatched the gauntlet from Rhiana's hand. He pressed it to his chest and offered her a condescending smile. She knew what was coming. "Dragons and armor? Really, my lady, did you miss your lessons in cooking and stitching?"

She rolled her eyes. "I had thought you different."

"How so?"

"Not so quick to form an opinion. Not walking about with preconceived notions of how a woman should present herself. We did meet in pursuit of a dragon. Or did you think I was just skipping about in the meadow collecting posies?"

"Well… Women have been known to gather flowers."

"At midnight, in the rain?"

"The moon is near full. Women are notoriously ruled by the

cycles of the moon. I cannot say, only that I guess you were chasing la Luna's wake."

Ruled by the moon? Must she bother to correct him? Oh, let him have his fantasies.

"Let me see it." She tugged the gauntlet from him and assessed which size rivet would be needed to make the repair. It was a simple fix.

Meanwhile, he studied the sword lying on the worktable, the one Rhiana had found in the chapel. "This looks of German make," he commented. Paul had yet to determine its origin, but he guessed it quite old.

"It traveled a great distance to be here," Macarius noted as he set the sword down.

"Think you?" Rhiana studied the sword with a keen eye. The hoard boasted all sorts of weapons brought from all places by the dragons. *Hmm…*

Macarius smacked his fist into his palm. "I itch to plunge my sword into a dragon's brain."

Turning back to the project, Rhiana threaded a rivet through the gauntlet plate.

Loose in his steps, Macarius stepped over to the fire and splayed out his palms to warm them. "Ah, fire. So seductive! So dangerous. Yet, it is my life's work, eh?"

"You never did tell me who, exactly, you are. How are you related to Amandine Fleche? A cousin or relation of some sort?" She punched the rivet in, placed the gauntlet over a small anvil, and gave it a good hammer. "Did he train you?"

"Train me." Macarius inspected an unburnished sword hanging from a wooden peg near his head. "He was my father."

"Your—" Rhiana swallowed back a gasp. Forgetting the gauntlet, she spun to face him. She had suspected… "But, he never mentioned children."

"Indeed?" Nodding and smirking coyly, Macarius walked on to the next sword hanging from the beam and tipped it with his finger. "I have lived dragons since I could toddle about in infant skirts. I dream of them. I talk of them. I slay them. And yet, the quest for my father's regard has always been fruitless. It surprises me little he did not mention me to you. And yet…" His jaw tightened. Macarius looked away from Rhiana. Fire flashes danced in his eyes. "I'll be at the tavern down the way. I could smell the honey beer as I walked by earlier. Come retrieve me when my armor is repaired, will you?"

About to answer with protest he should not expect her to wait on him, Rhiana held her tongue. She let him go with a promise the gauntlet would be soon ready.

Testing the riveted portion for ease of movement, she decided it required oiling. Rapeseed oil was the only kind Paul used for his creations. She dabbed a horsehair brush into a pot of the pale green oil and touched it to the gauntlet.

So Macarius sought his father's regard? How well she understood such a fruitless quest. For yet, Rhiana sought her mother's eyes. A simple look. A smile. A validation. Never would it come.

She and her mother stood at a distance from one another. Not out of hate, disrespect or even fear. Well, mayhap a bit of fear. Rhiana didn't know how to talk to her mother, and she suspected Lydia did feel the same. They walked parallel to one another, ever seeking eye contact, always forgoing a deep emotional connection in favor of something easier. A distant respect. An emotionless existence.

Was it possible Macarius might understand her?

Halfway to the tavern, gauntlet in hand, Rhiana nodded to Madeleine, a fine seamstress who often sewed Lady Anne's gowns, who skipped with her daughter Amanda at her side.

She and Madeleine had become friends a few years ago when Amandine had spent the summer.

"Rhiana?"

Shaking a sudden startling thought from her mind, Rhiana looked to Madeleine, who had lifted Amanda into her arms. The child was almost two, about as old as Rhiana had been when Ulrich had abandoned her. A thick froth of black curls danced upon Amanda's cherub face.

"What is wrong, Rhiana?"

"Er, forgive me, Madeleine. I…just lost my thoughts for a moment." She made a swishy dismissive gesture with the gauntlet. "So much on my mind of late. Amanda." She said the name as a greeting, but also, as a confirmation. The child had been named after her father. "So sweet. Dark curly hair. Keep her safe and indoors, will you?"

"I'm just to the smithy to pick up a cooking pot he fixed for me, then we're back to home."

Madeleine had been pursuing the blacksmith most aggressively the past year. If the man would take the time to look up from his work he might notice the gorgeous woman who held him in regard.

"Good day!" she called, as she strode away. Amanda waved to Rhiana with her chubby fingers.

Rhiana turned and walked right into Macarius's fine form.

"Distracted?" he wondered in a low, but hissing voice. "She is very pretty."

"Madeleine is a friend. Her child…" Rhiana looked after the woman and her daughter. Certainly introductions must be made. She tapped the gauntlet against her thigh. But not right now. "They are two sweet women, both mother and daughter. Hold out your hand."

She fitted the gauntlet onto Macarius's hand with a tug. Perfect fit.

"Now, come with me. We've planning to do."

They skipped up the stairs to the battlement walls. Passing through the barbican, Rhiana then leaped out onto a stone merlon and leaped from one to the next in an amazing feat of balance and skill. Like a child, constantly seeking adventure, Macarius thought at sight of her teasing encouragement for him to try the same.

Bending and leaning forward through the frame of two merlons, he scanned the outer grounds beyond the drawbridge. No one had claimed the boots yet.

Rhiana raced ahead, flipping and performing the most spectacular acrobatics. Finally, she settled and sat between two crenels. He joined her in the one next, and both dangled their legs over the battlement wall and looked off toward the sea. It was but a quarter league off, the sea, and the salted air did make Macarius hungry.

After a few minutes Rhiana stepped up to the merlon to his left and, propping her elbows on it, looked down at him.

While he cautioned his better judgment to keep apart, remain disconnected from the beauty who hovered over him, Macarius found his eyes straying to her hair, which plunged down in heavy waves and slid over his shoulder. Gorgeous, lush, and so much of it. Red, so red as garnets, not the dull, amber waves he'd usually seen on women with red hair. Surely a detriment to slaying dragons, unless she bound it back and out of the way. As well, a detriment to a man's desires.

"Want some?"

Did he. How he'd love to run the garnet strands over his face and drink in— "What did you say?"

He looked up. She offered him treats from the sack she had retrieved as they'd passed her home along the way. Fresh cherries.

"Thank you." The fruit was plump, ripe and juicy. Delicious.

Spitting out a cherry seed and landing it in the middle of the dry moat, Macarius checked himself. What was he doing? Ogling the woman as if a prospective companion? Here he sat—next to his competition.

A competitor who had lured him here with a coy grin.

Rhiana spat a seed. It landed the opposite side of the moat.

Macarius wound up, twisting the seed on his tongue to the tip, and with all his might, spat. It landed a stride short of Rhiana's.

"Want another?" she said, offering a plump fruit dangling from a limp green stem. He'd not seen fruit trees, though he had not walked through the entire village.

This village was quite rich. Though he would expect a sea-side village to trade and draw in much foreign goods and services, St. Rénan was quite cut off from the trade routes. The nearest landing was ten to fifteen leagues away. A good day's journey.

Macarius noted he'd yet to see a ragged heap stumbling about the village begging for alms. Nor, now he thought on it, had he seen servants bustling to the market this morning. Everyone was well dressed. And fine dress such as damasks and lace and much gold. All seemed the same social level as one another. Hmm… Perhaps they sent traveling merchants to bargain at the trade routes?

He turned to straddle the battlement wall, left leg dangling over the outside of the wall, the other hanging inside.

"Another?" Eyeing his miserable aim, Macarius shook his head. "Nay, my lady. You have bested me. I shall not continue to compete when all is lost."

"That surprises me. I know thee little, but I wager your competitive streak runs deep. To your very bones, mayhap."

"Speaking from experience, are you?" Macarius closed his eyes to the noonday sun and to the vision hovering so close.

It was odd of him to abandon a challenge so quickly, but he was tired from his travel and the peaceful mood demanded he relax. For this was the only peace he intended to steal. There were dragons afoot. "I only worry should a better slayer come along. I've not yet been defeated. I know I never shall."

She leaned closer, stretching her arms down the jut of the merlon. A spill of garnet hair washed over his arm. "You've not seen me take down a rampant."

"Your next may be your last."

"As well, yours."

Frustrating bit of fiery hair and tattered gown. Strange, Rhiana's was the only ill-worn clothing he'd noticed. Almost as if she had not equal consideration for her appearance as others did. Which made little sense to him. Did not women fuss and fret about their clothing and hair and skin and accessories until all hours had passed?

Her every movement called Macarius's attention to the tight muscles beneath the blue damask fabric. Muscles on her arms, her stomach and legs. Strong, she. Remarkable.

Coaching his fingers to be still—*do not twine them within the garnet strands playing teasingly across your flesh*—Macarius winced against the sun.

"Mayhap we should wager on the next kill?" he offered. Accepting another forbidden fruit, he then toyed the fragrant cherry against his mouth, eyeing her slyly. If he were to learn a competitor's weakness—and strengths—he must see him, er *her*, in action. "The first to take down the next dragon that flies overhead wins."

"What be the prize?"

A night nestled close to a fiery beauty. "Er..." Macarius retracted his hand from beneath her hair. "What think you? Have I anything you desire?" He popped the cherry into his mouth and waggled the stem suggestively at her. She did not look at him, her focus on the horizon where the land ended and plunged into the sea. "And vice versa. What is it you could give to me that I would deem worthy of a prize?"

Just one night? Didn't even have to be a night. An evening. Afternoon. A quick roust right there in the abandoned watch tower.

Rhiana reached to his side and tapped his sword. She perused the damascened steel sheath. It had been the only gift his father had ever granted without expecting something in return. To part with it would bring Macarius to his knees. Certainly a worthy wager, providing the woman offered up something equal in value.

She tapped the sheath and focused on him. And for the first time, Macarius noticed her eyes. So strange! One was green, the other—

"I want knowledge," she stated.

"Knowledge?" Macarius dropped the cherry down the side of the wall. Mismatched eyes widened above a teasing grin. "I don't understand."

Jumping upright, she stood, separated from him by the narrow merlon, hands to her hips. And those eyes! He wanted to jump up, hold her by her shoulders, and study her eyes. Never before had he seen the like.

"You know so much more than Amandine was ever able to teach me," Rhiana said. "You hold a lifetime of knowledge, while I was but granted a few months with your father. You know about the different stages of dragon life. And what of their mating rituals and their hibernations? Your father told me some about the maxima's torpor, but so little about mating. Do you know I have only seen females thus far? Not a single male!"

"That is curious."

"Isn't it? I know but the basics. Their flight patterns and habits. How to scent them."

"You can scent them?"

She nodded.

Damn. Macarius had trained for years to pick up the elusive scent of dragon and its variations, such as anger, mating, and playfulness. It wasn't something anyone could teach, it was innate. He counted that ability as the cream of his arsenal.

Rhiana pressed her palms to the merlon and leaned in. He tucked up his legs to his torso, leery suddenly. So dynamic a female. She surprised and startled and twisted his own sense of achievements askew.

"I possess the instinct," she said, "but you possess the knowledge."

"So, should you be the first to slay the next dragon, you wish me to give you this vast knowledge?"

She nodded. One green eye. The other…ah, it was gold! Fascinating.

Forcing a casual tone, Macarius cocked his head to avoid the glaring sunlight. "There is much that I know."

"I want to learn it all!"

Be this what had compelled his father to teach her—an enthusiasm bordering on infectious?

"I've already this instinct you claim so exclusively. I cannot guess what you could offer me in return…"

The notion crossed his senses with the desire to touch her intimately, and the need to know her very being. He decided in the next second, what he wouldn't ask for. He would not make a play for her intimately. What made this woman so powerful, so strong? Instincts?

She wasn't that good.

And yet, why had Amandine chosen to give her the training he had only ever given to Macarius? And to not tell him about it? All Macarius knew is Amandine had *met* a female slayer. He'd not once mentioned he'd trained her. For months?

Why would Amandine keep that very important fact a secret? Dare he ask if she'd had a liaison with his father?

"Can you judge the very moment the dragon decides to flame?" she said, her tone defiant, yet also beguiling. "What of its flight? Do you know the exact moment the dragon catches a high wind and can coast, lowering its heartbeats to near rest so it does not expend energy on wing? And in the dark, where the dragons lurk, can you smell their fear?"

"Their fear? Dragons do not fear. They have but two emotions: anger, meaning attack, avenge and flame; and procreation, which lends to anxiety, and a surreal arousal scent."

"They do fear." Rhiana leaned forward and touched his tunic, right over his heart. "Here. It is palpable in their heartbeats. I can feel it when I am near one. The momentary fear. They fear us!"

He laid his hand over Rhiana's. As he sensed a dragon's mood, he sensed the fire within this woman, glimmering in her mismatched eyes and in her potent words. For a moment his hackles stood to guard, as if…a dragon were near.

A dragon?

He had let down his guard!

Checking the skies, and standing to pull away from her touch, he scanned the blue open sky. Nothing. Not even a bird.

"What is it?"

"Nothing." He would not confess his false assessment, for the challenges the woman put forth were already far too many. "Oh, that my father did never tell me about you, fire chaser."

"I had thought he had. You'd said you traveled to St. Rénan to see the female slayer."

"Yes, but that is all he said. That he'd met a slayer, not that he had trained you. That, and you were so much the marvel one could only believe by seeing. High praise from my father. Let us see if you are worthy."

"The wager?"

Macarius nodded. "I shall grant you knowledge with your win. But for my win—" he blinked against the sun's brightness "—I will ask for proof."

"Should not a kill be proof enough?"

"Yes, but my kill will not prove your skills, warrior."

"Very well. What proof then?"

"You will enter the caves and bring me back proof you have walked amongst the dragons. Mayhap a piece from the hoard? Yes! That should demonstrate your stealth and instinct. To walk into the caves without being flamed by the rampants?"

Rhiana tilted her head forward. Liquid garnet purled across her cheeks. Her lips parted. She appeared to consider his wager.

Be not so foolish, Macarius thought. Know your limits, woman. No inexperienced man—or woman—could walk into a dragon's lair and come out alive. At the very least, the idiot would be dreadfully burned. This he knew from experience.

"Very well," she offered snappily. "It is a wager."

Rhiana leaped from her perch and strode the parapet toward the village gate, leaving Macarius quite speechless. He wasn't sure if it were her mettle or just an idiocy that knew no bounds, but the woman frustrated. And at the same time, she fascinated.

"Just my luck," Macarius murmured, watching her hip-swinging retreat. Even the long urgent strides betrayed her feminine attributes. Oh, that hair.

And those eyes.

"She is not the brute woman I had expected of one who could stand before dragons. Instead, she is a lackwit wearing the guise of beauty."

CHAPTER THIRTEEN

It neared midnight. The moon was almost completely full. The entire village had once again crammed into the castle to feast upon dragon and rose-hip wine. While gold meant little in the eyes of the villagers, meat and a full belly held tremendous currency. Though a portion of the meat had been packed in salt for curing, the hindquarter and belly provided delicious fare and must be eaten before it rotted.

"If they only knew," Rhiana said with a sneer over her shoulder toward the receding battlement walls.

Macarius, striding alongside her across the field circling the village kept her brisk pace. "That their lord is a self-serving, cold-hearted bastard? I wager they do, but merrymaking cannot go disregarded. I might try for some dragon meat myself, later."

"Hmph. Certainly they will feast until their bellies drag upon the ground. But it is only celebratory, not necessary."

"The meat will turn if it is not used."

"I understand. But we, none of us in St. Rénan, have need for free handouts. We are all quite well off."

"And how is that? I have noted the general lack of poverty."

"We are all aware of what is required to survive," she answered, in truth. "Everyone pitches in during planting to tend the fields, and returns for harvest. Elders are watched after by the younger, and the babes are raised by entire flocks of women."

"An entire village to raise one child, eh?"

"It is a good thing. Were you raised by your mother and father?"

"My father. I did not know my mother for she passed with my birth."

"I am sorry."

"No matter." He splayed a hand before him. "There were a few aunts to coddle me and chase me about and trip me into the wash bucket. I grew up fine and well."

Fine, well, and particularly handsome in this pale moonlight. Rhiana could verily feel the need to compete ooze from the man with every tense grip of his gauntlet or tighten of his jaw, his passionate determination seeped into her and made her feel much the same.

"Indeed," she said on a sigh.

"Think you?"

Now there was a question she must not answer.

Senses ultra-aware, Rhiana slowed her pace a bit so he could join her side. She had tromped these fields for two decades and was quite deft. But even the brilliant moonlight did allow an easy walk for one unfamiliar with the lumpy terrain.

Now Macarius's musky scent breeched the air and wrapped her in his essence. Interesting. Not at all like the dragons' scent, but equally as intriguing. It did not scream out anger, but cloyingly tossed with an earthy antipathy that demanded further investigation.

The night was bright, for the white moon illuminated the sky. It would be full complete in a few days. Yestereve's rains had left the field moist, but not so much that their footsteps were unsure. They headed for the caves, tucked discreetly beneath the mountain dotted with a half dozen megaliths. The valley before them curved at the base of the mountain and formed a counterscarp, though St. Rénan had not been to arms for decades and the ditch served merely as a divider for the plantings now. Perfect spot to lay low and await a dragon.

Normally Rhiana would think twice before such a ruse, chasing a dragon, mayhap risking it, in anger, to fly over the village. But she knew every man, woman and child was inside the castle, dancing to the dulcimer's song and marveling at the feats of swordplay the knights always performed out of vainglory. And wondering with wide eyes and open mouths at Sebastien's fiery display. With the night young, the festivities would continue for some time.

"That is interesting armor," Macarius called. Striding ahead, he turned, and walking backward, facing her, kept up the pace. "Dragon scales, yes?"

"My first kill. Paul designed this armor for me."

"Impressive. Your first was with my father?"

"Indeed."

"Of course. How was the armourer able to file down the sharp edges? Or did he?"

"He fashioned a sanding tool from a rampant's fore-talon. Used a tooth to puncture a hole in each scale so it could be laced to the undertunic. No man-made material is strong enough."

"Very clever, your stepfather. I imagine it is impervious to flame."

"Oh yes."

"Ease of movement, for the small scales move as if on a dragon's body."

She stretched out an arm to smooth her palm over the glossy scales. Each one had grown from the leathery hide of a rampant as if a petal upon a flower, but not so easily plucked. She and Paul had worked two months removing the scales from the hide and preparing them for armor.

"See this dragon dust?" She tilted her arm to catch the moonlight on the lightweight violet scales. "No matter how many rains or scrubbings to remove the dirt, they ever shimmer."

"Dragon dust is a valuable commodity."

"Think you?"

"Do you not know, my lady?" Macarius turned and rejoined her side, stretching his hand above to the stars as he spoke of strange enchantments. "The gift of flight, say some of the dragon's breath—for that is what the glittering dust is formed of—it is alchemized by the gold the dragons nest upon."

"Yes, I know! Your father told me. It is the dragon's lifeline, the gold. Their belly scales absorb the gold and create the dust...somehow..."

"Breath of fire must be added to the rub of scale over gold. As a result, dragon dust forms. The glittery substance covers the inner walls and lines the caves. It is their vitae. Should a man consume the dragon dust—legend says—they can then fly."

"Impossible."

"Oh, indeed." Macarius chuckled. "But that is the tale told, my lady. And the immortality!"

"Immortality?" She laughed and followed Macarius's sudden rush toward the counterscarp valley. "You mean should I consume this dust I would live forever?"

Macarius stopped at the ridge of thick emerald grass, muted a dull gray in the darkness. Rhiana halted behind him and he swung about and gripped her arms, sliding his palms reverently down the scaled armor sleeves. "I know not how it manifests such wonders. It is another myth. But you see—" he held up his palms and even in the dull light Rhiana noticed no sparkle "—it is permanently fixed to the scales. How should a man harvest such a substance?"

"Mayhap only in his dreams."

He drew his fingers across his tongue, perhaps hoping to taste the immortality? "Yes, dreams. Of finer times and dragonless skies." He looked across the sky. The night glittered with stars as if on a dragon's scale. "Are you not fearsome?"

"You have asked already. And yes, I am. But your father warned to never shy from what is within. Should I lose my fear I think I should lose my edge."

"My father taught you very much."

"I am lucky to have known him. Will you…tell me how he died?"

"How else should a slayer wish his life to end?"

"A dragon? Oh, my—"

"The beast perished as well. It lifted my father high and swung him about in his maws. Amandine was able to deliver the killing strike with his sword before the dragon flung him off through the sky. He landed, dead from the fall."

He recited the event with no emotion. Perhaps that was the only way he could relive so horrid a happening. Rhiana would not question him further.

"Sit with me." He settled upon the counterscarp that edged the valley, which was more as if a great boulder had rolled a wedge into the soil demarcating the flat fields from the rise that began the hill capping the caves. "Tell me about you and Amandine."

"I have told you all. He taught me for three months—".

"Where did he stay while you trained? In your home?"

"Oh no, my mother refused him bed. She does not favor my choice to chase dragons."

"Wise woman."

"My mother does not know my heart." Rhiana picked a strand of grass and folded it about her finger. "I often wonder was I a changeling she found in the cradle, so different we two are."

"Are you?"

"What?"

"A changeling? Ha!"

While Macarius chuckled, Rhiana couldn't completely abandon that wonder. She was so different from all in her family. Though she only had blood ties to Lydia, nothing about her mother resembled her. Lydia was dark and short and quiet. To know her real father would not so much answer questions, as quiet the long wonder that had carved a nest in her belly.

"Your father stayed with a woman who was widowed," she explained.

"Ah, I would have been surprised to learn otherwise."

"Do you hear that?" Rhiana spun about, rising to her feet, but remaining crouched. A swoosh of wing on air? A search of the sky saw the stars. No pulse beats. But a stealthy rhythm. Not dragons, but…horses? Standing upright, she searched the distance. A long way off yet, but heading toward the counterscarp. "Someone from the village?"

"There!"

At Macarius's shout, Rhiana wielded her crossbow to aim. Notching a bolt, she fingered the trigger. Instincts flowed to the fore. Now she could feel it. In the opposite direction of the horses. One heartbeat racing across the sky. A rampant soared out from the cave opening, and skimmed over the sea's moon-glittered silver ridges. It topped the sky at the edge of the cliff. Wings spread in great flaps, momentarily scooping the moon from the sky, until another flap released the bold white ball.

Macarius drew out his sword. "It is mine!"

Suddenly this competition changed to a very ridiculous tournament. This was no show performed in the lists in hopes of winning a lady's favor or a lord's respect. They could not, one or the other, stand back and allow the other to make the kill. If two people worked together, then their odds increased. And why fight over kill rights when one lost moment may see the beast flying toward St. Rénan—and the approaching horsemen.

"I'll go for the belly," she ordered. "You deliver the killing blow to the skull."

"Worry for your win, my lady. I've my own plan!"

He dashed along the counterscarp, his shadow racing toward the dragon's huge black outline gliding like a dark wraith over the grass.

Muscles tensing and her entire skeleton growing an inch in utter alert, Rhiana tracked the beast.

With a draw down of its head, the rampant lunged to earth. For its supper.

Rushing after the slayer, Rhiana intended to beat him to the target. He needed protection. Cover from the inevitable flame.

The rampant paused midair, hanging weightlessly, as a fallen angel that can never ascend to the ranks of the ethereal—and marked upon its forehead in proof. The dagged tail whipped just above the ground, parting the tall grasses. Wings spread wide, embracing the midnight. The belly expanded, sucking in air, gorging itself on the night.

Rhiana knew flame would follow.

Drawing up its long violet neck, the dragon's wings flapped slowly for balance. Wind from the wings tore back her hair from Rhiana's face. A devil's whisper, that brush of sage-tainted air. 'Twas the devil's flaming kiss from which she must protect Macarius.

The roar of flames preceded the fire, the sound like a thousand bold stallions beating the earth in free-gallop. And like an angel of vengeance descended from the heavens with flaming sword in hand.

As the first wave of amber and gold heat licked across the breeze-sifted grasses, Macarius dove over the mounded side of the counterscarp.

Had he escaped the flame? It was impossible to determine.

Using the dragon's suspension to her advantage, Rhiana set off the bolt. The heavy steel arrow hissed through the air. Contact, right at the base of the dragon's neck where the belly scales began to grow hard and become like armor. Aggravated at the angry touch of steel, it jerked backward and faltered. The beast cried out. The avenging angel dashed a narrow stream of flame past Rhiana's face.

The rampant's landing shook the ground. Clouds of earth and grass plumed up. A fox, rousted from its den near Rhiana's feet, scampered to safety. Its heartbeats were frantic, the scent of fear so strong Rhiana sneezed at it.

It had landed the valley. Right where Macarius had rolled.

"Did you see that?"

Rhiana twisted to spy the riders she had earlier noted, two of them, wearing the Guiscard coat of arms in angry hornet yellow.

"Not now," she muttered through a tight jaw. The last hindrance she required was two more bodies to protect. Retrieving another bolt from the sheath strapped across her back, she reloaded.

"It's the female slayer!" one of the horsemen shouted. Before Rhiana could get the bolt fixed she was stepping back from the barrage of horse hooves and slashing swords. "Do you not listen to Lord Guiscard, wench?"

How that word *wench* put up her hackles.

The scent of wine overwhelmed the angry stench of dragon.

Stunning that out here in the darkness and amidst this battle she could scent the filthy knights so easily.

"I listen to no man, especially not a sot. Did you not see the dragon?"

"Indeed! Your bolt knocked it from the sky."

"Not for long. Get you gone, lackwits!"

Another sword joined the first idiot's sword, both aimed for Rhiana's throat. "Did she call us a name?"

Rhiana took a step back. They followed.

The closer she got to the counterscarp, the closer she lured two innocent knights to their death. The notion teased for but a moment. Much as she'd favor sending these bastards to their fiery graves, they were merely drunk and not in their heads. She held resentment toward no man, even those who teased her. Ignorance was no crime—though, it should be.

The heat of flame filled the air. Behind her, dragon's breath lighted the sky as it shot flames straight toward the stars. An ebony taloned paw slapped the berm right behind her. She felt the earth part and ooze away, unsettling her stance. It was climbing out.

"Mercy," one of the men cried, dropping his sword at Rhiana's feet. "Get you gone from here, my lady!"

"It is you who should ride like the wind!"

"Indeed!" They heeled their mounts to a mud-spitting gallop.

Quick to accuse and torment, they were, but not so brave when heroes were required.

"Gallop back to your lady's arms," she muttered, then bent to sweep up the abandoned sword as another paw tore apart the soft summer grass. Chunks of dirt and grass blades separated in her wake and the air filled with earth and green scent.

In her peripheral vision she saw Macarius pull himself up to sit the berm. Still alive? Not a flat bit of bone and studded jack? Remarkable!

Breaths huffing from her chest, Rhiana worked to settle her anxiety. No one had been harmed. Now, to keep it that way.

A pair of gold eyes, large as a cooper's barrel, appeared behind the talons. A snort of hot air steamed about Rhiana, enveloping her in a deceptive sage cloud. The beast rose above her, casting midnight shadows across the grayness of the ground.

Rhiana stood strong, feeling every movement of the dragon's sinew as if her own muscles bending and stretching for power. Every pulse of blood raced from heart to extremities, bubbling like witch's brew, eager and angry for escape. She knew its fury. She also knew its fear.

The gaping split of its maws worked in her jaw. 'Twas as if she were a part of the beast. Through its eyes she saw herself, a speck upon the land, standing before hellfire.

And she knew its next move.

Twisting sharply, Rhiana thrust the knight's abandoned sword as if a spear. The blade entered the dragon's mouth and pierced the top of its jaw, exiting cleanly out through scale and horned snout.

A paw madly slashed the air. The tip of a talon nicked Rhiana's armor, throwing her to the ground in a hard fall. The crossbow crushed into her gut; she felt the bolt release into the grass as a thud against her breast. With the dragon looming over her, dizzily slapping at the sword lodged in its maw, there was no time to reload.

The head would next fall, Rhiana knew. Right on top of her.

Digging her fingers into the sweet summer grass and toeing herself to a crouch, Rhiana pushed forward, using pure fright to power her muscles and limbs into a run.

The beast's head pounded the ground behind her. The wind of its landing blew around her shoulders, batting her plaited hair against her cheek as if a whip.

Stopping and turning, Rhiana witnessed Macarius climb upon the dragon's skull. Footsteps sure, he avoided the horned tusks, which crossed toward the nose. As long as a man's body, the forehead to nose tip, and armored with tough scale and jutting spikes. The last walk a man should ever wish to make.

Lifting his arms high, Macarius pierced the kill spot with his sword and delivered the coup de grâce.

Rhiana felt her breath gush out. The deed was done. Despite her contributions to bringing down the rampant, this one was the slayer's kill.

Didn't matter. The beast was dead. Had it flown out from the lair to torment the village this night? Mores the better it had not gotten farther than this berm.

A huff of breath, the final death sigh, exhaled from the dragon's nostrils, steaming over Rhiana in a cloud of heady sage. So sweet, yet sharp with beguiling danger.

Closing her eyes she dove into the moment, drenching herself in the very essence of the beast. Arms spread wide, she welcomed the dying essence as it permeated her flesh in a hot bath of steam. Find solace in my feeble shell, she thought. I offer you respect. Forgive my call to protect my own.

It did not feel unnatural or wrong to stand there bathing in the fallen rampant's death. Very right, in fact.

Why? Why did she revere these beasts so very much, and yet, did not blink an eye to destroy them?

"Success!" Macarius lifted up his sword in triumph. Moonlight glittered upon the blade. One foot poised upon the horn sprouting from the rampant's temple, the other along its scaled nose, the slayer thrust both arms high to the sky.

Elation.

Wrapped within the dragon's death sigh, Rhiana knew the feeling.

She saw him swipe his fingers over the dragon's skull then

trace them across his forehead. It looked a ritual gesture. Only when he turned his head to the left, and the moonlight glanced over the substance did Rhiana make a small cry.

Macarius had drawn a bloody cross upon his forehead.

CHAPTER FOURTEEN

Another female. That made three females she had slain. Make that: two females for her and one for Macarius. Not one male. Very interesting. And a little disturbing. Surely, if the females were brooding there were males inside nesting? Which would prove more vicious? A harder kill? A hungry female, or a male protecting his offspring?

Tromping up to the fallen beast and needing to do something to keep from looking at Macarius, Rhiana pressed out her palms and ran them over the soft suede nostrils. Like a horse's snout, the one part on the dragon not of scale or the softer belly tiles, or talon and horn. Warm, this beast, like her flesh.

Curving a hand about the lower edge of a nostril she traced the moist leathery blackness to the thick scales that breeched its upper lip. Indigo scales. In the moonlight they gleamed like fine jewels, changing to violet as if alchemized by the heat. And over all, the dragon dust of mythical immortality sparkled like the stars in the heavens.

"Not of heaven," Rhiana whispered.

"From hell, and no doubt of it." Macarius joined her side,

slapping a boot heel upon the dragon's temple and leaning in to smooth his hand over the beast's half-closed eyelid. "A fine kill."

"Neither from hell," she quickly added. That he stepped upon the beast with so little regard sent up her hackles. She wanted to berate him, but at all costs she wanted to avoid looking at that bloody cross on his forehead. "Think you this beast from Lucifer's ranks?"

"None other could breathe the very flames of hell," he offered matter-of-factly. "A punishment for mating with the dark angels who fell from the heavens."

"But that doesn't mean the creature is from hell, merely that it— You think something that breathes fire is from hell?" Desperation warbled her voice.

"I don't think, I *know*." Stepping up onto the tusk curved out from the corner of its jaw, Macarius stood there, stretching his hands over the skull and continued his perusal of the slain dragon. "Did not my father teach you?"

Of course, Amandine had explained. All knew the legend of the fire-breathing dragon. The tapestries in the castle keep depicted the angels' Fall and their mating with the once fireless dragons, and the hand of God marking the beasts in shame.

"But…" Rhiana did have proof of neither heaven nor hell birthing these beasts. Amandine hadn't known, he'd allowed her to form her own opinions. "I have always believed them enchanted," she protested forcefully. "That which resides between the heavens and hell is enchanted."

"Speak you of Faery?" The slayer chuckled.

"Mayhap." Rhiana knew nothing of Faery. Nay, but it must exist if piskies roamed the land. And the Nose, she set out a bowl of cream every evening for the brownies that would march through a man's home in seek of treat or trick. "Amandine told me the legend of the shaming touch and the gift of fire by Hell's angels. But the dragons were already here. Earth creatures."

Macarius jumped backward to land the ground. Grace in his moves, and a cockiness to his motions called out for attention. Leaning against the closed maw of the dragon he crossed his ankles. Thick dark curls parted across his forehead as he tilted back his head to study the sky.

"My father did not know. He always left it to others to make that decision." A pointing finger speared Rhiana. "And that is all I shall tell you, my lady, because you have lost. I believe knowledge was only to be granted with your kill. And if I am correct, 'twas my sword which placed the killing strike."

"You are correct," she offered, but feeling no joy in that defeat.

Macarius lifted his sword high in declaration, "Dragonsbane!"

Rhiana smirked. "Be that the name of your sword?"

"It is, indeed."

She lifted an impertinent chin. "Methinks every other sword in the kingdom of France bears such a moniker."

"Oh?" He tapped the air with the sword tip. "And what be the name of your sword, fair lady slayer?"

She did not wield a sword, only the small dagger at her hip, which she hadn't touched. Her weapon of favor was the cross-bow, which was abandoned somewhere in this field. It had no name. But it was always there to serve.

"Ready," she stated. "That be the name of my weapon."

"Ready?" Macarius rubbed his jaw and finally shrugged. "Funny name for a weapon. No poetry. No romance. Ah, no matter. My kill. My win."

Rhiana could counter with her efforts: That 'twas her skill that thrust the sword through the mouth and first felled the beast to ground, making it easier for Macarius to deliver the killing strike. But she was not a poor loser. And she did know enough of the man to realize he would not take well to being bested by a woman, and certainly he would gloat on this for days.

"Fine and well." She paced the length of the dragon's body, finding its tail stretched down into the valley of the counterscarp where it curled at the end. How to retrieve her crossbow, which lay somewhere beneath the massive skull?

"Have you a portion of rope?"

"Whatever—" Realizing, as Macarius bent and slipped a hand inside the opened jaw, what his intentions were, she marched up to him and shoved him from the dragon. "You will not!"

"It is dead! I always claim a tooth as my prize before the vultures come for the carrion. Or in this case, your village should ride out to claim yet another fortnight's feast."

"It is barely dead, and you wish to tear it apart? Methinks I should rip a tooth from your jaw and see how you like it."

"My lady, so ferocious you are!" He stalked out into the meadow a pace or two and kicked at the high grasses. "Very well, have it your way."

Not sure she had actually won, or maybe the man would return later when she was sleeping, Rhiana nodded, content to leave it at that. She had more important things to contend. "So I am off."

"Where to?" He stabbed a thumb over his shoulder. "The village is the opposite direction."

"To the caves!" Striking onward, Rhiana marched down the ditch. The rampant's landing had impressed the usually loamy earth to a flat hard surface. "You did wager I should filch a piece of the hoard."

She heard the man's footsteps beat the ground behind her. His urgency made her smile. The greatest slayer in all the land could have the kill, but she would have the ultimate win.

"You cannot!"

"I wagered as much," she called out gaily. "And I have never stepped back from a wager."

Not breaking stride, Rhiana descended the valley. Still high from the challenge, she planned to use the feeling to counter her normal fears at entering the cave.

"It is late," Macarius protested. He slid down the packed wall of the counterscarp, landing unsteadily. "You are winded from the chase."

"Says you. A man who huffs and cannot find his breath."

"Stop!"

She did, at the opposite side of the valley, and looked down to where Macarius hung against the side of the counterscarp, huffing and fingers clawing into the dirt and great gouges torn out by the dragon's talons.

"Will you concede your win to me?" she wondered.

"No." She twisted a shoulder.

"But—wait! Perhaps I asked too much of you. Yes, surely. You but requested knowledge. The spoken word! I cannot require so risky a challenge in return."

"It is risky." Tapping the sky with her dagger, Rhiana took great delight in the man's sudden reluctance. "But I've never backed down from a challenge."

"You are a most frustrating woman."

"What trouble should my actions cause you?"

"Do you not imagine a man should be concerned for your safety?"

Hands at her hips, Rhiana paused at the base of the mountain. The moonlight was shaded here.

In the darkness she could not be sure of his moves; he yet had not gained the top of the counterscarp. Silence managed to overwhelm even the chirps of meadow insects. The leaves on the trees were absolutely still.

"I am off," she said, and swung about.

* * *

She was a frustrating bit of mettle, forged from the same indestructible substance as dragon scale. And dusted over with an impermeable measure of bravado.

Macarius was truly winded after his battle with the beast. Attribute that to his race after the beast, and the tumble into the valley. He'd almost been knocked senseless. And then the mad scramble to the edge of the counterscarp at sight of a dragon plunging out of the sky straight for him?

Dragging himself up the side of the counterscarp further exhausted his aching muscles. When he landed high ground, he collapsed there in the cool grass blades. Above and ahead, he saw the dark slender shadow tramp along the mountain, toward the cliff.

Was she so foolish? He should not have challenged her so. He knew those with competitive streaks could not see beyond their own safety, so determined they were to prove themselves worthy.

And how did he know this type of aggressive soul? The woman fair resembled himself. So similar, in fact, he knew be it him on the other side of the wager, he would have done the same. March into a cave full of dragons and not emerge until he had proven himself the successor.

But to have a woman show him up?

Injurious to his claim to be the greatest slayer.

"Blessed saints, she will be the death of me." Dragging himself up, Macarius forced his legs to a swift stride.

If she insisted on the risk, he must be there to scrape up the bones and return them to her family. And should she emerge successful? He didn't want to consider the humiliation.

CHAPTER FIFTEEN

Landing the cliff ledge, Rhiana marched to the center, where she had stood days earlier. Dragon's flame had danced about her. The breath of sage had entered her system. She had tasted danger on her tongue and in every pore on her body. Alive is how she had felt then.

Anticipation of questing into unknown dangers made her feel equally as alive.

The mouth of the cave stretched just wide enough to allow a full-bellied dragon entrance. Forged of limestone the opening glittered with mica flecks captured by moonlight, seeming more an opening to a fantastical land than that of a beast's lair.

To think on it, why shouldn't a dragon's lair be of fantastical design?

She peered into the cave, seeing only blackness. The cool breath of darkness whispered across her flesh. Evident scent of sage misted invisibly through the night air.

Who would risk the chance to stand in the midst of dragons?

"I will take that chance," she said to herself. A defiant smile shifted her bravado to the fore. The hoard was familiar, but the risk was now paramount.

Macarius, who followed her like a lamb to slaughter, touched ground precariously close to the edge of the cave opening. Wobbling, he struggled for balance, arms splayed and Dragonsbane cutting the night. For one moment Rhiana thought he would plummet over the edge, but his equilibrium altered, and he landed both feet squarely on solid stone. He turned to her, straightening his shoulders and assuming indifference for his near fall.

Much as Rhiana wished he'd stayed up top, she figured should worse come to worse, an extra hand—waiting outside—wielding Dragonsbane, could not be overlooked.

"You've been inside the caves before?" he wondered as he joined her side, keeping his voice to a whisper. The mail coif he wore slithered across the steel plates riveted to the shoulders of his jack armor.

Would a confession reveal her edge to this side of the wager? Of course, she'd never traversed the caves while occupied by dragons.

"No, never inside with so many dragons nesting." Not really a lie. "But I did reconnaissance the other day. I wanted to get close, get a feeling for the caves now that they've been reinhabited."

"I see. Does the cave go back, or is it just this cove?"

"The penetralia snakes in and about for quite a distance. Parts of it even go under St. Rénan."

"Really? And how is this evident? Have derring-do's followed the passages?"

"St. Rénan sits upon a salt mine. We've mined the salt for centuries, though not so aggressively the past few decades. It is a journey to the nearest port. But no dragons can live beneath the city for the tunnels narrow so even a man must crawl to access the mines. And why should we when it would open the village to such danger?"

"And now you venture into danger's mouth on a dare?"

Rhiana clasped a hand about the dagger at her hip and drew in the tempting scent of danger.

"I favor a dare." It felt exhilarating and dangerous. The adventure she had been born to. A way to prove to others she was capable.

She slapped Macarius on the shoulder and pointed to the dark opening with a stretch of her dagger. "Stay here, keep an eye and ear open for trouble. I'll be back in a bit."

"Is there nothing I can say to make you change your mind, my lady?"

"Not a thing."

"Perhaps I've not the desire to seek your bones to return to your family?"

"Stand firm, dragon slayer. I shall return."

"Perhaps I should accompany you."

"Then the wager would not be met. It is for me alone to bring back a piece of the hoard."

She had not lied about entering the cave the other day. But that didn't mean she had never before been inside. Everyone visited the caves when it was sure there were not dragons to fear. Or they once had. At one time there was so much, Rhiana decided should a man take a piece every day, and multiply that by the number who lived in St. Rénan, and stretch it over a decade, nary but a small niche would be carved into the hoard. That had changed.

Be that the reason Lord Guiscard wanted to keep Macarius from slaying the dragons? A slayer was due all he could take from the hoard should he extinguish the beasts. Not that Macarius Fleche would make so much as a dent in the hoard should he load up the largest of horse carts.

Nor would he find what he wanted. For, over the decades, a good portion of the hoard had been transferred to the penetralia beneath the village. An act of greed? No. An attempt to take away the one thing that attracted danger. Now, but little remained here in the seaside cave, which is why the number of dragons come to nest so surprised Rhiana.

But that didn't cohere with Guiscard wanting to keep Rhiana from doing the same. Not that she would claim any more than usual from the hoard. And it wasn't because she was female. No, Guiscard had a darker reason for denying slayers the right to hunt.

What was that reason?

Wandering along the inner wall, a view of the sky yet visible, Rhiana traced the cool, moist stone with her fingertips. A ritual she had performed thousands of times, as she'd walk along the bailey walls. At times, as a child, she was blind, darkly walking the world. Others, she'd sought that hidden stone that would move and open to an enchanted realm. Ah, but those were the days of her youth. Though, the spirit of her adventures was renewed with every step she took into this mouth to hell.

Roughly carved, these cave walls, not smooth like the building blocks that fortressed her city. Everything smelled of salt, a tang of the mysterious, for the sea offered no truths to Rhiana, only wonders.

Turning sharply to her left, she knew there was a narrow passage lit by strange rocks—too narrow for the rampants to pass through—paralleling the dragons' wider passage that led back to the hoard.

But what of the newling? The one that had been injured in the village was the size of a mastiff. It could easily navigate this tunnel. Was there just the one? Pray, it had survived.

Twenty strides in, the smaller opening to the narrow passage beckoned like a magical portal. Feeling a sinister chill ride her spine, Rhiana switched a final glance toward the oval of pale midnight framed in the distance. She could not sight Macarius's silhouette. Just as well.

He stood there. Waiting. Anticipating. She knew it as she sensed the heartbeats within the cave. The man had balked when he'd seen she had no intention to refuse his wager. Fine time to grow chivalrous. She would show him, once and for all, and put to rest his ridiculous rants against women slayers.

Turning, she drew a glance up the cave wall. A spider gamboled across the mica-flecked stone. She wasn't afraid of creepies. Very little did she fear. That which she did was more visceral, ingrained. Tales of the charcoal man stealing children who wandered from the beds at night still made her shiver.

Though this darkness did teem with…well, the unknown.

Here in the inner walls of the cave the *shushing* of waves against the seashore slipped away. Her footsteps made but muted noise. Expecting utter and frightening darkness, every step Rhiana made upon the chill stone floor the room brightened. In blue. 'Twas as though there were tiny firefly lights set into the stone walls. The walls were lined with a luminescent crystal, which glowed a soft blue as fathomless as the sea and as glossy as rounded glass.

"Such wonders," she said, always amazed.

Here and there the floor was mounded with angular black stones; they appeared molten lumps for the blue light did not illuminate down that far. Like Lady Anne's eyes, the glossy stones.

"It is a jewel box filled with sapphires and hematite," she said.

She held her hand before her and studied the blue shapes of light glittering upon her flesh. Had she walked through a mist of faerie dust? Not hell, this cave. "'Tis enchantment most grand."

Rhiana stretched her arms high above her head and spun in a circle. This was a room of wonders, of beauty and magic.

A deep breath drew in the scent of sweetness covered with ash. Not an awful smell. Just…curious. Citrus combined with a sweet wood-smoke flavor. Altogether, quite appealing.

Reaching out, she traced a fingertip along the sparkling wall. Fine particles glittered on her flesh. Rhiana sniffed it, and then, without thinking overmuch, she touched her tongue to the particles.

"Hmm…" Not horrible. Almost sweet. Like honey.

Her heel crunched on a smooth branch. She teetered, and fell. Bracing herself, she landed softly on hands and knees, clutching the cool black rocks, but her face aligned with the object that had caused her fall. Highlighted by a narrow beam of blue light, a bleached skull cracked a hollow grin.

Scrambling back and to the wall, she shuffled her feet across the floor, inadvertently tipping the skull so that it rocked. Empty eye sockets leered at her and shook a sad warning. *Indeed, this may be hell.*

A cursory study of the floor now spied a few bone shards, and a long bone, complete, not crushed. The length of her…thigh.

"Oh." Human remains? Were they…fresh? No. She could not bear to inspect.

Reverence for the great beasts was replaced by dread. *Be wary. This be their demesne. You are but food scampering close to hungry mouths.*

Moving forward, her steps cautiously avoiding the bones, Rhiana was suddenly drawn to the coin suspended about her neck. Clasping the small gold disk centered her. A gift from Paul, he'd presented it to her after a particular incident in the bailey.

Jean-Marque had been teasing her of being a witch, sticking out his tongue at her and making demon horns with his fingers to his temples. Quite tired of being teased by that point, instead of running, Rhiana had spun on her feet and thrust her arm against Jean-Marque's throat, pinning him to the wall of the battlements. For two long moments the boy's feet had dangled, until Rhiana had released him and stomped away to seek the armory.

Not long after, the boy and his parents appeared at the armory, insisting Paul admonish Rhiana for her harsh treatment of their son. Jean-Marque, muddy and beaten, stood smirking joyously at her while his parents had berated Paul for not keeping her in hand. When they'd left, Rhiana hadn't even opportunity to explain her quick anger and utter frustration. She'd read Paul's understanding in his proud smile. "The boy is a head taller than you. And you put him up against the wall!"

As reward for her bravery in the face of opposition, Paul had made her a medal. A coin he had saved from a hoard raid, for he favored the strong female profile on the obverse side. The medal of feminine strength, he had christened it, as he'd placed it about her neck. Rhiana never removed the coin.

Ahead the glow from the hoard spilled out from the inner cave entrance ahead. At sight of the glamourous illumination, she rushed onward.

Stepping onto a thin carpet of loose coins, Rhiana skidded and stumbled forward. Her hands crunched over a pearl rope and her face landed within inches of a bejeweled crown. The floor of the hoard was yet covered with treasure. But for how much longer? Here and there the stone floor showed through the glints of gold and silver.

Beguiled by the glitter of riches, she reached for a dented shield. Her reflection smiled back at her. The corner had been torn away from the thin steel shield, likely during battle. There were words painted across the top, peeling away, but still readable. The first letter was an *R,* which was likely the end of the first word. Following, *Valor* and *Truth.*

"Hmm." Tracing the words, Rhiana wondered at who might have wielded this shield. A brave knight marching in the battle against the Burgundians? Mayhap an ancient Visogoth warrior come from overseas to explore a land unfamiliar to him?

The flutter of wings buzzed overhead. Rhiana shooed at the nuisance insect. Soft green wings skimmed her shoulders. A purple-bodied pisky was joined by half a dozen more. Tugging at her hair, they grunted and spouted strange buzzing noises. 'Twas a swarm.

"As if they believe they can move me."

Rhiana swat at one particular pesky creature that buzzed around her face. A swipe of her palm skimmed its crisp wings, but it merely flew right back at her.

"I've not time for you," she admonished.

Then, checking her voice, she scanned the room. How easily her focus had been distracted by sparkling bits and piskies. No dragons in sight, though she could not see to the far reaches of the vast room. The reflection of the gold cast strange dances of light upon the walls so that a flash could, for an instant, be a creeping beast.

A pisky flew before Rhiana's face and hovered there, its skinny arms bent and hands on what might have been hips. Shaped like a human, but smooth of skin and devoid of any detail that might determine it a male or female. Its wings moved so rapidly they were but a blur whispering soft air across her cheeks. Wide green eyes blinked once as it looked her over. Then, with a finger hooked at each corner, it stretched its mouth wide and waggled its violet tongue at her.

"Rude little imp!"

Her voice echoed. Stiffening and pricking her ears, Rhiana

thought she heard a rustle. Breath held and her body stiff, she waited—and heard nothing.

Sitting back down, she lifted the shield and stared at her reflection, wavering with shadows and light. 'Twould be the proof Macarius required.

Thunk. The shield shook in her hands. She turned the shield around and shook off the stunned pisky.

"Serves you fine and well."

The glitter imbedded in the dent attracted her inspection.

Immortality? Well, she'd never before heard that, not even from Amandine. But surely Macarius would have all the proof of the dragon legends.

Compelled, Rhiana licked it clean, tasting nothing particular, or even sensing a preternatural shiver as the promised immortality coursed through her system. What she did feel was heat rising in her throat.

Mon Dieu, normally she could control it. In fact, she had to summon—

The burning sensation shot across her palate and exploded into a grand belch. A pouf of fire hissed at the heels of a fleeing pisky.

Rhiana winced. The ache of fire tightened in her chest and stomach. Always she suffered for breathing fire. But this small belch had taken her unawares, and this time there was little residual pain.

She stiffened at the sudden sound of coins clinking. Something larger than a pisky had moved. Had it seen her fire?

The huff of sage filled the room. A few stridulations began to click nearby. Was it nestled at the far side of the hoard? To even see to the other side of the massive room was impossible without walking at least halfway through. To judge from the clatter of shuffling plates and trinkets, something emerged from the depths of depleted riches.

A flicker of wings snapped the air. A bat? Could she be so fortunate?

A small cry, six eagles in volume, drew her attention to the circling black shadow that hovered above her head.

"A newling!"

Fascinated, but wary not to stand and reach for it, Rhiana kept her ears pricked—and heard another. A newling *and* its elder protector.

This adventure had come to an end.

Tucking the torn shield under one arm, Rhiana slapped a pisky out of her way and ran out into the tunnel.

Behind her the clatter of talons clicked across steel plates, copper pots, and gold coins. Long talons. Not small, bird-size claws that the newling possessed. She had alerted a rampant. It could not follow her out this narrow tunnel. But the newling could. Insistent chirps signaled her the newling kept close on her tail.

Swept from behind by a stream of fire, Rhiana hastened her steps. She felt the heat but did register no pain. She ran through the illuminated blue room, avoiding the bone pile and easily taking the black rocks. Moonlight flashed at her.

"Prepare!" she shouted to Macarius, who turned from his observation of the sea with a startled spin. "It is coming!"

Dagger raised and ready, she raced out onto the cliff ledge. Drawing the tattered shield defensively before her, Rhiana joined Macarius's side. He lifted his sword, looked to her—she nodded—and he turned back to face whatever might come crashing out from the darkened depths.

"You got a shield," he shouted, as the sounds of approaching scale and talon worked to a vicious noise. "You made it to the hoard!"

"I told you I could. But I woke up one of the rampants."

"You don't care for a moment of safety, do you, my lady?"

Smiling at his comment, Rhiana saw the newling skim out as if an arrow. Macarius's aim followed the small dragon.

"No!" She slapped a palm across his wrist. "It is but a newling. There is a rampant close behind."

"But—"

A hiss of flame ended but a stride before where they stood. Macarius forgot the newling and returned aim to the dark mouth of the cave.

The dragon's snout appeared. Jaws wide, it yowled the keening cry of anger. The emotion felt evident in Rhiana's veins. Her blood warmed and began to race. Without another thought, she rushed the beast, but veered to the left to avoid a head-on collision. Macarius could make the distance shot, but without her crossbow—still in the field—she needed to be closer.

She saw Dragonsbane pierce the rampant's mouth, right at the crease where it joined in the jaw. Not a good placement. A nuisance tap to the dragon, surely.

The head swung toward her, and she brandished her dagger fitting the curved black talon into her palm. A swing of her forearm. The blade sliced through the gold eyeball. Hot liquid rilled from the wound and splat the limestone beneath her feet.

Rhiana winced at the cut. She did not wish to make the beast suffer. A quick kill was preferred. Now it thrashed its head wildly, clawing at its eye. If she had her crossbow, she could deliver a killing blow, put it from its misery.

And then it occurred to her, if the kill spot rested between the eyes, should it not be accessible from *within* the eye socket?

Oh misery.

Avoiding a sweep of the tail with a deft skip over the slashing whip of scale, Rhiana saw Macarius dodge an abbreviated hiss of flame by lunging for a boulder set at the cave's mouth.

Rhythmically, the dragon rocked its skull, back and forth, yowling miserably at the pain. Pain, she had caused it.

When it returned to tilt its head toward her for a third time, Rhiana struck. Stepping onto the tail coiled near its neck, she jumped and delivered the dagger right through the eyeball. The angle delivered the blade toward the center and back of the skull—pray it hit the kill spot.

Thrown roughly to ground by a flip of the tail, Rhiana's jaw clacked upon impact. She rolled to her side to spread out the jarring to her bones, but it was too late. Something popped loudly. Brilliant white pain ignited in a streak from neck to arm. 'Twas as if a nerve were bared to the flame.

With one final hiss of fire that billowed along the upper curve of the cave mouth, the dragon's head dropped. The dagger loosened and the talon hilt clattered at the base of Rhiana's feet.

It was not finished. Not until the devil's mark had been breached. Groping for her dagger, Rhiana pulled herself up and climbed upon the beast's nose. The scales were warm, solid, like living armor. Crawling onto her knees, she lifted her arms high, clutching the hilt, and drove the blade vertically into the kill spot.

CHAPTER SIXTEEN

They left the fallen dragon where it lay on the cliff ledge. Rhiana sensed two more heartbeats deep within the cave. She could not know if they would venture out to discover their fallen brethren or if they would remain inside, fearful to their own fates. Nor did she know if the beasts would dispose of the remains in their own manner, but for now, she would leave it to them.

While the scales, talons, and teeth would hold some value in the village, now was no time to take advantage of such riches. Whosoever wished to risk their life for a few trinkets of dragon was welcome to return on the morrow to make the attempt. Besides, the smell of roasted dragon permeated the castle walls, and left Rhiana with no desire to deliver yet another feast to her home.

"Coming?" Macarius had already started to climb up the side of the cliff.

Rhiana nodded, but winced. Intense pain flashed white before her vision. She gripped her shoulder. It didn't feel right. An attempt to rotate her arm in the shoulder socket forced a groan from her.

"You are hurt?" He jumped down and rushed to her.

Backing away from his intense immediacy, Rhiana couldn't move much farther, or step off the ledge.

Macarius lifted his hand over her shoulder, and, making eye contact, asked silent permission to touch her. She shook her head no.

"Please, my lady, let me have a look. You may have pulled it from the socket." He gingerly touched on top of her shoulder. Rhiana bit back another wince but the pain was too intense to ignore, and a moan followed. "As I suspected. I've seen this injury before. It is common. I'll have to fix it for you, or you'll not make the climb up the side of the cliff."

"I can manage."

"Not if you faint."

"I will not— And how will you fix it?" She wanted to pull from his touch, but even the slightest movement shot arrows of pain through her arm and upper back. Instead Rhiana breathed through her mouth and closed her eyes, seeking inner calm amidst the storm. "You are not a leech."

"I'm even better." He turned and pointed to the boulder nestled against the cave entrance. "Stand over here against the rock. Come, my lady, we've not much time should other rampants creep out and inspect the commotion. Right here, press the front of your body against the stone but keep your wounded arm free so I can rotate it."

Blindly moving into the position he suggested—the pain made her thoughts muzzy and Rhiana simply wanted it gone— she leaned against the stone. "Why must you rotate a wounded limb? I don't trust you."

"That is fine and well. I've had my shoulder loosened from the socket more times than I care to recall. I know you are in pain. But I also know how to fix it from experience. So please, trust me?"

He leaned in close so she could focus on his eyes, shadowed by the night. Blue as a summer sky. Challenging as they comforted.

The pain drew up her bile. She did not like to feel so helpless. "Do it. And quickly."

"I'm going to stand behind you and put pressure on your lower back while I rotate your arm. Tell me if it pains overmuch."

The sensation of his palm to her back, pressing her belly firmly to the stone, momentarily changed the intensity of the pain. Touched by a man, and so intimately. His breath hushed over her shoulder, aside her ear. A firm palm cupped her shoulder and worked the bone a minute amount.

"Does that hurt?"

Hurt? She was concentrating on the connection of man to woman. His hard, firm body nestled into hers. He'd moved his hip against her hip and leg, forcing pressure against her lower back, which seemed to refocus the pain.

Rhiana laid her cheek onto the cool stone. Now he slid his hand down her arm and pulled it back. "How much longer?"

The cartilage in her shoulder socket creaked. A spark of pain made her wince. A tiny pop, and a fire burned through her shoulder muscles and across her back, and then it was gone.

"Done," he whispered. "Just remain in this position for a moment. Get your bearings."

That was it?

He had not moved from her body. Their contact, so intimate, had been what had kept her mind from the real pain. Yes? For certainly it must have been a painful procedure.

Rhiana blew out her breath onto the stone. He had touched her. The moment must not be lost, and yet, she could not lean here against the stone like an invalid.

She tried to move her arm, starting gently to shake it aside her body. The muscles ached, and yet burned, but a lift of her arm proved the bone and socket returned to position.

"I think you did it," she murmured.

He lifted her from the stone and turned her around. Gently he clasped her wrist and asked, "Let me help you. Just show me you can touch your opposite arm. Rotate it gently."

She did so, and the marvel at his skill gave Rhiana new respect for the greatest slayer in all the land.

"You'll have to take the climb slowly," he directed. "I'll follow."

"I can do it."

"I feel sure you can."

Once topside, Rhiana had adjusted to the minute ache in her shoulder. The muscles were likely bruised, Macarius said, but she would heal. 'Twas a far better injury than to have taken a talon or hungry tooth to a body part.

Together they clambered down the hillside to the counterscarp where the other dragon lay. This carcass would present a problem. It could not be left here to rot, contaminating the field where they grew their food. The butchery must be alerted and a team of horses would ride out to claim the carcass.

St. Rénan hadn't consumed fish for days. Red meat was welcome to their diet. Yet, Rhiana craved seafood more intensely when looking upon the carcass of the exquisite beast. A pity it had been taken down.

Was there another way? How to dissuade the dragons from attacking the villagers? Could they be diverted elsewhere? Herded like sheep?

An impossible notion.

Retrieving her crossbow from the earth where it had been pressed deep into the grass, she brushed off the dirt and checked for repairs. No damage. Combined, the steel and dragon gut crafted one amazing weapon.

The evening was young. It was yet gray. Rhiana kept her eyes to the ground as she paced quickly toward the battlement walls. The shield she'd claimed from the hoard was tucked under her good arm, dangling its pointed tip across the grass tops. After all she'd gone through to get it, she certainly would not leave it behind. As unusable as it appeared, Paul might melt it down or clip out smaller portions to make gauntlets.

"So we are even," Macarius offered in breathy huffs as he joined her side. Pumping his arms to keep up with her, his coat of plates creaked with every swing of his arm. "One kill for each of us this night."

"I do not keep score."

"I do."

She smiled. "I have come to know that. I don't understand why. Your father was not so competitive."

"Mayhap that is your reason right there." He thumped a fist over his breast. "I have something to prove."

"To a dead man?"

She heard his shrug in the darkness. "Do you mean to tell me you've nothing to prove? The very reason you took that wager was to prove to me you've the pluck."

She'd never thought of it that way. Was she attempting to prove to all who had taken her apart with words and pointing fingers that she was better than them? Jean-Marque had not spoken to her since that day she'd pinned him to the wall.

No, never better than anyone. Just more determined. Stronger.

Oh, very well, better—when it pitted girls against boys.

"Have I succeeded?"

"Eh. You are still a woman."

"Indeed, I am."

In the moonlight, the dried blood on Macarius's forehead taunted her.

"You are a woman; reason enough to wish to prove yourself. I will have you know, men do not appreciate a strong woman."

"And why must that be so?"

"Well…look! You rush to danger, and look at the results. You were wounded! I had to pop your shoulder back into its socket."

She could not argue that, but it had little to do with her prowess. "It could have easily happened to you."

"Mayhap." Macarius scanned the sky, one foot propped on a head-sized stone set like a pearl upon a furrowed row of rape. "Men. Well. We have preconceived notions of a woman's mien. You do not fit any of them."

"Bless the saints," Rhiana said.

"You are a threat to the common man!"

"How so?"

"How— Don't you know? Have you so many suitors you are blind to the differences that keep most away?"

He hit a sore spot and she didn't like it. She had caught Sebastien's eye! Maybe.

"Have you never been asked to marriage?"

"What?"

"I wonder that you have frightened all the men from your marriage bed."

She spun the shield on the tip of her boot. "That presumes I would find interest in any man who should ask."

"Ah, so that answer is a no. No man has asked for your hand."

She attempted a convincing tone of disinterest. "Mores the better."

"Do you plan to live your life alone and in misery?"

Quickening her pace, Rhiana called back, "Open your eyes, slayer. Women can be capable if they so choose."

Like every other male, he. A pity. She'd not before met a man who stirred her heart and ire so easily.

Macarius slapped a hand to her shoulder, and she swung about, thinking he attacked. Drawing up her leg with intention to kick him away, she stopped at his shout for mercy.

What a lucky man that he had not touched her wounded shoulder.

"Be still, my lady. Your back." He slipped about behind her. "Turn your back to the moonlight so I can better see." He slid a finger behind the leather strap securing the armor at her waist. "I had not noticed this when I was tending your shoulder. Your tunic, it has been burned away! The flesh is exposed here below your ribs. You were flamed by the dragon?"

"No." She snapped her shoulder away from his unwarranted touch and turned to face him. But he persisted in trying to get a better look by dodging about her, head bent. "Do not touch me," she warned. "You have been most personal with me this night."

"It is plain even in this poor light. Your tunic is half gone! The edges are burnt. I can smell the smoke and ash from where I stand."

Immensely not good.

"Mayhap a gust of flame flowed close to me as I ran from the hoard, but not close enough to cause me harm. This tattered bit of fabric burns easily."

"Yet, you did not feel it?"

"My actions must have snuffed out the flame before it could do serious harm."

He gripped her shoulders—the wounded one most gently—and try as she might to look away, his searching gaze would not allow it. Even in the darkness his sharp curiosity was evident. "Be you a witch?"

"Oh! Have you no more original accusation? If someone confuses you, you call him or her a witch? Just because my hair is red—"

"Very well then." He released her. "What are you, my lady?"

"I am Rhiana Tassot, fire chaser."

"More like fire runner. You escaped fire's burn? Impossible!"

She did not step away from his challenging stance. "And why should I not suspect the same of you? You, who deems to touch a maiden without her consent. And you, who possesses knowledge of the medical arts. What are you? A man, a wizard, a witch?"

"I am a man, a mere mortal. I burn, my lady," he said in a soft yet firm statement.

"Yes, it is evident from the scar on your neck."

"My neck?" He chuckled, tossing back his head to release a throaty dash of sound. With a little sigh, then a bow, he stepped around Rhiana and walked onward toward the village. "My neck, she says. Ah, but if only!"

Macarius paced right through the portcullis gate and out of Rhiana's sight.

She let him leave. He was distracted, and mores the better, for she did not want to discuss the fact that indeed she had felt the flames wash over her shoulder. And yes, she had felt the wool tunic melt from her flesh and drip to the floor of the cave.

And if Macarius discovered she'd awoken the rampant by breathing fire herself?

It was a secret she must guard with all her means.

CHAPTER SEVENTEEN

After a few hours of sleep, sprawled upon her bed in the tattered tunic and leather braies—armor and legs stretched to the compass points, as Odette often pointed out—Rhiana rose. The ache in her shoulder was not immediate, but a few prods to the muscle realized it did yet hurt. She would take things easy for a little while. Mayhap an hour or so.

A bowl of water and tallow soap sat upon the window bench; must have been placed there by Odette. She washed the soot and dirt from her face and picked under her fingernails. She had not pale, shiny nails like Anne's. Hers were strong and short, but always dirty. Good for clinging to cliff faces and for dragging in the dirt, as well, she could crack open a poorly riveted mail ring with a flick.

A few times Rhiana had watched as Lady Anne would dance to the minstrel's music. She used her arms to seduce, snaking them sensually and curling her hands upon her wrists. Such long and elegant fingers, feminine, and painted with the Nose's henna designs, were capable of attracting all the men's stares.

Has no man asked for your hand in marriage?

Lifting her unwounded arm, Rhiana tried a curling twist of her hand—mayhap the Nose would paint henna designs on her fingers?—but only succeeded in bonking her forehead with a knuckle.

"Bother."

Abandoning all attempts to grace, she tugged on her blue gown. Rhiana never slept overmuch. Four or five hours usually served. A ridiculous shortage to Odette's nine or ten.

Neither Lydia nor Paul had returned from the festivities last eve when Rhiana had come home. Likely they had curled up in the castle kitchen after the food had been passed around and a cask of wine had been depleted. They were a loving couple. Though, of late, Rhiana had noticed Lydia flinch when Paul touched her. And why did she walk about, scanning her periphery as if someone were after her?

Rhiana's night had not been lacking in event. Two dragons down, which left seven remaining. If her count was correct. She wasn't sure to tally the newling or not. Had the newling recently hatched? It didn't figure that the rampants would carry an egg to a new nest. So maybe the newling had hatched elsewhere. What had led the females to leave the nest with a young one for the depleted stores of the north hoard? There had to be a better reason they were here. But Rhiana did not know it.

And where there was one newling, could there be more?

Trailing a fingertip along a line of letters scribbled on the wall, she glanced to the gesso stub sitting on the windowsill, and sighed. No time for writing out her letters this day. Combing through her hair with her fingers Rhiana then headed down the stairs.

She checked the cupboard and found a half loaf of rye bread. The edges were crusty, but the inside was still soft and tasted fine. She forewent raspberry preserves, not one for the sticky mess. Eating on foot, bare feet, for to wear boots with a gown was most unladylike, she stepped outside to a silent village. Indeed, the celebration must still continue within the castle walls.

'Twas good the people had opportunity to laugh and forget their fears. She prayed the revelry would not be ended with the sudden arrival of a dragon. And so, she intended to return to the caves this day. After she had found Macarius. For she must admit a partner did serve no harm. They had taken down twice the dragons last night because of their combined efforts. She wasn't so pig-headed as Macarius that she could not accept help. She would even listen to any plans he may suggest.

Hell, she'd surrendered any echelon of knowledge or prowess when allowing him to adjust her shoulder. How he had touched her should be considered a sin, but a venial one, at that, easily erased with a visit to the chapel.

Knowing exactly where to find him, she strode past the closed shop windows and sleeping mutts that guarded the homes, and to the chapel. Dipping her fingers into the fount, she then crossed over her forehead and chest. Morning glittered across the benches in colored rays and focused beautifully upon the cross on the altar. As well, on the silver studding Macarius's tunic.

"This be not an inn!" Rhiana said, loud enough to rouse the man.

He shifted upright upon the bench, turning to set his feet on the ground and face the altar. Rhiana sat next to him and allowed him time to wake. Rubbing his eyes and moaning at the morning, the man managed an elaborate ritual of scratching, stretching, and yawns before finally acknowledging her presence.

"Good day to you, fire chaser."

She gnawed off a particularly tough piece of bread from her dwindling loaf. It was impossible not to notice the stench. "It will be after you've bathed."

"What?"

"You smell, slayer."

"I…mayhap I do. Dragon slaying tends to be dirty and strenuous."

"There is a public bath around the corner. If you go now, you may have it all to yourself, for most are still inside the castle."

"Now that is an order I can accept." He stood and with a clatter of armor and sword, strode away.

"I'll fetch you some soap!" she called, and was answered with a groan.

Champrey marched down to the middle level of the steps sprawled before the castle. The sun was high and a cart of faggots to fuel the keep hearth sat hobbled behind the steps. Children climbed upon it in play. One of them might take a fall…

He turned away and muffled his hearing to the gaiety and unrolled the formal parchment just inked moments earlier. Bits of sand scattered upon his boot toes. A small, but sizeable crowd had gathered following the trumpeter's retort. He nodded to the trumpeter, who grimaced, spat into the mouthpiece of his instrument, and gave it a rub with his forearm. Gauche bit of—

But to business.

"An edict issued by Lord Narcisse Guiscard, baron of St. Rénan, on this day, Saturday 17th, the year of our Lord 1437."

He paused to note all eyes were on him, save a boy juggling red bean sacks in the back of the crowd. Insolent. The faggot cart wobbled. Champrey looked away.

"From this day forth," he announced grandly, "all slaying of dragons shall cease."

A noticeable hush fell over the crowd, so Champrey quickly followed with, "This edict is issued for the safety of all who live—and wish to remain alive—in St. Rénan. Recently, a very unwise person—who shall remain unnamed—has seen to slaying the dragons come to nest in the caves of St. Rénan. This sudden violence has stirred the creatures' bile, and made them aggressive toward our village. Lives are at stake. Lord Guiscard has decreed it best we fall back, go into hiding. The dragons will leave. We all know the hoard is lacking. But should one more dragon be slain, we risk bringing the entirety upon us like a plague from hell."

"The entirety?"

"How many are there?"

"There could be dozens," Champrey hissed. He waited as the number fixed in the minds and horrified expressions. "Whosoever should even think to violate this edict shall be immediately arrested and thrown into the dungeon. That is all."

Champrey rolled up the parchment, and as he did so listened to the rumble. People were nodding, agreeing. They saw the truth in Guiscard's concern. No one would tolerate a slayer from this day forth.

The bathhouse was little more than a stone shed. Three round wood tubs dotted the limestone-tiled floor. Cecil, the falcon master, had rigged up an elaborate device to catch rainwater outside in a leather tank and had strung pipes to the three wood tubs for easy filling. Ingenius, but cold. Iron warmers were placed at the base of the tubs, but unless they were given a while to heat the water, a quick, cold bath was in order.

Tallow soap ball in hand, Rhiana entered the bath house to find Macarius sitting in a tub of water, his head back and eyes closed, arms stretched along the well-worn rim of the oval tub. Perhaps the water was lukewarm.

She checked the open warmer and fanned warmth across her cheeks.

"I brought some soap," she offered.

Her voice startled Macarius to a splash. He sat upright, flicking his lids open and gaping.

She tossed the soap ball up and down, acting nonchalant. The village women always accompanied their men to bathe, scrubbing their backs and bodies. It wasn't as if Rhiana's presence should be distracting.

Of course, that depended on *who* was the distracted party.

"My lady…" Words sticking at the back of his tongue like a prickle thorn, Macarius suddenly clamped his hands down into the water over his groin.

"I have seen many a man bathe," she offered as she tossed the ball of soap.

He grabbed for it in a spray of water, but again quickly covered his privates.

"I cannot see so deep into the water, slayer. Do you mortify so easily?"

"No, I just…you are a maiden, yes?"

"Of course." Much as she'd like to change that status. But who had the time to pursue romance when the skies were black with danger?

"I shouldn't wish to…well…"

With a heavy sigh, Rhiana approached the tub and pulled up a wobbly wood stool just behind Macarius's head. Propping one foot on a small log, she sat, knees bent and legs spread. A very unladylike pose. "Do you wish me to wash your back? I have done it before. I can do it again."

A mistruth. But she could not allow him to think otherwise. This day was the first she had entered the bathhouse, knowing there be but the one man—a stranger. But when had she ever walked away from a challenge?

"Don't sound so enthusiastic, my lady. You may just entice me."

"Hand me the soap and lean forward, thus protecting your manhood from my maidenly eyes."

He chuckled, but did as she asked. "The marvel of St. Rénan. She slays dragons and men with but a stroke of sword or tongue. The minstrels should like to sing of your exploits, lady slayer."

"Lady Slayer," she tried the title as she rocked her palms about the soap ball, getting them thick with the lavender tallow. "I like that. Oh."

Until now she had not really looked upon a man's flesh, other than to gauge a wound over Odette's shoulders as her sister sewed up the knights who frequently sought her skills. Macarius's shoulders, broad and straight were thick with muscle. Powerful strength forged by swinging Dragonsbane.

But she hadn't leisure to explore the planes and hardness of his form before noticing the angry wounds. The left side of his back shocked Rhiana so thoroughly tears loosened in her eyes to look at.

"You see, it is not merely on my neck," Macarius said. "Does it horrify you?"

"N-no. It makes me sad." Rhiana swallowed to keep her voice from betraying her utter horror.

Stretching from neck to below water level the scarred skin, pink here and deep red in some places, coated half his back. Puckers of flesh spoke of horrors too painful to imagine. Scars from dragon flame, no doubt.

Awkwardly held to the sight, Rhiana smoothed her fingers down her throat. Many times she had stood in dragon's flame. Had been literally surrounded by fire. This is what her flesh should look like. Why did it not? Why, by the heavens, did she not burn? And to breathe fire like a beast? She was human. Not an animal or supernatural beast.

"Did it hurt very much?" Forcing herself to move a hand

to his flesh, Rhiana's fingers lingered above the scarred shoulder. "Forgive me, 'tis a terrible question. Of course it hurt."

"All in a day's toil, my lady."

"You must have suffered for more than a day, surely!"

"Two weeks I was in bed, facedown, moaning against the pain of it. To this day, if I so much as smell a mustard plaster I feel my gorge rise. My father tended me. Had he not been there, I might have perished from pain alone."

"He is the one who adjusted your shoulder, as well?"

"Yes. Far too many times, as I've said. It's a trick shoulder, I've learned, and I must be ever careful with it."

"Amandine was a generous man."

"So generous he neglected to mention his family to you?"

He had her there. And to think of Amandine's family… Was this the time to tell Macarius the truth?

"He was focused," she tried an excuse that might lessen Macarius's obvious annoyance over his father's slight. "For months we talked of nothing but dragons and slaying them. I had so much to learn, and so little time to learn it all. I'm sure, had we taken a moment for leisure, he would have spoken of you."

"Your fibs serve well enough, lady slayer."

"I do not—" He was right. Why did she want to lie to protect him from emotional pain?

"Are you going to wash me, or will my shivers from this icy water turn me ill?"

"Sorry. Does it hurt if I touch it?"

"Nay, in fact, I've very little feeling there. Save when I stretch the muscles or deliver a killing thrust. Are you sure you wish to do this—mmm…"

At first touch of her palm to his back, to the right of the scars, for she would slowly work her way there, Macarius's satisfied noises told her she did no harm. No pain in her touch.

She relaxed her nervous fingers, easing them carefully but surely over the flesh.

He moaned as she swept her soapy hands over his muscles and scars. "Does that hurt?"

"Nay, do not stop," he breathed. "No woman has ever touched my scars."

That statement made her pull abruptly away. "Mayhap it is because you hide them from all the women?"

"You think I have very many women, then?"

"Oh, I wasn't asking. Well, yes I was. I shouldn't have— But. Oh."

"It feels a world better for your touch."

Tight, hard muscles pulsed beneath her massaging fingers. It was when Rhiana realized she had never touched a man like this before that she drew back her hands and stood.

"What is it?" Bold blue eyes searched hers over Macarius's shoulder.

Always Rhiana looked a man in the eye, for there she found truth, and there she would not falter, nor must he. To lower one's eyes when speaking to anyone showed you were eager to please, to submit and serve. Not a manner she often exercised.

The wonder fell from Macarius's eyes and he bowed his head. "My scars do frighten you. Forgive me, I should not have allowed you to touch them. I can do the rest."

"No." Sitting again, feet straddling the iron warmer, Rhiana picked up the soap ball and touched it to his scarred neck and drew it down his back. "Just tell me if I hurt you."

A smirking noise was muffled against his bent elbow. "You think a man who chases dragons shall not mind a little pain when it comes from a beautiful woman?"

At that statement she simply had to pinch the base of his neck.

Yelping, Macarius then pleaded, "Mercy! I promise to behave."

"Best you should. I can get to your sword much faster than you."

Dragonsbane sat by the middle tub, propped carefully, as did his coat of plates and clothing and boots.

"I thought knights bathed with their precious swords."

"Have the knights you've washed worn their swords?"

"Er…" Immensely not good. "Some…"

"I see. Interesting. So you've washed around a few swords?"

"Certainly." What did he mean by that, exactly? Hmm…

"I have become complacent in the company of humans. It is dragons that raise my instincts and make me act the sentinel."

"Yet we humans do bring the showman to your surface."

Macarius chuckled.

"You like the admiration," she said. "You cannot deny it, greatest slayer in all the land."

"And some parts of Spain and Wales."

"Not England?"

"Ach! The land is dull and flat, the air misty and gray. No dragon would seek to nest in that foul country."

Setting aside the soap, Rhiana smoothed her palms carefully down the rugged landscape of scarring. Smooth and yet puckered, it felt like flesh and not. And he could not feel her touch?

Working the soap carefully, she pressed a little firmer, noting the scar was very warm. Closing her eyes she concentrated on the connection of flesh to flesh. The contact heated, drawing up a definite burn to the surface of her palms. A pleasurable and comforting warmth, much like it felt when she held her gold coin. It made her smile.

"The water grows warmer."

She wasn't sure what Macarius had said, for she managed to focus so deeply that all other sensations, such as sound and sight, slipped away. Fingers splayed across the destruction of mortal flesh. 'Twas almost as if Rhiana could see the moment in her mind, feel the heat of the flame as it left the dragon's throat and wavered through the sky. Direct impact against the slayer's unshielded back, for he'd removed his armor to rest beneath an apple tree in the shade of a midsummer's day.

Stealthily, the dragon had approached from the rear, stretching out its neck for distance instead of taking another step that might vibrant the earth with its weight. The target slept. And then he did not. Seeing the mortal rise and lift a weapon—pain, that is what the dragon registered at the glint of steel—it reared back.

The blast always tasted sweet in its mouth. Delicious, undulating amber and crimson flame. The gift of hellfire after its ancestors had mated with the Fallen. Born of blasphemy, but used for defense, it was the counterbalance to its God-marked kill spot.

Curious. 'Twas almost as if Rhiana experienced the event from the dragon's point of view. "How is that possible—"

"My lady!"

Macarius's sudden movement startled Rhiana from her strange communion. Immediately she took her palm away from his back. At the same time, he scrambled forward, struggling in the tub. A red mark the shape of her hand had been burned into the flesh!

But even stranger, the water boiled.

The slayer tumbled over the side of the tub, grasping for a linen as he did so. Hot water splattered Rhiana's face and chest. It actually burned, so hot it had become! She flinched, for water could burn her.

And at her feet the iron warmer hissed up steam in the wake of the waves of water splashing over the sides. She looked at her hands. Had touching the scar born of dragon's flame somehow boiled the water? Impossible.

It occurred now that Macarius was no longer in the tub.

"Are you safe?" she called, leery to seek out the naked man. He'd tossed himself over the opposite side of the tub. Sensing he could be coiled into a painful ball, she saw a foot when she bent to peer around the side of the wood tub. "What have I done?"

Rhiana stood and backed toward the door. Gripping her skirts in tight, twisting fingers, she cautioned herself not to look. Leave him to his private pain. Yet, he needed help. "Tell me you are not hurt! Please!"

"The water became so…hot," he finally managed. "I will fare, my lady. What…"

"I must leave." A naked man lay within eyesight. And she had harmed him. Somehow.

It felt ridiculous, but it seemed possible.

"Tell me if you wish me to send another to aid you."

"No, leave me. I am just overcooked, is all."

Sensing he was wounded more desperately than he would admit, but not daring to look upon her destruction, Rhiana stumbled backward out the door and broke into a run to her stepfather's shop.

Had it been her doing? How? She had not the ability to lay hands upon another and cause results. Yet, she had seen the imprint of her hand upon his back! What was that from?

She rushed into the armory and ran around the stone water table to get Paul's attention.

Paul pushed back his leather mask to rest upon his bald pate and stopped pounding the ingot of iron that looked newly molten. Furrows creased his temples. Tender wonder changed his initial smile to a wobbly smirk. "What be wrong with you, fire chaser?"

"The dragon slayer." Rhiana frantically pointed outside. Gulping air, she gasped and choked. Tears spilled down her cheek. Never had she done physical harm to another.

"Rhiana?"

"I did not mean to do it. He is in the bathhouse. I think…I might have hurt him."

Paul Tassot's mouth wrinkled to a smile. His eyes danced.

"No! Not what you might think. I did not— Please! The water, when I touched it— The slayer, he is scarred by a dragon— So hot! He might be burned."

"You breathed fire on him?"

"No! But the water started to boil. Did I—? I don't know what I did."

"I'll go check it out." Paul handed the pincers to Rhiana. "This cannot be left. Can you cool it for me? What ever happened, I'll find out."

She shook her head.

Was that it? Her eyes had been closed. Had she…inadvertently sent flames out from her palms to burn the man? To heat the water? Never before had she done it without knowing. "Oh, *mon Dieu!*"

CHAPTER EIGHTEEN

This thing the troubadours called love was truly divine. Narcisse Guiscard's thoughts, as always, were fixed to his wife. Anne smiling. Anne laughing. Anne kissing him and making love with him. He loved her so!

It had been three years of bliss since they'd said their vows. And now, he was compelled to gift her with some grand token of his affection. But what would serve fitting for this exquisite woman who made him forget his very name every time he looked upon her pearl-smooth visage?

He glanced to the fire, blazing a hypnotic dance of red shadows upon the ivory dragon skull fashioned by his father. To slay the creatures was an abomination. Especially when they provided Narcisse with the dragon dust he craved every other moment he did not crave Anne.

Narcisse stretched out his back muscles, smiling at the burn to his flesh. Striding naked to the steam bath, he considered soaking for a while. The water was cold. So instead, he cupped his hands in the water and splashed his face, rubbing vigorously and slicking back his hair. A damask robe waited, folded neatly on a bench near the door. He slipped it on and drew the tasseled drawstring tight.

"My lord?"

Narcisse flexed his fingers and looked up to Champrey, who had insinuated himself in the doorway to the apothecary room. "Did you issue the edict?"

"I did, my lord." The seneschal shifted from foot to foot. Cleared his throat. "There's been an interesting capture outside the village gates."

"Are not the prisoners your concern, Champrey?" He licked his fingertips, slowly, eyeing the seneschal.

"I would not have dreamed to disturb you, my lord, but the prisoner is claiming he is father to the Tassot woman."

Tilting his head and peering up at Champrey, he asked, "Tassot?"

"The er…" He lowered his voice to a whisper. "Fire chaser."

Narcisse quirked a brow. "I thought the armourer was the wench's father? At least, her stepfather. Was she not a by-blow of some unnamed man?"

"Indeed, but this man, my lord, he has given his name. Jean Cesar Ulrich Villon III."

Narcisse muttered the overly long name, trying to fix his memory to the familiar sounds.

"He was once wed to Lydia Tassot, my lord. Disappeared two decades ago. Just, up and left his family. Though you do know the rumors."

Indeed, he did.

A man who left twenty years earlier had suddenly returned, claiming he is the father to the dragon slayer.

"What does he want?" Did he attempt to secure a portion of the hoard by claiming a relation to one who was owed such?

"That is the odd thing, my lord. He claims with adamant

fierceness his daughter yet lives. And he demands a party be sent to rescue her from the dragon. He believes we have sacrificed her to the dragons!"

Narcisse smirked.

"Why would he believe such a thing? St. Rénan does not sacrifice virgins. Although…" Tapping a finger aside his jaw he perused his options. The occasional sacrifice may appease the dragons, eh?

After a twenty-year absence, why would a man return?

"He has been detained?"

"Locked in the dungeon, my lord. I thought it best. He was raising a ruckus."

Ah, the dungeon. Narcisse did never go down there; he usually commanded the prisoner be brought to him, should he need question them.

Champrey, still in the doorway, lowered his head and looked across the outer hall.

"I will send for him later," Narcisse said to Champrey. "For now you will leave me to my privacy."

"Um…" Toeing the doorframe with a boot, Champrey did not leave, but instead acted as though the cat had dragged out his tongue and flagged it in front of Narcisse.

With a disgusted shrug, Narcisse implored Champrey.

"We've taken another man, forcibly, at your command. The dragon slayer."

"Still here?" A roll of his eyes, Narcisse stood, tugging his tunic closed. He paced over to the doorway and stood over Champrey. He towered over the man by a full head. "I thought that man had understood he was not welcome in the village. Did he not hear the edict?"

"He ventured off to the dragon's lair on his own last eve. With the woman."

Narcisse hissed out a breath.

"Killed another rampant. By the by, he had a nasty burn on his back."

"Tussling with the dragon? Lackwit! Why must I be troubled by the sort? And what is it about our dragons that attracts the damnable slayers from far and wide?"

He sighed and shrugged a hand through his hair. "I will speak to him. When I am ready. It won't be for some time. I've Anne to attend."

"Very good, my lord. Shall I show him to our best cell?"

"How hospitable of you, Champrey." A snap of his fingers sent the seneschal off.

Closing the door behind him, Narcisse kicked it with his heel.

The dungeon walls glittered with moist and stank of long forgotten dreams. Lady Anne never despised the dungeons, she rather felt them an adventure. She did not come often, but this day her chains had been broken. Pity.

She wanted to speak to the man she had heard had been imprisoned by her husband.

Slippered feet taking the broken stone stairs about the curve that led to the cells, she traced her fingers along the cool, seeping wall. The sound of her chain tinkling in the dimness of air and light and humanity put a smile to her face.

He must be here, somewhere. Narcisse had only recently mucked out the dungeons of the destitute and half dead. Surely, she smelled new blood just around—

Letting out a squeal at her discovery, Anne skipped up to the bars and peered inside the dim shadows. A tall figure startled at her approach.

"My lady?" the man said. He peered beyond her. "There are no guards?"

"Not this day."

In the darkness, Anne could make out but his dark curly hair and pale skin. He was tall and clad in parti-colored hosen that were likely dirtied from the rotting hay in the cell. Shoulders slumped and eyes tired, wearied by the world, be he. She was familiar with the feeling.

She drew a palm along a bar and pressed her side to another. She liked the coolness of the bars, and felt slinky and open. "You are not as I would have guessed, poor one," she cooed.

"My lady." He went on his knees. "You are the Lady Guiscard? My lord Guiscard's lady wife?"

"I am. And I find your prostration fitting. Stand you."

"I fear I should not like to know what finds so fine a lady in the depths of so foul a place," he offered. "Seek you me, my lady?"

"You have been wrongly jailed by my husband."

"Yes," he gasped. "I only sought…my daughter." He made a nervous glance to the side. Anne did not know what he thought to see around the corner. "I did not mean to offend."

"You are Rhiana Tassot's real father?"

"Oh yes, my lady. Well, er…"

Anne lifted a brow. She had heard the rumors. Lydia could not name Rhiana's real father. "Your name?"

"Jean Cesar Ulrich Villon III, my lady. I am most humbled before you—"

"Villon. Yes, indeed. The wizard's idiot apprentice?"

"Former wizard. And former idiot but for a fortnight, my lady. His Most Magical took me on, but quickly saw a means to dispose of me. Wizardry simply was not my calling."

"So I've been told by my husband. He briefly mentioned your tutelage. He was just a young boy when you apprenticed."

"Yes, I have come to understand that. Now. Though it has not been so long as you would imagine. But my lady, about my daughter—"

"You abandoned your child and wife decades ago, Monsieur Villon. Tell me why you come back now in seek to reunite?"

"Really, I've only been gone three weeks. It is very difficult to explain. I had been told Rhiana was sacrificed to the dragon."

"Sacrificed? Who told you this?"

"My wife, Lydia. Er, former wife. She has remarried now, I am told. Actually, that fact was pounded into my head with a very large rock."

"Why would she tell you so cruel a lie?"

"A...l-lie, my lady?"

Anne lowered her head and glanced up through her lashes at the man. Did he not have the truth? Hmm... "You believe Rhiana dead? What do you care, you, a man who leaves your family for another?"

"You would not believe my tale if I told it and so I shall spare you. I simply have come to see Rhiana once more."

Spills of laughter trilled from Anne's throat. She slid along the bars to the wall and caught her belly with a palm. "She is not dead," she said in slow and measured syllables. "She chases dragons, man!"

Clutching the silver chain in hand, Anne swung it in a twirling circle before her. "Sometimes my chains snap," she offered. A pouty smile was received with strange awe. "You won't tell Lord Guiscard I've been down here?"

"No, my lady. If you will tell me how I may see to my release. And how—she lives?"

"Is she truly your daughter? You look nothing like her. She's the wildest riot of red hair and is slender and tall."

"So she is alive? *Mon Dieu,* I had not imagined. But that means Lydia... Rhiana, she is my daughter here." He tapped his chest, right over his heart. "But not my blood, no."

Anne felt a giddy rush fill her belly. "Tell me more," she

hissed urgently. "Why do you not claim her as your blood child?"

"I…cannot. I married Lydia immediately following her attack. She was…"

"Violated?" Anne trolled.

"She told no one. It was the madman in the woods—"

"Teeeeee!!!!!!" Anne spun a gay reel, clinking her chains against the bars as she did. "I knew it!"

"What do you mean, my lady? What do you know?"

"I cannot tell. I cannot tell! Oh, great delight, and wicked horrors! He should be mine. She stole him from me."

A clatter of armor descended the stairs and Lady Anne spun into the arms of a startled guard. "My lady?"

"My chains have broken?" She offered a pitiful frown and showed the glinting chain she had smashed with the bottom of the bedpost.

"I must return you to your room."

"Please, my lady," Ulrich shouted as she was pushed up the stairs. "What of my daughter?"

"What of me?" she called back. "Is it not my right to learn my truths!"

CHAPTER NINETEEN

The battlements were sound, though they would do little to keep out a flying enemy. Iron pyres placed on the parapets between the towers hadn't been utilized for years. Someone must be elected to clear them and prepare firewood. A dragon's senses were dulled by smoke and fire. It was a small means to protection, but Rhiana would utilize any and all ideas.

Dancing across the narrow planks to the door guarded by Rudolph, she gave the password and the door opened.

She tried to slip by him, but the squirrelly fellow stepped around in front of her. A silly smile tugged his mouth to a crooked angle. Then he actually touched her. Pressing his fingers to her shoulder he tugged her hair, not so tenderly, and pressed her against the wall. Did he think to dally with her?

Rhiana would have nothing of this. "What is to you, Rudolph?"

"I require a kiss for opening the door for you this day."

"A kiss?"

Tucking her foot around one of his, a deft twist succeeded in toppling him—but, most unexpectantly, he pulled her down with him. Briefly, they struggled, like two children grunting and shoving to see who would win, until Rhiana kneed him in the gut. Extricating herself, she managed to stand.

"You've gone mad!"

Rudolph clutched his gut and sat with legs splayed. "For all the times I have let you in and kept your secret, I should think one little kiss a trifle payment."

"I don't want to kiss you! If you insist on payment I'd rather lay coin in your palm."

Standing, he swept away the offer with a gruff flutter of his lips. "Coin means nothing, you know that."

"Why the sudden need to kiss me after all these years? Surely you can have your pick of maidens to kiss."

"Oh, but indeed I do." A tug to his skullcap drew it down tight about his ears. "I just wanted to…try you."

"T-try me?" Rhiana sputtered. "I am not a sweet lying on a silver platter for you to pluck up and taste as you please."

"Why are you so tight with your affections? Your sister gives away her kisses quite freely."

"My sis—" Anger was replaced by utter consternation. Rhiana tilted her head inquiringly. "Odette has kissed you?"

Rudolph held up an arm and pointed to a small scar, and then another on his neck. "She stitched me twice. Each time I got me a kiss. All the men know to go to her to get their wounds stitched up. This time—" He tugged up his wool braies to reveal a narrow scar about a finger in length. Fresh white threading stitched it neatly. "Was self-inflicted. But she kissed me longest for it, cause it was so large."

"I—" Rhiana lost all notion what to say. How to react? He'd wounded himself apurpose to get a kiss?

But even more disturbing…Odette was kissing men? She knew her sister did stitch up the knights' injuries. Odette enjoyed the task, said it helped her to study the medical arts. But to give out kisses along with first aid? "Step aside, Rudolph."

She shoved him and strode away. Too angry to even form words, Rhiana stalked home, growling.

The first floor was dark, but at the sound of voices upstairs, Rhiana knew she had arrived during a medical procedure. Skipping lightly up the narrow stairway, she paused in the doorway as Odette leaned in to kiss Sebastien, the fire juggler.

Rhiana's heart plunged to her gut. A thickness curdled in her throat. Her hand moved to her dagger.

"Odette!"

A feminine squeak and a male grunt parted the twosome who sat on the bench by the window.

"Douce et belle!"

"Don't even try," Rhiana snapped, fighting the tearing in her heart with a staunch demeanor. "You use that silly name for all the women."

"But—" Sebastien's eyes moved across the floor guiltily, yet he found the presence to display his stitched arm to Rhiana. A tiny gash, hardly in need of tending.

Odette jumped up and smoothed out her skirts. "I didn't hear you, sister. Been off slaying dragons?"

"A far more noble venture than you've been to, Odette."

To look at Sebastien hurt so desperately. 'Twas as if a part of her had fallen out onto the floor and now spread in a puddle. Let no one tread this floor, for fear of stomping her heart.

Avoiding eye contact with the man, Rhiana said, "I see you're all stitched up."

"Yes, I—"

"Leave," she commanded in a not-so-gentle tone.

"Of course, *douce et*—er, my lady." He jumped up and scrambled to the door. Rhiana did not move, so he had to squeeze by her. He stumbled on the first stair, let out a yelp, and hastened onward.

"You are perfectly awful!" Odette announced once they'd heard Sebastien vacate their home. "I was working."

"Why him, Odette?"

"What do you mean?"

"You know I favor—"

Clapping her hands together and catching up a portion of her sunny amber skirt, Odette squealed, "You favor Sebastien? Oh, Rhiana, if I had known."

"I don't favor him. Not anymore." Pacing to the window, she eyed Sebastien's departure. He tugged on his shirt over those fetching muscled arms and glanced upward—she spun and stepped from the window. "You stitch up quite a few men." She approached her sister, arms crossed. "Most every day."

"Yes, I do." Plucking up her needle, threaded with fine, pale wool thread, she placed it carefully in the seeded needle cushion of suede. "I *am* a professional."

"Indeed. And for every procedure do you also deliver a free kiss?"

Odette twisted her head down shyly. "I do."

"You admit to giving away your kisses to more men than a sheik's harem?"

"It is merely a kiss! Nothing more."

"Odette! How dare you? You, why…you risk being labeled the village whore."

"How dare you? You who walks about in men's clothing?"

A feeble argument, but not unworthy. Rhiana stalked to the window, surmising her best defense. But yet her heart pounded. Betrayed. By a man. A man she'd never had real conversation with, and yet, many times she had stood hypnotized by his flame, swept into the language of his art. She had only ever fancied him from afar.

You admired his fire, not the man.

Yes, and best to continue that belief.

"I have been stitching up wounds for well over a year now, sister. Some days I see more than one man."

"Mercy."

So she had kissed very many men. And where were these men getting injured? Men who did not battle an enemy, but merely entertained friendly jostles in the lists. Were they self-inflicted, as well?

And while it frightened Rhiana, at the same time, the notion of kissing so many men intrigued.

But the scandal.

"You must cease this very moment. Not another man's lips must you kiss."

"But I cannot do that. I like to kiss, Rhiana."

Crossing her arms, Rhiana assumed a defiant stance.

"You are jealous because I kissed the fire juggler!"

Jaw falling open, Rhiana knew some snappy reply should be produced, tossed at her sister's cruel accusation like a swordsman's riposte—but no words came to tongue.

Was she jealous? She had just a moment ago wondered what it would be like to kiss so many men. Hell, even one man would be thrilling for her.

Should she have kissed Rudolph? Just for the purpose of discovery, of course, not to please him in any way. No. What fool thoughts she entertained! She would kiss a man when she wanted to. Or, should the moment ever present itself, when he held her in his arms and seduced her.

What of a man who touched her lower back, firmly, and leaned into her entire body with such purpose?

"Oh." Feeling her bravado wilt, Rhiana sank onto Odette's bed and raked her fingers through her hair. "Mayhap I am jealous! It is just...I am not so very attractive."

"Oh, sister."

"I hear what the whispers say about me. My hair, my face, my…ways. More a man than a woman. Is that it? Am I…runcival? Oh, please, let it not be that."

"You are most certainly not thick and manly. You are very…" Odette leaned before her, studying Rhiana's lowered face. A sigh. "Well, you are so very…much."

Rhiana could barely manage a smirk. "What does that mean?"

"You hair, it is *so* red. And your freckles, are so…much. And your voice." Odette straightened and paced the end of the bed. "You do not converse, sister, you command. And your walk!"

"What about my walk?"

Odette broke into a comical, foot-thumping march across the floor. She exaggerated her steps into long strides and wide, awkward steps. "You stalk about as an oaf. Never looking up to give a 'good morn' or 'bless you' as you pass people by, always so determined. And so serious!"

"Do I really walk like an oaf?" Feeling her arms shiver and a sudden quake in her gut, Rhiana lay back across the bed and stared up at the ceiling. A tear heated the corner of her eye. She swiped it away. "Is that why men don't want to kiss me?"

"Mayhap. You must be more feminine, Rhiana!"

"I don't like dresses, they hamper my—" Walk. Her, ugly, oafish awkward walk.

Oh, *mon Dieu*. Why had not Odette said something sooner? And only yesterday she was feeling so attractive when Macarius had commented on her gown in the chapel.

"There is no hope for me, Odette. I am doomed to become the Nose in my old hag days."

Odette's laughter sprinkled overhead as she bounced onto the bed beside Rhiana and lay down next to her. She clasped

Rhiana's hand. "You are pretty when you wear your blue dress and let your hair down from its plaits."

"I cannot slay dragons in a gown."

"True. And certainly I do wish you to keep them away from St. Rénan. You are brave, Rhiana. Moreso than any man I know. And I respect you for that."

"You do?"

"Very much so. You are unique!"

Rhiana blew out a pitiful sigh. "Unique. Ugg."

"Look you, at your fine skills! And this!" She tugged the dagger from Rhiana's hip belt, which made Rhiana sit upright, her eye keen to the ill-wielded weapon. "It is so pretty and dangerous!"

"Be you careful, Odette. That is sharp and can—you do not stab with it."

Fingers wrapped firmly about the talon hilt, Odette poked the air a few more times with the curved blade. "No stabbing? How then do you use this?"

Fascinated at her sister's naive curiosity, Rhiana thought to humor her, and so tilted her wrist and directed the blade outward.

"It is used to slash. Like this. Careful! Yes, like that. Slowly. You're very talented with a blade, Odette. Methinks I've competition should you take to slaying."

"Really?" Had such a delicious smile ever spoken so loudly before? Odette shrugged, then carefully turned the weapon to hand back to Rhiana. "You see, I am interested in things that ladies should not care about. I see you stalk about, so proud and strong. Mayhap you should not worry so much about your ways, nor should I encourage you to change. You are just as you should be."

"A deterrent to those men who would ask for kisses from you?"

The two giggled. Odette was the first to agree she would be jealous should Rhiana steer one single man from her lips. But she promised to keep her mouth far from Sebastien's should he ever again seek her care.

"It is no matter," Rhiana said. "Sebastien is a cad. He flirts with all the unmarried women."

"He is so tall and handsome. And so many scars!"

Rhiana sighed, but it ended in a smile. Odette and her attraction to wounded men.

"What of the slayer?" Odette said in lower, teasing tones. "He follows you about like a puppy dog. You should kiss him."

"He is not a man to me, but a partner."

"Oh, he is a man. A very fine man with broad shoulders, and scars and—"

"Very many bad, evil scars," Rhiana stated. She did not want to think on their miserable encounter in the bathhouse.

"Scars are attractive!"

"Not the sort Macarius bears. He has suffered, Odette."

"That's perfect! He needs a woman to soften memory of his suffering."

Rhiana stared up into her sister's twinkling blue eyes. She really was enamored of all things male and wounded. Perhaps she should attend to her sister's feminine ways more often, try to incorporate them into her routine. There would be nothing wrong whatsoever with kissing Macarius.

But how to convince him of her femininity?

Narcisse winced as the final glass globe was removed from his upper left shoulder and a hot towel that had been warmed over sizzling coals was spread across his back. Until it had all settled into his blood, the towel would prevent the dust from escaping out in a steam.

Bastian Totaire, the alchemist, set the thin glass globe on

the marble-topped table next to half a dozen of the same. A small clink rang musically. He then, as usual, bowed and left Narcisse to relax in silence. On the way out, Bastian passed Champrey, who entered and went to wait by the stained-glass solar window.

Knowing the man knew better than to interrupt these sessions, Narcisse squint his eyelids tight. The sting of the cups still lingered, yet they were all six removed. It wasn't a painful feeling, just tugging. Of course, that is how he knew the method worked, if not, for his youthful appearance.

He couldn't see Champrey, but he could hear the man breathing. Nasal, stuffy, nasty bit of breath. The man never bathed; he stank. Yet Narcisse could not deny the seneschal was a whip when it came to the administration of St. Rénan. Not a single tax was ever missed, nor levied too highly so as to cause discord in the village. Executions went off without a hitch, and usually with much fanfare. And the castle larders were so carefully documented Champrey would know it if a mouse so much as nibbled a kernel of corn.

And the secret was enforced with an iron fist.

Narcisse had little to do but hunt and make love to his wife. As it should be.

"What is it, Champrey?"

"Forgive me, my lord, but there is urgent news."

"Spit it out. Did one of the revelers fall in a drunken state upon the castle steps and twist his neck?"

"It's Lady Anne… She's missing."

A squire swept away rubbish and twigs as Rhiana marched up the steps to the castle.

And Narcisse Guiscard marched down the steps toward Rhiana.

"My lord, I've come to—"

"—help me find Anne."

All business and not wasting a moment for breath, he hooked an arm in hers and swung her abruptly about and down the steps. By the time they'd reached the ground a mounted knight and two additional horses waited.

"Anne?" Though she'd changed to a gown—conversation with Odette had prompted her to soften her appearance—Rhiana automatically mounted. Reaction was instinctual. "Where is she?"

"I do not know!" Narcisse mounted and swung a bejeweled suede boot over the horse's back. "She disappeared in the night!"

"But did you not chain her?"

The horses stirred, sensing the urgency. Sitting sidesaddle, Rhiana reined in her mount to steady.

"I forget atimes," the baron said. Beckoning blue eyes squinted against the sunlight. "We fêted through the night. She left at midnight to say matins, as you know she always does. And when I stumbled to bed she was there, asleep like an angel. I did not notice her drift from my side. And this morning I had assumed her already in her solar, tending her tapestry. We must make haste!"

"Where do you think she's gone? Why must I accompany you?"

"She's gone to the caves, I know it. It is all she thinks about. Now come!"

The caves. Of course, Rhiana also guessed it would be the first place Anne might wander. What mystical enchantments the dark corridors offered a troubled mind.

"I must retrieve my crossbow and armor." She ignored Narcisse's order and turned the mount toward Paul's shop. "I will meet you outside the north wall, anon!"

"Make haste, my lady!"

Not giving a moment's thought to why Narcisse would require her aid, when a few knights should serve, Rhiana rushed to the armory and ran inside. Seeing her urgency, Paul helped her on with her scaled armor and secured the points of her tunic to her leather braies.

"He believes she wandered to the caves?" Paul strapped on the baldric across the scales and fitted her crossbow upon her back.

"It is not a surprise," Rhiana said as she sheathed her dagger. Two bolts Paul placed in her quarrel. "Anne's mind tricks her. She does not reside in this world."

"But that of the dragon's world?"

Rhiana nodded. She had told Paul her suspicions. Lunatouched, Anne communicated with the enchanted in a way she could never imagine. 'Twas Anne who taught Rhiana how to communicate with piskies. "I feel compelled to her, Paul. I don't know what it is, but we two are alike."

"Do you think she breathes fire?"

"Or can set a tub of water to boiling? What of the slayer? Did you speak to him?"

"He is well—just a little surprised."

"No damage?"

"None. Now, off with you. Bring our Lady Anne home safely."

"I pray we find her before she stumbles into trouble."

CHAPTER TWENTY

Narcisse and Jacques san Marque, one of St. Rénan's best archers, heeled their mounts to a gallop as Rhiana rounded the battlement wall. Crossbow strapped to her back and dagger at her
hip, she was ready.

That Narcisse wore no protection, and merely brandished
a saber could not bode well. He looked the vision of a chivalrous knight, bejeweled with garments fine and golden. Mayhap he could not concern himself with proper attire for he
worried about Anne. A knight flanked him to his right, and
Rhiana to his left. Pray, he knew to get out of flame's way and
keep from harm.

They crossed down and through the counterscarp and began
up the side of the mountain. As the megaliths dotting the
mountaintop came into view, Narcisse pointed. "There!"

Rhiana spied the figure walking along the meadow, near the
very megaliths she had tracked the twice-wounded dragon to
last night. Ghostly white robes, so ethereal, floated out against
the periwinkle sky. Overhead an enormous crow circled. That
was not a crow—

Heeling her mount to follow Narcisse and the knight, Rhiana shouted, "Be cautious! We do not want to frighten her. There is a newling circling her head."

"Kill it!" Narcisse commanded as she sided him. "You are the slayer!"

"It will not harm Lady Anne. It is but a babe."

"Jacques! Destroy the beast!"

Now he wanted to kill a dragon. And this one would never cause anyone harm.

Rhiana heeled her mount to a gallop, but it couldn't catch up with Jacques's swift destrier. Clinging to the horse's back with but his thighs, the knight drew up his bow and notched an arrow to it. Rhiana did not believe the man could get a precision aim while riding. He risked hitting Anne.

"No!" Rhiana fired a bolt. The target, Jacques's bow, bounced from the knight's hand and flew into the air. "You will hit Lady Anne!" she reprimanded, as she passed up both men and dismounted into the thick heather.

Jacques fisted an obscene gesture at her insolence. "Witch!"

Oh, but the village men needed to develop a new oath against her. Witch was so tired.

Lady Anne had yet to notice the approaching entourage. Which could prove a boon. She would not flee.

Rhiana stalked toward the meadow. Narcisse dismounted and gripped her by the shoulder. Her wounded shoulder.

"Don't touch me!" She turned and made a fist, but at the baron's admonishing look, she spread out her fingers and stepped back. "It is my shoulder. I hurt it yesterday. Forgive me, my lord."

"You hampered my man's best shot!" He huffed angrily at her.

"He could have hit Anne," she insisted, easing a palm over her aching shoulder. "You asked me to help? Then allow me the lead. The newling will not harm her. But should we harm it, it may send out a cry that will alert other, much bigger dragons, as happened yesterday. Now, will you follow?"

Narcisse looked to the knight and back to Rhiana. A nod verified his acquiescence—but he wasn't about to appear pleased. "Lead on."

Sweet summer perfume stirred about their legs as they crossed the meadow of heather. A fat humble bee disturbed from gathering pollen protested by buzzing about Rhiana's face. She shooed it away.

Behind her Jacques muttered oaths about precocious women under his breath.

Anne walked the thick grasses that capped the caves, weaving toward the narrow-spaced megaliths. Her strides were flighty, pausing every step or so to reach up to the newling. She spun in a circle, delighting as the black shadow of a newling spun matching circles above her.

Rhiana reached back, signaling with a hand for Narcisse to join her. Much as she wished to rush forward and tackle Anne, she knew the safest method. The baron flanked her side. Crickets chirred at their feet, and from above, the menacing shadow of the newling briefly darkened their faces.

"You must approach her," she said. "Use soft words and mark your pace slowly."

"Yes, my fragile Anne." He stepped forward, the sword he wielded dragging the grass-tips at his side. "Anne, my sweetness," he called out cautiously.

At the sound of her husband's voice, Anne startled from her reverie and stumbled. She fell to her side. Her hand slapped the megalith. A scream sent the newling to a dash high into the sky. Branches snapped. Anne disappeared.

"No!" Narcisse rushed to the stone.

Rhiana raced behind him. *Mon Dieu*, but she had forgotten

the hole the dragon had escaped into. She arrived at the megalith to see Anne's groping arm.

The frantic baron lunged to the ground, gripping his wife's arm high by the shoulder. But that did not stop her descent. Narcisse dropped prone. He slid along the ground, pulled toward the hole by Anne's frail body.

"Grab his legs!" Rhiana ordered Jacques.

Jacques tugged the baron across the ground. Narcisse drew Anne up and laid her across the ground. Grass fluttered over her eyes and shoulders and pale gown. A pisky fluttered up from the depths of grass, hovering about Anne's face. Narcisse slapped it away, and then bracketed her face with his palms. "She is dead? No!"

"No, she cannot be." Scrambling to Anne's side, Rhiana looked into Narcisse's tearful eyes. "Is she hurt? Is there blood?" She scanned Anne's body for sign of injury. If a broken branch had poked her she could very well be wounded. But not dead, no. "Touch her throat. Listen at her lips. Do you hear breath?"

Pressing his ear to Anne's mouth, Narcisse closed his eyes and listened. After a few tense moments, he nodded. "She breathes. She is alive. Hurry, we must return to the castle and have Totaire attend her."

Jacques helped Narcisse mount and propped Anne against his chest so he could put his arms under hers and hold her upright.

Slamming her left fist against the megalith, Rhiana leaned over the hole. She could not judge the depths, but when marking the distance from the cliff edge, and in her mind pacing it to the forest's edge, she wagered the hole dropped right down into the hoard.

Still tense, for she would not relax until she felt assured their scuffle had not woken any dragons below, she worked her fingers at the knot tightening at the base of her neck.

"Come!" Narcisse called. He waited astride, Anne's dark tresses spilling over his left arm. "We must see my lady wife to safety."

"I will remain and investigate," Rhiana offered. She knelt before the hole. "It is curious. Why have I never before discovered this hole? And then to see it twice in so little time…"

"You will return at my side!" Narcisse barked. He nodded to Jacques, who walked Rhiana's mount over to her and tossed her the reins. "I may need your help with Anne."

Bowing her head, Rhiana looked askance at the commanding baron, and for a moment held his gaze. He did not require her help. There were plenty women in the castle, maids who every day tended Anne and who knew her eccentricities.

Did she stare into benevolence or madness? Did he tread lunacy far more delicately than Anne? His emotions quickly flashed from kindness to violence. He controlled—yes, that was it, the baron wished to always have control. Over all. Be it a frail woman or an entire village, even a doom of dragons.

With a glance back to the hole—she would return—Rhiana complied. "I will accompany you," she said as she rode up alongside Narcisse. "On one condition."

"What be that?"

"Release the dragon slayer."

"The slayer shall be released after he's had a few days to think on the error of his ways."

"The error— He seeks only to prevent what might have happened here," Rhiana protested.

"There is an edict against slaying dragons, you should be keen to obey!"

"Since when?"

"Since this morn. If you would read the posts in the bailey, you would know that. Mayhap you cannot read?"

"I can!"

"Then you must have missed the section where it banned the slaying of dragons. I have no mercy for ignorance."

Feeling the muscles in her arms tense to form her fingers into a fist, Rhiana tightened her lips and inhaled deeply through her nose. She beckoned inward, *just calm, my furious heart.* If anyone were ignorant it was the baron.

"What if Anne had fallen into the caves?" she blurted out. "If she had survived the deadly fall, then surely she would have become a fine dinner for a hungry dragon."

"Cease with your babbling, wench. Your logic does not serve my intentions."

"And what be your intentions? To see the village ravaged by the wings of hellfire? Four have been taken and eaten!"

His mount stomped the ground. Narcisse wrestled to rein it calmly. He swung about to hiss at her, "I know what is best for all. The more you stir in the nest of dragons the more voracious they become for human blood."

Gasping out a protest, Rhiana pulled back and took up the rear of the cavalcade. "It is a doom, not a nest."

Her logic and his intentions? Of course they were at opposition. But why did Guiscard believe his intentions the best for all? Her slaying did not, in turn, turn the dragons against the village. It did not. It could not.

Guiscard did not believe his own edict was for the good of all. It was merely a statement. A means to control.

And that was the trouble.

They avoided the drawbridge and instead galloped around, past the small entry Rhiana used at Rudolph's discretion, and to the east side of the great castle that looked over St. Rénan.

Dismounting, a waiting squire received their horses and wandered off with Jacques to the stables.

"I was not aware of this entrance." Rhiana, eager to learn of its secrets, trundled behind Narcisse. The moat was boarded over with a wide walk, capable of holding the two of them side by side.

"No one is. It leads directly to the dungeons. This walkway is laid out only when I request it." Anne in his arms, Narcisse tromped across the creaky, but sturdy walkway.

Rhiana followed, finding no challenge in the walk and noting her sullen mood was likely because she was not to action, back at the hole where she should be, but instead nursing a capable lackwit.

The door was designed of tightly lashed beams, blackened with oil, each very narrow, likely quite strong to keep back, or as the case may be, keep in. The earth around the entrance had been dug down a good leap to meet the base of the door, leaving the surrounding ground unstable and crumbling at every step. The least obvious place for an exit, Rhiana mused. What protection, besides a dry and very crossable moat would keep away the enemy?

St. Rénan had become complacent. Not set upon for decades by attack, the village, with all its secrets, was ripe for invasion. Would she see real battle in her lifetime? She expected so.

"It's not lit and very dark." Narcisse stepped aside as sign Rhiana should go in first. "It twists about twice, very sharply. Just step slowly and keep your hands pressed to the walls. I'll follow. Should I stumble—"

"I'll catch Anne," she hastened.

Thinking the stairs would be chilly, Rhiana was surprised at the humid air. Never had she been in a dungeon. Just another adventure into a dark pit filled with suffering souls and sorrow. It was a lacking visit she'd wished to keep so, but she would remain with the baron until she was reassured Anne was well.

Pressing both hands out to her sides to skim the walls, she

tested the first few steps. Each was triangular, and no wider than her foot at the greatest end. An easy stumble.

The heavy wood door closed behind her, completely blacking out the stairway column.

"Pity we are not alone," Narcisse's voice slipped over her shoulders like snake scales. Much smaller and colder than dragon scales.

"You love Anne," she said as she carefully stepped lower. Now she remarked that Anne had not yet returned to consciousness. Might she have been harmed? "Why do you wound her with your indifference?"

"It is merely talk. If you actually believe I should ever lay with a witch—"

"Why does everyone insist I am—" Missing a step, Rhiana groped for hold, leaning into the wall, her cheek kissing the warm stone.

How Guiscard managed the steps with Anne slung over one shoulder was incomprehensible. Mayhap he took these stairs often? For what reason?

"Be I a witch I would have bespelled you to a warty toad years ago."

The baron chuffed out a husky chuckle. "You risk burning at the stake with that statement, wench."

Burning? That would prove a long, miserable death. Rhiana shuddered to consider how she would startle more than a few should they ever fix so heinous a judgment against her. How long would they roast her before they realized mere flame could not kill her? If anything, she would die from inhaling the smoke.

"You know I am not a witch. You've had conversations with the Nose. I've seen her visit the castle late at night."

"Yes, but what *are* you?"

"Did not the Nose tell all?"

"The woman knows little more than anyone else."

A solid wood door blocked Rhiana's farther descent. She released her held breath and pressed her forehead to the door. The question that ever troubled. *What are you?*

What sort of person is impervious to flame? And not simply dragon flame, but all flame, even from a simple hearth fire or the fancy five-pronged torch Sebastien juggled?

"Lift up on the handle, jerk it to the right, and twist left."

The curved iron handle moved easily and the door opened to a stretch of hallway. Thirty strides away a torch blazed and the narrow aisle hooked sharply to the right.

"Have you many prisoners in your dungeon this day?" she wondered as she held the door for Guiscard and waited until Anne's filmy skirts had cleared to close it behind them.

"A slayer and an idiot. There is room for one more," he called as he took the lead.

They rounded the corner by the torch and passed cells barred in iron rods, and yet some were merely fashioned of thick wooden dowels. Rhiana knew she would find Macarius here. She hoped to see him, for the other option did not sit well with her; his absence could only mean his death. Dare she believe that he had been released and left St. Rénan? *Without a word of farewell to her.*

Neither option was as desirable as seeing him.

With much relief, she sighted in a man who sat in a cell to her right. He did not move from his position on the floor as she and the baron passed by. Knees bent, back to the wall, his wrists rested upon his knees. The clink of Guiscard's sword rattled against the iron bars.

The jailed man turned. Their eyes met, and Rhiana, thinking quickly, lifted a finger to her lips for silence. If he knew she was planning something—which she was not…

Should she have a plan? The notion to break Macarius out from the dungeon hadn't occurred until now. Hmm…

"Quickly, witch—er, Rhiana," Guiscard insisted as he rounded a corner and arrived at the stairs that led up to, she hoped, the castle—and freedom.

"Rhiana?" A pale hand shot out from the first cell around the corner. "Is it you?" the prisoner inside cried. "Oh, so lovely you have become."

Walking wide to avoid the man's grasping fingers, Rhiana slowed and peered between the iron bars at the man with dirt-smeared cheeks and pale blue eyes. How did he know her name? Rather, had he heard Narcisse name her and thought to plead to anyone who would listen?

"It is me," he insisted, fingers reaching and groping. Rhiana remained at the opposite cell, shoulders pressing to the hard cool bars. "Jean Cesar Ulrich Villon III!"

Her heart fell into her gut. That name. It meant so much.

And so very little.

Scrambling forward, she gripped the iron bars and peered inside as the man stepped back. He stretched out his arms, displaying a gaunt frame and parti-colored yellow-and-green hose beneath a long black cape. Shoulder-length black hair curled upon his shoulders.

He did look a little familiar. It had been so long. Had he ever truly been a part of her life? Her…father? Well, he wasn't her *real* father. She couldn't recall being so young, or naming him father…

He had abandoned her and her mother!

Rhiana spat upon Jean Cesar's face and swung about to march past Guiscard and up the stairs.

"Do you know him?" the baron demanded as he gripped her shoulder, stopping her on the bottom stair.

"If he is who he claims, he was the man who was married to my mother when I was born."

"Your father?"

"He does not deserve that title. Paul Tassot is my father."

"I have heard of this man. The man who abandoned your family? Never to be seen again?"

"Indeed."

He twisted a curious look around to the cell where the prisoner wiped spittle from his cheek. "But he looks so young. Very much your age. How can that be?"

Not caring for further conversation regarding a man who had broken her mother's heart, Rhiana ran up the stairs.

CHAPTER TWENTY-ONE

Still armored and bearing her crossbow, Rhiana marched straight for the main gate and out of St. Rénan. Macarius could sit tight for half a day. Right now she had more important things to check on. Namely, the hole in the ground Lady Anne had stumbled into.

Tugging back her hair she twisted it to a knot. The day promised to grow warm, mayhap even hot. Though the scaled armor was surprisingly cool, her mail chausses and tunic already itched. She was in need of a bath—but not in the public bathing house. Bad things tended to happen there.

Spreading out a steady palm before her as she trekked onward across the field of sunny yellow rape, she wondered how her hand had caused the water to boil. And yet, these very same hands could press back fire, were impervious to flame. Had contact with the remnants of dragon's fire on Macarius's back been the catalyst to the boiling water?

It was all she could figure, but so far beyond comprehension.

Of course, her entire life was beyond comprehension. Why

was it so difficult to accept she may have inadvertently harmed the slayer? Though, Paul had said Macarius was fine.

Macarius would have many questions. Which is why she had avoided speaking to him in the dungeon. No reason for her to display their camaraderie before Guiscard and force him to imprison her on collusion.

And then to see Jean Cesar Ulrich Villon III? What foul day this had become! That man, why, she had not seen him in twenty years. And yet, he had seemed familiar. Oh! He was the reason for she and her mother's distance; Rhiana knew it as she could sense a dragon's heartbeat. Why was he here, and in the dungeon?

Did Lydia know? She could not. And yet, her mother had been acting rather queer of late. Hmm…

So much to trouble over. But fore, Rhiana must look beyond her personal worries and strive to protect the innocents.

With those innocent souls in mind, she trekked onward.

Narcisse would be busy with Anne and so should not send his knights to follow her. As she crossed the field and trundled down and up the counterscarp, she had only to keep an eye out for beasts on wing.

On the seaside of the megalith, broken branches jutted up like a messy haystack about the circumference. A deadly step. Surprising she had not stepped into it during her many treks here. It could have only been uncovered, or formed, recently. Rhiana decided if she could not cover the hole with something secure, like planks, she must mark it so she and others would take note in the future.

What had compelled the pale lady of the castle to this particular site? Be it the caves that called to her? Had the newling led her to this hole?

Even more puzzling…

Why was Anne so attracted to the dragons?

Squatting and leaning over the hole, Rhiana could not determine its depth. It reeked of dragon and earth. Poking her dagger inside hit upon nothing. Stretching out her legs in the long grass behind her, she reached into the darkness. What she hoped to grasp upon, she did not know. And in her next thought she abruptly pulled out her hand.

What fool thrust their hand into a dragon's lair?

A flutter of commotion emerged from the hole. Swatting at the nuisance insect, she cursed the pisky. It chattered and flit its wings before her nose.

"Is it the hoard just below?"

Kicking a leg out at her nose, and missing, the violet pisky then flew up to disappear into the sky. Obviously in no mood to communicate.

"Fickle piskies."

Giving thought to the newling she had seen earlier, Rhiana searched against the blinding sun for a darker, larger shadow than the pisky. None but a flight of white seabirds sailed against a tuft of clouds.

Leaning forward a bit more cracked the branches around the edge of the hole. Splinters scratched her armor. Rhiana's body lurched forward until her head dangled. And then she noticed the ladder.

A ladder?

Obviously not for dragons to climb up or down. Only a man might use it to descend into the…?

"It is the hoard," she whispered.

She wondered how long this entrance had been here. And who knew of it? Was it included in hoard raids? Or was this a secret entrance some used to procure their own stores of wealth?

"Who would be so foolish to visit when the caves are inhabited? And for what reason? We are all well off. What use is greed when gold does nothing more than decorate?"

The bane of a village, rich in gold, was that gold ceased to be of value, for everyone held it.

"Someone is trying to increase their standing?"

It made little sense, but one must wonder. There was one way to find out.

Shifting around, Rhiana stabbed her legs into the black void and dangled until her feet found a rung of the wooden ladder. She descended into darkness for over two dozen steps. And then the dark grew brighter, as if illuminated by a captured sun, its rays striving to touch all crevices of its surroundings.

Cool yet verdant, the air inside the cave. Welcoming, almost as a baker's shop on a winter's morn that offered abundance and sweets. Rhiana's foot touched earth, yet she snapped back to cling to the ladder, taking stock of her surroundings. Indeed, she had lowered herself into the hoard. Everywhere, gold and silver and bronze and other metals glittered with a thick coating of the dragon's dust.

The hoard stretched across the vast room. Even plundered and lacking, this room contained riches. No one in the village had ever put forth a guess how so much could be gathered by the beasts. Surely this room had once held tens of centuries of plundered riches.

Cautious to scan for sleeping dragons, Rhiana assured herself this side held none of the golden-eyed creatures. Yet, she had missed a hidden rampant last night when fulfilling the wager, so she would not relax her guard.

The gold compelled and spoke to her with soft whispers.

Safe here. Home. Touch us. Spread your arms over the riches and close your eyes…

Focus. Do not become complacent. Look about.

How strange, the area about the ladder was cleared. By rights the hoard should scatter to the walls of this massive room. Certainly a concerted effort had been made to remove the bulk to the penetralia, but there yet remained a layer of riches over most surfaces.

Did someone from the village have a lust for the treasure that they risked their very life to mine for it? It made little sense. Gold was like sand to the villagers. So common, easily gained. A man could not trade a gold coin for a loaf of rye bread; the baker would sneer at his own wealth.

One hand clutched to the ladder rung, Rhiana leaned forward and drew her gaze up and over the pots and urns and various coins.

Such peace here. Safe even. 'Twas the most comforting feeling. And yet, that feeling troubled. Why did she feel as if she were in her mother's arms standing amidst a dangerous doom of dragons?

She noticed the layer of dragon dust to be so thick that she could trace her finger through it. If the dust beneath Odette's bed sparkled like this she would sweep more often, Rhiana mused.

She swept a finger across the dust and then slipped that finger into her mouth. No taste, not a sensation or smell in the dust.

"Hmm." There, along the cave wall where much of the dirt floor was exposed she noticed the scrapes, like fingers dragging through a pudding.

"It's not the gold. Someone is mining the dust," she said in wonder. Her thoughts matched her confusion. "Why?"

Immortality? As Macarius had mentioned.

Impossible. Man only gained immortality through death and the remembrance of his brave and valorous life.

"About as impossible as a woman breathing fire," she answered her thoughts.

Reaching for a scoop of the dust, Rhiana turned and leaped to the ladder. She had nowhere to put the handful, and so ascended the ladder with one hand. When she topped the ground, she studied the dust under the sunlight.

Like holding minuscule jewels in her palm. It sifted easily, and yet it possessed a viscous thickness that would not allow the soft breeze to trickle away her prize.

What fool in the village thought to steal dragon's dust in order to expand his lifetime? And could it really work?

"Mayhap Macarius will trade some of his knowledge for rescue?"

Retrieving her crossbow, Rhiana stood and turned to face three knights wielding sword, mace, and vicious grins.

CHAPTER TWENTY-TWO

She was roughly shoved down the dungeon stairs after one of the knights had gone to Lord Guiscard with the small bit of dragon dust that had yet clung to her fingers. The baron's orders returned swiftly: to the dungeon.

As she was shuffled past Jean Cesar's cell, the man inside rushed to the bars and began to plead the men to have mercy upon her. "You cannot imprison a woman! It is cruelty most horrible!"

Rhiana would speak no argument. Breath was not worthy to be wasted on these wastrels. The knights took pleasure in shoving her along. If she wanted to act the valiant, they mocked, she should not expect mercy.

She exchanged cool glances with Macarius as she was placed in the cell opposite his. The iron door was secured with massive rusted hinges. Keys clinked and soon the dungeon quieted as her jailors' footsteps echoed away and up the stairs.

"Well met, fire chaser," Macarius offered.

He leaned against the cell wall so his head was not visible behind the iron gate, but his legs, at a slant, were. Thigh-high suede boots crossed casually. The mail rings on his sleeves scriffed against an iron bar. *Mon Dieu*, but he was attractive, and Rhiana could not even see his face!

"What mischief have you been up to? Wait." One blue eye peeked around the iron gate. "I've heard tell, no more than a public bath will serve to put a man behind bars in this village. So you must have done something quite awful. Dancing about with unbound hair?"

Smirking at his jest, Rhiana reached back and unknotted her hair. She was in no mood to return the humor. What idiot locked up the only hope to protect his village from the violent skies?

"I hear there's an edict against slaying," Macarius sing-songed. "You weren't out slaying without me, were you?"

"Slaying? Are you well?" Ulrich called. "Rhiana?"

"Yes," she answered curtly. She didn't want to have a conversation with the man who had abandoned her. Why now had he returned?

No—she did not care to know. He was of no concern to her.

Besides, dire situations called for immediate reactions. She had no intention of loitering about to make conversation with Ulrich and getting to know her mother's absent lover.

Pacing to the far wall and staring at the floor, she tapped her toes and drew in a breath. *Concentrate. Open the mind and focus.*

Heartbeats settling, Rhiana closed her eyes. For the moment all sound ceased, she did neither hear the rustling of Ulrich's pacing or the flicker of the distant torchlights. The world became very small and she stood in its core. And just when she thought to spread out her arms and encompass the world, she heard it.

A heartbeat. Not her own, but that of…a dragon? She knew it as none other than a dragon.

Stretching her gaze across the floor, Rhiana jumped at the intensity of sound vibrating beneath her stance. She focused in on the origin of the heartbeat. Beneath and…far below.

"In the salt mines?" she whispered. "Impossible. The tunnels, they are too narrow for a…"

She could mistake the beat pulsing in her blood as nothing but dragon life. *Mon Dieu.* This was not good.

Immensely, not good.

She had to act. Fast. Hands jittering near her hips, she surveyed the small cell, looking floor to ceiling and over the iron bars. Of course it was possible to get out of here.

Anything was possible.

"Right. Anything." Clutching the cell bars, Rhiana looked across the way. "You ready to bust out of this place?" she called to Macarius.

The slayer twisted on his heels. One shoulder poked between the bars and his head tilted into view. "Don't tell me, you have a plan?"

Rhiana surveyed her options. The walls were of earth and thick stone. The floor was covered over with dry straw. Iron bars faced the cell. A rusted lock hinged the door to her confinement.

Rusted?

A catty smile slipped onto Rhiana's face. It may just be weak enough to bend when heated. "I think I do have a plan."

"She thinks?" Macarius's partial face and shoulder slid out of view.

But enacting her plan would mean exposing her secret to Macarius. And Ulrich, whom she currently could not see, because his cell was around a corner and to the left. She wasn't sure what to feel about the man at the moment. Why now had he suddenly reappeared in her life? What did he want from her? The brief moment she'd looked upon him earlier he'd appeared so young. Merely a child, himself. She'd once thought he believed her a witch, and that was why he'd fled the family. No matter how many times she'd pleaded her mother for answers, Lydia would never give a solid reason. Rhiana had decided her mother knew little herself. Ulrich had just…left.

So she wouldn't concern herself with him.

But Macarius was another problem.

He had said earlier that if it breathes fire, it was from hell. She had never been one to hold back truths—but the one. Was he deserving?

He could be. She barely knew the man, yet, she felt she knew his heart, for was he not Amandine's son? Her trainer had embodied valor. Surely Macarius would not consign her to the same ranks as the dragons she sought to kill.

Turning her back to the cell bars, Rhiana held out her hands and spread her fingers. Closing her eyes, she drew her focus inward. Intense placement of self, Amandine had once described the method of centering. *Go inside, seek the quiet and know the way.*

And do not return to the heartbeat below your feet.

It would take some time to heat the bars. But she didn't need to burn through the iron, only heat it until she could manipulate the molten metal as Paul did when he worked his pieces of armor and swords.

Might she risk smoking them out? Mayhap the smoke would attract a guard before she could finish.

"I'm waiting," Macarius called tauntingly. "Does the big bad fire chaser have a plan or not?"

"I do!"

The slayer challenged with every breath he made. On so many levels. And not all of them physical. Some were emotional. He made her think of things like weaving flowers into her hair and walking less like an oaf. Of kisses and touches and— And emotion should not interfere right now!

Time to get out of this place, and put the slayer in his place.

Breathing fire took a lot from her; it was not to be used indiscreetly. She would be out of sorts and achy for a while following. Much like she received a good punch to the gut, yet from a flaming fist. Was it worth it?

"Do not call out in fright," she directed both men. "You must simply trust me."

"I do," Ulrich hastily said. A hand reached around the wall, signaling his closeness.

Macarius shrugged and slid his head back out of view.

Rhiana didn't need to impress the man. This was for her more than anything. Because to sit any longer than necessary in this cell she would go batty.

Stepping to the rear of the cell, back still to the bars, Rhiana closed her eyes and stretched her mouth open. Fire breathing was like channeling a miserable ache in one's belly. It started as a small flicker and grew swiftly. 'Twas painful to summon, and made her gut muscles clench so tightly as her jaw.

A hiss of flame passed out her mouth. Catching it, she worked the stream of fire into a ball. Cupping it with both palms, it was about the size of a babe's head. Small, but it should serve with a bit of handling.

She wavered. Though the act of breathing fire was simple, rather quick, it was as if the flames continued to burn in her belly. She crouched, fighting against the debilitating pain in her gut, but managing to retain the ball within her palms. Stumbling to the wall, she propped herself there, knees bent. Leaning forward, the fireball glowed in her hands.

She had only discovered this skill when she'd reached her teen years, days following her first monthly cycle. One summer she'd been lying in a meadow, looking up at the clouds, and a belch had blasted a fiery wave above her. Following, had come the worst cramps that she could not associate later with simple monthly pains. Initially shocked, she'd quickly resumed a manner of calm and had checked that no others had seen. She'd learned early on to disguise her differences. From that day forward, she'd worked to learn control and anticipation of the skill. Paul and Amandine were the only others who were aware of it. Neither had an explanation.

And it was the lacking answers that troubled her more than the fact she could actually breathe fire—as if a dragon.

The weight of the fireball increased as she moved her palms over the flames. Letting out a moan at a particularly nasty bite in her gut, Rhiana breathed through her nose. The cramps subsided. Finally, she was able to regain control.

Straightening and holding up the fireball in outstretched hands, she smiled. When it felt liquid yet solid like a mortar of mercury, Rhiana turned and approached the lock. Holding the fireball in one hand, she slipped her right through the bars and to the opposite side of the U-shaped link in the lock. Pressing the fire onto the link, she caught it with her other hand and held the flame over the iron.

"What in the seven hells?"

Now she had Macarius's attention. He stared between the iron bars like a stuck pig.

"My lady? What—how? You will kill us all!"

She tilted her head to eyeball Macarius. "I said to trust me."

"You hold fire in your hands! How do you do that?"

"Have faith," Ulrich called. "Let the woman work her magic."

"Magic?"

"It is no magic," Rhiana was quick to assert. "I am not a witch!"

"Claims the red-haired beauty who conjured flame from out of nowhere," Macarius protested.

"Beauty?" Rhiana fixed her gaze to Macarius's pale blue eyes.

He'd called her a beauty. The longer she held his stare, while the flames worked at iron in crackling licks, the more his face softened. Until his mouth parted and he smiled.

"You know you will have to explain this," he said. "I wager it is much the same as your methods to boiling water."

She winced at that reminder.

Well, if she was going to come out as a freak, might as well do it complete. In full view of the man, she coughed up another flame and caught it in her palm.

"Oh!" she gasped against the burning within.

"My lady!" Macarius cried.

"Quiet," she managed. Bent nearly in half from the pain, Rhiana pressed her good shoulder against the iron bar and pushed hard as a means to counterbalance the pain she felt in her gut. It worked minutely, yet managed to allow her to continue her focus.

Working the second ball of flame into the first fireball, she focused on its growing weight. Amber and yellow flame followed her direction, seeping about the iron and eating at its rusted exterior.

A glance to her side pinpointed Macarius, his mouth open, eyes remarkably wide, framed between iron bars.

Chuckling at the hilarity of at all, Rhiana cautioned her attention and focused on her work. Should the hay at her feet catch fire, she would have a blaze to deal with. Not that she worried for her safety. But one secret a day was enough to reveal.

The rusted iron heated rapidly. Soon it blazed redder than the fire. The flames remained contained, morphing about the smoldering metal, edged with a violet border, as her flames always burned. It was pretty. A marvel.

In order not to become bespelled by the rhythm of the fire, Rhiana looked across and fixed to Macarius's stunned stare.

"Unbelievable," echoed from across the hall.

She smirked. Belief required evidence, and the evidence was right here. So what was there not to believe in?

That you are not completely human? You know it. You wonder. How else do you do what you do?

Not a witch, the Nose had said, but something so much more.

Rhiana did know wizards commanded the elements. Mayhap she was a fire wizard? No. They had to study. And surely she would know if she were a magical being? Yet, Ulrich had studied with His Most Magical, a wizard Rhiana barely recalled, and only because Lydia had, once or twice, mentioned him. No wizards resided in the village now. Not even a female who did not know if she were a wizard or just a freak.

Not a freak.

It felt right, standing here, holding flame. It was as if flame drew her and comforted at the same time. Home, it called. It is you. You are flame. Accept it.

"Believe," she murmured, feeling the need to draw that acceptance from the man who she considered her equal in every manner. "But do not tell."

"What is there to tell?" Macarius called. "That I am enamored by a beauty who breathes flame? I should never be let out from this dungeon, for madness would claim my bane."

Enamored. Beauty. The words Macarius used titillated Rhiana's sense of identity. He used them without thought. And yet, did he know how such language made her feel? As if he desired her. As if, for once, a man looked upon Rhiana Tassot with beguiled interest.

You should kiss the slayer.

Tilting a look down over the lock mechanism, Rhiana determined the iron had begun to thin and stretch. In fact, the lock had settled lower. The iron glowed red. With force it would break.

Amandine had taught her to deliver a powerful blow with her body. Using her entire skeleton to weight behind the impact, she needed balance, forethought and an exact placement.

Taking two brisk steps toward the wall, Rhiana bent at the waist, bringing up her left leg. In the next movement, she stomped the iron bars with her foot, focusing all her energy on the one spot. Flames licked at her flesh as if water streaming over stone.

The lock snapped and separated. Tumbling in a rain of fire and ember, the iron door ripped from its ancient daub plaster and went down, spilling into the hallway. The crash snuffed out most of the flame, leaving but small tufts of fire flickering here and there.

Leaping up to climb over the door, Rhiana jumped over to Macarius's cell. He reached through the bars and gripped her forearms, pressing the scaled armor tight to her wrists. He did not speak, but his eyes searched her face for a tense moment.

"Now what?" he finally said. "There is no time to perform another miracle. The noise will bring the guards upon us!"

"What has happened?" called out from around the corner. "Rhiana?"

"Bestill your tongue. I will be there shortly. The key. It must be down here somewhere."

Dashing around the corner, her loose hair dusted over Ulrich's outstretched fingers. Rounding another corner to the steps she spied the ring of keys and grabbed it.

Macarius's cell opened with ease. But before opening the iron door she stared him down. "I'll ask for payment."

"Of course." He raked a hand back through his hair. "Does the lady desire a tumble in the hay? I've many skills that would be of interest—"

Slamming the door shut, she spoke her displeasure. Now was no time to ask for a kiss. She would have it on her terms, not his.

"Knowledge," she commanded. "That is the payment I require. Agreed?"

"Again she requests mere words?"

"I will leave you, slayer," she threatened.

"Very well. But for every question I answer I will expect an explanation."

"That is not the way it works."

He crossed his arms again. "Then I'll stay and take my chances."

"Lackwit!"

"I need to trust," he countered. "I have seen many a curious sight this day."

Oh, but he did try her patience!

"Very well." She opened the door. "We are in accord to share information?"

"Agreed."

"We're going out the back way," she said, directing him to climb over the fallen timber. She turned to Ulrich. She didn't know how to comprehend this man. Standing there. Returned for her?

"Why did you leave us for twenty years?"

He wrapped his fingers about the cell bars and poked his nose through them. "It has been little more than a fortnight to me."

"I don't understand."

"I love both you and Lydia. I would have never walked out the door and out of your lives. But that is what happened when I stepped into the faery circle."

"Faeries?"

"You are beautiful, Rhiana. I am saddened to come home to

Lydia's hate and your sad eyes. But I am gladdened to know she remarried and had a man to take care of her and you."

"I need no man to take care of me."

"I can see that."

The sound of footsteps hastening around the corner alerted her.

Ulrich touched her hand, and squeezed. "You must leave with the slayer. I'll stay behind and distract attention. They will not hold me overlong. I've a companion in the village who waits for me. Gossamyr—er, Verity. She is my love. Go, quickly! Do what you must to save the village from the dragons."

"Thank you," Rhiana said. And she meant it.

Twisting, she sped into a dash, climbing the timbers and snuffing out a small blaze with her foot as she did so.

Macarius stood on the other side and caught her as she leaped to ground. Slipping from his grasp, Rhiana ran ahead. "There is a stairway and a door just ahead."

CHAPTER TWENTY-THREE

"Where do you rush off to?"

Macarius, arms pumping, carried Dragonsbane. Short crop of curls bouncing, he tromped across the north field. Rhiana knew exactly where he was headed. Focused and determined, he did not turn to her.

Doubling her strides, she caught up to him.

"You've missed nothing in the time you were locked up," she said.

"I've a theory about the hole," he finally offered.

He could not actually go look into it. For then he would learn the secret. And begin to wonder why dragons choose to nest there when— But how to keep him away?

"Someone is stealing dragon dust," Rhiana blurted out.

That statement brought him to a halt.

Good. Now, turn around and march back into the village. And leave the secrets alone. For if he pressed, well, Rhiana could not lie!

Breaths hissing at his exertion, Macarius heeled a palm through his sweaty hair. "Dragon dust?"

"That is not *your* theory? It is mine."

"And how did you come by that theory, fire chaser? You went down the hole?" He joined her, curious now. Breaths still huffing, his chest heaved against the coat of plates that fell to his hips. "But of course, why should I expect anything less. Without me to hinder your steps you've been crawling about the caves, exploring. You've been in there once before, now you are curious. So tell me what you found."

"Tell me your theory first. Back in the village." She turned and made to walk, but Macarius remained planted in place. This wasn't going to be easy. "Are you not hungry? You can not have eaten since yesterday, and even then, I'm not sure what."

"Hunger be damned! A slayer's first and only concern is how to find the dragon and where. I will not return until I've looked upon the situation for myself." He turned and began to march toward the mountain.

"Do you not fear repercussions to going against the edict? Again?"

"This be a reconnaissance mission. No slaying. I promise."

She believed that like she believed piskies were striped. Which they were not.

Besides laying him out flat, there was nothing Rhiana could do but join him. He stomped across the field toward the counterscarp. To follow the edge of the forest was longer, but an easier walk. She would not suggest it. Keeping facts to themselves was not lying. But her conscience got the better of her.

Rhiana hastened to Macarius's side. "The hole leads down to the hoard. Which is how I formed the dragon dust theory. It is very plain the thick viscous dust has been scraped away from the walls. I took some out myself, but I lost it when Guiscard's knights abducted me."

"Did they harm you? And what—" He swung around, stopping abruptly in front of her. Macarius gripped her by the shoulders. His face all seriousness. Now he was willing to talk. "I have been able to think of nothing since we left the dungeon."

"The dragon?"

He grimaced. "No. You. Your…display. Where did you get the fire? It was a trick, surely. No one can…" He did not finish the statement. He already believed otherwise, but logic, and a certain male bravado, wouldn't allow him *not* to argue. "Was there a torch close by your cell?"

Rhiana shrugged, and scanned the sky. She wanted to tell him. By certain means, she already had. And he had likely guessed the truth, but his challenged logic wasn't as quick.

"I thought we were talking about dragon dust?"

Macarius blew out a frustrated breath. So blue, his eyes, like sapphires beneath a dragon's paw. "Why would anyone want mere dust when there are treasures galore to be had? Although…"

Something sparked in his vivid eyes. The man did think. And a thinking man meant trouble.

"What?"

"If there be one thing I have noticed since arriving, is that St. Rénan is quite well off." He crossed his arms over his chest. "Why is that? Be it because you raid the hoard when the dragon is not to be found?"

"You know, as well at I, there are many more than one dragon."

"Stick to the question."

"What was the question?" She paced away from him, taking two wide strides to mount the curved lip of the counterscarp. He knew what he was doing, questioning her so. And she would do well to turn the other cheek.

"The village, my lady. Why do I see no beggars or poor?"

"We've no need of the treasure." He had guessed correctly.

"Should we require coin, we simply sit back until the dragons leave and we can again raid the hoard."

"You *all* raid the hoard? You?"

She walked onward. Exploring the hoard was looking better every second—anything to avoid his interrogation.

"So you have been inside the hoard? *Before* last night when I thought you risked your life for our wager?"

"Of course. But I stay away when there are dragons. Everyone knows to keep away when the caves are occupied. The gold belongs to all who reside in St. Rénan."

"The treasures in that hoard belong to whosoever should slay the beasts and stake claim to it."

He spoke truth. It was an unwritten law of the land.

"So that is your intention? To claim the prize?"

Obviously affronted, Macarius pressed a fist to his chest. "Am I not owed that for extinguishing the horrible evils?"

"Extinguishing? That remains to be seen, slayer. You've killed but one. I have slain three this week!"

He discerned her cautiously. Not keen to hear she was ahead of him by at least two kills, no doubt. "And where is your hoard price? For each kill should you not be granted plunder?"

"I've no need of gold trinkets."

"Says the woman who wears a gold coin at her neck."

Rhiana clasped the coin. "It was a gift! You cannot understand the way we live. We don't want for a thing. Materially." It was the emotional things that Rhiana wondered about. Like sharing conversation with her mother or…kissing a man.

"And seven remain." Macarius whistled. "Such riches! I'll split the booty."

"Split— Do you not hear me? I have no interest."

"But I do."

"Should you slay the dragons, Lord Guiscard will allow you a cart of treasure."

"Should I slay even a dragonfly your Lord Idiot will have me in the dungeons again. That impossible edict! He proposes to protect the villagers from the dragon's wrath. A wrath, by the by, that puts the blame to you."

"Me?" Thus far, Rhiana had only heard bits and pieces reported to her by Paul.

"Yes, you slayed the first dragons. You stirred up their ire. Or so that is how the baron's seneschal put it to me. Now the rampants seek vengeance against the people."

"You know that to be untrue!"

"I do, but the idiot villagers believe Guiscard."

She was not surprised to learn the baron had succeeded in directing the blame to someone else.

"Why does he wish to keep the beasts alive?" Macarius asked. "It makes no sense to me. Has it to do with the hoard? Surely then, he would wish the beasts slain immediately so access to the riches is not cut off."

"The hoard raids occur bi-yearly. This infestation of dragons has come midseason. There is no concern for lack or access to the hoard."

"Hoard raids?" When Rhiana did not answer, he shoved her, not hard, but trying to get her craw.

Rhiana bristled. "Do not touch me, slayer."

He shoved her again. "I shall do as I wish. Does that put up your ire?" A swaggerish grin lighted his face. The scoundrel toyed with her. "Come, show me your mettle, fire chaser. Spin me a ball of flame and perform for me!"

Her dagger tip found its mark against his throat. She could silence him with but a sweep of her hand from sternum to gut. Slicing, not stabbing, as she had taught Odette. But he was too pretty to gut. Arrogant, yes. Boastful and far too much pride, indeed. But certainly worth preserving, for the answers she sought after touching his scars.

"It is not for me to discuss the matters of the hoard with you." She lowered her dagger. Though she certainly had, hadn't she?

Macarius bowed his head and speared her malevolently. "Then why tell me anything?"

"I…cannot keep secrets!"

A chuckle echoed out across the field. It did not put Rhiana to contentment, to be laughed at, but it seemed preferable to him shoving her. The man was mad, surely.

"You have a right to know you will be paid for your services, be they wanted or not. Champrey pays out to the slayers. Not that any have been successful over the years. Save myself."

"Yes, the remarkable lady slayer."

Macarius stepped so close his breath tickled over her mouth. Rhiana did not know how to react. Her stance stiffened. He did not touch her, but she could feel his presence like palpable heat, even through the dragon scale armor.

He took such careful inventory of her. Eyes drawing over her face like metallic-colored insects marking territory in slow steps. What thoughts flittered behind his gaze? "What are you?"

"We've had this conversation before."

"Nay, not a witch," he agreed, and reached to hold her shoulders so she could not tear away. "Freckles and red hair are a comely mix. Witches, they wear warts and grey hair. But, mayhap you are a wizard? One who can command the elements? There was not a torch near your cell. I saw the truth of you. I saw the flames leave your mouth. You, my lady, breathed fire." He stepped back. A blink of his eyes and a shake of his head. So difficult to order his beliefs to rational thought, when rational thought was so far out there. "Like…like a dragon?"

"You saw it with your own eyes." His own stunning blue eyes that she did only want to see smiling upon her, not looking at her as though she may bite him. "Like a dragon."

Rhiana strode past him, along the lip of the counterscarp, wishing to leave it at that. She knew an explanation was required.

If only she knew that explanation.

Ahead, the counterscarp stretched from sea to village. A seabird keened sharply and dove toward the silver waves, disappearing from her view. It was yet mid-day. No midnight darkness to conceal her reluctance. It was very important to her she be truthful with this man, a hidden streak of honor and the quest for integrity would not allow a mistruth.

"I have no answers," she finally offered.

Yes, speak of it. Do not add this secret to that which the village holds so tight. Let him in. As much as you can manage. Be softer, Rhiana. *Speak the truth always, even should it mean your death.* Paul had once said that, and it ever remained a part of her being.

"I've…had the ability to breath fire since I was twelve. Mayhap ten years now."

A series of expressions moved over Macarius's face, starting with shock, then concern, then wide-eyed disbelief. But he found his tongue, and asked the least expected question. "Did my father know?"

"Yes, but he did not speak to me of it."

His silent nod made her wonder that Amandine had never told his son of the fire-breathing slayer. Interesting. The dynamics between the two men were certainly intriguing. A dynamic she was overly familiar with for she and her mother lived in the same world yet tread different dimensions.

"You breathe fire," he stated. Splaying a hand out, ready to postulate, he snapped it to a fist and pounded the air. "Mayhap there was a torch, and I simply did not notice—"

"It is my truth, Macarius. There was no torch."

"Yes, of course. I am trying to put a twist on something I

witnessed, yet could not believe. So!" He poked the sky with Dragonsbane, a fierce stab that drew from his frustration, likely. "A woman who breathes fire. Very well then, you are half dragon," he insisted.

"Ridiculous."

"You know otherwise?"

She shook her head. Unwilling to look him in the eye, to search for the trust she must have from him, she again shook her head. "I know nothing."

"Ah, that is why you wager words instead of actions. You do not have quite all the knowledge on dragon lore, fire chaser. My father did not give so much to you as I had suspected."

"You know something that may give me answers?"

"Not sure."

"Knowledge was promised if I got you out from the dungeon."

A heavy sigh preceded his long gaze across the sky. Rhiana joined his search. There, be dragons formed of clouds and a young child's imagination.

"There is legend that dragons can communicate with mortals," he said. "The elder maximas. Centuries old, they are rumored to have the ability to shift into human form. Though how, I cannot know."

"But that has nothing to do with me. I am not a dragon! I would certainly know if I was."

"No, my lady, you are only half."

As Rhiana processed Macarius's voice, the words sounded credible in her mind. She listened. He explained carefully. But all the while a roiling built up in her gut. Familiar. Burning. She knew what was coming.

"Why they would desire the human form is beyond my understanding," he continued. "Father did not know either. It is only for a short while. And these elders can then speak with we humans. Some say they can speak to only a chosen few while in dragon form. Others claim that they seek the holy. I don't believe that. That a beast can talk?"

"And yet you simply accept they can change to a form so unlike their own?"

"I did say it was legend. Legend be myth, marvel and mystery."

"This coming from the greatest slayer in all the land. Are you not legend?"

"I aspire to it. Some legends be true. What of St. George, the dragon slayer?"

As he spoke about brave knights and their regal history, a woozy strangeness swirled in Rhiana's body. It birthed from her center and simmered, but quickly began to…boil.

No.

She clutched her gut. This was not so strange. *Not…now.* Please!

Trying to maintain calm, she swallowed back her fiery bile. She could not guess why this was happening now, but it would not be stopped.

Flames rose in her throat.

"Are you winded? Rhiana?"

She must act quickly. He could not witness, but—no, not so close! Giving a shove to Macarius toppled him from his feet. He tumbled down the counterscarp away from her.

Twisting, Rhiana tilted back her head redirecting the coming torrent. The fiery burn emerged. Flames rushed past her lips. A violent burst of flame painted the air wavery reds and amber and gold. The next gasp of flame 'twas unstoppable. And the next, which felled her to her knees.

Palms hitting the blessedly cool grass, Rhiana dropped her head, and kneeling on all fours, panted. Cramps clutched her gut and jerked her skeleton to a tight bend. Moaning, she clenched her jaw. Rolling to the side, she spread out her arms and landed her back. Huffing against the pain, tears filled her eyes and burned across her cheeks.

Exhausted by that outburst, she had never before experienced such an uncontrolled escape of flame.

Why now? In front of a witness! Was she changing further? Had Macarius's talk of dragons speaking to humans and changing to mortal form infuriated something within? Some instinctual part of her that knew he spoke truths, but yet wished to deny them?

"Pray you are not hurt!" Scrambling up from the valley, Macarius landed her side. He patted her gently upon the stomach, smoothing his hand up to skim along her neck. There he pressed his knuckles beneath her chin. "So hot. It is as if you've the fever. Rhiana, talk to me."

She could but shake her head. Still woozy and achy, she prayed that had been it. No more flame.

Drawing back a lock of her hair loosened from the leather ties, Macarius moved onto his thighs and sat aside her, bending to seek her eyes.

Never had she felt so fragile. Sick almost, as if she were losing her gorge. Yet a compassionate soul sat nearby wishing to comfort. It did not feel right to have his compassion. She was not sick.

Or was she?

No, this was merely the result of breathing flame. Weak and dizzy from that outburst, Rhiana flattened her weary muscles to the sweet summer grass. But a single cloud sailed the sky shaped like a winged beast. The day drew to a close yet the sky was still light. It must be nearing vesper time.

His face appeared above hers. Brows wrinkled over seeking blue eyes. "Take deep breaths," Macarius coached. Concerned, he touched her forehead as Rhiana had often seen her mother do to Odette when she'd linger in bed and complain of painful courses.

"What was that?" he whispered. "I mean, I understand you can—well, breathe fire. But… It took you by surprise?"

"Yes."

"Never happen before? So…much flame? So forceful? Unexpected, like that?"

"Never," she gasped.

"And you are hurt now?" He held a shaking palm over her chest, tilted it in wonder and then sat back. Legs bent and elbows on his knees he pressed his forehead into his palms. "I don't know how to fix this!"

"Worry not, I will be fine," she offered, sensing his inability to figure this all out, and surprised at his frantic need to make it right.

"I am humbled and stunned and worried all at one time. Please, Rhiana, tell me you will be well."

A chuckle could not be stopped. And that burst of laughter cleared her head. She pushed up to her elbows. "Do not fret for me, slayer. My head returns to normal with each breath I take."

"Your head is not right?"

"Just a little woozy."

"I must imagine, after… That was a very lot of flame. Almost as much as a rampant—"

Macarius stiffened, his gaze fixed to the sky. Without another word, he drew his sword from the sheath and started up the mountain.

All Rhiana could think was that her flaming outburst must have called a dragon.

"I can smell them!" Macarius hissed.

But she did not. Rhiana trundled along behind him. "Mayhap it is merely me?"

He turned such a strange look to her, Rhiana felt as though he touched her, right there, on the center of her forehead. The dragon's kill spot. "You?" Dragonsbane bobbing the air, he stepped closer.

He stopped and looked to the sky. "I was wrong." With that, he resheathed and marched down the counterscarp and across to ascend the mountain. "It was this final megalith, yes?" he called, but did not wait for her to answer.

CHAPTER TWENTY-FOUR

Rhiana descended the ladder after Macarius and found him standing in the hoard room, arms stiff and gaze fixed to the floor of the depleted chamber. A thin layer of coin, shield and pottery covered but half the floor.

"It is all but gone!"

"Shh." She stepped up behind him. "Be careful. I sense another heartbeat. There is yet some gold. A good cartload if one pokes into the corners and seeks for every last bit."

"What has become of this hoard? This is ridiculous! Have your people taken it all? Why would any dragon choose to nest here? I don't understand."

He knelt and toed a single gold coin, not bothering to pick it up. Head bowed, he huffed out a heavy breath.

What to say? She was surprised, as well, that the dragons came to nest. And all females?

"Why do I remain in this crazy village," Macarius muttered, "with crazy lords and feisty women who carry crossbows and march about in armor? Why do I allow myself to be jailed for nothing more than walking this earth? And to be smitten for nothing more than gazing upon beauty?"

What was he yammering about?

"I am sure some means can be rallied to help you collect the remaining gold," Rhiana said. He was so single-minded, focused on the end prize.

In a fury of clacking armor, he stood and spun to stand right before her. With but the light from the hole entrance beaming down over them she could feel his anger ooze from him in tangible waves. Almost like the dragons' anger scent, but she knew better. Nothing was so feral as that.

"Did my father know about this pitiful hoard?"

Rhiana took a step back from his forceful mood. "Yes."

"Yes." Clapping a hand over his forehead, Macarius stepped to the ladder and pressed his hand and head against one of the rungs. "The old man knew that I would find nothing more than…"

"Than what?"

Macarius spun and shook his head. A smile traced his mouth briefly, and he chuckled and then smashed a fist into his palm. "You, fire chaser. You!" With that, he turned and began to climb. "Of all the underhanded… I cannot believe he sent me on this trek."

"Me?" Remaining at the base of the ladder Rhiana watched Macarius climb, utterly at a loss by what he had meant. "Why *me?* It doesn't—"

His father had sent him on a trek. For the purpose of…

Because Amandine wanted Macarius to find her and… marry her?

What a silly thought.

Mayhap?

What other reason could the trainer have wanted Macarius to find her? And yet he'd never once mentioned her to his son? Then surely he could not wish him to marry her?

Mayhap, prove her the weaker slayer?

Amandine had always been so prideful of her skills.

A shout from aboveground startled Rhiana from her confusion. Boots clicking across the gold coins, she took the rungs quickly, and surfaced to spy Macarius running toward the cliff's edge.

A black shadow skimmed the sky overhead.

"Be wary, slayer!" Rhiana reached for the grassy edges surrounding the hole and pulled herself out with both hands and feet. "He's going to be dragon food!"

The rampant banked sharply to the right. Wings spread wide in a glide, the setting sun beamed through the pellicle fabric separated by the long fingerlike bones. It swooped low toward Macarius.

Rhiana had seen a dragon snatch up a man far too many times. But she could not look away. 'Twas as if to look would keep Macarius safe.

"Please, let him be safe."

Talons lowered, the beast swept over Macarius. The slayer slashed against the massive scaled beast, but his sword did not find its mark. What fool did he become? Should not the greatest slayer in all the land know to take cover? Or was he so overconfident of his skills that he would stand down a dragon alone?

Like she had.

His body hooked up by one taloned paw, Macarius's feet left the ground.

Reacting defensively, Rhiana spat flame, but it did travel no farther than a leap. Again she spat flame, but this time into her palms. Quickly rolling a tight heavy ball, she thrust it into the sky.

Flames splashed against the dragon's hind foot, doing little more than showering the sky with red ember.

Fool! That she had expended her energy to use fire against

a beast impervious to flame! Rolling into a tight coil against the inner defiance, she slapped a palm into the grass.

Macarius's cry shuddered through Rhiana's skull. Defiant in its tone, he would not succumb to fear even as the dragon flew over the cliff and toward the sea.

Groping for hold in the grass, she pushed to her knees and stumbled forward. Feeling as though the muscles in her gut were tearing and contracting at the same time, she managed to get to her feet. Staggering, she gripped her crossbow and forced her body to move against all compulsion to collapse.

Rhiana rushed beyond the megaliths and to the cliff. Even dangling from a talon, she saw Macarius yet slashed with his sword. His strokes had to serve a nuisance bit of damage to the dragon's foreleg. It appeared as though the beast had hooked him by his armor, and had not the fortune to dig a talon into flesh. And then....

...a man's body fell freely. Arms flailing, Macarius's feet hit the silvery surface of the water.

The rampant banked sharply and headed back toward her.

Thoughts did not even form. Instinct reigned.

Notching the bolt onto the crossbow shaft, she fumbled. The heavy iron bolt slid, but she caught it from falling to the ground. Darkness suddenly fell. A cloud of sage misted the air. The dragon screamed like a thousand eagles. A flap of its wing stretched farther than Rhiana anticipated it could. A female, none too pleased that humans were dawdling about in her hoard.

The dragon flew low. Wings flapped. The very tip of one wing swung toward Rhiana. She took a hit against her shoulder and toppled. Crossbow landing the grass, she cursed the beast for striking her sore shoulder. At the least, it had not tried to pick her up.

Yet.

Seeing the dragon soar high and coil into a tight circling turn, Rhiana searched the ground frantically for her crossbow. Crawling forward, she kept one eye to the approaching danger. So close! To remain low and flat would give her opponent greater challenge.

Sensing the flame just as she touched the tip of her crossbow, Rhiana closed her eyes against the force of fire that scurried over her body and melted the grass around her, laying a gutter of fire in her wake. The beast drew out its flame all the way to the cliff edge.

Undaunted, she blew ash from her face.

Pushing her hair from her eyes and scrambling to sit and crabwalk her way to the crossbow, Rhiana wondered did the dragon circle the sea in seek of its abandoned prey?

No. It returned in a flash of wing and such speed Rhiana had only time to lift her crossbow and release the trigger. The bolt disappeared in the sunlight. Target missed.

But the rampant did not swing back to her, instead, it flew toward the village.

"Mercy," Rhiana breathed.

It would take another from the village.

She looked to the sea. Macarius was not to be sighted. Back to the village. The rampant circled the field. She could not make it to the village in time to rescue any who might be swept up by the dragon. But she could get to the sea.

CHAPTER TWENTY-FIVE

Impact blackened his senses.

It was the coming to his senses that pained like no dragon's fire ever could. Macarius opened his mouth to cry out. Water rushed down his throat. Liquid muted and clogged each shout. He choked and struggled against— He was in the sea! Deep within the sea, smothered by deafening water.

Where was the sky? The air?

Kicking his feet and slapping his arms against the weight of his armor, Macarius worked for the glimmer of pale silver that had to be the surface. Pray God, it be the surface!

A hot poker had stabbed through his shoulder—the dragon's talon. It was difficult to move his left arm. His muscles tensed, but his arm merely flailed in the surrounding grayness. But that did not keep him from scrambling his other limbs, slashing and kicking and fighting for air.

Breaking the surface felt like crashing through a sheet of winter ice. Macarius gasped in the entire sky. Lungfuls of air. Delicious life.

The shore was nearer than he'd thought. Stretching out his

legs, an overwhelming sensation of relief gripped him when his feet touched soggy sand. He would not drown at sea. But he might die from the cut he knew sliced through his shoulder. The dragon's talon had hooked him by his coat of plates, and in doing so, had torn open his flesh.

Stepping once more, Macarius slapped through the hard surface. He was almost to shore. But he could not see around the massive boulder that glimmered with sunlight. Did it call out to him?

The water tasted salty, different, like wildness and freedom. Like Rhiana, a beauty with long shimmering tresses and movements so seductive she could not be aware of their power. A beauty who could breathe fire.

Not of earth or sky. So far from the water beauty who winked at him—

Ah, but he must be delirious. Imagining a woman in the water before him?

Squinting, Macarius noticed something did move. No, not something, but…someone.

He had not imagined it.

There was a woman—but not a whole woman. Half human, and the other half… There were two! One of the creatures sat, a line of sunlight beaming upon the wet stone and glinting in the flip of her tail. A siren? Until now he'd only heard tales of such creatures.

Macarius spit out water and swiped a palm over his face to clear his vision. Yes, two of them.

Slowly, he must approach. If frightened, they might slip into the water and away from scrutiny. So close, the sounds of their song coiled into Macarius's thoughts as if a gypsy mist drenching a room with exotic scent. One arm outstretched, his wounded arm floating freely and to his side, he crawled through the water.

From the corner of his eye he spied the second siren, bobbing some distance out in the waters. Behind him, she dove, the sparkling green tail fin flipping spittles of water into the sky. Moments passed. Macarius followed the ripples upon the sea surface. The second mermaid resurfaced closer, near the boulder.

But a hands-reach from the stone, the siren on the rock slid over the side, her tail disappearing into the water.

"No," he whispered, stopping. "I won't harm you. I…just want to look at you."

The siren made a sound a bit like a giggle. It bubbled like colors upon the water. Joined cautiously by her mate, the two creatures clung to the side of the boulder, which Macarius figured must be twice the size for the portion he could not see beneath the water's surface.

He winced at the spread of heat through his shoulder. No judging the damage. But right now he could not concern himself with pain. A wise man would search the sky for the return flight of the aggressive rampant. But wisdom had been drowned in the depths.

Sirens!

Slowly, Macarius squat in the shallow water, to show them he would not move farther. Flipping his bangs from his face was matched by a move from one of the sirens. One narrow silvery hand slid over her head, pushing away a liquid stream of viridescent hair.

Silver disk eyes held him. Their faces were the shape of his own, yet the flesh was slick and gray. Not a deathly pallor, but that of watered silk worn by fine ladies at court. Small mouths opened in Os and there—Macarius pressed a hand over his mouth—there was not a nose of the sort he expected, but only two nostrils. Smooth, their faces, no angles or juts of brow and cheek. And might that be gills on their necks?

One of them tilted her head. Silvery-green glossy hair spread across the surface of the water. She swam forward, one arm extended, and as she did so, the other siren began a trilling song.

Beguiled, Macarius crawled forward, his palms sinking into the sand and the water lapping at his elbows.

A webbed hand broke the surface but inches from his seeking fingers. The siren paused, treading before her. A smile Macarius had only seen on the temptresses in King Henri's court curled onto her gray face.

They are sirens. They seduce. They are wicked.

Reaching out, he placed his hand onto a cold palm.

The sky darkened. A sudden chill trickled down Macarius's spine. The siren clasped his hand. Tightly. Jerked forward, he swallowed water. His free hand sank into sand and muck and suctioned firmly into the depths.

Skimmed on the side by scales and tangles of hair, Macarius managed to lift his head above the water. But he was immediately pulled under. He grasped, but felt only air—

—and fire.

The water blazed amber and crimson. Keens segued to cries of terror. Macarius sensed the heat. Only, he could not determine where the water's surface was. Up, down, or to the side? Water siphoned into his lungs and he struggled against the pull of the siren.

Everywhere the water blazed with fire. How could water burn? And in his next thought he knew that it could—for it had not a day earlier.

He surfaced, floating, free of the siren's touch. A mighty warrior stood above him, hands to her hips, blocking out the brilliant sunlight. Luscious garnet hair curled about her arms and danced against her hips like waves upon the shore.

"Be gone with you, evil sirens!" she commanded loudly.

Another blast of flame. Macarius felt the water lurch and his body swayed with the tide. Just at his peripheral vision he saw a green fin smack the surface angrily and dive.

"Nasty mermaids," Rhiana said as she hooked a hand around Macarius's unhurt arm and pulled him to shore. "You survived being picked up by a dragon. A fall into the sea. Near drowning. And yet, you'd give your soul to one of those slimy bits of scale?"

Choking up water, Macarius could not answer. His lungs felt on fire. Indeed, the humiliation of his near death hurt. He turned his body, allowing water to seep from his lips, and laid his head upon Rhiana's leg.

The sun had set by the time Macarius roused. Rhiana was concerned for the gouge out of his shoulder. It was on the left scarred side. Blood had ceased to trickle, but the flesh remained open. The talon had scooped out a chunk, but had not dug so deeply that it revealed bone. Stitches would be required. Mayhap Rhiana would not allow Odette near this particular wounded man.

"What happened? Oh…" Macarius winced and shut his eyes against the sunlight.

"Don't move," she cautioned. "I'm still assessing your wound."

Certainly he would have to stand and walk back to the village. Soon. Rhiana didn't like their position below the cave opening. The dragon that had picked up Macarius was last seen on wing. Headed toward the village.

"You've an injury on your shoulder."

"Yes, it feels the devil's own pitchfork is yet stuck in my flesh."

"Did it pop out?"

"No, blessed be." He tried to sit up but the weight of his coat of plates anchored his shoulders to the shore stones. Macarius set his head back and winced as skull thudded dully against stone. "Methinks it is not so deep as the injury to my pride."

"I do not judge you for your foolishness with the mermaids."

"Foolishness? I—I was seduced!"

"Of course you were. I'm sure every day another knight falls to the seductive beauty of those big silver eyes and slimy fish scales. And gills!"

"It was their song. Did you not hear it? So canorous. Never have I heard so sweet a melody. Only angels can match it, I feel sure."

"And you have heard angels?"

"Fire chaser."

"Think you not their song changes when you are under the sea and can no longer scream for your life? I heard but their wicked giggles, slayer. They sought another hearty man to lay upon their bone pile at the bottom of the sea."

"Indeed, I am hearty." He slapped a palm against his wet armor. "I survived flight with a dragon! Did you see?"

She smirked. Well, it had been a remarkable thing. But what good be his pride if the dragon carried him off for a fine meal?

"So you have flown and survived. Something no man has done before. I'm sure the ladies in the village shall swoon to hear the tale."

"And I shall tell it. By evening the troubadours will have composed a song about the slayer who flies with the dragons."

"Remarkable," Rhiana said, both to his astonishing pride and his fearlessness. "I shall bind your wound with strips of your tunic, if you will allow."

The scaled armor clinked as she carefully moved her leg out from under his head and helped him to sit upright. Removing his coat and then the undertunic was a challenge, but he persevered when she had to lift the sleeves over his head. Men could growl and moan and cry out all they liked, and women thought only that they were so brave. Women, on the other hand, mustn't show their pain. It troubled men, Rhiana knew.

Ripping off long strips from the bottom of the linen tunic, she kept one eye on her handiwork, and the other on the scars marring Macarius's back. Nay, there be not a handprint. Only angry flesh. And a gouge.

"You rescued me," he said as she twisted the shirt tightly across his back and over his shoulder to keep together the parted flesh. "With your breath of fire. Ouch!"

"Sorry. I must make it tight. I don't think you'll die, but we must get you to the leech right away. He'll have a mustard plaster for you."

"No mustard plasters, please, my lady."

She recalled his mention of the remedy for his scars. How the smell must remind him of that horrific pain.

"Sorry. Mayhap a lavender ointment?"

"We must find an answer," he said, pounding his fist into a palm with a soggy smack.

"To what?"

"To why you breathe fire."

"Is it so important to you?"

He sat up straight, rotating his wounded shoulder to feel at the bindings, then turned to her. Rhiana knelt in the watery sand.

"Is it not to you?" he queried. "Or know you already the truth and you keep the secret from me? That must be it, the entire village holds their secrets dear. Makes sense that you should keep your own close to heart."

"I know not how I came to breathe fire, slayer. I have told you no lies, nor do I intend to."

"Concealing the truth when not asked the proper questions is as close to lying."

"I have done nothing of the sort!" That he should even consider accusing her of dishonesty… "Ask me all you wish, I shall not tell a lie. But it gives me to wonder why you care?"

"You are important to me."

Aghast at that easy reply, Rhiana laughed. "I think the impact of hitting water knocked your senses askew, slayer."

"Think you?"

In the evening light, Macarius's face softened. Eyes seeking hers, he dipped his head to look up at her. A wince stretched his bluing lips. He was cold, and yet, the intensity of his gaze felt palpably warm. 'Twas almost as if he wanted to kiss her. But, Rhiana had never seen the sort of look on a man—and Rudolph's attempts did not count to the measure—so she could not be sure.

"May I, fire chaser?"

"May you what?"

"Kiss you?"

"But—"

A kiss? Well… He *did* want to kiss her!

But— Did the man always *ask* before doing? Wasn't it just…done?

Rhiana had not before been kissed by a man. Certainly such an advance must be put off. Putting distance between themselves and the dragon's lair remained fore. But that was not the reaction that burst from her mouth.

"Please."

Macarius leaned forward, but let out a moan, which stopped him less than a hands-width from her lips. "Damn, but it pains me to move overmuch. My lady, will you kiss me?"

"But I don't know—" Almost to the point of admitting she had not the skill to do something, Rhiana stopped her silly retort.

She could slay a dragon; she could kiss a man. Yes? Wasn't so difficult. She'd watched Odette steal that kiss from Sebastien after she'd sown up his wound. Just pucker your lips and press. Giggles seemed to be appropriate as well. Hmm…

Drawing in an imperceptible breath, Rhiana leaned in to press her mouth to Macarius's.

Contact felt different than anything she could have imagined. His lips were salted by the sea. The scent of him was also of the sea. A merman risen from the depths.

Opening her eyes wide, lips still pressed to his, Rhiana saw he looked at her. His eyes were so close, she crossed hers to look. And she giggled, because it all seemed so silly.

"Come, fire chaser, you can do better than that."

"But your eyes are open. I cannot kiss you like that."

"I will close them." He did so, and puckered his lips, but then added, "You close yours, too."

"But then I shall not see where I am kissing."

"Makes things much more interesting." His grin moved the sun-browned crinkles at the corner of one eye.

Reaching to touch those pale creases, Rhiana went with the feeling of discovery, and learning.

Kneeling over him, one knee to each side of his legs, she smoothed her hands over his wet curly hair. He kept his eyes closed, bless him. And for some reason she felt powerful, as if she commanded him. *Drink you, fine knight. Taste me and fall to my charms.* Again she pressed her mouth to his. Soft, and warm, his mouth, the feel of him tempted her to delve into the kiss.

It was nice. His lips moving over hers, pressing and softening, yet stirring parts of her anatomy far from her mouth. The kiss made her tingle. It made her smile deep inside. And it made her sigh against his mouth. Actually, this was better than nice. Rhiana might label it splendid.

"I have never kissed a man before," she admitted. Drawing out her tongue, she flicked it quickly over the plumpness of Macarius's lower lip. "You taste like a merman."

"Oh? And how many sea creatures have you kissed to know such a thing?"

"But this one." She delivered a quick kiss to his beguiling smile. And then another, for this newly learned skill begged more study.

"You taste like fire, lady slayer."

His hands slipped up her back and when they moved across the scaled armor, Rhiana wished that she did not wear it so she could feel the pressure of his wide hands trace her flesh.

About them, the sea *schussed* against the shore, kissing the smooth boulders, carving its impression in the solid stone for ages to come.

Macarius carved an impression of himself into Rhiana's being as he breathed his life into her mouth. She shared his breath. The notion startled, and yet, it pleased her tremendously, to be taking part in this man.

"It is a little disturbing," he whispered. Tugging a strand of her hair he drew it into his mouth and spoke around the tresses. "You are armored, and I am bared to you."

She looked upon his hard, firm chest, bared to reveal a fine sprinkling of dark hairs about his nipples and down to his belly. The thought to touch him was immediate and nagging, but Rhiana kept her position, her palms sinking in the sand at either hip.

"I must protect myself against rogue warriors and lusty knights who wish to steal my virtue then slip away, only to then immortalize the event in a troubadour's song. Think you, this armor effective?"

A tap of his knuckles rang dully against one of the indigo scales. "Most effective." He twirled her hair about his finger. "Will you let me steal but another kiss?"

"I give it freely."

"Mmm, you are warm, Rhiana."

The sound of her name startled her. And at the same time as she drew away, Macarius appeared out of sorts. He looked up to the sky, sniffed, and then slapped the rocks for his absent weapon.

"Do you smell them?" he asked. "More dragons. Close?"

"In the very caves above." Rhiana concentrated momentarily, closing her eyes and listening beyond the sounds of the sea and her racing heart. "But I do not smell them, nor do I detect a noticeable heartbeat. They are far into the penetralia, they will not bother—"

"I can feel them very close!" Macarius pushed back and made to stand, but he paused, staring hard into Rhiana's eyes. "Can you not scent that? Their…mating scent? It is so strong. Almost as if one of the beasts looms over my shoulder." He jerked a look over his shoulder.

It must be that he did take a good knock on the skull from that drop. The man could not scent what Rhiana did not smell, for she knew her senses were keener than his. He continued to search the sky.

Sadly, he'd lost all interest in kissing her.

Just as well. A woman could not slay dragons when she stood in the arms of a handsome man. But might she slay her heart's desires?

CHAPTER TWENTY-SIX

The sky grew dark by the time Rhiana had helped Macarius shuffle along the shore to the dock that the fishermen used to land. One small boat was moored to a post, crusted with barnacles.

When they arrived home, Odette was upstairs sewing. Rhiana gestured Macarius follow her up the narrow stairway. The bedchamber she shared with her half-sister was cool in the evenings for the windows faced north.

"I've something for you to sew up," Rhiana called as she topped the stairs.

Sitting upon the window bench, knees bent and toes tucked under her pale lavender skirt, Odette tended her stitchery. She liked to embroider her dresses, decorating them so elaborately they would fit well at Paris's finest courts. A halo of pinks danced about her crown of curly hair.

Odette tilted her head and studied her bedraggled sister. "I don't do armor, I've told you that. Especially not dragon sc— Oh."

Macarius stepped into the room. Bared to the waist, he'd drawn more than a few curious stares as they had walked through the village. All of them from women. Rhiana had walked a bit taller for the inadvertent attention.

"He's a wound on his shoulder," she said. "It needs a few stitches."

"Oh, certainly!" Always eager to help a man in distress, Odette jumped from the bench and gestured Macarius sit on the bench.

"Watch yourself," Rhiana warned. How to insist Odette keep her lips to herself without making Macarius aware of her jealous thoughts?

"I understand completely, sis— Oh, but he's the slayer." Odette gave Rhiana the most awful look, as if she'd eaten a rotting sweetmeat sparkled with stale sugar. "Lord Guiscard does not like this man."

"That's one point in my favor." Macarius stretched out across the bench. Swinging from a dragon and battling lusty mermaids tended to tire out a man.

"But the edict!" Odette argued.

"Does not say anything about stitching up a slayer's wounds," Rhiana finished calmly.

She tugged Odette before her and pushed her—one reluctant step after another—across the room. Sometimes the girl could be so obstinate!

Macarius fit the length of the window bench. Closing his eyes, he then turned to his stomach, which revealed the nasty cut on the back of his shoulder.

"That's a bloody mess! And look at all those scars! Oh, splendid!" Unable to resist, Odette stepped closer and bent to inspect. She prodded at the bandage then loosened it. "Bring some water and linens," she directed Rhiana. "I'll need to use fine white thread for this one. Oh, it's so large!"

Rhiana caught Macarius's hopeful glance. She shrugged. "The wound, slayer, she speaks of your wound."

"I am not the greatest for nothing." He winked, then closed his eyes. "Two women tending me, how fortunate can a man be?"

After the wound had been cleaned, Odette set to sewing up the cut.

"Let me guess," she said as she touched the needle to Macarius's shoulder. "A dragon?"

"Yes." Rhiana paced the wall before her gesso writings, not focused on anything in particular. She was tired. She was antsy. She wasn't sure what she was. She wanted another kiss, she did know that. From a man who had come to St. Rénan to put a challenge to her, whether or not he'd intended to.

Did he realize his presence stirred such interesting, exotic feelings inside her breast? Feelings of fancy and admiration and yes…lust.

"I thought you had killed it?" Odette said. "The dragon."

"You know very well there are more," Rhiana answered bluntly. She was too tired to summon compassion or discretion.

Yet Odette's shiver was so noticeable, Rhiana felt compelled to explain. "Seven more."

"Give or take," Macarius commented.

"Seven," Rhiana said with an admonishing tilt of her head his way.

"And you believe that you and this man can slay them?" Odette asked. "All of them?"

He put down his head between his crossed arms and closed his eyes.

"We will try. So long as Guiscard's knights do not hamper us." As they had almost done in the field. "I hate to think that I now have to sneak about to do some good."

"The baron claims you roused them to violence," Odette said. "That is the reason for the edict."

"Would it have been better had I stood back and allowed them to snack upon the entire village?"

"Don't say things like that! Oh, I'm so frightened."

"Please, Odette, know that you are safe. So long as you remain indoors and away from…easily burnable things. Remember that. Seek shelter the instant a dragon is sighted. For if you are out in the open, they are difficult to outrun. Don't ever forget it."

"I don't like being frightened. I need…a man to cling to when I am afraid. Like you have a man."

"I do not have a man, Odette."

"What of him?" She drew out the needle from Macarius's flesh. Odette's stitches always healed nicely, with a barely visible scar, yet tiny little stitch tracks along each side of the scar. It was her trademark. She was quite proud to notice her handiwork on many of the knights in the village. "Do you not favor this slayer? He's quite fine. Well, if he would bathe. He smells fishy."

"Odette." Rhiana sighed but a tired smile was irrepressible. "You know, he can hear you."

"Nonsense, he's fallen asleep. Else he would be wincing with every poke to his— Oh!"

Macarius's movement made Odette pause, mid-stitch.

"I *can* hear you," he murmured. "I have very little feeling where the flesh is already scarred. You women gossip about men like two old hens. I do not smell fishy, either. I just bathed this morning."

"Yes, you do," Rhiana said. "You'll be needing another bath."

"Will you wash me again?"

Odette nearly broke her neck twisting a curious eye to Rhiana. Such delight in her dancing eyes.

"Nay, I will not. And you needn't put suspicious thoughts into my sister's head. Heaven knows it be an easy leap for her to make."

Rhiana sat on her bed and faced the wall as Macarius chuckled and again closed his eyes. Odette began to absently hum a tune. Rhiana caught her sister's frequent glances to her on the bed, and so focused determinedly on the wall where she wrote out her letters.

Memento mori. Remember that you must die. Yes, but not before she had ensured her family's safety.

"My father, the armourer, he finds you favorable," she heard Odette say to Macarius. "You could ask for my sister's hand. He would grant it, I'm sure."

"Is that so?"

Not wanting to hear this dalliance, Rhiana raised her hands to cover her ears, but it didn't help.

"She is a fine woman," Macarius said. "She speaks softly, yet carries a huge crossbow."

"It is Rhiana's bane," Odette said on a sigh. "All the time she wishes to be the man. This dragon slaying nonsense is ridiculous." Another sigh. "Does her mannish desire to chase dragons put you off?"

"Not at all. The woman beguiles me."

"Well." The sound of a careful snip clued Rhiana Odette cut the thread. "The day is quite pretty, yes? I wager Vincent will return early from the salt— Oh."

"Vincent, eh? So you've a man, Odette?" Macarius asked.

Rhiana bolted upright. The salt run? She jumped from the bed and rushed to the window. Stretching over Macarius's prone figure, she looked to the ground and up the street to where Vincent usually kept the salt cart parked. It was there.

"Tell me the men have not gone on a salt run this day."

"The stores in the kitchen have depleted. Mother mentioned it a few days ago, and I…may have suggested to Vincent…"

"Dragon's bane!"

CHAPTER TWENTY-SEVEN

An eternal pyre was kept lit near the entrance to the salt mines. It sat at the edge of the cliff, and puffed up a constant cloud of gray smoke thanks to the holly that was burned. Rhiana was halfway down the cart road, which snaked west toward the sea and the stone steps that led a precarious descent to the shore, when Macarius caught up to her side. Huffs and bites of pain punctuated his steps.

The man did follow her like a puppy dog. He was impossible to shake. Of course, he was a handsome puppy.

"Your sister tried to make me stay," he huffed. "I had to bodily lift her and place her away from the door. She had a giggle about that."

"You should have remained at the house." Flirting with her sister? "You need rest. You've been wounded."

"What is the salt run?"

"Exactly as it sounds."

Vincent must have gone on his own at the flirtatious urging of Odette. Silly girl, she did not realize the danger he could walk into! Vincent could not know what Rhiana knew, what she had heard when she was in the dungeon. That one deep heartbeat.

She stopped abruptly. Macarius crashed into her so forcefully they both went to ground in a clatter of scaled armor and weapons.

"You see! You are not well, slayer. Now get you back to my house. I'll return soon, to see to your health."

"You prideful bit of—" He'd landed on her body as if lovers embracing, and now he lifted himself over her. Cushioned by the thick grass that edged the path, every movement released the sweet tang of summer and earth. "Do not nag at me, woman."

"Get off me!"

He planted a palm upon her gut, keeping her firmly to ground. "Not until you tell me what it is that set you off like fire to a forest."

"I fear no fire."

"You are avoiding the question!"

"I've no time for this. There are men in danger."

"From dragons?" he wondered breathlessly.

"I don't know!" The truth, for she had not seen what she had heard. There was always a possibility she had not heard right. However, what else could it have been?

Shoving hard, Rhiana managed to push him from her. Perplexed, she sat there, legs sprawled and elbows propped to her knees. It was important she got to the men, and quickly. If her senses were correct—had she really heard the heartbeats while locked in the dungeon?—they may be walking into a dragon's lair. How had it broached the narrow tunnels?

Kneeling, both fists pressed to the dirt path and his knees bent, Macarius wheezed. He required time to recuperate. But if he had a measure of fight in him, Rhiana could not deny his usefulness. And the boon of Dragonsbane.

"You can come along," she offered.

"Be that where the village keeps its hoard?" he wondered. "The real hoard? I should have guessed it would be in a location more difficult to reach."

Rhiana stood and offered Macarius a hand up. He did guess at her secrets too easily. "Do you favor me as Odette would like to believe?"

A smile to reveal his white teeth flashed at her. He nodded. That small affirmation should have set Rhiana to a dizzy-headed reel. He fancied her! But she only nodded in return. Remain stoic. No time for silliness.

"Then pledge to me you will speak of nothing you see."

"But—"

Straightening her shoulders, Rhiana drew herself rigidly before the man. Battle posture. If he had thoughts to argue…

"Very well." He drew out his sword. "Will I need this?"

"If there be dragons below the village," Rhiana said as she turned to walk to the cliff edge. "You'll need Dragonsbane, and prayer. *En avant!*"

The tunnel that twisted to the penetralia beneath St. Rénan sloped at a thirty-degree angle toward the city. Not a difficult descent, but an arduous return for the men who hauled leather sacks filled with booty up the slanted run. A decade earlier the plan to dig straight down beneath the village into the heart of the salt caves was over-ruled by Pascal Guiscard. It would weaken the structure of the village, he had argued, and why should it not be a task to mine the riches?

Here within the tunnel, torches were lit. Signal that, indeed, there were men inside. The rush lights provided enough illumination so a man would not stumble on his journey. Carved of limestone, the walls began to lighten and smell of the sea the deeper in they journeyed.

Rhiana was aware Macarius's curiosity led him to scrape at the wall with his sword. "Salt," he whispered.

"We do live by the sea," she warned. "The caves are ahead. Usually three men go inside, with a guard left out by the cart. Vincent may have taken one or two others with him. The fool. We must find them quickly, before the dragon does."

Scanning the ceiling all about him, Macarius asked, "We are beneath the village now?"

"Yes."

"And how do you know there are dragons down here?"

"Dragon. I heard it earlier when I was in the dungeon. One heartbeat, strong, but slow and very close."

"I heard no such thing."

"It is a part of me, the instinct to their kind."

"I have instincts."

"I know that you do, but—" But she would not argue. "I have never sensed them so deep within the caves before. I had not thought these caves would draw them."

"Perhaps they seek the hoard? The gold is their vitae."

"Yes, but…" Rhiana stepped into the vast carved out cave. "The passages from the other caves are too narrow. A single man who arrives at the caves from the north hoard, must eventually squirm like a worm to enter the salt caves, so narrow be the passages. I cannot believe a dragon could get through. It is unthinkable."

"What of a newling?"

"Possible." Of course, she couldn't sense them, for some reason unbeknownst to her. A newling could be circling overhead and Rhiana would not know unless she spied it. And why was that?

"Mayhap a newling has nested here so long, it is now a rampant?" Macarius scratched his head and dismissed that idea with a shrug. "Impossible. But what of the path we have taken? Why would not the beasts enter in this manner?"

"The pyre by the opening is constantly lit. No dragon would find the opening through all the fire and smoke."

"A task to keep it lit?"

"It is a great honor to be chosen to watch the pyre. Six men rotate each year, and following their duty, they may then be elected to the Hoard Council."

Rhiana's feet crunched on the ground that was not solid. Two massive torches were lit, flicking at the air. No sign of the men.

"Mon Dieu." Macarius crunched up alongside her, twisting his head to take it all in.

Great mountains of crystal salt landscaped the vast cavern. 'Twas a delicate color, almost pink, but when piled high and fathomless it glowed a brilliant white. But a dip in the center, a path that led to even more rooms filled with the precious commodity. Water trickled from the underground springs. The ancient drilling machine used to mine deep for the salt sat still, its bamboo pipes fashioned in seesaw fashion the only sign of human intrusion.

"Does St. Rénan mine salt?"

"Not for decades. We've become…" Complacent, rose to mind. "There was once a port right below the entrance where the pyre burns before a rock fall closed it off to ships that sought the valued salt.

"They must have gone farther in." She signaled with a gesture of her fingers Macarius followed. "Keep to the center aisles. If you step into a thick pile, the crystals will take away your balance. We want to be stealthy."

"Yes, fire chaser. But…so much salt! This is far more valuable than a hoard. Why, kings pay a ransom of gold for such. Your city is very rich, indeed!"

"Shh!"

And then she heard a voice that belonged to neither she nor Macarius. It wasn't a statement, but a scream.

CHAPTER TWENTY-EIGHT

Flame filled the second room of salt. As Rhiana entered, her shoulder was brushed by Vincent, who fled like the devil bit at his heels.

"Run!" he yelled.

Another man from the village scampered close on his heels. He shrieked, "Why is it here?" He recognized Rhiana, but did not slow as the flames licked at his heels. "Laurent is dead! You did not kill them all! There are more, and they've penetrated the mines!"

"Macarius!"

"Right here." He joined Rhiana's side but for a moment, then, Dragonsbane at the ready, he dashed into the next room and ducked behind a mountain of the crystal salt.

Taking the opposite direction as Macarius, Rhiana waited until she could place the origin of the flames. Pressing her toes securely into the layer of salt, she scanned the room. The few times she had been down here, there were but the narrow tunnels from room to room and the holes in the upper walls. Small entrance holes, too narrow for a rampant.

Drawing up her crossbow, Rhiana aimed high as she scanned the walls and ceiling. Not a dragon in sight. Could Macarius's guess about the newlings have some measure? Not that one had lived here so long as to become a rampant—that required decades—but it could have been but a small dragon that had chased out the men.

A head popped through the small hole in the upper wall. A violet-scaled rampant. Its neck filled the diameter of the hole; its body could not enter. But that didn't make it any less a danger.

Releasing a bolt, Rhiana quickly reloaded. She was so far off aim, she had not even watched for a hit.

"They cannot get into the mines!" she yelled to Macarius.

"There is another man!" Macarius yelled and stepped out from his shelter.

"Stay back! He is dead!"

But the fool slayer did not listen. He had a death wish, Rhiana knew it. Running rashly toward death and not caring if he got caught up by dragon talon or mermaid seduction.

A smile took Rhiana, quite by surprise. What a fine man, indeed. Fancy him, she did. For he feared nothing, and growled at whatever should growl first at him. A man of her mettle.

If he wanted to play the bait, she could come that.

Following Macarius's dodging path, Rhiana kept one eye to the hole high up in the wall, the rim coated in thick salt deposits. Swinging his sword and boldly declaring a challenge to any beast within range, Macarius's voice echoed in the chamber.

"That's good," Rhiana whispered. She drew aim on the hole, finger soft upon the trigger. "Draw out the beast, and I shall reward you heartily for your bravery, fine knight of the dragons."

Standing in the center of the room and surrounded by mountains of salt, Macarius appeared a small insect one might flick out from the saltcellar. No rampants to be seen.

"I have frightened it off!" He turned a brazen smile to Rhiana.

Never turn your back to danger.

Now. Rhiana released the trigger.

A gust of flame lighted the room. Macarius dodged to avoid the fire, plunging into the crystals.

The dragon cried out. It smacked its head against the inner wall. Direct hit!

Quickly reloading, Rhiana prepared for another attack. There were others close. She could feel them.

The dragon's head fell slack, dangling out from the hole. No room for any others to get through.

She scanned the darkness, knowing the tunnel at ground level led to another salt room and yet another.

Salt crystals tinkled like prized beads Odette kept locked in her cedar chest as Macarius spread his arms across the white mounds upon which he lay. He noticed the rampant's head, dangling lifelessly.

"You've earned your salt, fire chaser," he said.

Propping her crossbow upon her shoulder, Rhiana laughed, loudly, and heartily. And falling to her knees beside Macarius, she splayed out next to him in the mountain of salt.

"*I* am the greatest slayer in all the land," she declared.

"Nay, you are the second greatest."

"First."

"I am too tired to argue, and I think I have ripped open my stitches."

"So I am first by default?"

"Never."

"I beseech you: what is required to best you?"

"Why do you wish to be first, woman?"

"I don't want to, I just—" What *did* she wish for?

A world where dragons did revere human life as she did

dragon life. A simple confidence with her mother. A fine man to ask her hand in marriage.

"We should go in farther," he suggested.

"The tunnels are all similar. All entrances are through small openings either high or ground level. The others have retreated, can you not sense that?"

He closed his eyes, listening. "Yes, you are correct."

"We must figure what to do with that dead dragon up there. We cannot leave it to rot—"

"But it will not rot, my lady. The salt should cure it."

"I had not considered that." Rhiana nodded. "And if we leave it, one hole will be stopped up. But that only proves the caves are expanding. No dragon should have been able to get so far. And what of its sisters? Will they remove the carcass?"

"I expect so, but worry not. They'll not get any farther than this one did. So, tell me where is the hoard?"

"You are guessing, slayer."

"Nothing else would draw the dragons to this room. Certainly not the salt, for it must dry their scales. Tell me true, and I shall keep the secret so tight as the village does."

Oh, this man. How he did dally with her sensibilities. And that constant glimmer of challenge in his eyes...

Rhiana thumbed a gesture toward the far cave opening. "It's back there. You will be able to claim a lifetime's riches from it, surely."

"You think the baron will grant it? I have broken the edict. Mayhap it would be simpler for him to do away with me?"

"Not if I have any say about it."

"My lady, have I told you how much you beguile my heart?"

Feeling a blush stain her cheeks, Rhiana searched the ceiling, for nothing in particular. "No."

"Then I shall speak it once, and once only." Salt crystals tinkled as he turned to stroke the back of his hand under her chin.

"Bewitching, beguiling, and bewildering, this woman of the garnet hair and fiery kiss. She tempts me truly, but puts me to guard. Ah, the lovely lady slayer."

"You speak poetry?"

"It is a wonder what a little fancy will do to a man."

And he kissed her there in the cathedral of salt.

As they topped the cliff, Macarius stretched up a hand to block the setting sun as he looked over the sea. Cooing at a passing crow, Rhiana tossed a smooth stone down from the cliff and waited until she saw the small white splash. The roar of the waves was muted, standing at the edge of the world.

She felt she could stand forever by Macarius's side. No commitments, no promises. Just freedom.

No dragons. For the moment, let the world be freed of the sky creatures, thunderbolts delivering cruel flames to earth.

The memory of Macarius, nodding in answer to her question about favoring her made her smile. And from behind, he embraced her. It felt so right, so natural, as she had seen men embrace women in the village. She did not want to think for fear to curse her luck, but it was impossible not to. This man did favor her.

Remarkable.

"You can be first for this day," he murmured aside her ear.

"It is not important to me. I was merely teasing earlier. You are the greatest."

"Then you are the most beautiful slayer in all the land."

The title, silly as it was, felt good. She had won the man's regard. How? When she was the least feminine and pretty in the village. And oafish! Didn't matter. She wasn't about to lose it.

"If you continue to speak so of me, and to touch me so boldly, you may very well have to speak to my stepfather, as Odette suggested."

"Are you propositioning me, fire chaser?"

"I don't think I know the first thing about propositioning a man."

"Oh, you are tricksy. You know, Rhiana, you've merely to laugh that bold laughter of yours and a man should fall to his knees before you."

"My laugh?" Turning to Macarius tore the smile from her face. Behind him the village was in view. "The devil!"

St. Rénan glowed against the darkening night sky. The city was in flames.

CHAPTER TWENTY-NINE

While they had been beneath the village, half a dozen rampants had attacked, was the report Rhiana pieced together from random cries and shouts as she and Macarius moved through the city.

Dozens of shops burned. Anywhere there was wood the fire took hold. Here and there, a stray lick of fire nibbled at a parked cart or at the corner of a roof. Men stamped out the smaller flames and doused them with water from the well. Women, wide-eyed and frantic, did their best to tend the burned and injured. Children clutched at their dogs and blankets.

Rhiana strode past a little girl, but the sight of her was too much to ignore. Backtracking, she rushed to the child. Her leg bubbled with vicious red burns. So many must have been outside. The dragons had to have swept out of the sky, surprising them all.

Drawing in a breath, she squeezed out a tear from her eyes. If she had but the power to give her resistance to flame to this child, to erase the angry welts! She knelt before her, but was pushed back by the mother, who shook an angry fist at Rhiana. "See what you have done!"

Caught around the waist by Macarius, Rhiana stumbled away from the weeping child and angry mother. "They think I am to blame?"

"No. It is Lord Guiscard who twists their beliefs."

"Mayhap I am to blame. Had I been here to protect them—"

"You cannot be in all places at once! And you certainly could not have slain all the dragons. This was bound to happen."

"My family!"

Tearing from Macarius's grasp, Rhiana raced blindly through the village. Red ember flurried in the sky like an angry snowstorm. Her home yet stood. Blessings! Rushing through the door she sought out Odette, Paul, her mother. There was no one inside.

"No," she cried. "Please let them be safe."

Stumbling out into the ember-stormed night, she looked about. Vision distorted by the flickering embers, she swished a hand through the air to bat away the nuisance. Faces marred with soot and dirt stared at her as people numbly wandered about. Accusations silent but sober glittered in tear-soaked eyes.

Dashing to the armory, Rhiana was relieved to find Paul and Odette inside, shuffling the wounded in and out. "Children first!" Odette ordered a knight who offered a bleeding arm toward her. "Pick up that child and let me take a look at his leg."

Toward the back and near the fire, Lydia handled strips of linen, tearing them into bandages and soaking them in water.

"Rhiana, you are safe!"

She plunged into Paul's arms, the only real father she had ever known. In that moment the image of Ulrich, still in the dungeon flashed in Rhiana's mind. She prayed he had gotten out, and that he had found the companion he had spoken of. Did Lydia know of his return? Oh, but that her family was safe!

"Where have you been?" Paul asked.

"I am come from the salt mines." She exchanged glances with Odette, who knew well why Rhiana had been there. Her sister bowed her head over a seeping wound.

"What were you doing there?"

"There are dragons beneath us, Paul. They attacked the men on a salt run."

"But… Why were they there? There are no scheduled runs. It is idiotic with the dragons nesting."

"I don't know. There were three of them. I could not save Laurent. But while we were occupied—oh! I should have been here."

"You went where you were needed, and now you are here. They attacked as a group. Five, maybe six, I could not get a count. We were not prepared. Lord Guiscard's edict keeps us all afraid and ill prepared to fight them off. You would have perished had you attempted to stop them. I am glad you are alive."

From behind, Rhiana felt a pair of arms embrace her. Odette sniffled and began to cry. "When will it end?"

"I…I don't know."

Torn bandages in hand, Lydia looked across the fire to Rhiana. A nod acknowledged her in ways that words were not required. She was glad Rhiana was safe. She stood and dipped a copper tankard into the clean water supply and offered it to Rhiana.

"I was worried," Lydia said.

Rhiana looked over the rim of the tankard into her mother's soft green eyes. "Thank you." She handed her back the tankard. "I am glad you are safe."

"The dragons?" Odette prompted.

"I had thought the few remaining were concentrated in the north caves, until this morning when I heard something beneath the village. There is one, a dragon."

Rhiana paced to the center of the armory. The doors were open to let in the cacophony from outside. But now the screams had changed from fear and urgent reaction to emergency mode. "Why would they seek the salt mines?"

"The hoard, surely," Paul answered. "Though I thought the tunnels from the north too narrow for anything larger than a small man?"

"Indeed, the one I killed could only get its neck through to the main salt mine. But behind it the body is large. The tunnels must have become larger. Have they dug through?"

Had her visit to the hoard alerted them? Could the attack on Macarius this afternoon, and the resultant injury to the rampant, have brought them to gang? Were the dragons such thinking creatures that they could even form such a notion as to band together and attack the village?

Surely, they must have been out carousing.

Horrible remains they left behind.

Rhiana must not wait another moment. She must…gather men. Weapons and support. The doom must be exterminated. Lord Guiscard's edict, be damned.

Where had gone Macarius? She looked about. The boy Odette had tended wobbled out, a fresh bandage on his calf, with the assistance of his older sister. A few men and women waited tending. Lydia washed the face of a weeping woman. There, by the doorway, the night rained red fire.

The slayer's absence felt like a wide space in her gut, so wide as the open doorway. Something missing. He could do so much at her side, as she could at his side. Together, they could defeat the dragons. She knew it. And, if many more joined to arms to help them.

If only that idiot edict…

"I must speak to Lord Guiscard," she hissed and stomped out from the armory.

Rhiana met Macarius moments later—he was helping the Nose douse the burning pile of faggots near her home. A frill of flame licked along her roof where she'd hung dried herbs.

"I am on to the castle." Rhiana punched a fist into her opposite palm. "Guiscard must see that we need to do something about the dragons. I'll ask for knights to accompany us."

"Luck to you, fire chaser!" Macarius called as he soaked a wool blanket with water, then beat at the flames. "I will help where I am needed!"

Momentarily taken at the sight of a man who held no ties to the village, yet risked his life to help others—

"Madeline!" Rhiana rushed to the young mother's home. Her face was streaked with soot.

"I can't find Amanda!" Frantic, the woman clawed at Rhiana's arms as she sought to comfort her. "Where could she be?"

At that moment, Macarius swept up behind them with a child. "This who you're looking for?"

"Maman!"

"Amanda!"

He deposited the teary-eyed waif into Madeline's arms. "She was just behind the well, crying for her maman."

Macarius glanced to Rhiana. Now was not the best time, but—it was a time.

"Macarius," she said, clasping his hand and then placing her other palm to Amanda's head. "This is Madeline, the village seamstress. And this be Amanda. She is…your sister."

Madeline gasped and clutched Amanda tightly. "You are Amandine's son?"

Stunned, Macarius could but nod.

"Your father has told me about you."

"H-he has?"

"I will leave you two to talk," Rhiana said, and she backed away. They would not have the leisure to share stories right now. But 'twas fine she'd had opportunity to introduce the two.

"Slayer!"

Walking toward the castle, she spun and sighted Christophe de Ver, who wielded a scythe. Sooted and bleeding, he raised his weapon. "I will join you in your fight!"

"I will come for you, Christophe. This night!"

So some would help. Yet, Rhiana felt leery to ask for help. Lives would be lost. Did she want that tragedy to bear?

If she did not bear it then so many more would be lost. It was not for her to question why she had the gift to slay, only she must use it properly.

Lord Guiscard stood upon the castle steps. As Rhiana approached he swept off his ornate cotehardie, trimmed in gold lace, and offered it to a woman, weeping and displaying her burned arms before him. He offered consolation—which startled Rhiana to her very core.

That the man showed empathy when he was the very one who had worked to allow the beasts free rein!

He stood, his back to her, and Rhiana noted the small red circles marking six places from shoulder to shoulder on his flesh. Cupping marks. But these were different, in that, usually when one is cupped a small cut is made in the center to allow the bad humors to escape. There were no cuts.

The baron swept about to face Rhiana. It seemed a lifetime that he held her gaze.

Arms stretching out in helpless surrender, he asked, "What do you want, wench?"

"We need to talk, Guiscard." No thought to bow or soften her anger.

"I shall not bandy words with you. As you can see we are in the midst of a disaster."

"A disaster," she said through clenched teeth, "you could have prevented."

He stiffened.

She should not have spoken such accusing words. As if he alone had the power to control the dragons. He did not. Not even she could claim so much might. And much as he thwarted attempts to annihilate them, the baron could not be blamed for what had occurred here tonight. Shamed at her retort, Rhiana looked away.

"Do you accuse me of this travesty?"

She shook her head. "Forgive me, my lord."

Yes, propriety. *Or you'll never get what you need.*

"I…I just want to take a moment to strategize. If you could grant me a half dozen of your men, or better, a dozen. The dragons have infested the salt mines below the village. We could go to the caves this night and smoke—"

"You wish to add another dozen to the dead list? I will not have it!"

"Then we will all burn!"

The baron drew up regally, yet his eyes lowered upon her with the disdain one reserves for a leper. "You would do well to aid those who are in need of care instead of avoiding responsibility by chasing after beasts you can never control and only make angrier with your attentions. This is your doing!"

With that, he swept past her and bent to inspect another villager's wounds.

Standing beside the woman shivering beneath the ridiculous

comfort of the elaborate cotehardie, Rhiana took his words deeply. Avoiding responsibility? But— She did not— She only ever thought of her family. Well, mayhap…

In truth, she avoided much by chasing dragons. Daily tasks required within the household, the quest to femininity, emotion, her mother.

Her doing? *Mon Dieu.* Was it all for naught, her quest to bring down the dragons? Had her stirring the doom angered the creatures and set them after the village?

How could her good intentions become so twisted?

Clutching the gold coin at her neck, Rhiana lifted her head and closed her eyes. *What have I done? All my life I have rushed toward this moment. Have I plunged over the edge?*

Turning, she looked over the remnants of destruction. Embers glowed over all, raining through the sky in storms of amber mixed with white sooty flakes. The darkening night discreetly disguised the wounded, yet it could not mask their moans and cries.

Lord Guiscard was right. So many were helpless. She must turn from her selfish pursuits.

Rhiana knelt to smooth a hand over the woman's back. "Are you well?"

The woman nodded. Rhiana stepped down beside the baron and knelt over a crying child. She cupped her hand under the child's dirtied jaw, and searched for wounds. Just tears and the stilted huffing breaths of fear.

Rhiana asked Guiscard as they worked alongside one another. "Is Lady Anne safe?"

"Yes, she is inside, being watched." He paused and nodded, approval of her actions. "Remove your bravado, my lady. A tender touch is required this night."

Slipping from the hardened warrior to a different hardened exterior—one that must not flinch in the face of tragedy—Rhiana went from person to person throughout the night.

Most were simply frightened and stunned immobile. She helped them to their home, and if it was on fire, gathered them into a castle keep. Those with injuries she carried, or helped hobble to the armory. Now a dozen volunteers aided Odette, along with the leech and the Nose in tending the wounded.

Exhausted, and fighting the pull of her muscles to simply sit a moment—for to sit, she might nod off—Rhiana swung her arms forward and back to stir her blood as she marched down a pathway pocked with water puddles.

Ahead, a great blaze had attracted many with buckets. The cries of fear pricked at Rhiana's tired senses.

"*Mon Dieu*, the chapel! It is the only wooden structure." Rhiana rushed onward and joined the circle of people congregated outside the chapel doorway. Mary Yvette wailed to the heavens. "What is it? Is someone inside?"

"Her child," a whisper over her shoulder informed. "The flames are too high. We cannot get in to rescue the child!"

Indeed, flames whipped across the doorway where the wooden threshold lay. Wicked fire ate up the doorframe, as if the gates to Hell instead of Heaven. Through the flame Rhiana could see not all inside was afire. The altar was still clear.

Without further thought, she shoved aside a man standing before her and strode across the threshold.

Behind her shouts of terror abruptly ceased as Rhiana, arms held out and fingers spread to trace the lace of flame licking about her hips, entered the chapel.

The heat of the building sweltered. Sweat beads trickled down her face and neck. She scanned about; the north and south walls burned and the east wall had begun. The west, where the altar stood had not taken to flame, but above her, the roof rolled with thick amber fire.

There, a child, choking and sobbing, huddled beneath the cross.

Unfastening the leather straps at her sides, as she ran to the front of the chapel, Rhiana slipped off her scaled armor. She plunged to the floor at the child's side. The girl was about five, she guessed.

As soon as she saw Rhiana, thin arms wrapped about her neck and knees clamped to her waist. *"Maman!"* she wailed, but it ended in choking sobs.

"You will be safe," Rhiana explained, as she tried to pry the frightened clinging thing from her body. "But you must do as I tell you. I have a magic tunic that I'm going to wrap about you. No fire will touch you within this."

Sniffles and soot-streaked tears turned to study the indigo and violet scales. Wide eyes shrieked. The child shook her head and buried it against Rhiana's neck. "'Tis a dragon!"

Overhead, the thick pine beams creaked. A chunk of dried mud that was once part of the ceiling fell. Sparks rained down. Rhiana shooed at a few and clapped a hand over the girl's hair to extinguish a simmering crystal of ember.

"Listen to me! This dragon skin will save you from the fire. Stand back. Let me wrap—" The tiny arms clung like a goat to the teat, but with a firm tug Rhiana pulled her free. Before she could jump to cling again, Rhiana spread the tunic about the child who wrestled against the thing as if it were fire itself. "Trust me," she said. "Please."

Knowing the more time she wasted, the less chance of their survival, Rhiana decided to let the child cling. She managed to pull up the armor over her head. Thin legs were exposed, and wrapped about her waist. That wouldn't do. Tucking up her legs and holding the child as a babe against her chest, all bits were finally sheltered inside the armor.

Fire rained over her head. Rhiana dashed down the aisle toward the door as a beam crashed upon the altar. The cross burst into flame. Screams thudded against her ribs.

Rhiana soared through the flaming doorway and into the pale evening sky, lit by dozens of rampant flames. Opening the armor to reveal the child brought a rush of people upon her. The child claimed by her mother, Rhiana clung to the dragon scales and stumbled back to distance herself from the strange whispers and glorious cries.

CHAPTER THIRTY

Macarius arrived at the chapel to witness the stunning rescue of the child. Rhiana stood upon the chapel steps, flames licking at her ankles and burning up along her mail chausses. Framed by wicked fire, she looked a flame goddess burst from the fires of hell. Gorgeous. Powerful. It hurt his very heart to look upon her, for he could not imagine possessing one so divine.

She could not be aware she stood right in the center of the fire. How could the woman feel no pain from fire? But though it harmed her little, her wool tunic had begun to melt and expose her arms and stomach.

Rushing through the crowd—all stood in awe and could but point and gasp—Macarius lunged and gripped Rhiana's arm. She did not struggle. Exhausted, she merely followed his lead.

Picking up the dragon scale tunic, abandoned at Rhiana's feet after the child's mother had claimed her, he tossed it over a shoulder.

"You expose yourself, fire chaser," he whispered as he drew her close and clasped his arms about her. He meant that she could stand in fire, but also, her tunic sifted into ashy remnants across his leather tunic, revealing bare flesh. "Let's get you safe."

"But I must help?" she murmured, so tired, and little energy in her voice.

"Yes, and you have helped many, and will continue to do so. But first, let's to the armory. We'll get you strapped back into your pretty armor. Can't be saving lives bared to the world."

"Oh." Realizing her exposure, Rhiana's body changed in Macarius's arms. Clasping both hands to the front of her fire-eaten tunic, she slumped, then softened, falling against him. The moment was so remarkable, Macarius could but press his head aside her neck and close his eyes. This woman, seeking strength from him. And suddenly he felt lacking.

Once back at the armory the scaled armor was strapped onto Rhiana's arms and torso and she set out into the night, along-side Macarius.

She did not cease in her efforts, and only when exhaustion closed her eyes did she settle next to a stone wall and indulge a few winks as the sun rose upon the horizon.

Rhiana opened her eyes to a beautiful young woman with long blond braids bracketing her narrow face and beaming brown eyes. Her cheeks were smudged with soot, her hands were dirty, and her simple blue gown soiled. She must have worked through the night. As had so many.

Rhiana eased a finger under her chin. Oh, but her throat ached to breathe. So much smoke she had inhaled last night. Often she had shouted orders and called to claim a rescue. 'Twas as if she had eaten ash by the spoonful.

"Are you well, Rhiana?"

Quirking a brow, Rhiana wondered how this unfamiliar

woman knew her. She did not recognize her as from the village. While seeming young, about her age, she could not place her to a family or even as one of Anne's maids. "Yes, I am well, just fell asleep. I must help."

"Most have been taken to the keep where we've set up a triage. The armory was too small to house them all. The few dead are being buried right now."

"H-how many dead?"

"Three. Two men and a child."

Wincing at that, Rhiana reasoned three was not so much, but at the same time, it was three too many. And a child? *Mon Dieu,* until now, only adults had suffered the dragon's wrath. It was not fair. Children were innocent!

"I should go say prayers for them." She stood. The woman did not move, but remained looking upon her kindly. The chapel, it was a loss, surely. But she wanted to look upon it, to witness. Had she really exposed herself to all by standing before them, surrounded by flame?

She asked, "What is your name? I've not seen you before in St. Rénan."

"Verity d'Ange," she offered. "I've traveled here with Ulrich, your—"

"He is not my father." So, this be his companion? What did the man want from her? To send his mate in his stead?

"I know that Ulrich loves you as if you were his child. He is sad the years were stolen from you and him. He wanted to watch you grow."

"I do not believe his nonsense about stepping into a faery circle."

Verity touched her arm softly. Utter lightness befell, as if a sprinkling of spring rain kissing her soul. "Believe, Rhiana. I know it to be truth. It is in your heart to understand. You have witnessed many marvels with your eyes. Go within. You must open your heart to see beyond the common. I know truths can set a person free."

"Truth has always been mine. It is the falsities of those who would abandon me I must endure." Rhiana gestured toward the chapel. "I should go. There is much left to be done. Have you…found Ulrich? When last I saw, he was in the dungeon."

"Yes, he was released this morning to help where needed. He's around here somewhere. Last I saw, he'd organized a bucket brigade to flood the smaller fires. I am so honored to meet you, Rhiana, and to know that Ulrich's worst fears—that you were dead—are not real."

A startling comment. Rhiana turned from the chapel. "He thought me *dead?*"

"Your mother told him so."

"Lydia told—" When had her mother talked to Ulrich? And to not tell her he was in the village?

"It is a truth for you." Verity bowed and smiled.

Confused at the woman's gentleness and ease, Rhiana walked away, looking back once at the luminescent woman. Kindness radiated from her, and strength marked her invisibly, but Rhiana felt it like heat. She was a fine person. 'Twas good Ulrich had someone like that to love.

But why would Lydia want Ulrich to believe she was dead? She must find her mother. If not to get answers, to at least ensure she was safe.

Striding purposefully up to the chapel, Rhiana was pleased to see it yet stood. Partially. The roof over the altar had caved in, yet the four walls remained. The iron cross at the gable was charred with black soot, but a glint of sunlight caught one section where the ash had not settled. A crowd lingered outside, whispering prayers, lost in a reverent worship.

Macarius, arms crossed, and looking as weary as Rhiana felt, appeared from inside the dilapidated chapel and walked up to her. Soot blackened his face, as it did every face Rhiana looked upon. Tragic masks.

"I've paid my respects," he said. "They say three perished. But so many more were burned. They are being tended in the keep. An assembly has been formed to brew up soothing plasters and stitch up wounds. It is a pity."

Yes, a pity, when she might have been here to do something. Enough self-pity though. She had been where she felt she was needed, and that placement had allowed her to take out one dragon.

Yet, another man had died in the salt mines. *You did not save him.*

Are you stirring up the doom to a murderous rage?

Troubled at the push-pull inside her head, Rhiana turned to focus on Macarius in an attempt to avoid her inner moral dilemma.

"Have you slept?" she wondered.

"As little as you have." He wiped a hand over his face, drawing streaks through the ash. Blinking and stretching his mouth, he yawned. "I saw you curled up by the well and thought to leave you to peace."

"Have you had your wound tended?" He yet wore no shirt, and the bindings about his soot-dusted shoulder and chest were blackened and loose. Dark blood crusted and trickled in a solid line down his arm. "You should let me clean it or it will become infected."

"The bathhouse is overflowing."

"I'll take you to my home. Besides, we need to strategize."

"Indeed, we do."

"Rather," Rhiana said as she walked alongside Macarius. This would be difficult to admit, but it was the right tack to take. "I think the time has come to step back. To leave the beasts to their nest. I think it was us, poking about the lair, that brought the rampants upon the village."

"You can think that all you like, lady slayer, but it is not the truth. Sounds like you've been talking to the baron of this tattered little village."

"Lord Guiscard spent the night tending the wounded. Underneath the lascivious exterior, he is…a good man."

"Rhiana, don't turn on me now."

"I've not turned." *You have to open your heart to see beyond the common.* "I'm looking at the situation in a new light. With…my heart."

Macarius stopped. Fisting the air, he sighed, then said, "You have a purpose, fire chaser. You walk this earth for one reason."

"Why only one? To slay dragons? Why can I not have a greater purpose? Is that all I am to you is a machine who kills?"

"It is what I am."

"And am I like you?"

"You are." He stroked a finger along her jaw. Wiping away soot? "It is like that saying carved into your crossbow. We both know death will be ours—and we do not fear it. Mayhap that is why I favor you, even though you look something dug up from the fire pit."

"I care not if I look a wraith. So many others have real wounds and losses. If only I could take away their pain."

"You can. *We* can, by slaying the remaining dragons."

They arrived at her home. Odette snoozed by the hearth, a tangle of linen strips for bandages spilled from her lap to the stone floor. A heap of wilted henbane, the roots clamping dried dirt lay on the table. The henbane was used as a painkiller; Odette must have literally ripped it from the Nose's gardens, and had intention to brew it up. Rhiana would not disturb her.

The night had been too long, a few minutes sleep was needed if Odette had intention to work through the day.

Lydia must be to the castle. Even through the tragedy, the people must eat. Likely, she would be busy brewing stews and helping the bakers distribute food to those who hadn't the time to eat, for their medical efforts, or had lost their home in the fires.

Checking the water bucket by the hearth, there was about a finger's depth inside, Rhiana gestured Macarius follow her into the kitchen, where she seated him on a low stool with a red fish embroidered onto the silver damask and began to unwrap the filthy bandage.

There was so much soot on his flesh she could not determine if the wound had begun to fester. "You are as black as a Moor," she commented as she drew the wet cloth over his bicep. The soot smeared and sludged up, making many rinses of the cloth necessary.

"Have you seen yourself this day, my lady?"

The thought she was equally as black surprised, and then made her laugh.

"It is good to hear laughter," Macarius offered. "It is a tragedy, yes. But we must not be pushed back in the face of our greatest challenge."

"Why do you care?" she asked. It was something she had begun to wonder about. "I fight for my family. For the lives of those I know and call friend. But you, you've no ties to St. Rénan. Is it still the hoard you seek?"

"A man must have a purpose."

"Indeed." Greed, then, drove Macarius to risk his life. Which made little sense. Even the most idiotic would not allow greed to push them so far. Surely, Macarius had other reasons for wanting to stay and slay the dragons.

"You...spoke with Madeline and Amanda?"

"Very little, but there was not time. My father told her all about me. A sister… It gives me great joy."

"I wish it had been more favorable circumstances, your first meeting."

"We will talk more when the skies are clear."

He traced a hand along her waist as she walked around in front of him and wiped the cloth over his face. The man's touch tempted. Rhiana did not think amorous play should be considered this day, but she did neither move away from him.

"You've the softest eyes," she said. "Barely blue. Distant, almost. But they touch me."

"Like this?" He pressed a palm to her belly, where her tunic had burned to reveal her belly button and lower rib cage and was rimmed with a lace of blackened fibers, and drew it up to below her breasts. He did not touch them, but the anticipation startled her.

"Yes, like that." She swallowed and continued to wash him. Black streams ran down his neck and shoulders and across his bared chest.

"I like touching you, with my eyes and my hands."

"I…favor your touch."

"What if I were to kiss you?" he asked.

"Now?"

"Am I too dirty?"

"No, I am!"

A giggle from the doorway clued them both Odette stood there. Rhiana whipped her head around to spy her fleeing skirts.

"We are being watched."

"Yes, but she is finding laughter this day. Is not our little show warranted, if it gives her such glee?"

"Mayhap, but I shall never live this down. Odette chatters to everyone about everything."

"Well then, we should give her something to really chatter about."

"Oh? Do you want to kiss this blackened, dirty face, dragon slayer?"

"Mayhap."

"So indecisive. I shall decide for you." Rhiana grabbed him by the tunic and kissed him soundly.

She kissed like a man. Or, as a man chose to kiss a woman. Forceful. Taking. Commanding. Her lips burned across his like a safe fire that threatened, but could never harm. Yet, while Macarius thread his hands about her scaled armor and pulled her closer he found himself pushing her away as well.

The scent, pungent and sweet, filled his nostrils and spun a heady wave in his brain. It reminded—

Startled to defense, Macarius shoved Rhiana off from him and unsheathed his sword. Head filled with the scent of dragons and their mating rituals, he thrust out his arm, bringing the tip of his sword blindly to Rhiana's chin.

Eyes wide, and her hands going up by her shoulders to placate, she demanded, "What be wrong with you?"

"I…" The end of Dragonsbane wavered. But his aim was always true, and always drawn to the danger. "There are dragons? I smell them."

Rhiana searched the ceiling, then closed her eyes, sensing. "I do not. Stand back, slayer! You dare to threaten me?"

"You don't smell them?" Racing to the window, Macarius surveyed the sky. Nothing. But he knew the scent. It was unmistakable. Sweet, like sage, and tainted by musk. Tilting a look over his shoulder, he squinted at Rhiana. Had it come from inside this room?

Impossible.

Mayhap?

Sword falling to his side, he slumped against the wall. A startling thought creased his brow. Was it her? Did something about this woman remind him of—the devil take him—dragons? For every time he kissed her—*at the sea.* He always thought to smell dragon scent. "I cannot do this."

Shoving his sword back into the sheath, Macarius rubbed a palm over his head and barged past Rhiana. "Sorry, I feel…angry. It is the dragons. And you. You…confuse me."

"I do not mean to—"

If he remained, he would either kill her or go mad from the mating scent that filled his senses.

Rhiana watched as Macarius raced down the street toward the chapel. Seeking salvation? Going to beg mercy for kissing her? For acting so odd?

She confused him? Well, he very much confused her. What man kissed a woman, then immediately drew his sword upon her?

Diverting her gaze to the heavens, Rhiana sniffed back a tear.

This day the sky, wicked and gray, promised rain. Yes, please bring the rains to snuff out the embers that simmered over all. To wash away the ash and to renew spirits. But to snuff out the pain?

To look away hurt far worse than suffering the cut.

Why had Macarius pulled from their embrace as if she had burned him with the fire within her?

Stripping away her armor and tunic, she stood naked in the room.

Was that it? Could he sense her fire? Bearing the burns of dragon flame, could Macarius sense the pain she could cause him?

Why should she not allow that if she could breathe fire, then

Macarius could sense her danger? *He is a hunter.* Did his predatory instincts single her out as prey?

Touching the scaled armor, she spread her fingers over the glossy scales. Lifting it onto her shoulders, she smoothed it over her bare chest and closed her eyes.

What am I? Do these scales belong to me, are they…part of my very nature?

Looking aside, she saw her blue gown in a lump on the floor where she'd abandoned it hastily yesterday morn. It would not serve to don the impractical garment. Instead, she must dig another tunic out from the rosewood chest and strap on the chausses.

From this moment onward, let no dragon try her mettle.

CHAPTER THIRTY-ONE

"The kitchen garden is a complete loss," Lydia said on a sigh as she entered the second floor of their home. "I was able to rescue but these few items." Lifting her skirts she deposited a few turnips and a head of cabbage onto the cutting board.

Rhiana rushed to catch the cabbage before it rolled onto the floor. Fully armed, she clicked and creaked as she moved.

Soot coated Lydia's skirts and her normally pulled-back auburn hair was scattered about her ash-smudged face. She managed a weak smile.

"I saw you helping last night, daughter. Are you well?"

Rhiana nodded. "As well as one can be after witnessing the disaster. What of you? You should lie down, Mother. You've worked through the night endlessly. Where is Paul?"

"He's busy tending the wounded in the keep. So much was lost."

"But so many lives were spared because of the buildings in stone and slate tile. Sit down, mother. Rest for a while. There's something I want to tell you. Or rather, ask you."

"What is it? I am rather tired. Perhaps a few winks, then I've got to get back to the castle. Lord Guiscard has opened the doors to any and all who require food and shelter. Oh, I shouldn't even be sitting now."

"Mother." Rhiana grabbed her mother's arm, but released it as quickly. Though her mother possessed no flame, to touch her burned that part of Rhiana that craved contact, for it was not a common action. "I saw Ulrich."

Exhaustion fluttered over Lydia's eyes but was replaced with a glossy fear.

"Ulrich," Rhiana said. "I saw him yesterday."

"He is back again?" Lydia's voice literally shrieked.

"Again? What do you mean— Has he been here before, mother? A time you did not tell me about?"

Watery eyes took in the scaled armor with leery discernment. If he had been here…that may be the reason her mother had been acting so oddly of late.

"A fortnight earlier he returned." Lydia pressed her palms to the butcher table. Shaking her head, a few splats of tears landed the bruised cabbage. "I thought I'd sent him away for good when I told him you were dead."

"Dead?" Pressing a palm over her racing heart, Rhiana didn't know what to say. Lydia had told Ulrich she was dead? To punish him for leaving twenty years earlier? How could she be so thoughtless—no; Rhiana knew it must have been a reaction to seeing one long lost. Lydia had mourned for so long, and then to have him suddenly show up…

"He was here," Lydia said, head still bowed over the table. "Two weeks ago. The man simply strode into our home, insisting not a thing had changed since the day he had left twenty years ago. I hadn't intention to tell him so heinous a lie, but…I panicked. He was mad! I chased him away from our home. I did not know what to do."

"Where was I, mother?"

Lydia gestured absently. "Off playing slayer."

The comment cut like no dragon's talon ever could.

"I didn't want him to see you," Lydia continued. "He has no right! Why has he returned? Can I not be rid of that man?"

"What if I had wanted to see him?" Rhiana slammed a fist onto the table, upsetting a turnip to a wobble. "You had no right to send him off."

"He abandoned us, Rhiana."

"Yes, but mayhap he holds answers."

"Answers." Lydia nodded then smirked. "Ulrich knows nothing. Where did you see him? Did he approach you?"

"It was…in the dungeons. Guiscard locked me up for a while yesterday."

"You did not tell me that. Rhiana, are you hurt? What did you—oh, the edict."

"I am fine. I was able to get out… The bars in that dungeon are old and rusted. Just a bit of strength required." And breath of fire. Lydia had no clue her daughter possessed such a talent.

Be it a talent or a bane?

Clutching her forehead in a palm, Lydia sighed. "I thought if I told him you were dead, that would be the last I'd see of him. I have a good life now, Rhiana. And you, do you not admire Paul? And Odette, she loves you."

"As do I. Paul is the only father I have ever known. I do love him. I'm sorry to upset you, mother, I just…. I feel there are yet answers to my life you hold. How to ever get them out from you?"

Lydia straightened, sniffing back tears. "You may be wrong."

"I am not. But I will not press you. Now is not the proper time. For worse dangers threaten the security of St. Rénan. I must see to the slayer. We've plans."

"Plans to chase dragons?"

Rhiana nodded. How could her mother disapprove even as the skies were dark with violence and flame?

"You must be cautious of Guiscard's knights," Lydia said. "They'll be watching for you now."

"And why must I be the pariah when I only wish to help?"

"It is your cross, Rhiana. We all bear a cross. Some are heavier than others."

Before she got close enough to see inside, Rhiana heard the conversation in Paul's shop. Slowing, she paused outside beneath the chain-mail sign that signified out Armory and listened.

Paul talked to a man and a woman. No tension in their tones. She knew those voices. Had they somehow become friends? Paul could not be aware who the man was. As Rhiana had left her home, Lydia had gone back to the castle kitchen.

Was that it? Her mother avoided life by occupying herself with her work. No time for you, Rhiana, I've work to do. *Very similar to how Rhiana faced her deepest troubles.* And if she did not speak to her then she did not have to remember Ulrich or that other man, Rhiana's real father. *Just tell me about him. I must know!* So easy to avoid conversation with a wondering daughter when the bread was to burn or the salted fish needed to be rinsed and repacked.

Just inside the smoky air of the armory stood a portion of her past. Jean Cesar Ulrich Villon III had been in her life but two years. Rhiana could not even recall him. Could anyone envision their life when they were so young? The earliest thing she remembered was tripping over a cuirass on the floor of Paul's shop and splitting open her palm on the sharp, unburnished edge. She had been five then. A faint scar still traced the meat of her palm.

"We should speak to Rhiana," Paul's voice said.

Ulrich agreed. As well, his female companion added, "We will give her all the help she requires. I've not fought dragons before, but I am itching to try."

A willing female? Rhiana liked her already.

Twisting around the corner she entered the coolness of the armory. The wood window canopies were lifted on the south side to allow in grey morning light. Paul winked at Rhiana's entry. He stood at the worktable, half seated, half leaning, his ankles crossed casually. The fires were low; he had little time to attend the usual work.

Upon her entry, Ulrich stepped forward but, with a grimace, took a step back. Rhiana noticed he slipped a hand into the woman's hand. Verity, that was the name she had given. Truth, eh?

"So you've met?" she asked, looking only to Paul.

"I introduced myself," Ulrich answered. "Your father, er...*met* me a few weeks earlier. I was in St. Rénan briefly."

I told him you were dead and chased him away.

"Yes, I just found that out. I'm sorry, my mother should not have chased you away."

"Lydia is confused," Paul interjected. "Don't be too harsh on her, Rhiana. I've spoken to Ulrich. He is a good man. Circumstances changed his life drastically."

"I would never have abandoned you," Ulrich said, stepping forward, but for the hand Verity held and, keeping him from stepping too close.

Rhiana nodded. Faery circles, eh? Well, she did communicate with piskies, so there was the slightest chance...

"We've been trying to come up with a plan," Paul offered as she joined his side.

She didn't know how to feel, what to do. Did one acknowledge their former father? Not really a father, but he had been wed to Lydia. He had cared for her for two years. She wanted to touch him. Somehow. And yet, it was easier to stand near to Paul, close to the safety she had known for years.

Ulrich looked so young. His eyes brilliant and his stance tall and strong. Did she not know better, Rhiana would think him her age, or very close. Where Paul was rugged and sun burnished, Ulrich was frail and elegant, a courtly man. Faery circles? Had he danced so long that he had not aged? Curiosity put the questions to her tongue, but a sheepish discomfort kept her quiet.

"Verity and I offer our sword and staff to the fight. We are yours to command, Rhiana."

Rhiana looked over the elaborately carved staff Verity clasped high near her shoulder. Now she noticed the gown the woman wore was not so much a gown as a long tunic that revealed underneath a man's set of braies. And she was eager to fight dragons? More and more to like about this woman.

"I do not have a count of the remaining dragons. There are six, maybe more. Somehow they have infiltrated the penetralia beneath the village. I don't understand how they can traverse the narrow tunnels, but mayhap they have discovered a larger tunnel. I intend to scout out the salt mines this day."

"I will join you," Ulrich rushed out.

"Alone," Rhiana said sharply. No need to invite the many thousands of questions that strived for answers by spending time alone with the man. Besides— "I've a better chance going it alone. Less for me to worry about."

"You cannot!"

"I can, and I will." She looked to Paul, who nodded approval.

"She knows what she's doing," the armourer offered. "While she's gone the two of you can help me with the trebuchets. There are three or four in storage at the artillery."

"And the pyres along the battlements must be cleaned and

prepared. The fires and smoke distort their senses," Rhiana added in explanation.

"But, Rhiana," Ulrich said. He splayed his hands in query, and then dropped them. "There is much to be said between the two of us."

"It will have to wait," she rushed out. Now was no time for tearful reunions. Not that she would cry. No, she wouldn't. This man did owe her an explanation. But it could wait. And for some reason, by spending too much time with this man, she felt as though she were betraying Lydia.

"Paul, you gather as many men—" she glanced to Verity "—and able females to work the trebuchets. We'll need long spikes to launch at the rampants. And boulders. Big ones that crack dragon skull."

"There are a few already who have volunteered," Paul said. "Cecile and Christophe. The cooper and the falcon master." He scrubbed a hand over his bald head. "Do you think a day attack or night?"

"It could be any time. After last night's disaster I do not believe they'll let up. The rampants are vicious and intent on destroying life."

"Why?" Verity posed. "There must be some reason the rampants are so aggressive toward the village. I know nothing of them, but is it normal they fly in packs and attack like this? And females, all of them."

"No, it's not normal." Rhiana paced the wood floor between the gathering. But that was merely a guess. Amandine had not taught her about the dooms that dragons formed—literally, packs of dragons.

"Usually but one dragon nests for a time in the northern caves. Why they've come as a doom…"

Well, if she were honest with herself, she already knew the

answer. They sought the hoard. The massive treasure that sat beneath the village. To the dragons it signified life.

The village sat right on top of the one place they chose for safety. Could it be the dragons thought to extinguish any chance of interference? It would make sense.

"If you two are going to help," she finally said, "you need to know the truth. We stand upon a massive hoard. For decades St. Rénan has methodically moved the northern hoard to beneath the city, in hopes the dragons would cease to return, for access was once, at least, impossible."

"I know this," Ulrich offered. "But what of the hoard to the north? That has always been the one to attract the dragons. It is far enough off to keep them from the village."

"No longer. The north hoard up by the cliff openings has been depleted. I had not thought they would dig so deep in search of more. Hellfire, I'd not thought they *could* dig. Somehow the creatures must be attracted, can sense it."

"Quite a lot of work to reach the hoard," Verity interjected. "But if it is their vitae…"

"It is."

"Wouldn't it have made sense to leave the hoard alone?" Ulrich asked. "At least, keep the dragons at a distance?"

"They will always kill, and what man wants to always walk with one eye to the sky? It was decided by Pascal Guiscard, before his death, the hoard should be moved. But that was with the thought the dragons would go elsewhere to seek a hoard. Not, below the city."

"And now his son says we must cease to protect ourselves."

"We won't let them destroy our homes," Rhiana said. "I won't."

"Neither will I." Verity stepped up and thrust forward her staff.

In a show of solidarity, Rhiana placed her hand above Verity's on the staff, clasping it firmly.

Ulrich followed, placing his hand below Verity's, and then Paul placed his fist below Ulrich's

"Let's do this!" Rhiana announced.

Plans to venture out to the salt mines were stalled when Rhiana returned briefly to her home. Macarius was there, eating a trencher of stew. He smiled, but did afford little effort to speak, so focused he was on the food. But what startled Rhiana was that Odette tended a man near the door. She had cut his hose all the way up to his knee, revealing a strong thigh.

"Sebastien," Rhiana acknowledged him.

"*Douce et belle,* good morn to you."

At the fire juggler's sweet moniker, Macarius stopped eating. Spoon held before his mouth, he slid his gaze to the doorway.

"I was helping the ferrier move the stones that had fallen from his stable and, well, I guess I'm clumsy with some things."

Macarius chuckled.

Rhiana held back a smile. "But a master with fire. It is fine you've been helping."

"We all have. It is a travesty, the dragons, but what can we do?"

"I've an idea."

"You cannot go after them all yourself, *douce et belle.*"

Macarius stood, loudly shoving back his stool and crossed the room. "*Douce et belle?* So, fire dancer, you like your women soft?"

"Oh yes," Sebastien answered. "And beautiful."

Macarius dropped a hand onto Rhiana's shoulder. "I prefer them strong and unaware of their beauty. And don't fret, this strong, gorgeous woman won't be going it alone. She has me."

A brow above Sebastien's darkened eyes lifted. The two men

took silent measure of each other. And while Odette smothered a grin behind her cupped hands, Rhiana could but stand there, posturing proudly.

CHAPTER THIRTY-TWO

Rhiana rolled over in bed; finding sleep was elusive. She should not sleep, but exhaustion had other designs upon her body. So she focused inward, drawing away from the world and into her belly, where all feminine power reigned.

Heartbeats thumped below her. He was there. A creature, old and wondrous…

Rhiana heard the dragon's ascent over the horizon before she saw it. When the beast rose into view, its massive size blocked the sun, blacking the dragon's silhouette. Wings stretched to span a great distance—far longer than a rampant's span. The scent, so bold, yet steeped to a subtle tang, spoke to her differently. *This one is not the same.* This one she had never before encountered. This is the one Amandine had spoken of.

A maxima.

Each flap of the dragon's wings moved warm summer air across her face. Blinking, she smiled at the sweetness of meadow grass mixing with the new smell. Another sweep of wing was stronger, more forceful. Stumbling off balance, Rhiana caught herself and planted her feet squarely to ground.

Dagger at her side and crossbow lowered and held against her left arm, she thrust back her shoulders, defying the approaching enemy.

I will not falter. She focused her thoughts. *I must not.*

The first paw to touch ground did so in a rumble. The earth beneath Rhiana's feet shook. A skitter of winged mayflies swirled up from the grasses before the dragon and high-tailed it away from danger, the flutter of insects breezing over Rhiana's head.

Fear, she did not feel. Truly.

Anger did not exist.

'Twas reverence that swelled within her, calming her breaths and relaxing her finger on the crossbow trigger. Never before had she witnessed so splendid a beast. It was three times the size of a rampant, and would likely fill the castle keep with outstretched wings.

But for the presence of the dragon, she could not determine the beat of her heart from that of the beast's heart.

Tilting back her head, she followed the maxima's movements.

It perched at the edge of the cliff, wings flapping the air as great ships' sails harnessing the air, yet slowly it drew its wings close to its body to cleave against emerald-scaled torso.

The head, so large as five or six destriers, Rhiana figured, tilted this way and that. A curious entity taking her in.

Did it see her as she saw? As a creature, not the same as it, but as a living, breathing thing that feels pain? Could the dragon smell her? Sense her various moods with a mere sniff of the air? Judge her slightest movement and anticipate whether she would run, draw weapon, or merely faint?

Fainting be for maidens and luna-touched women.

Here, be dragons.

Here, be the testing field for courage.

Rhiana stood proudly before the ancient beast. If there were a manner to communicate with this, the elder of all its kind, she did not know. Yet, Macarius had alluded to it. And Amandine claimed to have spoken to the great maxima he had once encountered and allowed to live.

Was it the same one? Might it converse with her in a language she could comprehend?

A pouf of delicate thistle seedpods spiraled before the beast and swirled about its head, a summer storm, as furious as it was delicate. The dragon pulled up its tail to curl about its forelegs, much like a cat settling to roast in the sun. Rhiana found this movement curious, and for the moment, forgot her smallness as she took further inventory of the beast.

Much as the creature was a murderous, bloodthirsty thing—it had once been a rampant like those that tormented St. Rénan—it wore the guise of beauty. Enchantment, so evident before her. Bold emerald scales decorated the dragon as if a jeweled creation set out upon a hawker's tray to glitter beneath the sun—the bold coloring marked it female, but she sensed otherwise. It sparkled all over with a fine sheen of iridescence. Dragon dust.

It grants immortality.

It be legend, myth, all of it!

And yet, legend suddenly felt very real.

The dragon's maw was studded at each dimple with huge ivory tusks that could rip a man's body open with a mere tilt of its head. Along the upper ridge of its snout and around back toward the eyes grew smaller horns. Deep gold eyes held an arrow-sight on her.

Rhiana let out a forceful gasp, which succeeded in loosening the dam of anxiety welled in her throat.

"Please, I have not come to harm you," she said, though her voice did tremble. No matter, the beast couldn't possibly comprehend. But to speak loosened her apprehensions.

Her voice stirred the maxima. Its head thrust forward, bringing them face-to-face—woman to dragon. The massive crocodile skull was frilled about with dags of sharp scale and horn. Like the spikes set about St. Rénan's battlements, the head was armored for protection. The climb to the kill spot would be perilous. Yet, there it was, the kill spot, touched by Him, and cursed for winning flame from hell.

But Rhiana had difficulty placing hell's grace to this maxima. Not of hell, but merely cursed to suffer for its ancestor's mistake.

A gold eyeball, as large as a cooper's barrel, fixed itself to Rhiana. The pupil slashed a black line through the center, from top to bottom. A blink of the soft leatherlike lid purled a viscous clear substance down the dragon's scaled jaw. The drops that splat upon the ground hissed then dissipated to red smoke.

"Please…" she whispered now, not sure for what she wanted to plead.

For life? Unthinkable. For her family's sake she would sacrifice. But would her death keep the dragons from further tormenting the village? Mayhap, for she had been the one—oh, but Macarius would surely rally to bring them to a wicked frenzy. She did not sense an anger scent. The beast was not prepared to kill. Not yet.

How to communicate? To show it she meant it no harm— so long as it would promise the same.

The dragon moved quickly. Rearing onto its hind legs, it drew its head up high until it leveled the treetops. It spread its jaws wide—

Rhiana opened her mouth, but she shut it abruptly. She knew what would follow. And she did not fear.

A filigree of amber flame licked through the air. One moment it formed a wisp of steam at the corners of the dragon's fang-lined jaw, the next, it shaped into a rippling cacophony of heat and fire that encompassed Rhiana's body.

The force of contact pushed her from her feet to land the slimy blades of grass melting into the earth. She could feel the heat. It was smothering, yet intoxicatingly dreamy as it wavered images of the world before her. Emerald waves of leaves dripped overhead. Distorted crystal sky. A frenzied blotch of scale and fang and fire.

She could not breathe. Her lungs expanded, then sealed up. Her chest felt bloated, stopped up. Would this be the killing flame? There was so much of it, everywhere, surrounding, invading…

A moment of clear vision ascertained the flames had ceased.

But the dragon drew in another breath.

Another blast of flame. She thrust her hand out, a feeble blockade against the inevitable. But she did not feel the pain of fire sizzling at flesh. She did not hear the sound of her screams. Did not feel the ache of flesh melting upon her very bones. She did not black out and chase her soul up beyond the reach of earthly evils.

She did not burn.

Once again the dragon reared back—yet, this time, it did not release another blast of flame from its velvet black nostrils.

She did not burn.

Rhiana winced. *Of course I did not burn.* Odd to be thinking such, when there was so much else—she was still alive.

Triumph bubbling over, she fisted the air and shouted defiantly. "Can you come that, dragon?"

It merely looked at her.

The beast's fiery kiss had scorched the clearing to smoking blackness. Multitude of simmering smoke-pots tendriled up hazy smoke curls surrounding her. A barren wasteland to be renewed with the spring.

Rhiana flicked ash from her hand and her feet. Her tunic had melted away from her flesh, leaving her naked beneath the scaled armor. But completely unharmed.

She is not the one. Not...her.

"Who said that?" Rhiana called. She spun and scanned the area. Now was no time to be concerned for her revealing attire. Not when a spy lurked somewhere close. "Show yourself!"

Rhiana twisted her head up to look into the tired gold orbs of the beast. Well, indeed, they did appear tired. Smoke hissed from its nostrils. It inclined its massive skull forward, stretching the distance of the clearing, right up to where she had fallen and now sat in a circle of ash and melted grass.

I spoke to you, mortal. Heat puffed from the beast's nostrils. Sage, sweet and heady, misted over the foulness of burnt grass and meadowsweet.

"Y-you? I have gone daft. That is the way of it. The flames have burned my brain to a crisp."

Silence!

Rhiana flinched at the command, then glanced from side to side. Did the mad direct themselves to silence, then? So she was to become like Anne, tormented by things unseen?

Dragon sired, came the resolute voice. *Not my mate.*

Flicking its tail about to encircle its forelegs, the dragon settled to a sitting pose.

Mon Dieu, but it was the maxima that had spoken.

So this was it? The communication between dragons and mortals Macarius had spoken about. Blessed mother, if she did not hear it, Rhiana would not believe it. But she had heard the voice. And...could she believe it?

She dropped the crossbow, unaware of its weight leaving her hand. The dagger she yet clasped tightly. Ready. Not so foolish as to abandon all safety.

"I am Rhiana Tassot of the village St. Rénan. Can you speak to me?"

Dragon slayer.

The beast did not mince words. Rhiana bowed her head and then went forward onto one knee, pointing her dagger tip into the ground as a knight who would kneel before his lord to pledge fealty. Genuflecting to the inverted cross of hell.

No, not of hell. But whence did it come? Was it a beast of Enchantment?

Do you deny you are a slayer?

"Your kind destroy my people," she stately plainly. "I protect my own."

Why do you not now rush me with your meager blade?

"Because it *is* so meager against one so old and revered. More so, I wish you no harm, great one."

Even should I flame your entire village?

"That has been left to your minions. The female rampants destroy without regard."

The dragon stirred, sifting a huff of warm breath through its nostrils. Sage enveloped Rhiana, briefly making her woozy. She put out her arm to balance; her blade slashed the air.

The village sits upon my hoard.

"Your—" Caution, Rhiana. Though she was impervious to flame, her frail bones served little resilience against one fierce snap from the dragon's jaws. "I will not slay another dragon if there is a way to keep them away from my village."

The young ones cannot be controlled. Your violence toward them only stirs them to frenzy.

"Equally met with a frenzy to survive, to protect one's own," she countered. "If they cannot be controlled, they must leave."

You ask very much.

"In return, you may have the hoard. Great riches to provide you with the life-giving vitae you require." She hadn't the authority to grant such a prize, but it seemed the thing to say.

A hoard so large cannot be moved.

"Keep the females away, and you've it all to yourself."

A female in estrus cannot be kept back. Besides, I lie in wait of the most deserving. I must continue my legacy.

So they had come to mate. The maxima's scent attracted the female rampants, though they could not reach it. Not yet.

"You are very wise, old one. Help me to understand, to forge a bond between the dragons and the mortals."

The maxima made a dismissive noise that seemed to sound only in Rhiana's head. Not impressed by her offer.

"I will slay you if I must," she warned. A foolish statement. One snap of the dragon's jaws and she would cease to exist.

Bold female mortal. You slay your own kind?

"I've never taken the life of a human being."

You are but half mortal. Know you not your origins?

"I…" Half mortal? That was certainly an odd statement. She was completely and entirely—

On the other hand…

She did breathe fire.

The other half was what?

Rhiana stepped backward. *You are but half mortal.* The magnitude of that statement—why, to even fit the notion into her brain…

"You speak to trick me!"

Discover your truths, dragon sired. Return to me when you are ready to accept your fate.

With that, the beast rose onto its back legs. Shadows swept over Rhiana in a sudden chill. She grasped at the ground for the crossbow, but could not force her legs to bend to retrieve it. Wings swept fiercely, moving hot air over her body and this time successfully knocking her from her kneeling stance. She landed the grass, arms splaying and body stretching out. The great beast took to air and fly before the sun.

"Dragon sired," she whispered. And then all the years of not knowing coalesced into one real truth.

Still asleep, Rhiana murmured out loud, "Yes."

"So, you had a dream?"

"A dream. A vision. Some such," Rhiana said to Macarius as they took the road past the armory where they'd met. "It felt real. Like I had left my body and had actually stood in the meadow. I could smell the maxima."

"And it spoke to you."

"Yes!"

"Tell me what went on between the two of you?" Macarius asked carefully.

Rhiana walked swiftly toward the castle. The kitchen was resting before preparations for supper began. There was but one person who held the answers the dragon had beseeched her to seek. Lydia.

"What did it say to you?"

"The maxima has no control over the rampants."

"Hmm…according to your dream."

"I know it to be truth! He was quite forthcoming."

"He?"

Rhiana stopped. Hands to hips, she exhaled. "Yes, though it was boldly colored. He spoke to me in a male voice."

"With…with his mouth?" Macarius tapped his lips. "What did it sound like?"

"He spoke in my head. It did not move its mouth."

"That sounds incredible."

"After all you have witnessed since coming to St. Rénan, *now* you don't believe me?"

Quick to placate, Macarius shook his head, agreeing even

while his crossed arms and smug grimace proved he yet doubted. "I believe everything, lady slayer. Even be it a mere dream. You tell it to me, I will believe it. Nothing is remarkable anymore and everything is incredible. I have never before seen a person stand in the billowing flames of dragon fire and survive. When you walked out of the chapel with the child shielded by your armor… And the flames, they touched you, but 'twas almost as it they leaped away in your presence. For one moment, the opening to the chapel was engulfed in flame and mixed with your hair and… Even your hair, it is all fine! Not a single scar!"

"I am sorry."

"For what?"

She shrugged. "You are scarred."

"I am not immortal."

"*I* am not immortal." She swung a look up toward the south tower hugging the castle. Guiscard's solar; his apothecary spent much time there. Doing what? The baron appeared healthy. "But I think Lord Guiscard might be trying to touch it."

And the way to immortality? Keep a dragon beneath your feet, perched upon a hoard, to constantly manufacture the precious dragon dust needed for extended life. Did the baron know about the maxima? Did he suspect it nested below St. Rénan? If he had been sending a man to retrieve dragon dust surely he would have the entire system of caves mapped out and monitored. Mayhap that is what Vincent and his cohorts had been to yesterday. She did know he was jockeying for a position in the garrison. And where to keep a map but in a…library?

The last time she'd seen the baron he had been helping the wounded—why, he'd even offered his own clothing. And what she had seen on his bare back—

"That's it!" Rhiana broke into a run. Macarius kept her pace. "The cupping marks."

"Explain, fire chaser."

"It gives perfect reason Guiscard would wish to keep the dragons alive. Why did I not think of this sooner!" She sped ahead, leaving Macarius calling behind her.

CHAPTER THIRTY-THREE

Rhiana entered the keep. It had been transformed from an eating hall, where the villagers made merry and danced and sang and lived, to a triage for the wounded, and a hideout for the fearful.

"It is the slayer!" a boy cried as Rhiana strode past a clutch of small children playing stones under the watchful eye of a parent. "Why did you make them come after us?"

"She is the one who walks in fire," another child warbled. "Devil!"

Not about to admonish a child, and wincing at their biting diatribe, she held her head high, yet quickened her footsteps away from the innocent accusations and slipped into the hallway that led to the baron's solar. None of the adults had chastised their children. Because they believed the same?

"What have I done?"

Destroyed the innocence of a child? Made herself a devil in their eyes. She had been out of sorts after rescuing the child from the chapel. Bless Macarius for drawing her away from their horrified stares.

Crossing herself, Rhiana looked to the heavens. "If it is so wrong, you will stop me. I trust you. You must trust me."

Pray, the villagers could find a morsel of trust beyond the false betrayal they held against her.

Before stepping too close to the open solar door, Rhiana heard Guiscard instruct his priest to make haste. "She is out of holy water."

"I just blessed fresh stock yesterday," the priest argued.

"Damn the house, man, she needs more!"

"It is not midnight."

"Don't argue with me, priest. Get more!"

The priest exited in a flurry of brown wool robes. Rhiana swung into the doorway, opened her mouth to speak to the baron, and received a slammed door. She heard him bar it on the inside.

"Be gone, wench! I am in a fine temper."

Beating the door once, Rhiana decided to grant him the moment. There was another room she wanted to check out while in the castle. Turning, she walked right into a solid male chest.

"Macarius," she hissed lowly. "You are following me?"

"I had thought the invitation implied. Were you to speak to the baron?"

"He is in a temper."

"Shall I speak to him for you? Yes, let me by—"

"Not right now." She felt him flinch. She'd denied him the man's call to chivalry in the face of a scorned female. "There is something else I want to do. Come along." She skirted him and started down the long hallway that paralleled the keep on the second floor. Arrow-slit windows, looking over an inner courtyard cast long, pointed patches of white sunlight on the floor. A robin perched in one window chirped gaily as they passed. "Up ahead. The library."

"Ah, but of course, perfect time to settle down with a hefty volume—when dragons are upon us."

"Be quiet," she chastened in a loud whisper. "There could be guards."

"*Sneaking* into the library?" He joined her side, hooking an arm in hers, and whispered, "Could prove most adventurous. What are you looking for?"

"Hold your tongue until we're inside." Rhiana stopped at a turn in the hallway and peered about the corner. The door to the library stood right outside Anne's bedchamber. She also had a connecting inner door to the small room of books, but rarely used it, for her disinterest in any activity that required one to focus for so long. And such a singular task!

"Can you move without creating a great commotion?" she asked Macarius, with a glance down his coat of plates and sword, which *chinked* at his hip with each step.

"I can. Lead on."

Together, the two tiptoed down the narrow hall, hands to their weapons. Rhiana moved inch by inch, for her scaled armor did clink overmuch. Passing Anne's door—the lady of the castle surely slept within—she inhaled and did not exhale until she reached the fancy carved door to the library. 'Twas fashioned after a rood screen, Anne had once explained to Rhiana. All the grand cathedrals have them.

Pressing a hand to the wood carvings, she slowly blew out breath and turned to Macarius. He gave her a lifted brow, encouraging to open the door. She tried the pull. It did not open outward. The keyhole glared like a one eyed serpent, taunting her lack of key.

"Your dagger," Macarius whispered.

"What about it?"

"Hand it over."

While she did so, Rhiana decided if he were going to use it

to pick the lock— "You cannot." She gripped his wrist, stopping him before the tip of the blade touched the iron keyhole. "You will damage it!"

"Is what you seek behind these doors of great importance?"

Caught in his endless dreamy eyes, Rhiana could but nod. She understood what he was asking. Was not a mere weapon worth sacrificing for knowledge?

"Yes, there may be answers that will help us defeat the rampants. Go on," she said.

Within a few heartbeats, Macarius had mastered the lock. The pull clicked and the door breathed inward. He held her dagger before him to display the undamaged blade. "A fine weapon. I shall have to convince your stepfather to fashion one for me before I leave."

He had plans to leave?

As Macarius entered the cool darkness of the small round room, Rhiana lingered, her fingers brushing the iron door pull and her toe jutting through the entrance. The man would soon leave St. Rénan. And her.

Well, of course he would. He did claim no village, city, or land his own. The man roamed freely, seeking adventure in the kill. He may never be content to remain in one place, with one woman…

"Fire chaser?"

"Yes," Rhiana breathed. She winced at the shudder of her heartbeats. "Never content. Hmm? Oh. Yes, I'm coming." She closed the door behind her, and rubbed her palms across her thighs, burnishing heat to her chilled fingers. And redirecting her straying thoughts. "Pull back the screen from the window and let in some light."

Sunlight beamed through the arrow-slit window to softly illuminate the circular room. But a single high desk that would hold a wide book and a pair of elbows centered the room. A person must stand to read upon the desk, so obviously the room had never been meant for leisurely study. The walls stretched an arms reach higher than Rhiana's head, and volumes stocked the shelves in a circle from one side of the door to the other. All were dusty and thick. Gilded titles attempted to gleam but the dust was too thick.

After much perusal, there, on a bottom shelf, did Rhiana spy what she suspected would interest her. She knelt and carefully drew out the heavy marble scrolls.

"What is it?" Macarius looked over her shoulder as she laid the scrolls on the desk and decided to unroll the thinnest rolled side first.

"Pascal Guiscard, the baron's father who passed away about five years ago, was rumored to have quite a large collection of books on dragon lore. He traveled far and wide for volumes, and had special couriers he'd send out on hunts for books and scrolls. He paid insurmountable sums for some of these. See here, this marble scroll? And the gorgeous artwork," she said as she unrolled the parchment to view the text. The borders were painted in azure and red and gold. "I think this is gild, yes?"

"Mayhap." Macarius leaned in and placed a finger upon the text. "Latin. Can you read it?"

Rhiana shook her head. But for the dragons dancing along the borders, and spewing fire at small fleeing figures of men, she determined this scroll would hold the answers. "I can write my letters well enough, but only French. Can you read Latin?"

"A bit." He perused the text, drawing his forefinger along it slowly. His lips moved, which made Rhiana grin. "I guess this is the legend of the Fallen angels mating with the dragons and gifting them hellfire. Let's unroll it farther."

The desk was too small, and so, at Macarius's suggestion, they laid it on the floor. The sunlight did not beam directly onto the tiled marble floor, but they could yet make out the text so long as neither leaned directly over the parchment or blocked the single source of light.

"Is there anything about dragons speaking to mortals?" she wondered. It had been but a dream, but if Amandine had also mentioned it… "What is that?"

Rhiana tapped a finger on a diagram that showed a priest anointing a man with holy water, just as she did every time she entered the chapel, just as Macarius had drawn the cross with blood on his forehead. There was one grievous difference. The man in the drawing had a tail.

"I don't understand," she said. "What does the text read?"

"There is no accompanying text," Macarius said. He unrolled the parchment to the end of the scroll, where a gorgeous ebony-scaled dragon was revealed, its tail erect and a human body dangling from its ivory maws. "It appears the man is receiving a blessing. But, why the tail?"

Tilting a curious look upon the man with the tail, Rhiana wondered why the image troubled her so.

"There is nothing about a dragon changing to a man?" she asked absently.

"There may be…" Macarius moved on his knees to study the length of the scroll. "I can't see the tiny script so well in this light, and my Latin is rudimentary, at best."

A rattle from the outer hallway alerted them both. Quickly working, one at either end of the scroll, they rolled it back up. Macarius wrapped an arm around Rhiana's waist and pulled her to him, behind the door. They both listened. Tiny clinks sounded from the hallway.

"Anne's chain," Rhiana whispered. She closed her eyes and focused. Did the sound move closer, or farther away? And could her heartbeat not pound so loudly? And why, oh why, did Macarius hold her so?

A warm breeze tickled her cheek. The day was sunny and—Rhiana realized the breeze was actually Macarius's breath. Eyes closed, and head bowed, he must be concentrating on the action outside. He clutched the scroll tightly near her waist. His thumb pointed into the space where her armor was joined by the wire-reinforced leather ties.

Touched again, inadvertently. She tilted her hip, moving closer. Macarius opened his eyes, fixing his urgent gaze upon her.

The sound had ceased. Anne had either exited her chamber, or had gone inside. Though, they had yet to hear a door close.

Drowning in the depths of sky blue focused on her, Rhiana felt her jaw slacken. 'Twas as if his look intoxicated. So many goblets of rose-hip wine she must consume to feel the same warm, wondrous ease. Her breaths panted and a woozy wonder softened her brain.

Without thinking, Rhiana tilted her head to kiss Macarius.

She felt the scroll fall and grabbed for it, just as Macarius lifted both hands and cupped her head. He did not break the kiss, but instead deepened it. Scroll clutched to her belly, Rhiana followed the woozy wonder to a delicious reality.

"Fire chaser, you confuse me," he whispered against her mouth. "Do you not realize you are as a dragon when I kiss you? I can smell it, your mating scent."

"What?"

A hard kiss stopped her from protest. Immediately he pulled away and shook his head, but then again kissed her. Battling the urge to kiss her?

"What is it?" he murmured. "You smell—" he closed his eyes and inhaled of her so deeply Rhiana felt sure she would melt and permeate his very flesh "—wanting. What do you want from me, Rhiana?"

"This is what I want," she gasped. His palms pressed her shoulders to the shelf of books behind her. "Your kisses. Your regard. You…"

"I am torn between wanting to kiss you and—" he pushed himself away from her and unsheathed his sword, turning to stab the ceiling high above the arrow window "—and wanting to slay you!"

The scroll slipped, and Rhiana hastily bent to clutch it upon her knees. She did not want to damage the valuable item. But as she bent there, looking up into the strange gaze of the dragon slayer, she briefly wondered would he really do it. Slay her?

He thought to notice a mating scent on her? Did she put out a scent when impassioned and enthralled in his kiss?

Still he held Dragonsbane at the ready.

Rhiana slowly slid upright. She held the scroll as if a staff, ready to deflect a blow. "I am not a dragon, Macarius. S-stand down."

"I cannot!" He clenched his jaw fiercely.

"Slayer!"

"No!" Slashing the sword through the air, the tip swayed very close to Rhiana's scaled armor. She felt the air of the sword move across her hand. "I must be away from you. Forgive me."

He took his escape, leaving the door wide-open behind him, but taking no concern for the noise his exit made.

Clutching the scroll to her chest, Rhiana exhaled. That was close. She swept out her tongue, tasting the remnants of his kiss. So sweet.

Why did their intimate contact always end in the slayer wishing to kill her?

CHAPTER THIRTY-FOUR

He would not have harmed her. He could not fathom harming her. But, he had slashed his sword in that small room, knowing there had been ample room, and yet, he'd had to hold himself from leaning in to stretch his reach.

A woman who breathes fire had captured his fancy. How? His father had not told him of the slayer. It had been a lie to insinuate himself into Rhiana's trust. He'd heard Amandine mutter about her in his sleep. That Amandine had not let him into his private life was a cross Macarius must bear.

He knew this cavalcade of dragons would rouse his father if he were still alive. It hurt to recall that evening when the sun had glinted on the horizon, momentarily blinding Amandine from the approaching danger. They, neither of them, had sensed a dragon near. It had appeared over a cliff ledge as if the devil rising from hell. Macarius had slain the dragon, but not in time to prevent the beast from whipping Amandine's helpless body about in the air and breaking his neck. His father had whispered a few dying words: "I love you, my son. Go to St. Rénan. There, you will find a woman…"

I love you, my son. Words Macarius would always cherish. But, that in his dying breaths Amandine had thought to send Macarius looking for Rhiana stunned. For what reason? Had his father known she would need help to battle the doom? Or was a more personal reason, that of perhaps introducing his only son to a woman Amandine must have deemed most worthy.

A few words his father had once said returned to him now… *Find a woman who knows you better than you do, and you will already love her.*

Indeed?

But what if that woman made him want to kill her every time he kissed her?

Rhiana, she must be…half dragon. How was that possible? That he even considered it did not startle him so much as he felt it should. But to achieve a result like that—a female human had to mate with a male dragon. Impossible. Although…if the dragon had transformed—which Macarius still did not believe.

Macarius had seen Rhiana breathe flame. She walked through flame like the devil himself. But the woman was no demon, far from it.

Douce et belle? That damned juggler, who did he think he was, naming her so intimately?

And why hadn't *he* come up with a pretty little name for the pretty little slayer?

Because, Macarius knew, while she may be pretty, she was nothing so little. Rhiana, the fire chaser, was bold, valorous and brave. And he would do to learn from her ways. But would he ever be able to kiss her without wanting to kill her?

"Easy," Verity directed Paul as he pushed against the left rear wheel of the massive trebuchet. Three other men flanked the

armourer, and Verity had lassoed a rope about the front wheel
to steer. "To the left!"

All men groaned and dug their toes into the ground as they
shoved. The old battle machine creaked and did as much
groaning. It had sat in storage with two others of its like for
decades. Paul could not even recall a time when St. Rénan had
been to siege and had to utilize the machines, and he had lived
here all forty-one years of his life.

Nor could he recall being surrounded by so many powerful, strong women. Impressive. It gave him an impish feeling
of joy to work alongside women. Put a spark right there in his
belly. They were not the lesser breed, but equals. Which is why
he admired Lydia and her daughters so much.

Even Odette had rallied, digging out a pair of Rhiana's braies
and walking around issuing commands and orders as if a field
chief. And the surprising thing? The knights listened to her. Of
course, Paul had noticed more than a few of the knights swoon-
ing. His daughters were beautiful, he would not deny that.

But no man would ever be their match.

Lydia was in the kitchen, poking at the smoldering embers
in the hearth. Mid-day offered a respite. Those who worked in
the kitchen had either gone home to tend their families or rest.
Though, some jobs were never finished. A husk of hares huddled in a wicker cage waiting slaughter. Surprising, for the
smaller animals had been scarce of late. One guess where they
had gone to.

The apprentice baker sat snuggled in the corner, snoring;
she stacked the fresh breads in the pantry and swept the floors.
Lydia had begun to show her how to mix pastry. She did not
stir as Rhiana passed her.

"You look hungry," Lydia noted as Rhiana stepped across the
swept stone floor and stopped before the low hearth fire. A

square chunk of ember had spilled from the fire and onto the stones a good stride from the hearth. "There's almond-milk pudding and bread. I'll get you some."

"No, Mother, we need to talk."

Yes, she was doing this, and she would not back down.

"Oh?" Lydia twisted her fingers into her flour-dusted apron, avoiding Rhiana's eyes. "Daughter, please, I heard the accusations in the keep as you passed through earlier. You should not take the words of a child to heart. You are not of the devil."

"Then what am I?" Rhiana toed the ember, and with a gentle kick, delivered it to the fire with a smack of sparks against the inner hearth wall. "I need to know about my father."

Lydia met Rhiana's eyes with abrupt aim. She could not recall when her mother had looked so directly at her. It felt as though she reached out and touched her. For the first time.

"I have explained…"

"Yes, that neither Paul nor Ulrich are my father."

"You name that bastard so easily?"

"Have you spoken to him this day?"

"I will not. I pray he does not seek me out." Lydia sat upon the smooth beechwood-stump stool before the fire. Fire reflected in her pale green eyes. "Am I not allowed freedom from the past? Ever?"

"I am sure he won't approach you. He's…his own life now." Certainly she would not tell Lydia that Paul had befriended Ulrich. The man walked a fine edge by remaining in St. Rénan. "There was a good reason for his absence."

"Absence? Rhiana, twenty years is a lifetime. Absence is two days, three or four at the most!"

"It was not his fault."

"Have you spoken to him?"

"Briefly. When I was in the dungeon."

"You speak so casually of one who abandoned you. Us, he abandoned us, Rhiana!"

So the hurt ran deep. Perhaps far deeper than the hurt Rhiana felt at her mother's indifference to her. Had she ever put herself in Lydia's place? To have a man who claimed love for you, and then to lose him? She had not, for the experience seemed alien to Rhiana. When had she known a man's intimate love?

Well, very recently. But must it always be served with a terrifying ending? *Macarius will not harm you.* She did believe it, if only *he* did.

As a child, the sudden loss of Ulrich had been merely as if a friend had not come to visit. Though, she would never forget her mother's tears. Long days of tears, following Ulrich's disappearance, which had seemed to go on for eternity.

"I cannot explain it all now. But Ulrich and his companion have returned to St—"

"His companion? Oh, Rhiana, dear child, do not tell me these things if you wish your mother to remain whole and well. I had put the man from my mind!"

"He would have never left had he not been forced. Well, in a manner." Rhiana still wasn't sure if she believed his tale herself. A faery circle? It was ridiculous. But there was something about Verity, her presence, that made Rhiana believe in other worlds. "He is miserable over his absence."

"I care not to hear another word about that man. I have a husband now. Paul is a fine man. That is why it troubles me you wish to speak of the other when we've gone beyond that."

"Can one go beyond something they've never really known?" Rhiana paced the vast kitchen to stand before the hearth. The flames bewitched and beckoned.

"Sorry, Mother. You're right. This matters little now especially with what torments our lives—all of us—right now. But that is the reason I must have answers. I…have discovered a strange truth."

"Really. I feel I may regret asking but, why so strange?"

"It is the reason Lord Guiscard wishes the dragons be kept alive. At the very least, one of them. A maxima nests close by, I believe in the hoard beneath the village."

"What?"

"Right below our very feet." She would not reveal her suspicions were founded by a dream.

"Is a maxima a dragon?" Lydia wondered.

"Yes, it is a large one, the elder of their breed."

"It must be very large."

"Very."

"How can it get in? The salt mines are difficult to traverse, very narrow. Rhiana, it troubles me that you gallivant about in those caves. They are dangerous."

Rhiana smirked. "No more dangerous than dragons, Mother."

"Oh, when did I fail you, dear child? Mayhap if I had not allowed you to go with Paul to the armory, and instead kept you close in the kitchens. And Odette! She strolled in this morning wearing men's braies. She follows every step you make, Rhiana. Do you not see how she looks up to you?"

"I had not realized until today." The sight of Odette proudly walking about in braies and tunic had caught the eye of many a knight. "But I get off course. I should not think to ask you this, but I need to know. Mayhap you need to speak it. To purge the past from your mind, so you can be free."

"I don't understand. I thought I had—"

"Tell me about the man who is my real father. Was it a man from the village?"

"Rhiana, this is of no import."

"He is my father!"

Lydia shrugged her hands up her arms, looking cold and so

small. She searched the vast polished marble counter, where she made all her creations.

"You've always told me Ulrich was not my real father. That there was another."

Finally, in the smallest voice, she said, "Though Ulrich and I were soon to be wed, we were not having relations when you were conceived. And you will kill me if you make me speak of it now."

"Mother!"

Lydia actually cringed. She did not want her to feel horrible. Or to make her mother angry, but she was so close to learning all that she felt belonged to her.

"Very well." Deciding there was but one way to dredge the truth from her mother's tight lips, Rhiana turned to the hearth. The sizzling embers hissed and snapped warnings that she would not heed. It was time she took mastery over her life. And the only way to do that was to know exactly who she was.

Drawing up a breath, Rhiana spat flame at the embers.

Lydia shuffled against the wall where a soot-dusted tapestry hung, recoiling from Rhiana's wobbling approach.

The breath of fire had been small, but yet Rhiana bent in pain and clutched at her gut. "Yes, I breathe fire," she said through clenched teeth.

"You are in pain!"

"Momentarily." She shrugged a hand through her hair, tugging at the strands to redirect the pain.

"You—you." Lydia swallowed. "You?"

"Breathe fire. I have since I've gotten my monthly courses."

"No! Do not speak of it!" Lydia pressed out her palm, a field of protection that could only appease her haunted memories. "It is a trick. Magic such as Ulrich once performed."

"I have no magic, Mother. I have only this." Rhiana leaned back, tilting her head, and breathed fire high up into the rafters. The violet-edged flames danced liquidly over the oiled beams, but did not alight on the wood. It was a silly display, but warranted.

This time the force of such a display felled her to her knees. Rhiana landed the stone floor with her palms. Her gorge rose. The acrid taste of fire lingered on her tongue.

When she again looked to Lydia, tears streamed from her mother's eyes, drawing creases in the fine dusting of flour that smudged one cheek.

"What am I, Mother? Only you can tell me. Am I...half dragon?"

"Oh, *mon Dieu*." Lydia slid down the wall, her knees bending until she landed in a squat. She wrapped her arms around her calves.

Rhiana felt a moment of regret—stop this; you will kill her if you push—but the urge to know vanquished sympathy.

"It sounds remarkable. Nonsense, even," Rhiana said. "But you have witnessed my fire. I believe in all that can be possible. Dragons fly the skies. They can even shapeshift to human form. This, I have learned from Macarius Fleche, the slayer who aids my quest. Mother, talk to me!"

"I know well they can shapeshift." At that statement the room fell silent. Even the wisps of flame in the hearth settled. Lydia nodded and twisted her head down. "I have...ever wondered."

"Mother, what is it?" Rhiana scrambled to her and brushed aside Lydia's soft brown hair. It felt strange to touch her mother. So rarely the two came in contact. It was like touching history, her very being, a gilded entity she had ever worshipped but had never known. For all the secrets the village kept, Lydia's guarded veneer held back even deeper secrets.

"I have learned much about dragons from the slayer," Rhiana said softly.

"That man spends too much time with you."

"Paul approves of him. Have you two not discussed this?"

"Actually, we have. Paul sees the good in people. I tend to see the darkness that shadows us all. The slayer is too boastful of his skills. One should not take pride in murder, be it for the good of mankind, or other."

"We've both the same goal. Macarius is…fierce."

Lydia shrugged. "Like you, then. Not that you are boastful, but, well, you have a manner about you that is so strong. Fierce."

She considered that a compliment, and her mother had not formed the word to make it sound ugly, but rather, prideful.

"The slayer tells me the maxima dragons are able to shift to the shape of a man. Very rarely, but it is possible."

"Do not tell me this."

"Yes, Mother, you must listen. I need to know what I am. Speak to me. I think you hold the answers. Why I am like I am. Why they can change shape. How? And for what reason?"

Lydia put up her hands between her and Rhiana, a feeble blockade to her tear-streaked face. She wanted distance; Rhiana felt the utter loss of power melt from her mother. She hated herself for making her mother pain like this. Mayhap she would do to leave her be. It had been twenty-two years. It was not right she ask her mother to relive so painful a memory.

"It is the consecrated water they seek," Lydia murmured in a pale figment of voice.

"Holy water? I don't understand."

"Neither did I. But I do now."

CHAPTER THIRTY-FIVE

"His eyes, they were different," Lydia recited in a distant, yet dreamy tone. "The moon was full. Piskies fluttered over my head. I had been gathering cowslips for wine in the forest and had fallen asleep beneath an oak, only to wake in darkness. But I wasn't afraid to be by myself. Not even when I came upon him. He wore no clothes and wandered as if in a daze."

"No clothes?" Rhiana gasped.

Lydia merely shrugged. "You've seen one naked man…"

Rhiana wasn't sure how to feel about that startling glimpse into her mother's mind-set. She was comfortable with seeing a naked man?

"He was strong and handsome," Lydia continued. "But his eyes, as he held me, I looked into his eyes. Gold."

Rhiana touched her cheek below her left eye.

"Yes, gold like that one," Lydia said. She sighed, clasping her hands before her in her lap. "They were pierced with a narrow black pupil, like that of a snake. He was not real, Rhiana. I thought him a dream. And yet, he seduced me with an unholy attraction. I closed my eyes after that."

"I am sorry. He must have hurt you terribly."

"Actually—" Lydia's tone lilted softly "—he did not. He was very gentle. Mayhap that is why I carry dreadsome regret. I understood that he wanted to connect. I gave myself willingly to him. And he made me feel, well, splendid. Oh, Rhiana you were born of great pleasure. I should not say it. It is not right."

"Mother, it is your right to take pleasure from a man."

"But you tell me he was a beast. A dragon!"

"I cannot know for sure." Tangling her fingers in her hair, Rhiana knew nothing but what she could see, feel and touch. And yet every word her mother spoke felt more real than the tangible. "It certainly would explain my breathing fire."

"Indeed. *Mon Dieu,* does it not burn your throat?"

"Momentarily. Please continue, Mother. Tell me, did you ever see him again?"

"On the following day I returned with the favor he asked of me."

"You returned to him?"

Lydia nodded.

"Wh-where was Ulrich?"

"We were to be wed in a se'nnight. I was ashamed for my actions—giving myself to a man not my betrothed—and yet…not at all. The man in the forest gave me such strength. And all he asked for in return was holy water."

"What for? Did you know he was not a man? Did he have a tail?" Like the picture on the scroll! "Mother?"

"I suspected he was not of this realm, but no tail. No man is so attentive and gentle, so…curious. And of course, his eyes were not human." Lydia lowered her head and smirked. "I fancied he might be the fair folk." She shrugged. "One never knows. I had had dreams as a child. Well, don't we all?" Girlish charm brightened her mother's eyes. Indeed, Rhiana had dreamed of meeting a handsome lord of the forest. That, and to swim with the mermaids.

To know that her mother was not so different from her opened her eyes to the possibility that they could have a closer relationship than they'd had.

"What did he do with the holy water?"

"He asked me to bless him. To trace the cross upon his forehead. At first I refused. I initially thought it sacrilege. But then I knew by virtue of the action being performed—*ex opere operato*—any one could give a blessing with the sacred water. So…I did."

"And?"

Lydia shrugged. "He did not change before my eyes, if that is what you guess. But he did flee immediately after. I never saw him again. My fancies dreamed he'd flittered off to an enchanted land."

"Did you…return? To search for him again?"

Lydia tilted her head in what appeared a nod, but it wasn't quite.

"What of a dragon?" Rhiana insisted. "Did you see a dragon in the sky that day after he left you?"

"Actually, yes," Lydia said on a sigh. "Well, no, I didn't see it with my eyes, but a watchman reported seeing a dragon fly over the sea. The entire village was relieved to hear it did not seek to nest in the hoard."

The affirmation entered Rhiana's heart on a whisper no louder than her mother's sigh. Lydia had known, but to have never voiced so fantastic a tale had ever tormented her. Rhiana's father was no faery—he was a dragon.

"Why did he wish to be blessed?"

"I did not ask. I was…enamored, Rhiana. He was comely, so tall and muscles on every inch of him. You do know what it is like to be attracted to a man's appearance?"

"Oh, yes," Rhiana answered quickly. Too quickly. She looked into her mother's smiling gaze, and for the moment, the two shared a common bond. It felt…new. Like something she ever wished to hold close.

"His hair was dark," Lydia said, dreamy in her tone, "as well, his essence."

Rhiana toyed a curly end of hair through her fingers. "Not like mine?"

"No. Well, you've hair the color of nothing I have ever seen. Save fire."

"And you've never thought that curious?"

"Yes. No. I…"

"Have you always known, Mother?"

"Known?" Lydia startled out from her reverie, directing her soft gaze upon Rhiana, but still not really looking. "Mayhap."

"That you've never told me— Do you know how I struggled when first the fire came to me?"

"You never told me. Rhiana, had you said something…"

But they both knew that by then their relationship was already strained. Rhiana had felt safer telling Paul, than telling a woman she had never really been sure of.

"Ah, child, what have I done to you? I have not wanted to be so distant. I have always stood aside, reluctant. Not knowing how to embrace you. I had thought it would be the two of us after Ulrich left. That we would grow together, forging a strong bond. But instead—I don't know how to explain it—I did not want to get too close, for fear of surrendering to the wrong I committed that night in the forest. I thought if I let you know me, you would see my ugly core. The woman who did something wrong, so dreadfully wrong. Can you ever forgive me?"

"There is nothing to forgive. And there is nothing ugly about you. Mother, you were following your heart. I do not blame you for your passions."

"My passion." Lydia sniffed back a tear. "I have convinced myself that I was evil. That I must never show the world that side of me. That…to stand alongside you would scream loudly 'look at me!' I have done this. Condemn me how you will."

"I am not one to condemn. No man should be so quick to judge. Yet, are you…ashamed of me?"

"No." She shook her head. "I am proud of what you have become, Rhiana. Despite me. Despite my distance, and my struggles to keep you from all you rush upon and wish to become. You are a fine woman. Know that."

"Even if I've a propensity for men's clothing and chasing dragons?"

"Even so."

"You have raised me well."

"What will you do now?" Lydia asked. "Is there any hope to save St. Rénan from the dragons? And…what if they are your own?"

Rhiana had not thought of that. If indeed a shifted dragon had fathered her, then must she count the beasts as her own? How odd to even consider.

Of a sudden her gut muscles tightened. 'Twas as if she had breathed fire, without the pain.

"I'm not sure what I'll do, Mother. But I will stand and defend the village. Whatever it takes. They are not indestructible. With help, we can defeat the beasts. I require a few good knights to stand behind me. I've got to go, Mother. I need to find Lord Guiscard."

"You shouldn't trouble the man."

"And why not? This is his demesne. He should watch over his people. Instead he wants the dragons to live! To what? Kill off all who have not a stone castle to protect themselves? It is time he answered to me."

* * *

Still structurally sound, the chapel had been cleared of all benches. The walls were sooted and the wood eaten away to reveal stone. The cross hung from ropes at the fore of the room; fire had eaten at the left arm of it, but it had not been defeated. The holy fount had been refilled and blessed. Rhiana traced the cool water across her forehead.

Suddenly aware of what she was doing—the connotations— she pulled her finger from her forehead and stared at her fingertips, still wet with the blessed sacrament.

He asked me to bless him.

Why would a dragon, shifted into human form, seek a mortal blessing? And it had obviously not mattered that the blessing did not come from one in the holy orders. Could the dragon-man know the difference? Was it the blessing he had sought?

Or the holy water?

Someone knew about this. The someone who had created the images in the scroll she and Macarius had read. There was a connection.

She rubbed her fingertips together, feeling the divine enter her flesh. Had this water some boon to the dragons? For to risk a transformation and travel, weakened and in an unnatural state, amongst mortals who sought only its death, was risking very much indeed. At least she could only guess a dragon in human form might be weak.

"Rhiana?"

She felt the slayer's presence as a tremendous bubble that surrounded but did not weight her. He lightened her, made all things possible.

Macarius walked around in front of her, yet, she did not move. Curiosity kept her sight affixed to her fingertips. The mystery of this holy water startled.

And looking at Macarius, she did not immediately meet his eyes, but instead, she focused upon his forehead, where days earlier he'd drawn a cross with dragon's blood. And his maniacal grin of success. Triumph over those creatures believed to wear the devil's curse in the upside-down cross upon their skulls. The kill spot.

The beast's only vulnerability.

And if they received a blessing of holy water, placed to that very cursed spot?

The risk would be worth it.

"My father asked for a blessing," she blurt out. "Lydia gave it to him. She traced his brow with holy water. Macarius!"

"Rhiana." He folded his arms about her shoulders and drew her close. "You are shivering? What crazed notions trip through that busy mind of yours? What blessings do you speak of? And your father? I thought the man long gone?"

"He was a dragon."

Macarius's grin exploded to a burst of laughter. Still holding her, his chest vibrated with mirth against her cheek. "Did you hear what came from your mouth, fire chaser? You said—"

"My real father was a dragon. Lydia told me. Initially, she did not see him as a dragon—though later, she heard evidence to corroborate her suspicion. He went to her in the forest, and made love to her. She wasn't violated. She desired him. And together they made me!"

"Hold there, Rhiana. I think I'd better check for fever." He made to place the back of his hand across her forehead but Rhiana flinched away and stood.

"Macarius, the dragon-man asked my mother to bring him holy water. And to then bless him. Right here—" she touched his forehead "—upon his forehead, did my mother draw the sign of the cross. Upon the dragon's kill spot!"

"Wait—"

"Do you think it changed him? Made the dragon…stronger? Why else would the creature seek a blessing?"

Striding up the nave, Rhiana stopped but a hands width from the hanging cross. Looking over the symbol of Christianity, she sought answers within the grains swirling through the hard wood.

"You speak the truth?" Macarius asked.

"All of it." And she knew she did speak truth as she breathed the very air. And as she breathed fire. "It is why I breathe fire."

Reaching up, Rhiana pressed her palm to the wood cross. It had survived the fire, was remarkably intact. A miracle she had no need to question.

"Makes an odd bit of sense." Macarius broached her side. "Your fire breathing abilities…because your father was a…"

He would have difficulty believing. The man tended to embrace that which he could see, hear and clutch in his fist. But her fire was real. No trick of wizardry or magic. Neither was it from the Fair Folk.

"I have never heard of the creatures seeking holy water." Macarius slid a thumb along the base of the oiled wood cross. "Surely my father would have mentioned it if he had known. Why else should they risk changing to frail human form but to seek that which could—"

"Heal them!" Rhiana gasped. Heartbeat jittering, she slapped the air with a fist. "The holy water heals the kill spot. I know it as I know my own heart. It has to be."

They held gazes, eyes dancing with the possibility. Rhiana saw in Macarius's blue eyes trust and wonder. And a delicious openness that welcomed her in.

"You believe me?"

He nodded, imperceptible at first, and then he gave a shrug

and really nodded. "Yes, I believe. Damn me, but I do. Where is this dragon? Your...father?"

"I don't know. It was two decades ago. Surely the dragon that is my father is long from the French coast."

"You are getting excited."

"I am overwhelmed asudden. I think I know how we can defeat the rampants."

"With holy water? Will that not make them all the stronger? If your theory on healing the kill spot is true...?"

"The holy water will not be for the rampants. But if there is a maxima below us, mayhap the elder dragon will help us."

"It was just a dream, fire chaser."

"Trust me."

Macarius whistled lowly.

"My lord."

Anne's chambers always granted reprieve to Narcisse. Scented with myrrh, that he always purchased greedily for her from the merchants who docked up the coast.

He rolled away from Anne's warm body to flash a glare over his shoulder at Champrey. Much as he abhorred being interrupted while feasting upon flesh, he had given Champrey orders that he must be called at any moment something untoward occurred.

"It is the dragon slayer," Champrey offered. The man's eyes searched the ceiling, avoidance not his strong skill as they fell to Narcisse's bed and the creamy landscape of Anne's back and bottom. "I've detained her in the solar—"

"Her? Don't tell me the Tassot wench insists upon breaking the edict?" Narcisse slapped the air with a fist and jumped from the high bed to land a wobbly stance. "Must I string her up and have her burned as a witch?"

"Not wise, my lord. Despite the fires, some of the villagers have begun to stand behind her. As well as the other slayer, Fleche."

"He's not been run out of the village? What are you to, Champrey? Why does my seneschal not order my troops with more accord? Should not the slayer have packed away the moment he was released from the dungeon?"

"Er, he wasn't exactly released—"

"I know that! Insolent wench."

Wandering the room naked and searching for a robe, Narcisse turned to find Champrey offering his long, turquoise damask cotehardie. He shoved an arm into each sleeve and tugged it closed.

"Rumor tells," Champrey began, softly, for Anne lay sleeping, "the dragons are nesting in the mine below the city."

"Dragons?" Narcisse perked. "As in, more than one?"

Champrey nodded.

Snapping his fingers as he sought—something—Narcisse scanned the room. There. His freshly polished sword and gauntlets lay upon the leather-wrapped chest that displayed a thick black candle the Nose had given him as a wedding gift. For fertility. Fat lot of good that had served. He should not think to get Anne with child for fear it would come out like her—touched. Thus far, he had been lucky; she remained barren.

"What does the wench want now?"

"To speak with you, my lord. I've already explained—"

"Yes, yes, in the solar. When the dungeon would have—"

"Not held, obviously," Champrey tossed out. Both were aware of Rhiana's break from the dungeon. Neither could figure how she had gotten the fire to melt the lock, such intense heat and a length of time would have been required. "I'll escort you there."

"You'll remain outside this room. Should Anne wake, she is not to leave my chamber, you understand?"

"Is she chained, my lord? Perhaps you should secure her before you—"

Narcisse swept out the room, leaving Champrey wondering
if he should attempt to chain up the naked waif. Better
thoughts hustled him out the door and to stand guard.

CHAPTER THIRTY-SIX

Prepared to leave the solar and go in seek of Lord Guiscard herself, Rhiana jumped back to avoid the slam of the door inside the room. Narcisse Guiscard stormed into the solar, searching and hissing. The small room took on the heat of his sweltering anger. Like the dragon, he sighted her and moved in on stealthy wings of damask and ire.

The baron used her astonishment and succeeded in pinning her against the stone wall near an embrasure. Pressing her shoulders to the wall, he spat each word, "What must I do to be done with you, wench?"

"I have important news regarding the dragons," she managed to say in a firm voice.

"I'll not hear it." Now he slammed his entire body the length of hers. Formidable in height and strength, he held her there with ease. Dark eyes took her measure while his body gauged her every tense muscle.

"We are at daggers drawn. You tangle about my hair as if a nuisance insect. Why are you not home baking breads or washing the walls? You—you…firebrand! You have far too long a rein for my comfort. That is it!" His expression changed quickly from anger to a lascivious glint. Rhiana flinched. "You are young and wild and, as yet, untouched. Yes? You need a man to tame you. Be that the bitter medicine you seek?"

He slid a palm over her hip.

"Unhand me!"

Slapping his palm along her jaw, Guiscard roughly shoved Rhiana's head. Her skull hit the stone behind her. She tasted blood at the back of her tongue. The urge to burn him in her flame must be pushed down.

"You need a good rutting to show you who commands. That it is a man who rules over his woman. And that it is best for all if you meekly crawl back under the sheets and await yet another night."

His knee pressed at the juncture of her thighs. Had he intention to violate her? That would teach her none of the idiot submissions he rattled on about, only that this one man was as vile as she suspected.

Narcisse's grip clamped under her jaw and lifted her high, so that her heels left the floor. Rhiana scratched the walls for support. She lifted a knee to kick, but thought better. If she wanted to be free to fight the rampants, she must not be in the dungeon.

"A dragon nests beneath us!" she managed.

"I know that," he said.

"Yo-you do?"

"Leave the beasts to themselves," he barked. Utter darkness filled the centers of his pale eyes. The pupils expanded. For a moment Rhiana thought it he who harbored half a beast inside of him, not she. "They will cease to torment St. Rénan the moment you draw back your bolt and crossbow."

Her face hot and flushed, Rhiana choked. The baron released her. Unable to catch her stance, she wilted at his feet. Gagging for air, she struggled to right herself.

He knew that a dragon nested below the village?

Guiscard spun and paced two steps from her, but turned back with a viper's precision.

"What bargain must I strike with you?" he hissed. "Do you not understand your every kill sends my wife into greater melancholy? My precious Anne! She reveres the beasts! And I want only to please her."

"Do not use poor Anne to justify your twisted desires. You want the dragon dust," she dared.

Finding her stance, Rhiana tugged down her tunic and approached the intimidating lord with as much muster as he blasted at her. "For immortality, yes? You send a lackey to the hoard to steal the dragon dust and then you infuse it into your body through the cupping marks on your back. I have seen them. I know it is what you do."

"Well." The room silenced. Dust motes danced in the sunlight spraying through the arrow-slit window. "Aren't you the clever witch?"

"I am no witch."

"Right. A fire chaser, then? A queer-gotten bastard is what you are. That you carry the Tassot name at all is blasphemy. How dare you? You who were born to one not your blood? We all know Villon was not your father."

"What care I for names or titles?" Rhiana ventured. Pushing down the clinging shame, she rallied all the bravery and courage she had learned from Paul and Amandine. "Names are but words. Words tossed about as if pieces of gold or diamonds. Worthless to any who holds valor to their heart."

He grimaced and dismissed her bold words with a gesture. "How I do tire of chivalry. Name him, then. What be your father's name?"

Rhiana faltered.

"You do not know. Bastard. Fact is, you seek acceptance through violence."

"I merely wish to save innocent lives. How is it you can deny your own people that safety? Do you not hear the whispers? The rumors that you care for no one but yourself? My lord, it is in your best interest to allow the dragons be slain."

"Never!"

"You risk lives for your selfish fixation. Immortality is not yours. It is myth, legend. A farce and a faery tale."

"I do have a cell in the dungeon that is fashioned entirely of stone. I will arrange for you to be taken there posthaste."

"Wait!"

He would do it. As tainted as it was, Rhiana had no doubt regarding the baron's sincerity. "What if I could guarantee you one dragon would remain?"

A tilt of his head. His hand slipped from the gold door pull.

"One dragon is all you require," she continued. "Mayhap the biggest, which would produce the most dragon dust?" If he wanted to risk his life mining the dragon dust, then it was his death to tempt.

He turned and leaned a shoulder against the door, defying her with forced disinterest.

"It is the rampants that attack without concern. They are the ones that will kill each and every villager if given opportunity. They are wild, voracious, and have little need for the hoard but to replenish vitae perhaps once a month."

"But there is an elder that nests deep below us?"

So he must have seen it! Her dream was true. "Yes. I know not how it managed to enter the hoard through the narrow tunnels."

Attention piqued, the baron straightened. A languorous and stretching roll of his head focused an intent stare upon Rhiana.

"The elder dragon usually nests in peace for decades. It has little need for sustenance, such as meat or vegetation—even human flesh—for the gold it nests upon renews its vitae."

"You think you can kill them all but the largest and fiercest?" His laughter ended in a choking, red-faced hack. "Lackwit."

"Grant me the chance. Please. Defeating the rampants would put you in the right place with your people. I swear it to you—should it be so—I have no desire to slay such an old and wondrous beast. Please, my lord."

Dropping to her knees, Rhiana subjugated herself before him. It was a humiliating performance, but Guiscard would appreciate the move. She hoped.

"Anne is not safe from the rampants. You can lock her away in the deepest stores and the rampants will yet smash out all the walls and flame the entire village until we are but ash. Do this for Anne."

She looked up to him. He stared back. But he did not see her, so distant his gaze. Thoughts moved about in his creaking disaster of a brain. He considered. Yes, for Anne. Rhiana prayed she was right, and that his self-involvement was not so deep he did not include Anne in his ventures to immortality.

"There will be no mention of my desire to keep the one dragon to myself?"

Rhiana agreed with an effusive nod. So close…

"What if you are snatched up and killed before all the rampants are destroyed? Who will lead your glorious quest then?"

"Macarius Fleche."

"He will demand a dragon's purse!"

"And he will be given all that he can take from the hoard. It is what he is owed, and nothing less. The people will gladly pay him, why will you not? Your greed is not so great it could ever consume the massive wealth which sits beneath the roots of the village."

"Very well!" He stomped his heel to punctuate his declaration. He reached forward.

Rhiana suspected he was going for her hair again, and so slipped to the side. He caught her arm and drew her to him. A reflection of her inner fire danced in the baron's bold stare. It singed her without so much as a burn. "But you will stand by our agreement. One remains. Promise me."

"I promise you, my lord. One remains."

"And Anne."

"What of her?"

"She must never learn of the destruction."

"But if we go to battle— It will be impossible to conceal such!"

He shrugged. "I will shelter her away for a few days in the far tower to the north. There are no windows. Will that give you enough time?"

"I pray so, my lord. With your blessing?"

"The only blessings you will receive from me are those to your taming, wench. You will yet be brought to heel. If I must wed you to my most vicious and brute knight, I shall tame you."

Waiting for him to release her, Rhiana countered her brewing anger with deep breaths.

"Might I leave now, my lord?"

"You may."

She opened the door, but paused and looked across the floor to the bejeweled slippers of the baron. So ignorant of human life.

Not this way. No man was going to rebuke her.

"You cannot tame the wild at heart," she said boldly, feeling her inner fire. "'Tis why you shall never truly have Anne, and must chain her to keep her with you."

He lifted his jaw, defying with his gaze.

"As for myself." Rhiana matched his defiance with an open, ready stance. "There are no chains in this kingdom, be they brute knights or thick iron, which can bind me to submission. Know that, and be warned."

Lord Guiscard thinks she required taming?

Him first.

Rhiana stormed out from the castle, but as the breeze whisked sooty reminders of the previous night under her nose, she checked her foul mood.

There was no reason for her anger. Guiscard had agreed to allow her to hunt the dragons. And she would stand good on her promise to keep the elder alive. It would harm none. The dragon only sought sanctity. She did not kill indiscriminately. If the baron wished to risk his life by continuing to harvest dragon dust in the presence of a maxima, then that was his problem to deal with.

Immortality. Ha! No man could live forever. What man would want to? Once the body ages, it only slumps and withers. Should a person live beyond sixty, or even seventy years that would be so long!

The sounds in the village this day were industrious. Just over the battlement walls Rhiana saw a trebuchet release its pointed wood bolt. Excellent. They were practicing and readying. This dragon hunt would prove a success!

Spying the familiar steel-studded coat of plates moving through the bustle of townspeople, Rhiana swerved between two children carrying buckets of ash swept from the remains and skipped ahead. But she paused when she saw Macarius spoke to Gerard Coupe-Gorge. Cut-Throat Gerard.

The brutest and most vicious knight in all of St. Rénan.

I will marry you to the most vicious knight…that will put you in your place.

Gerard Coupe-Gorge, a recent import from northern France, was known to beg to lead any battle. He carried a halberd and cut his enemy's throats and was rumored to lick his enemy's blood from his fingers. Why he had been content to remain in St. Rénan the past few years never ceased to make her wonder, for the lack of blood and fight must gnaw at him.

Sizing up the pair, Rhiana saw Gerard's shoulders sat a good hand-span higher than Macarius's shoulders. His thick black hair, cut high above his ears and in the pudding-basin shape, capped a square face with an angry nose that seemed to want to flee the face, if only a few more whacks with a mace, and it could.

As she drew slowly toward the twosome, Rhiana's eyes began to water. Did not Macarius smell the man? He was foul! Like hogs in a sty.

"Ah, fire chaser!" Macarius gestured Rhiana join him.

Gerard straightened as she approached. Was he posturing? Trying to look more appealing? Interesting.

Rhiana joined Macarius's side. "What be the plans this day?"

"We wait for your instructions," Gerard said. Both front teeth were missing, so his words were lispy, juvenile. "I want me some dragon scales for armor like you, my lady."

My lady? Of a sudden she had gained respect from one of the castle's knights?

"I've just come from speaking to Lord Guiscard. He has granted us permission to take out the rampants."

Macarius's jaw dropped. Rhiana knew the feeling.

"The baron is a good man," Gerard said. "He is concerned for his people."

Right. So long as he benefited and could control the situation to serve his desires exactly.

"Who's manning the trebuchets?"

"Lady Verity," Macarius said. "She is a whip with the machines. Already trained half a dozen to man the three we pushed out to the field. Paul is outfitting the volunteers with armor right now. They'll need maximum protection out in the open."

"And what are you two doing?"

"Rallying the troops," Gerard said with a huff of his burly chest. The movement plumed a fresh wave of his staleness toward Rhiana. "We're placing archers on the battlements and scouts in the field. We'll be ready for them. We await you to flush them out, my lady."

The man could not tame her if he wanted. With force he might violate her, but never could he touch her soul. That part of her was reserved for another…

Rhiana looked over Macarius. Share her soul with him? At what risk to her very life?

"Flush them out?" she repeated. A tap to the gold disk at her neck calmed her sudden fast heartbeat. "That I can do. In fact, I'm headed for the caves right now." Not to do any flushing. No, right now, she had to know the truth. "I'll be going through the salt mines."

"I'll have your back," Macarius began to walk alongside her, leaving Coupe-Gorge smiling stupidly at her retreat.

"How could you stand there when he smelled so awful?"

"I did not notice."

Rhiana swung a look to him. "In truth?"

Macarius shrugged.

"He was so foul as to kill flowers merely by walking through a meadow. I think you've had your nostrils singed by dragon fire."

"If that be so, then I could not smell a dragon." They passed through the portcullis and Rhiana stopped to watch the trebuchets practice. Macarius leaned in next to her ear. "Nor could I smell the flower standing next to me."

"Save the poetry for troubadours, slayer. I don't want a milksop as my first man, I require a warrior."

"First man?" Macarius stepped around in front of her, blocking her view as a pine log rocketed by the trebuchet, soared into the spacious blue sky. "Are you drawing rank, fire chaser?"

"This *is* my mission. You've not plans to compete against me, do you?"

"I shouldn't wish to. But if you think you can command the troops—"

Rhiana gripped Macarius's coat and aimed the most serious gaze possible upon him. "I don't *think* anything, slayer. I know." She released hold and stalked around behind him. "I can command, and I will. But while I am in the caves, I need to know I can rely on a strong partner to keep the village in order. A man who can gauge the coming danger, and who will strike if needs be."

"Partner?" A dark brow tilted above a mirthless blue eye.

"Be that acceptable to you?"

"I'm not sure. Do partners kiss?"

Averting her gaze to the trebuchets, Rhiana spied Rudolph, who waved eagerly to show his skills. It was all she could do to keep her mind from that tantalizing question. Kiss?

"They do not," she said. "Not for all to see."

"In private then?"

"Mayhap. But not if you insist on beheading me in return for a simple kiss." She nodded once, exacting her command. "I am off. I won't be overlong. The longer they have to practice, the better chance we have to take them down."

"What of the maxima?"

"What of it?"

"You're going to speak to it, aren't you?"

"I—"

"Yes, I believe there is one down there. Will you ask it if our theory about the holy water be true? You should not come right out with it, but rather, slyly determine if the maxima has that ulterior motive."

Relieved he'd not admonished her for her intentions, Rhiana nodded.

The woman Ulrich claimed to be his companion marched behind the three wooden machines, shouting commands, staff marking her pace as she easily handled the task. Another woman capable of commanding.

Macarius was outnumbered, two to one. The thought put a smile to Rhiana's face as she waved to Verity, and walked on toward the pyre at sea's edge.

CHAPTER THIRTY-SEVEN

Rhiana had always loved the salt mines. When she was younger, Lydia would tote she and Odette along on her runs to bring back salt. Retrieval had been more casual then, for dragons had never nested in the salt mines, nor had any feared that the beasts would. But now, she crunched across the crystals with a leery eye to every corner of the dark caverns.

Choosing not to carry a torch, but instead relying on her instincts and the inner glow the salt crystals gave off, Rhiana navigated her way back to the hoard. She sensed but the one heartbeat. Slow, steady, booming. The elder maxima. It was here.

Before she stepped into the glow of the hoard she sensed the beast stirred. It had sensed her as well. She did not fear, only did not wish to frighten or startle.

The hoard room held a natural illumination for the enormous treasure that glittered and glinted and winked from every angle. Even the walls glinted with diamonds and rubies and gilded mirrors. It had been years since Rhiana had been in this hoard, and she took a moment to take it all in.

A dented suit of armor lay not five strides to her right. The damascened gold and silver elaborately spoke of the former wearer's position—quite high, mayhap a king. "Oh."

Five finger bones splayed out from the gauntlet attached to the armor. Obviously the owner had not wanted to give up the prize without a fight; the quarrel hole pierced through the cuirass, evidence of that. Sage overwhelmed.

Here, be a dragon.

Having almost forgotten that she was not alone, Rhiana wavered, but caught her stance and moved inward toward a high berm of stacked gold objects and coins.

Climbing upon the hoard, her feet slipped and sought hold in the piles of metal pieces. Groping for purchase, she levered herself to the brim of the hoard, and there she looked over treasure so vast, it could feed the entire country of France for a decade, she felt sure.

Home. So right.

Nodding, Rhiana reminded internally that she must remain sharp.

The dragon had made a nest, burrowing into the center a little cove, embroidered about with gold and silver of every shape, size and sheen. Its head lifted, scenting prey, as Rhiana emerged at the brim.

For long moments she remained silent, reverent before the beast. She would make no move to startle it. It must be allowed to determine her threat—which she did not offer. Now, she realized what she had dreamed to be emerald scales before, were actually a violet so deep as to be black. Glints of gold danced in the lush deep violet. Everything glittered with dragon dust, including the deadly ebony talons but a leap from her feet.

The air hummed with anticipation. The flutter of small wings—a bat or a pisky—circled overhead in the high darkness of the cave ceiling. Rhiana's belly pulsed. This moment felt surreal. And yet, she trusted.

With a graceful move, the elder laid down its head before her. A sign of trust or a daring temptation?

"I—" she started carefully. If it could understand her, well, what must her first words be? "I mean you no harm."

Dragon slayer.

So startled at that voice, inside her head, Rhiana slipped in the coins. It did really speak to her!

"I can't believe this."

Speak wisely, mortal. Do not waste a single word.

"You have made yourself at home." She searched the walls and spied two dark holes where the small narrow tunnels opened into the hoard chamber. "How do you get inside? Can the rampants come in?"

They are unable. I…am.

"But how?"

So many questions?

"Questions cause little harm. Answers will teach me, allow me to understand your kind. You are an intelligent beast, you should know as much."

Do not berate me, mortal.

"I simply want to learn. I mean you no disrespect. I just don't understand how…when the only entrance requires a thin man to climb in as if a worm…"

And yet, you entered. On hands and knees?

"No, I… The passage I took is narrow, but traversable. I know the rampants could not traverse it, let alone one so large as yourself."

You are aware the gold transmutes against our scales to create a substance valued by man?

"Dragon dust. Yes, but what has that to do with your entrance to the hoard? Can you fold back your wings so tightly?"

I transmute from scale to mortal flesh. It is our incarnation.

Rhiana slipped upon the gold and slid a ways down the inner berm of the nest. Her heel stopped against the dragon's talon. The click of hard leather heel to glossy talon rang dully.

Lying spread out, staring up into the dragon's nostril, she took a moment to get her bearings. Blessed be, but she was so vulnerable. One tap of that talon and she would be gutted. One snap of its jaws—history.

Her crossbow was not to hand. She'd left it at the base of the hoard near the entrance. Her dagger, fashioned from a talon one-tenth the size of the maxima's, rested upon her hip. A futile defense.

You understand?

Rhiana nodded. "Completely. I know maximas can transform to mortal shape. But I had not considered until now... So, as a *man* you can enter the cave."

Indeed.

"And as a man you can also mate with mortal females?"

There is no compulsion to do so.

"But—"

It is only the female of our kind that seek mortal connection, in order to strengthen our bloodline. The result is a newling which bears the blood of mortal man.

"But my mother. And you said... How can a mortal walk the earth as a half dragon, if the males do not—"

I did not say the males could not.

No, it had not. Which meant it was very possible that a male dragon could mate with a human female. "Are...are you my father?"

A snort of steam hissed from the nostrils, clouding sage and warmth over Rhiana's body.

"I just mean...I talked to my mother. She was...she...made love with one like you."

Made love? I hold no love for humans.

"You eat them!"

If they are in my way.

"My mother said it was mutual. That the man was gentle with her, but that later, she knew she had lain with a dragon. And I was conceived."

I am not your father. I have never mated with a human female.

"But you admit my mother's words are true? I could have been fathered by a dragon?

Yes. Now you understand, dragon sired?

"Dragon sired. Yes. Which explains my resistance to your flame."

You are more powerful for it.

"Indeed." Rhiana clung to the slithering stream of gold coins that poured toward the dragon in its wake. Were she not careful, the rush of coin could bury her alive.

Great bellicose laughter filled the cavern. The dragon fluidly curled up onto the berm, leaving Rhiana to clamber for higher ground.

Watch you don't become buried.

"Should I go under that would be an easy kill for you."

Indeed.

The beast's easy agreement for her death did nothing to settle her nerves. Rhiana struggled, gripping plate rims and stuffing her foot into the mouth of a dented urn, pulling herself up to the top of the gold.

Mon Dieu, that the baron was worried Macarius would request a dragon's purse for his slaying the dragons was ridiculous. The man would not even make a dent in this fortune should he carry out two or three carts loaded high and covered with tarps.

What have you come for, dragon sired?

"I want to bargain."

I don't submit to mortal ramblings.

"Your life for the lives of the rampants. The villagers have rallied. We are ready and prepared to take them down. With your promise not to interfere I shall grant you your life."

The dragon's head slid closer. Rhiana could feel the hoard shift. She shuffled her feet over the side of the berm. Should she go sliding again, it would be toward the entrance, and a quick escape.

When she focused again on the dragon it was to stare right at the thick ivory tusk that hovered but a leap from her body. A weapon the size of the sharpened logs Verity ordered the villagers to fire from the trebuchets.

A blink of the gold eye dispersed a heavy droplet of moisture that sizzled as it touched the gold and hissed to steam. Gorgeous glitter coruscated in the wake of the steam. Dragon dust.

"Is it a wager?"

Do you know why I nest beneath your village, slayer?

"For the hoard."

Another snort of sage steam. *Not at all. There are hoards aplenty throughout the land. This one is generous but the sea air is troublesome. Too moist.*

"Then why here?"

She is here. I can feel her. I had mistakenly thought you to be her, until I looked into your strange eyes. Not her.

"Who?"

My mate.

"There are no— One of the rampants?"

The younglings are wild and untamable. They will not mate for a long time, yet they've scented my presence and attempt to cajole me into a silly mating dance. The first female to get to me shall have proven her worthiness.

"Then who?"

She is lost in mortal form. We can, we elders, incarnate, as I have explained. It is used rarely. It is difficult, and the shifting of bones and flesh can sometimes go awry. Very rarely we…forget. Our animal brain succumbs to the mortal coil.

"You mean your mate is a mortal? Or walks in mortal form?"

Exactly. You have seen her?

Stomach rising to her throat, Rhiana swallowed hard, but the lump would not be pressed back. She had not to think any longer than a moment. Of course, she had seen his mate.

It made so much sense now she thought on it.

"I…I don't think so." She would give nothing to the maxima until he agreed to her terms. "There are none in St. Rénan who resemble a dragon. Well, there are a few rowdy knights—"

She cannot remember her origins! But I feel her close.

"Well, if she cannot remember—"

Then she cannot shift back to dragon form. It is so simple as restoring her memory to make the change. But first I must find her.

"You alter the conversation to your needs. I want a bargain you'll not prevent the annihilation of the rampants."

For the longest time the wide, gold eye held Rhiana as if fixed by a spear through the heart. Could the creature read her heart? Know she had spoken a mistruth? To hand over a woman who could not remember—'twould be cruel as a virginal sacrifice.

Very well. You have a bargain. On one condition.

"No conditions."

I can take out half your village with one breath, slayer.

Truth. And not so much a threat as a promise. "What is the condition?"

Bring the consecrated water to me. This night.

* * *

One moment he flapped his great wings, effortlessly cutting the air with his powerful strength, the next, he was stumbling, changing, *becoming* in a most painful manner.

Bones had begun to liquefy. Muscles tightened, shrinking to a different shape. Organs moved, reshaping, lengthening, and then shortening. Scales became flesh with the stinging razor of transformation.

The mind—for he could not claim possession in this state; he was neither dragon, nor man—was wide and open, a sponge to the pain. Fierce, blinding, paralyzing pain.

As his beastly moans took on the timbre of man, he clutched with talons that shed the hard glossy coating and gave way to soft, raw, sore human flesh. He buried his face in the cool, dirt tunnel path, but it was not soft. Still so out of his mind, he could not gauge softness. Darkness surrounded, hiding the wicked transformation.

The movement of his spinal column from dragon form to man shape was the most awkward and painful. Such transformation whipped the human limbs this way and that. The wounds, slashes and cuts he'd received from such gyrations never did heal properly, and so the open cuts only multiplied, making every touch, every sensation a thing of pain.

And when it was complete—dragon had surrendered to man—he lay panting and weeping. So alive. And so open to the pain.

A man in shape now, he rolled over to face the narrow opening that led out from the hoard. His limbs, still numb from the change, flopped in follow. He did not open his eyes. The adjustment to his feeble mortal sight was always a shock, for the dragon's sight was formidable. Colors, scents and sounds were always lesser in human form. He rarely opened his eyes for hours after transforming for everything was but a blur.

The bubble of foul air burst past his lips in a human belch. Smoke puffed out from his mouth, leaving in its wake a sticky sulfurous tang clinging to throat and tongue.

As usual, he was too tired to move. The transformation drained his strength. But it served the purpose. For the hoard offered vitae.

There was something warm close by. Mortal fingers dug into the hard-edged warmth of coins and plating and various metal objects. To move stirred the pain to a wicked alchemy that taunted mind and bone.

Here he would lie for a very long time. Taking in the gold to feed his vitae. The transformation back was equally as painful, but it would not be necessary until he had walked above ground and found the elixir. He did not trust the dragon slayer. He must act now.

Spreading mortal arms across the mass of coins he lay there and exhaled heavily. So weak this mortal coil. Nasty and small, the mortals. And so many of them close by. But that would change soon enough. The rampants would destroy the enemy.

He would see his mate returned to him.

And never again would he fear death from a mortal weapon.

CHAPTER THIRTY-EIGHT

A billow of amber flame rolled along the horizon of burnished copper. 'Twas as if waves of fire washing upon the meadow of pinks that edged the cliff. Rhiana stood upon the battlements, directly above the barbican.

Sheer helplessness shuddered through her. To stand and witness the line of rampants heading toward St. Rénan. To be unable to do a single thing to stop them—not until they got closer. To merely watch as death flew in on wings and scale and fearsome flame.

But she didn't maintain the feeling for long.

Lifting her chin, Rhiana eyed the lead rampant. "This day you will not win. Can you come that?"

Rudolph manned the alarm, trumpeting a staccato of short, then long, toots. Below and behind her, within the deceptive safety of the battlement walls the villagers hustled. Deceptive, for the walls, even the wooden-spiked battlements, could not keep out the rampants.

The pyres were lit, sending up black smoke at a dozen spots along the battlements. It would keep back the dragons—maybe; at the very least Rhiana hoped the smoke would cause some confusion, slow them down.

As the alarm shrilled, men rushed women and children to safety. Half a dozen knights mounted fully armored destriers—they would ride the fields. Carts loaded with weapons were drawn to central locations.

Stacks of sharpened timbers sat beside the trebuchets waiting outside the castle, each to one point of the compass. The south was left unguarded, but they had no choice in that matter.

A petite woman with long blond hair braided down each side, and staff held high above her head, gave the command to "Load!" Her seconds heeled their mounts to a gallop to deliver the command to the east and west locations.

To watch the men she knew, who had never before faced such adversity, take to the task with vigor and intent made Rhiana proud. That Guiscard had consented to this granted the villagers a freedom to pursue their own valor, to protect their own, and to make the world right.

The first dragon pulled ahead of the approaching doom and arrowed toward the village. The men at the trebuchets hustled into action.

A trebuchet was launched. Creak of wood and the hiss of the tightened rope sling flinging its weapon sailed through the air. The spike fell short of the incoming danger. Disappointed groans rose from the ground, but were quickly replaced by another call to arms.

The second trebuchet was dispatched, while the first was reloaded.

Another miss.

The rampant swooped low, banking its wings to a V behind its glittering indigo body. The men manning the third trebuchet took cover beneath the massive wood base and under wide iron shields Paul had dug out from storage. The dragon was too close; they could not release the weapon.

At Rhiana's feet sat the dented, torn shield she'd retrieved from the hoard. It was more a symbol of her intent than a real defense. But she would use it if must needs. Drawing a bolt onto her crossbow, she took aim as the rampant landed the trebuchet below. Its hind talons curled about the man-sized wheels of the mechanism. Wings flapped, sweeping the ground and swirling dirt and grass into the air.

Cries from the men beneath the trebuchet cut through her heart, but they were muffled by the shrieking howl of the dragon.

Rhiana released the trigger, yet at the same time swore an oath. At the very moment her bolt took to air, the beast reared back, shifting her target. The trebuchet lifted from the ground. One man dangled from the long pivoting arm of the machine.

Reaching behind her back and into the quiver for another bolt, Rhiana's arm was brushed by Macarius's studded coat of plates. He drew back a fletched arrow in the longbow he wielded. The arrow hissed through the sky. The dragon cried out at a direct hit between its eyes and dropped the trebuchet. A mass of scales and wings fell backward and landed the ground with a thud.

"One for me!" Macarius gave her a delightful wink. "Can you come that, fire chaser? You don't want me to win, do you?"

Smiling at his competitive mien, Rhiana surveyed the ground below to ensure there were not casualties. The trebuchet had been damaged, but no men were harmed, not even the one who had fallen with it. Even as she made sure that all were safe, the shadows of a half dozen more beasts grew closer.

"Good one, slayer. But I care not who brings down the rampants, only that they are brought to ground. I should check the village. So many are yet racing about. Did they not hear the alarm?"

"They are frightened. They need direction."

"Would that I'd more time to train men for just that. I'll have to do it myself. Will you man the battlements? Someone has to watch the pyres and call out should the outer defenses be defeated."

Macarius gripped her by the arm and tugged her to him. A hard kiss and a glad eye brightened his effusive, "Yes!"

The man was in his element. Fired for the cause and hungry for blood.

And just standing next to him sucked that fire from his spirit and emboldened Rhiana further. An affirmative nod confirmed her trust in him. A punch to his shoulder sent him off.

Licking the bruising kiss from her lips, Rhiana then spiraled down the stairway to the ground. No time to consider the sweetness of that moment, but it did fortify her courage in a curious manner. She and Macarius shared an intimacy. Splendid.

But now, back to matters. Macarius's kill had been entirely too easy. She guessed the rest would require more fight.

The *schroom* of a dragon flighting low overhead, wings spread to cut the night sky, hastened her steps. There were still people outside. Easy targets for a blast of dragon flame.

A hearty cheer rose up from outside the battlement walls, giving Rhiana pause. One of the trebuchets must have been successful. Either that or it was a late cry of celebration for Macarius's kill.

In that moment, Rhiana closed her eyes and settled her huffing breaths. And she focused on the heartbeats flying high. Four. But four!

Rushing into a jog, Rhiana gripped the arm of a man who walked a crooked path, his gnarled oak cane tapping the ground, and directed him to cover. He nodded and hastened for a slate-roofed home. Madly yipping dogs could not be quieted. She wasn't sure if they would attract or dissuade the dragons, but in such a roused state she wasn't about to attempt silencing them.

Clapping a gloved hand over her chest made the scaled armor *ching* musically. "There will be plenty more fodder for scaled armor before the night is finished. Mark my words, beasts of fire."

Ahead of her, a man strode purposefully toward the chapel. Rhiana grabbed his arm, yet he tugged away from her.

"Take cover!" she shouted to be heard over the cries of the frantic villagers and flames. "The chapel is not safe. It will collapse with further flame. You must to the castle keep. The chapel there is safe."

He looked her askance. Blinked.

And Rhiana sucked in a breath.

Those eyes. Her heartbeat pulsed heavily at the recognition. Not human. The pupil drew a narrow slit in the gold eyes. Had she...spoken to this man before?

Man? Was he—?

Swinging around and away from her, the man rushed across the ground. Rhiana took off after him, seeking a tail, but her path was diverted by the cries of a child. There, standing before a blazing haystack, a boy, no older than three, screamed.

Rhiana scooped the crying infant into her arms. "All will be well," she murmured. The child's face was red with fear and tears. Spinning about she scanned the surrounding homes. No sign of the man with the curious eyes. The chapel door was closed, but he had not entered. There. An open door.

The child's mother received him as Rhiana graced the stoop. "He is not harmed," she said, and fled without waiting for thanks.

Where had the man gone? She glanced toward the chapel; still closed. Had he changed his path for the keep, as she'd directed?

He was not a man.

To think such a ridiculous—but, yes, she could believe. His eyes were not human. The maxima? And he'd been headed for the chapel.

Come for holy water, no doubt. And she had diverted his course. To the castle, and...Anne.

Searching the sky, Rhiana sighted the spiraling flight of two rampants, performing a danse macabre above the village. Too high to reach with weapons, they merely tormented now.

Sighting in Macarius atop the battlements, along with dozens more armed knights, Rhiana nodded, sure the safety of the perimeter was in good hands.

Rushing for the castle steps, she headed for the far tower.

The keep was quiet; all able hands were in the battlements surrounding and protecting. Women and children huddled in a quiet circle, eyes to the ceiling and sobs dampened to better hear should the horrors approach. A few men guarded them; perhaps their presence provided some comfort. The tang of fear misted the air. Salted sobs on one child's cheek were cleaned away by the castle's three-legged mutt.

Racing across the rushes, Rhiana kept an eye out for the mysterious man—beast—she'd seen outside. He'd worn a long brown cloak, similar to a monk's vestments. Did he wear clothes beneath? She'd not seen. Where would he—it—get clothes?

Was it really the maxima? Or did her eyes play games with her, making her believe something so unreal.

You are dragon sired.

Not impossible. "And very real," she muttered.

Taking the stairs up to the third floor in strides that skipped every other spiraling step, Rhiana exited to the parapet that crossed to the south tower, the windowless one that Guiscard had felt sure would keep Anne safe.

Up here the air stirred with an ominous chill that thickened in places and then thinned in others. Clouds of black velvet hung in the night sky, but between those clouds glinted rose and violet light, reflected from the setting sun.

She could see the tower door across the parapet. It was wide-open. Pray the baron had gone to comfort his wife, or take her below to the dungeon where it was safer. All those huddling in the keep should have been directed to the dungeons. One falling dragon, or a stream of flame through the keep windows could prove disastrous.

Crossbow in her left hand and dagger in her right, Rhiana marched purposefully toward the open tower door. Anger rising at the gall of the creature—to walk amongst the mortals—she could not prevent what happened next. Tilting back her head, she yelled out a battle cry that birthed from her angry soul. Flames burst from her mouth, but this time Rhiana embraced the pain. Tightening her stomach muscles she focused the pain into determination and held her stance.

This half dragon would be the aggressor this day. Let no one stand in her way.

"Can you come that?" she muttered to any dragon close enough to hear.

Anne's screams hastened Rhiana's footsteps. Dashing into the round tower room she came upon the man, bared to the waist, but a brown wool cloak tied about his hips, standing before Anne.

He turned to Rhiana. Indeed, the eyes were not human, but that of a beast.

He growled, "She is mine! Let me take her away from here and return her to all she has known."

"Touch her and I sever your head from that feeble mortal shell you wear." Rhiana slashed her dagger before the beast in warning. "Stand back!"

"You believe I am mortal in this form?" The man/beast chortled deeply. "I've the blood of angels in me!"

"Angels. But…" But, of course. The diorama depicted on the tapestries. The dragons had mated with fallen angels. So should one incarnate…

Shivering upon a trundle bed and cowering in a puddle of pale blue damask, Anne reached toward the man. Silenced by fear, but some part of her wanted the connection. No silver chains bound her from wandering this night.

"She will never remember." Rhiana dodged between the beast and Anne. Eyeing him down the blade of her dagger, she fixed to the soft gold eyes.

Soft? Did she see the ethereal in the man's gaze?

He had come to claim his mate. Surely he mourned and pined for Anne's return to his arms. Not arms, but…paws. Wings?

"Leave now!" she commanded.

A scramble of limbs and damask whisked by Rhiana. Luscious dark curls kissing the night air, Anne fled out the doorway. Anne was not the one she had wanted to flee!

In an unexpected flash of wool, the beast drew up the cloak, blocking Rhiana's dagger, and escaped.

Close on his heels, she entered the night. Racing across the parapet, her footsteps were suddenly shadowed by a massive gray shape. High in the sky, a dragon's cry pierced the velvety blackness. No time to discern the situation, only Rhiana ran for all her might as she sensed the beast descend toward the battlement stretch that separated her from the safety of the keep.

But it did not clutch her up in its ebony talons, nor snap off her head with a bite of its iron-clasp jaws. Instead, the beast flew through a cloud of black smoke and collided with the tower Rhiana had just exited. Wings flapped, faltered, and the body rolled to the side. The head slapped the floor of the stone parapet behind Rhiana.

She paused, turned. A wooden spike pierced the dragon's body. Excellent aim from the trebuchet. It appeared an ichor-glittered spine poking out along the dragon's back. But the beast would not die from the spike alone. The kill spot was the only way to silence its macabre growls.

Biting her lip, feeling the urge to continue chase—Anne was in danger—Rhiana decided she must do what was necessary.

This rampant could not be left to somehow work the spike from its body and then to torment those within the battlements.

She ran toward the dragon. It had landed awkwardly, the hind legs stuck between the crenellations, and its neck twisted along its body so the head rested atop the battlement walk.

Caution did not exist. Rhiana saw only the need for urgency. As she mounted its snout, the head lifted and jerked. Just as her dagger pierced the kill spot, her feet slid from the knobby scaled nose.

Her hands clutching the ebony dagger hilt, her body sailed through the air. The dragon pounded its head upon the parapet. Once. Twice.

Rhiana's left hand flailed from the talon hilt. Her right held tight to the hilt. The blade remained rammed deep into the beast's skull. The sway of her legs slapped her body across the dragon's armored nose.

She stared down along the battlement walls. The spiked tail swung up and swatted at her but missed.

With one final shudder, the beast's head settled. As her body slid from the scales, Rhiana gripped for the tusk at the corner of the mouth.

Dangling, both hands gripping the tusk, she closed her eyes and waited. For another movement to shake her loose. For a grand death roar. Flight.

None came.

"Whew!" Eyeing the ground through the frame of her dangling feet, Rhiana knew a fall would crush her bones, if she did not first land the thresher that should cut her to ribbons.

Swinging, she managed to secure hold on the opposite tusk with her feet and worked her legs until her knees bent over the tusk. Now she dangled like a ridiculous embellishment beneath the dragon's maw. An impossible position. How to get back to the battlements?

CHAPTER THIRTY-NINE

"Memento mori," Rhiana repeated for the third time.

The statement held one simple truth—we must all die.

But not today. She had more pressing things with which to concern herself.

Dropping her tight grasp on the tusks, Rhiana swung freely. Her knees were hooked over the opposite tusk, and for the moment she viewed the world upside down. Flames washed the sky. Yet, a dragon or two roamed the air, seeking violence. But what had once been cries of fear now sounded more joined, rallied together. The villagers were claiming their freedom from the tyranny of fire.

A string of sage-scented drool dripped from the dragon's open maw and along Rhiana's body.

"Immensely not good." She swiped off the viscous substance from her arm.

The beast was dead. She had no revulsion to climb about its carcass to save her hide.

Swinging hard she bent and drew herself up, grasping the tusk to either side of her knees. Now she could press back her shoulders against the jaw of the rampant. Twisting, she drew up her leg and knelt upon the tusk. The skull wobbled. She reached for the horn that sprouted from its temple. A few grunts, and finally she was able to grip her dagger hilt embedded within the forehead, and pull herself upon the skull of the beast.

Straddling the long nose, she, for a moment, spread out her arms across the face and pressed her ear to the skull aside her weapon. No heartbeat. Sadness whisped out in Rhiana's sigh. This mighty beast should not have been slain—none of them, to be truthful—but for the dangers to those she loved; she'd had no choice.

If only there were another way. To herd them elsewhere, away from humans?

A fool idea. These female rampants sought adventure, sustenance and mating. The value of a human life had no meaning to them. They were instinctual and would fight when threatened.

Drawing out her dagger released an ooze of dragon dust and sage from the kill spot. Rhiana smeared her palm through the glittering blood, and then swiped it across her cheek. Then she traced her finger across her forehead, in the shape of a cross as she had seen Macarius do previously. An ancient ritual, a compulsive move, a flirtation with immortality.

And to think upon immortality brought her back to one urgent need: to find Anne. The lady of St. Rénan had fled toward the keep—the dragon-man in pursuit.

Jumping to the floor of the parapet, Rhiana hooked up her crossbow and resumed chase. The aisle to the spiral stairs passed before Guiscard's war room. The door was open. Rhiana glanced inside as she passed—and stopped. She backed up.

Inside, the baron stood with outstretched arms while his squire fitted him with pauldrons at his shoulders and damascened greaves strapped about his calves.

Vacillating on whether to continue chase, or rally Guiscard to her side, Rhiana decided on chase. But the baron's voice stopped her.

Clamping a gauntlet upon the door, he strode out from the war room, fully armored, and clutching a battle sword. He looked most regal, a true knight. But Rhiana had no confidence in his actual martial skills. Though, he had shown her his strength when he'd held her against the wall in the solar.

"Whence do you come, fire chaser? The dragons are outside, not in—" His attention fixed to the battlements—one could see the fallen dragon spread across the crenellated parapet. And beyond that, the north tower. "What the— You've been to see Anne?"

"I sought to protect her from the dragon who seeks to make her his mate."

Steel plates of armor clattered up behind Rhiana as she hastened toward the stairway. "You speak nonsense!"

"I speak truths, my lord. Truths I believe you know well. Did you not see Anne run past your door?"

"I just opened it. She…ran?"

"She was being chased!"

Frustration twisted her sense of urgency. So much she felt this man knew, to the detriment of all, and yet he cleaved to his secrets.

Guiscard clattered down to join Rhiana. A mail coif covered his head and pooled over his shoulders. He was ready to fight dragons. Or at least looked the picture of a brave knight. Though, she could not be sure he would make it farther than the keep doors. "Why did you not protect her? You are in my bad books, slayer!"

Heaving out a breath, she asked, "You know Anne's truths, yes?"

He bowed his head. No answer.

"Though you cannot imagine that truth valid. Merely suspicion, on your part," Rhiana continued. "I have seen the maxima walking through the village this day. As a man."

He clutched for her scaled armor, but his gauntlet merely slid with a scratch over the glossy indigo scales. "Impossible."

"Do you not wonder whence she came? What it is Anne cannot know? What details are lost inside her soul? The truth of her! Do you think she could be—"

"No! To speak it will only make it so." He shoved her roughly. Rhiana's scaled armor clanked against the stone wall curving about the stairs. "Where is she now?"

"Last I saw—before a dragon dropped on top of me—she was headed toward the keep. With the dragon behind her. He wears a long brown cloak wrapped about his body, bared chest and arms. He has no clothing, and for all appearances, looks a man."

Though he was not a man. Could not be. A fallen angel, the dragons claimed as blood ancestors. So this form the beast now took must be that of…no—it could not be!

"Let's make haste!"

For once the man had a good plan.

Leading the way, Rhiana flew down the stairs and landed the keep with a dash that took her past the huddled women and children. The high table was set with toppled gold goblets and crimson wine spilled across the white damask cloth.

There in the center of the rush-strewn room stood Anne. But she did not stand proud and beautiful, queen of her seaside village, rather she struggled against the hold of the dragon-man.

"I will kill you!" Lord Guiscard rushed the twosome.

Rhiana wasn't able to stop him. Nor, did she wish to. She would allow this to play out, remain close, and wait for the precise moment.

In that moment the dragon-man released Anne and she stumbled away and into her husband's arms. Guiscard did not approach the man, his wife claimed, he merely flashed his sword and sneered wickedly. Rhiana had to give him credit for *appearing* formidable.

But now, crossbow ready and pace cautious, Rhiana drew around behind the creature that stood erect and vigilant in the center of the keep. He was a head taller than she, a match to Gerard Coupe-Gorge surely. Bared to the waist, incredible and imposing musculature wrapped his borrowed body.

He be not an angel, she coached. For to even consider the implications of doing harm to such a creature!

To her right, six men stood along the wall. None of them knights, or armed. They were alert, but wary. At the end of the keep, by the hearth, a huddle of women and children observed silently. The mutt barked once, but a glance from the dragon-man silenced the dog into subservient whines.

"You will deny me my heart?" the creature asked Rhiana.

With a great cry that reached into and clutched Rhiana's very soul, the man in the center of the room stretched out his arms. He had come to claim his mate. It would not be allowed. 'Twas as if he were being pulled all directions. His legs shot out and he collapsed. Once coiling into himself, and then in the next scream he prostrated himself in a tight bend of limbs—

Limbs that began to change and move and grow.

"Mon Dieu." Rhiana rushed to Guiscard and Anne, gently but firmly pushing them to the wall. "Get back! All of you! Leave the keep!" She shouted to the women. "Get the children away from here!"

As if prodded along by red-hot irons the women quickly vacated. Children's cries filled the air as they were swept up by the men, but no human wail could overwhelm the horrendous shriek of transformation.

Rhiana took it all in, so awesome was the sight.

Scales began to form. A slashing tail grew out from the base of the morphing figure. Soon it no longer resembled a man, but a rampant birthing into this world. But 'twas no rampant, a creature that could be taken down with sword and might.

The beast quickly grew. Human appendages melted away, changing and hardening into armor of scale and razor-sharp talon. Ebony scales cut the rosemary-and-fennel-scented air in popping slices and hisses of sage-tainted steam coiled up and around the beast as its neck stretched high to the beamed ramparts of the keep and the wings swept out to clap at the air.

We had a bargain, slayer.

Standing with arms stretched to blockade the baron and Anne against the tapestried wall, Rhiana called up to the dragon, "She does not remember you! You cannot take a mortal woman away from the only home she knows."

"Do you speak to the dragon?" Guiscard snapped. "What does he want? A sacrifice?"

"He wants Anne," Rhiana said over her shoulder. "He claims she is his lost mate. A dragon that incarnated and cannot remember her origins."

"Pretty, so pretty," Anne murmured, close at Rhiana's side.

Let me speak to her. No, I shall not ask your permission. I shall merely do it.

And though Rhiana could hear in her mind the sounds made by the dragon, and recognized them to be some sort of communication, she had never before heard the language. Dragon speak. 'Twas musical and deep, a lullaby, as if the armourer's hammer to her soul.

Weapons held at the ready, she twisted to look at Anne, who

stared, mesmerized, up at the dragon's fierce gold eyes. She understood. She must.

Anne stretched out an arm to grasp at the air, pleading with the dragon. Her husband wound a gauntleted fist about the fine chain at her waist and with a rough jerk drew her to him.

He must release her.

"Does she understand you?"

"He speaks to me in music," Anne trilled.

"No, my love." Guiscard tugged at Anne's chain, but she stretched out both arms, grasping for the air in childish scoops. "It is a beast! It wants to devour you. Kill it, slayer!" he commanded Rhiana.

The command made a lot of sense. And required little thought.

Turning to face the dragon, crossbow at the ready, Rhiana searched its eyes. It had stopped communicating with Anne, though the pale waif struggled for release from the only compassionate arms she might have ever known.

And yet, had Anne been this maxima's mate? Did beasts know love and compassion as only humans could know?

How desperately we sought our origins. And to know the truth?

Do not blindly follow the lackwit's command to violence. Think you with your heart, slayer. You are one of us. You breathe fire. The blood of my ancestors flows through your veins.

Rhiana felt the fire within her. Forged by a beast very much like the one looming before her. She could not kill this wondrous creature. But neither would she allow it to take away Anne. Dragon or not, Anne did not remember.

The keep doors slammed open and amidst cheers and hoots, Macarius burst into the room and shouted, "The last dragon has fallen! Oh—"

Noticing the massive beast looming over the keep, Macarius struggled to unsheath Dragonsbane. As he charged, loosing a battle cry dredged from blood and revenge, the maxima swept down its head and opened its maws.

Rhiana jumped before Macarius, plunging them both to the rush-strewn floor as a plume of gold and amber flame soared over them. Heat burned into her flesh and lifted Rhiana's hair in a fan that blocked the flames from Macarius's face.

"Stay down," she commanded. "I've got this one."

Now the dragon stretched out its pellicle wings. The stained-glass windows set into the domed ceiling burst with a thrust of bone and wing through the fragile glass. Releasing a cry to the heavens, the beast thrashed its skull against the keep walls, loosening stone and mortar.

Anne's cry was muffled as the baron pushed her to ground and huddled over her to protect.

Macarius, heeding Rhiana's orders, grabbed her and pulled her away from a falling stone. The heavy rock hit the rushes and crashed to particles.

The ceiling opened to the night sky and the dragon took to wing.

"My love!" Free of restraint, Anne took off, rushing toward the stairs that led to the battlements.

Clasping hands with Macarius, Rhiana lifted him to his feet.

"What in the seven hells was that?" he barked.

"The maxima. He entered the village as a man and tried to kidnap Lady Anne."

Rhiana didn't wait for a plan, or even permission. Instead, she gestured Macarius follow and took off outside.

Behind her the baron cursed her and ran after Anne. She sensed his efforts would be futile.

They pushed through the rejoicing villagers who stood on the steps to the castle, and who had now began to cry out in fear at sight of the maxima soaring over the castle.

Macarius cleared her path with his sword, shouting to all to take cover.

It was Lydia whom Rhiana ran straight to. Her mother, in tears, fell into Rhiana's arms. "Odette is missing!"

"Where did you last see her? In the kitchens?"

"I just came from the kitchen. Odette was with me, but she went to find Vincent after the news that the dragons were all dead. Where did that one come from? It is so large. A devil from hell. Oh, I pray to Saint Agatha's veil!"

"Go find Paul," Rhiana directed. "Stay with him, and under cover; he will keep you safe."

Lydia's eyes poured out tears, the question in them so loud and painful.

"I will find Odette, I promise!"

Leaving her mother behind was one of the hardest steps Rhiana had to make. Lydia hurt, she was confused, she simply needed contact. A reassuring hug.

'Tis you who requires such.

Yes. Contact. Can it be so simple as taking it?

Rhiana turned. Lydia yet stood at the edge of the madness, staring bleakly toward the sky.

Yes, take it.

Rushing over to her mother, Rhiana took her into her arms. It surprised her how small her mother really was, and how easily she folded into Rhiana's embrace.

"All will be well," Rhiana offered. And in her heart, she knew it would be. For this clutch, this longed-for embrace opened her to possibility of a closeness and new relationship with her mother.

Sight of Ulrich and Verity running and shouting Odette's name redirected her. "I must go. I will find Odette!"

The beast swept from the sky. Fires blazing along the parapets and in the courtyard hissed up red-hot embers in the swirl of ash and soot that became a part of the midnight sky. The dragon's cry did not sound so alien to Rhiana. She did not interpret it as a word, but as a feeling. Anger. And loss.

And she knew for certain the maxima would not leave until it had claimed what it had come for. Anne.

Talons spread and aimed toward a fleeing woman, the maxima landed the ground just inside the main gates.

"Let me by," Rhiana shouted as Ulrich turned to stop her. "It has Odette pinned!"

"You cannot battle one so large!" Ulrich protested, even as she shoved him from her path.

It was Verity who slashed about with her staff to block Ulrich from further attempting to stop Rhiana. For a moment Rhiana held Verity's brown eyes. Valor and honor burned brightly there.

"Go," the woman said with a nod of her head toward the portcullis. "Save her. I'll come up behind you."

They both nodded in accord.

"Release her!" Rhiana shouted to the dragon as she gained the beast.

Here, out in the open air, the beast appeared three times larger than when she'd spoken to it in the hoard. Then, it had been coiled and hunched under the cover of mortal dwelling. Now, its wings were stretched wide, its spine arched and popping up the vicious spikes in defiance of any who would attempt to fight it.

The dragon held Odette pinned to the ground. A cage of ebony talons captured her spread arms and legs. From what Rhiana could determine her sister was unharmed, only frightened and screaming.

Huge gold eyes turned to her. Flames hissed about her body, encompassing in a reckless wall. Rhiana did not flinch.

You broke your promise. Now I shall take something of yours.

Argument felt ridiculous. Who could reason with a dragon?

For one moment of clarity, Odette twisted her head to look up, aside a talon, and into Rhiana's eyes. Cheeks were smeared with dirt, tears washed runnels through her creamy flesh. She spoke silently, but her wish was plain: do not let me die.

And the dragon's talons began to move, ever so slowly, scratching deep gouges into the ground, closing about Odette's body.

In her peripheral view, Rhiana sighted Verity. The blond warrior shouted, "Look, in the sky!"

Tugging her gaze from her sister's fate, Rhiana sighted a line in the direction Verity pointed. It could not be! But it was.

"Stop!" She raced to the dragon's foot, and clutched about one wide, sharp talon. "Look there!" Rhiana pointed to the top of the castle battlements, where, wonder upon wonders, yet another transformation was taking place.

CHAPTER FORTY

What was once lost to her, now flooded her mind with a gush of being. She had forgotten. The incarnation had taken the animal mind from her and abandoned her in a feeble mortal shell, amongst the mortals who walk the earth.

In mortal form she had sought salvation. Had bathed nightly in the holy, unknowing the reason, but compelled to it. And yet, even as her body began to ache and shimmer and embrace the change, she grasped on to a few mortal memories—*must keep them.*

Narcisse Guiscard. He had loved her, without question and unconditionally. Had he not taken her as his wife she might have starved or worse.

She had known kindness. Never would she lose memory of those bright blue mortal eyes.

Releasing her last clutch on mortality, Anne closed her eyes and thrust out her arms to the sky. Time to return.

"She changes." The words left Rhiana's mouth in a wondrous whisper.

Of a sudden, the heavens flickered and the sky dripped out rain. Soft, tickling droplets that signified renewal and hope.

From the ground where she stood, Rhiana could but see the twist of animal limbs struggling upon the battlements. A dagged tail, lengthening and growing, swished the sky and slashed out two stone merlons. Shattered limestone hailed to the ground where villagers dashed to get out of the way.

And there, flying before the transforming beast, a white dove soared into the night. Must have escaped from the castle's mews. The beauty of the soft white feathers, superimposed before the deep violet scales of the changing dragon put a lump in Rhiana's throat. She reached out, grasping for the unattainable bird.

The rains increased. The baron topped the tower. Ripping the mail coif from his head, he tossed it in his wake. An angry cry stretched his mouth wide as he dashed for his wife who was no longer a human and not completely a dragon.

A woman's cry redirected Rhiana's awe.

"Let her go!" she called, meaning Odette. Any attempt to move the talon was like budging an oak root from the ground. The maxima had sighted the same thing, and had almost forgotten its pinned catch. "Your talons are sharp and will cut her, for she struggles."

She remembers.

"And she changes," Rhiana agreed. "Release my sister. Go to your mate!"

And with that the dragon lifted its talons from Odette. A twist of its body, and a flap of the maxima's wings, propelled it to flight.

Rhiana lunged to the ground beside Odette, who had passed out. A long slash across her thigh bled, but it did not appear deep. Other than that, she was sound and breathing. Signaling to Verity to come assist, Rhiana left her half sister to the woman's gentle care.

Striding through quickly forming puddles, Rhiana raced for

the battlements. As she topped the stairs and began the long trek about the parapet to where Anne still changed, she sighted Macarius broach the tower and go after the baron.

The dragon that was once Anne stretched out her wings. Much larger than a rampant, but still smaller than the maxima, she wore violet scales so dark and rich, they were like velvet upon a stone. A kyrie to the heavens blasted from the dragon's mouth and was followed by a release of red and violet flame.

Returned. In possession of her real destiny.

Rhiana knew the moment. 'Twas indelible, yet imprinted upon her soul. For she had been granted return to herself— *you are dragon sired.*

A tip of Anne's left wing swept across the parapet, clipping the man who stood close. The baron. The wing hooked his body fully and lifted it into the air. The lord of St. Rénan cried out as he slid from the leathery wing and his arms thrust high, spilled over the crenellated battlements.

Macarius tossed his sword to the stone floor and jumped. He managed to grip Guiscard by the foot and held. The baron dangled between two merlons, obviously knocked out, for he did not make a move to climb to safety.

The ebony maxima lighted onto the battlements beside Anne. The two dragons twined necks—a lover's long-awaited embrace. Dragon keens filled the night sky, along with the staccato stridulations.

Halfway there Rhiana stopped. Pressing her hands behind her, she touched the cold stone battlement. Everything was wet and cold.

They had found each other. All that Anne had lost, she had regained. No longer must she wonder. Never would a silver chain and greedy platitudes of possession in the name of love bind her.

But as the elder drew back its neck and opened its maws,

Rhiana's dread grew. She shouted, "No! You have her back, do not harm any others!"

The dragon abruptly stopped from what would have been a forceful blast of flame. If dragons could sneer, it sent such a look at her.

This mortal kept my mate in chains!

The maxima wanted to flame Lord Guiscard. And it would.

"He thought only to protect her frail mortal form from danger!" Dashing forward, Rhiana drew up her crossbow.

Another draw up of its neck stretched the maxima to full size. Its wings spanned beyond the entire width of the castle.

Rhiana could not breach the distance quickly enough to deliver a killing blow. Even could she send her dagger like a spear through the air, she would never find target between the dragon's eyes.

As the elder lunged to snap at Guiscard, the female dragon twisted her neck and blocked the attack. The two dragons gnashed fangs. Strong battle scent permeated the air. And then, as quickly, the scent changed to the sweeter more musky mating scent.

Anne had given Guiscard the gift of life in exchange for her mortal shell.

The female dragon, satisfied the elder was not going to flame her human lover, took to air with a single flap of wings. Sage rushed over Rhiana's face and swept back her hair, freeing it from the binding leather ties.

Spreading her arms out wide, Rhiana called out to the elements, to the female dragon, to all who would listen. "I am dragon sired!"

To know the freedom of flight must be a wonder. Yet, to finally know her truth was as much a wonder.

As the maxima lifted its breast high in preparation to flight, Macarius stood, brandishing his sword.

"No." She could never get to his side in time. Rhiana set to a run along the battlements. "Do not do it!"

The slayer remained focused. Macarius did not hear her.

The elder flapped its wings. The massive, taloned paws lifted from the battlements.

Dragonsbane soared through the air, fitting its sharp silver blade into the dragon's belly. Not a kill shot. Far from it.

Snapping angrily, the beast knocked Macarius from his feet with a slap of wing, and then turned away and joined the female in their flight through the sky.

Falling, arms spread and looking as if a stuffed effigy, Macarius's descent to the inner bailey lasted for hours in Rhiana's heart. His cry to death echoed in her veins. And he landed the solid ground with a clank of armor and bone.

Not dead. But speaking to angels in soft murmurs that slipped from his lips as Rhiana bent over Macarius's prone body. Blood oozed over his lower lip and from his nose. Eyes closed, he smiled when she leaned in.

"Memento mori," he whispered.

"No, you must not say that!"

Rhiana looked up to the crowd that had surrounded. Would no one help? Where was the Nose? She needed to save this man. He would not die this day. He must not!

"Rhiana." A firm hand clamped her across the shoulder. "You…are the greatest slayer in all the land."

"No, I don't want to be. Macarius, please, you will live. You will!"

"Here comes the leech!"

Rhiana felt someone kneel beside her. The leech was a reedy young man, who spent his time drawing anatomical studies of wounds and organs, and a curmudgeonly sort, especially for his age. He began to inspect Macarius, and ordered Rhiana to unstrap his armor. She did so, quickly removing the pauldrons and leather coat of plates.

Macarius groaned as she lifted his shoulder to unbuckle the leather from the back of his arm.

"You feel pain?" she said.

"Most certainly. My shoulder…oohhhh."

"Good. That means you are too stubborn to die. Can you come that?" She searched the leech's face, seeking the positive answer she prayed for.

The man could but shrug. He could not say for sure that Macarius would survive.

Of a sudden, screams ignited the calmness.

Rhiana twisted and saw in the sky the line of flame burning over the castle banners, and heading toward the village. The maxima had returned.

Mon Dieu, would they never be granted reprieve?

"Don't die," she said. Leaning in to kiss Macarius, she felt him smile against her lips.

"I'll try not to. Though it played the deuce with me, that dragon. Take this." He lifted his sword. "Go. Kill that bastard."

"Already dead," Rhiana muttered.

She sprang up and pushed through the crowd.

Arms pumping, she strode purposefully forward. Heaven help the cursed beast, if it did yet seek revenge.

Flames blazed down the center of the road that led from portcullis to castle steps. The maxima's dark shadow circled the sky and banked. It was coming in again. Determined to lay waste for reasons Rhiana could not fathom. It had its mate back. Why further punish the village?

As she ran toward the wall of flame, she knew the answer to her futile wonderings. The maxima had no concern for human life. It required food and shelter and the hoard—that sat below a bustling community. All the better should its hoard be safe from human interference.

The flames whipped higher than Rhiana's head. She saw the

maxima swoop and bank to the left, away from where she stood. And the vision was lost behind the wall of flame.

Stepping through the fire, Rhiana emerged, Dragonsbane held ready and hair flowing in great waves. She embodied flame. The maxima was a part of her.

But Rhiana Tassot was mortal, and would not suffer her family, her friends, the innocent people of St. Rénan, a death she could never know—that by the flame.

The maxima's shadow arced. It drew back its head and turned in the sky. Rhiana could not sight in the female dragon. This danger was singular, large, and imposing, but it could be fought.

Swallowing back need, want, and the greedy desire to success, Rhiana surrendered her life for the better good, and raced down the road toward the dragon that dove low and flew along the same road. They were headed for a collision.

Releasing a great battle cry, she rushed the dragon. Flames licked at her face and momentarily blinded her path. But as she emerged from the cacophony of amber flame the dragon's head was right there.

Rhiana did not swerve. She did not duck to avoid a collision with a body that could crush her upon impact. She did neither thrust Dragonsbane in a blind attempt to wound any part where the blade could find purchase.

Rhiana leaped.

Airborne, her arms thrust forward to force her momentum, and her legs stretching as if to run across the frill of flame, she landed hard scale.

And immediately took to flight.

Clutching the small horn that dotted the dragon's nose, Rhiana clung with one hand. The maxima soared upward, snout bulleting the air and body streamlined in its wake. Her legs slipped down the length of the head, arrowing between the eyes. Sword arm flailing, it was all Rhiana could do to hang on to the weapon.

The air, cold and crisp, thickened as the dragon darted through a cloud.

So high! Too high to consider a safe landing. And yet, she had surrendered to fate when charging the dragon.

Now, Rhiana felt the maxima had reached its pinnacle. A death dive would follow. As it hovered high and straightened its position to a horizontal pose, she released hold of the horn. Her body slid.

Foolish human!

Feet hitting the massive horns that jutted from its temples, Rhiana found position. Lifting both arms high, and supporting her stance with her stomach firmly to the dragon's temple, she plunged Dragonsbane in deep.

In mortal form the dragon had not gotten to the holy water. It was still vulnerable. Rhiana prayed it be so.

Her blade entered the kill spot with ease. The beast cried out, jerking its head—flinging Rhiana into the air like a baby bird abandoned from the nest with a swift brush of wing.

The midnight sky, muddied by clouds and dragon flame, bit at Rhiana's face with the cold finality of death.

As her body plunged toward the earth, she saw below her the spiraling descent of the maxima, struggling against the blade firmly inserted into its skull. A talon scratched its skull, but only succeeded in bloodying an eye.

It was dead, and if not, the fall and contact with ground would surely deliver St. Rénan from the evil.

Closing her eyes to the fast rush of earth Rhiana spread out her arms. Air moved swiftly through her fingers and hair. A smile could not be stopped. So free. Flying.

Remember that you must die.

And when death should have risen and slammed her body to the ground, Rhiana felt her soul lift up and soar. 'Twas as if her entire being floated. Impact hadn't registered as pain or agony.

Would death be so simple, then?

Curling her arms about the warm surface of slick scales, Rhiana suddenly jerked her head up and looked upon what it was she clung to. Violet scales so dark they were almost black.

They soared through the sky, fire chaser clinging to the back of the dragon that had once walked the earth as an abandoned soul and had now returned to her very essence of being.

Lady Anne.

Realizing she clung to the dragon's neck, Rhiana wrapped her arms tighter, not wanting to fall now she had been given new opportunity to life. She sensed no danger from this magnificent beast, but would remain cautious should she show sign of returning to the village to finish what her mate could not.

Laying her cheek aside the warm violet scales, Rhiana looked down over her village, spotted with flame, so small when viewed from above.

Down there, Macarius lay, wounded, so close to death. She could not fathom his loss. Right now, all that mattered was the freedom, the flight.

The dragon soared over the sea. Moonlight twinkled upon the water like a hoard of diamonds. It stretched for leagues, but the dragon did not fly so far. Turning slowly and wide, so as not to dislodge its passenger, the dragon made for the shore and the village.

"Thank you," Rhiana said. She stroked a palm across the warm, pliable scales. "I had no choice. He would have burned the entire village."

I understand, fire chaser. You have ever been kind to me.

"Where will you go?"

The hoard is wonderful.

"You could stay."

There will always be danger in living close to man. And I will not risk incarnation again to access the hoard.

"We cannot move the village."

I cannot move the hoard. I will go elsewhere, but the village will never be free from the threat of others like myself. You cannot slay us all.

"I don't wish to. I simply desire that we exist alongside one another."

It is a thought…

"Let's look to the future," Rhiana said. The dragon soared high over her smoking village. "Mayhap together we can make a change."

Perhaps. I will let you down by the forest—

"No, in the village, please."

They will come at me with all manner of weapon.

"Not if I am there to protect you. Please, it will be a beginning."

The dragon that all in the village had known to be Lady Anne set down in the bailey. Rhiana slipped from her neck and stumbled forward, getting her land-legs back with a few testing strides.

Surrounded by angry-eyed knights wielding all manner of sword, mace and bow, Rhiana settled their ire by embracing the dragon's nose, slipping her palm over the suede nostrils.

"She is our Lord Guiscard's lady wife!" Rhiana announced. "We will respect her. She wishes us no harm."

"Preposterous!"

"It is a beast. We have battled through the night. Many are dead!"

"No mercy!"

"Stop!" All eyes turned to Narcisse Guiscard. He descended the castle steps, tugging a clean damask cotehardie over his soot-dusted armor. He approached Rhiana and the dragon. Silence punctuated with gasps and sniffing children surrounded.

The baron spread out a palm and did not touch the dragon, but held his hand very close. "This is she?"

I know he loves me. I love him for that.

"She loves you," Rhiana explained, for none in the village could hear the dragon speak. "She knows you loved her."

Face wrinkling from anger to disbelief and then to a wilting sadness, Narcisse tentatively reached to touch the dragon's nose. Sage smoke puffed out around them.

"If we don't kill it now," shouted out from the crowd, "it'll come back for us when we sleep!"

Agitated, the dragon swept out a wing. The villagers screamed and shuffled back. One knight remained in the fore, his crossbow drawn. Gerard Coupe-Gorge.

"Stand down," Rhiana ordered the knight. She leveled him with the evil eye. "Or risk my wrath."

Gerard looked to his lord and master. He would not take orders from a female.

"The dragon slayer has spoken," the baron said. "This dragon will cause us no harm. For indeed, it is truth, she was once my lady wife."

A hush fell over the bailey. The lord of the village had declared his marriage to a dragon!

"Go in peace," he said to the dragon. He bent forward and kissed the creature's scaled nose. Smoothing his palms where scale met the soft leather nose he pressed his cheek aside the brilliant violet scales. "Forgive me the chain, I only wished you safe."

And with that permission, the dragon stood tall and lifted into flight.

Rhiana, eyeing Gerard, saw him follow Anne with his bow. She lunged for him, knocking him to his back on the ground. Curling a hand about his neck she challenged, "Will you mark me your enemy?"

Gerard dropped his bow.

CHAPTER FORTY-ONE

Jean Cesar Ulrich Villon III had spent the morning being interrogated by Lord Guiscard. The baron was quick and agile as he paced before Ulrich, his hands gesturing madly with each question. Dark circles curved beneath his eyes and his hair had not seen tending this day.

It was obvious the baron believed Ulrich had stumbled onto the key to immortality. When Guiscard tore off his linen shirt and showed his back, Ulrich nodded miserably.

"No, that is not it," Ulrich said, then confessed all. He explained, in great detail, exactly what had occurred to bring about his youthful appearance. Three weeks earlier, he'd left Lydia and Rhiana (then, but two and toddling about) for a few days journey down the coast. Ulrich did not mention he had been seeking work; at the time he'd been serving His Most Magical, under the baron's father's command. The wizard was abrasive and Ulrich had had enough.

Anyway, not a day from St. Rénan and Ulrich stepped into a faery circle and had danced. Yes, danced. For an afternoon. He'd finished dancing, exhausted and exhilarated, and had returned home, forgetting his search for work, and only desiring to see his wife and stepchild. Only then did he learn how different time in Faery is from mortal time.

He danced away twenty mortal years. While he had thought a mere half day had passed while the faeries danced him to a mad frenzy, his wife had lived twenty years. Rhiana had lived twenty years. And all they knew was that he had abandoned them.

"You speak the truth?" Narcisse said, finally coming to stillness before Ulrich.

Ulrich nodded.

He suspected the baron fool enough to attempt to grasp immortality.

And later, as he wandered down the castle steps in seek of his companion Verity, Ulrich wondered who, in Guiscard's absence, would step into the baron of St. Rénan's shoes. For should he find the immortality he sought, a great price would be exacted. St. Rénan did possess a leader; Rhiana could step into the position. But she would not. She was a free soul. Set on a course to change the dynamics between predator and prey, dragon and man.

She could do it, Ulrich mused. Rhiana embodied fire, in soul, determination, and spirit.

A complete day passed before Rhiana found herself finally seeking the comfort of her home. She walked by Lord Guiscard, who, fit out in complete battle armor and walking toward the main gates, raised a hand and nodded at her. His effervescent smile captured her momentarily, so that she but stood watching as the baron strode out from the battlements and off to heaven knew where.

Mayhap he'd intention of scouting the caves to ensure there were no dragons? Likely, he had thought to mine the dragon dust. No matter to her.

She'd spent the past day tending the wounded, the burned, the terrified children who needed a few moments wrapped in the arms of someone—anyone—until their fears calmed and their parents could be located.

The castle would need to be rebuilt; it was an entire loss, for the maxima's flight from the keep took down all the walls save the farthest south tower. Many houses in the village were spared, and those who were without homes had been invited to stay with others.

The chapel stood proudly, like a battered beacon, the holy water inside untouched by any dragon that would defy fate and seek a seal against death.

A few knights sprawled on the main floor of her home. Lydia cooked a savory fish stew for the men, and Paul stoked the fire. The climb to the third floor bedroom took forever. Rhiana felt she had to cling to the stone walls and pull herself up each stair, exhaustion clung to her so. But sleep wasn't even to mind.

"Fire chaser!"

Greeted by a smiling—and not dead—Macarius, Rhiana rushed across the bedroom to the window seat where he sat, one leg stretched across the bench, the other to the floor. He wore but black hose. Odette was checking a bandaged wound on his arm.

Rhiana plunged to the floor beside him and looking up to his face saw a cut along his jaw had been sealed with tiny careful stitches.

"You approve?" he said, gesturing to the scar.

"Why is it men must wear their scars so proudly on the outside?"

He shrugged. "Why is it women must hide their scars away?"

"We would never attract a man if we showed our scars," Odette chimed in, "be they physical or emotional."

How precise Odette's comment.

Macarius touched Rhiana's cheek. She must look a fright. She did not care about hiding her scars. Let the world see them! She was stronger for all she had endured, physically and yes, emotionally.

"Odette."

Her half sister peered over Macarius's shoulder.

"There's a bleeding knight downstairs I think you missed."

Glee lighted in the girl's eyes. And a giggling nod. "I'll leave you two to your scars. Oh!" She hugged Rhiana. "Thank you for saving my life, sister. I have never been so terrified than when pinned by that monster."

"You were very brave. You did not even faint!"

"I didn't." Processing that with new boldness, Odette's posture straightened with pride. "I survived a dragon's attack! Can you come that, brave knights?" she called as she gathered her needles and thread into a basket and slipped down the stairway. "Here I come, the dragon tamer!"

Chuckling at Odette's bold step into confidence, Rhiana turned back to Macarius, and he caught her hand in his.

"Come, sit closer." He beckoned to the bench before him.

"Your leg?"

"Broken. Paul and the leech straightened the bone early this morning. Hurt like no flame has ever burned. Odette put a comfrey poultice on it."

"Yes, it smells—"

"Much better than a mustard plaster. Both the leech—and your sister—pronounced me able. The leech is fashioning a splint as we speak. I'm not supposed to move until he returns." He spread a palm over his bare chest, gliding it across the damage, all black and blue and slashes of dried blood. "I've a few cuts and some broken ribs, but otherwise, I am whole."

"Incredible." Rhiana sat on one bended leg upon the bench

before Macarius. "You fell from the battlements! I cannot believe you are not…"

"Dead?"

She cringed, looking away.

"I was ready."

Now she sought his liquid blue gaze. "Really? You would have—" Her heart pounded madly. He would have given up so easily? This bold knight?

He shook his head. "I prefer life. Especially…if it includes you."

She lifted a brow and felt her heartbeat slow. Relieved, Rhiana said, "Life is good."

"Rhiana…" Macarius drew her hand up to his mouth and brushed his lips over her knuckles. The touch drew her out from the horrors of the past few days and danced her into a surreal softness of soul. He searched her face, smiling slightly—but something about his expression remained tight. Blowing out a tremendous breath, he finally said, "I asked your stepfather for your hand in marriage."

"You what?" As if stung by a bee, she sprang to her feet and backed away from him.

That was a very sudden and surprising statement. Now, everything inside of Rhiana jittered, more profoundly than any booming heartbeat. Gone was the soft soul. 'Twas as if she'd been called to arms. Could he have not wooed her into a more accepting state?

"Your anger scent rises," Macarius said woefully. "I can smell it. I do not mean to raise your ire, Lady of the Dragons." He sighed heavily. "Worry not."

"Paul refused?" He had better. No man—

"He wondered if I had asked you first," Macarius said. He smiled and chuckled, but the action made him clutch his ribs. "I should have known better. I thought to do things traditionally by first going to your father. But you are not the traditional woman."

"Paul knows me well." Unlike Macarius, Rhiana thought. The anxiety coiling her to rigidity softened. But that he had asked... To have jumped into so bold a future without consulting with her?

She did not want to think on it. She would not.

"So, you will obviously be in St. Rénan for a time. Until you heal. Where will you stay?"

"Rhiana." Macarius shuffled on the bench, made to turn, then gave up with a sigh. He was too badly injured. "You are changing the subject. And much as I favor getting down on one knee before you, it is quite impossible."

"Your knee?"

"Fire chaser, you know me better than I know myself. Which, I now know, is the quest my father sent me on—to find that woman. So...will you marry me? Would you have me as a husband and put up with a man who will never be satisfied to stand back and allow you the win, but is always eager to compete for the title of greatest?"

A smile tickled Rhiana's mouth. A marriage proposal and a challenge all in one breath. Intriguing. An exact fit for her.

"What of my mating scent? I do not wish to perish for kissing you."

"That...is something we will have to address. I know not why I scent you so strongly."

"I am half dragon; you have been trained to kill my kind."

"Your kind. Yes. Who would have thought? I will never harm you, fire chaser, you have my word."

Striding toward the wall where she practiced her letters, Rhiana traced a finger along the first letter in her name. Now that was the way to approach her. Truthfully, and without fanfare.

"Very well, then, I believe I will marry you."

"Can a man get a kiss to seal that agreement?"

She spun and spread out her arms, looking over her attire for the first time in a day. Still she wore the dragon-scale armor, so comfortable it fit her. And with her arms spread and head tilted back, she felt a return of the moment as she clung to the female dragon's back and soared through the sky. Freedom.

This moment felt right. And Macarius was a part of the moment.

She skipped over to him and knelt on the bench before him, leaning in close to his face. "Promise me one thing, slayer."

"The world for you, my love."

"I don't want the world, I merely want to be allowed the lead half the time."

"The lead?"

"When we are traveling the world, slaying dragons."

"Is that what we shall do?"

"That, and…I've plans to work with the female maxima. We both believe that something can be done to bring man and dragon to accord. It will take time, but I am determined."

"You mean talk to the dragons and convince them not to kill us all?"

That she could still marvel him, after all he had learned of her in the past few days, put a smile to Rhiana's face.

"I mean, work with the dragons so we both can learn about the other and live alongside one another in harmony."

"You've great dreams, my love."

"It is all—you called me love."

He shrugged. "I love you."

Rhiana plunged into Macarius's arms, eliciting a groan because of his tender muscles. "I love you, too. So long as you allow me the lead."

"The lead, eh?" He considered, rubbing his chin with a thumb. "So you will continue to try to come it over me?"

She nodded.

"Can I still claim the title of greatest slayer in all the land?"

"You gave it to me when you thought you would die!"

He smirked and drew her onto his lap. Careful not to sit upon his broken leg, Rhiana wrapped her arms about his neck and leaned in to kiss him.

"Promise," he said. "We are equals."

"I love you," she said upon his lips. And she truly did.

After changing to her blue gown and scrubbing the soot from her face (all done in the kitchen; there be a man in her room!) and allowing Odette to stitch the few cuts and scratches along her arm and left leg, Rhiana returned to her bed chamber and combed out her hair as Macarius, still in the window seat, watched.

"A finely dressed lady and her knight have arrived at the gates," he said.

Rhiana leaned over him and peered out the window. Macarius pushed his fingers through her hair as she did. A shiver of rightness spiraled through her being. It was difficult not to lean in and kiss the man, but only because her curiosity was so much stronger.

Who were the strangers below?

Ulrich and Verity had gone to meet the new arrivals. The lady, mounted upon a fine black destrier, was dressed in braies and wore a flowing cape trimmed in jewels. Braies?

"I'll be right back." She kissed Macarius and tore away from his wanting hands.

"Not too long, my love!"

"Yes, my crippled one," she called as she ran down the narrow stairs, barefoot and determined.

Night fell beautifully upon the village, moonlight glistening in the pools of water that had doused the flames. A blue moon. Rhiana recalled now what Amandine had told her about the blue moon. 'Twas the only time a dragon could incarnate.

Stone buildings, crumbled by a slashing dragon wing or blast of flame, dotted the grounds. All craftsmen had set to re-creating the village, along with their industrious wives. But even in the devastation, children laughed and chased after dogs.

Paul joined her side. He held the tattered shield she'd stolen from the hoard. "I don't think I want to cause it further damage. You should save it."

"I will," she said.

"Where are you headed?"

"There are visitors at the gate. Come!"

As they approached the gates, Ulrich turned and nodded.

The couple that had arrived remained mounted. The woman cradled a babe to her chest, so small, it could be but a newborn.

"Rhiana." Ulrich thread his fingers into hers, and she allowed it. So proudly he beamed at her as Verity stepped forward to kiss her aside the cheek. "I want you to meet Sir Dominique San Juste."

The dark-haired man dismounted, flipped his cape over a shoulder and bowed before Rhiana. "A pleasure, my lady. I understand you've been flying through the sky upon dragons' backs and saving the lives of the innocents?"

Rhiana shrugged. What could she say? Was it a trick of the moonlight, or did the man…sparkle?

"Already Ulrich has detailed your adventures over the past days. You remind me of my wife," he said with a white-toothed smile. And indeed, when he turned to clasp hands with the woman, a sweep of faint glittering dust followed in his wake.

Verity stepped beside Dominique and clasped hands with

the mounted woman. "Rhiana, I'd like you to meet my sister, Seraphim San Juste. She and her husband have journeyed from the Valois Wood, north of Paris."

"That is a very long journey," Rhiana offered. "Especially with one so small. The two of you must stay the night. I offer my home."

Seraphim nodded thanks. "Verity," she said, and carefully handed down the bundled babe. "She's sleeping." She followed by dismounting grandly, and stepping up to kiss both of Rhiana's cheeks. "You are a marvel. I wish I could have been here to see you take down the dragons, and then to tame one and fly upon its back."

"My wife favors adventure," Dominique said over her shoulder. "Both she and her sister are attracted to danger."

"Sounds wonderful," Rhiana peeled. "What of the babe? She is so small."

"Yes, but the small ones are excellent to travel with," Seraphim said. "The gentle rocking of the horse keeps her happy. Her name is Mihangel."

"She's going to be just like us," Verity said as she embraced both Seraphim and Rhiana. "The world can always make room for another strong woman."

Seraphim looked over Rhiana's shoulder at Paul. "I can't believe it! My shield!"

"Yours?" Paul stepped forward and handed it to Seraphim.

Dominique embraced his wife from behind. "It is the shield you abandoned in your family's home?"

"I saw that shield when I first traveled in this Other Realm," Verity said. She looked to Rhiana and shrugged. "There are many things the d'Ange sisters must share with you."

"And it found its way here," Paul remarked, "to the hands of another powerful woman. Mayhap you three were meant to come together?"

Each of the women beamed, for they each knew it in their hearts to be true.

"Are you traveling far?" Rhiana asked Seraphim, who now unclasped her cape to reveal her choice of men's clothing complete.

Rhiana had to smile at that.

"Far? Oh, yes," Seraphim said. "We set sail for the Indian Ocean."

"Really? That sounds splendid."

"Oh, indeed." A glint of brilliant white lighted in Seraphim's eye. "It will be an adventure."

"Joy!"

And dancing. Circling to the right and then stop and to the left.

Lifting his feet high and barely remembering their touch to ground, Narcisse followed his fellow revelers about as the music and the gaiety worked his body almost against his will.

But he was happy. And so eager to dance. Will was not required, only submission.

They looked as he, but had wings and violet eyes. Their pace was frantic, but it never did seem too fast for him to keep up.

This was the key to immortality, to prolonging one's life. The Villon man had said so.

It hadn't taken Narcisse overlong to locate a circle of toadstools within the forest. He'd plunged right in. And now he danced.

Endlessly after.

She soared over the sea. Silver waves winked up at her. The *schuss* of water against stone at the imminent shore invited. An entire day she had flown north, seeking distance from the horrors behind her. Crossing the expanse of sea she passed over a great island and finally settled upon a causeway barely revealed by the cool sea water.

Gray-winged birds circled her head like an ethereal halo. The water slapped at her scales and tail.

It felt right here. There were no visible cave openings in the rocky cliffs that hugged the sea, but she would scout and find one.

The dragon dipped her head and lapped at the water. Splaying out her wings she laid them across the surface, cooling her tired limbs and sinking her belly into the depths. She floated for a long time, eyes closed, her head back and wings the only parts visible in the cloudy sky.

An intense *knowing* filled her completely. A newling formed in her belly. Its presence hummed in every portion of limb, scale and talon. And it was good.

She could but recall bits of that time she had walked the earth in ethereal form. A mortal man had loved her. He'd given her a gift that would be born a very powerful dragon. Born of dragon and man.

The birth filled her with anticipation.

Michele Hauf lives with her family in a suburb of Minneapolis. When not feverishly writing or plotting her next book, Ms. Hauf indulges her other creative outlets by tending her faerie garden, giving dragonflies glamorous makeovers, playing guitar and violin, and spending far too much time coloring. (Yes, that's right, coloring.)

Readers can write to her at P.O. Box 23, Anoka, MN 55303 or find her current e-mail address at the Web site www.michelehauf.com.

LUNA™

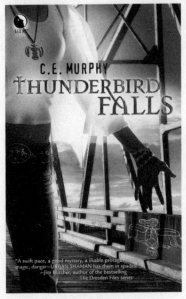